First in the Series:
And Also Some Women

Twelfth Year

Sherri L. Sechrist

Dedicated to

Mary Ann Van Weelden,
my inspiration, friend and mother

&

my husband Steve Sechrist,
for his loving faith in my dreams.

After this, Jesus traveled about from one town and village to another, proclaiming the good news of the kingdom of God. The Twelve were with him, and also some women...

Luke 8:1-2a NIV

CHAPTER 1

She knew what the two men thought of her without a word being spoken. Their opinions could not have been more different, but neither could stem the lump rising in her throat.

The corners of the second man's mouth twitched. Anyone else would have guessed a scrap of a smile might follow, but Leah knew better. She did not know the stranger, but his lips pulled into the sneer she expected, nothing but scornful disdain for the girl that stood before him. His insolent eyes swept over her. The smallest convulsion of shame ran down her back at his openly lecherous stare.

But there would be no salvation for Leah from the second man standing next to the stranger. She stole a quick glance at him only to feel a familiar weakness come over her. Knees shaking, she prayed she would not do anything that might further embarrass him before this unknown man with his mocking leer.

The second man spoke. "Leah." So much hatred captured in one word.

"So this is the girl you would offer me?" Leah flinched at the sarcasm in the stranger's voice, even as the enormity of his words washed over her.

Leah's father muttered something she could not hear. The stranger barked a short laugh and looked at Leah, a hard, appraising stare that made her feel naked, worthless. She did not know why, but she knew she had shamed her father.

"I trust you will present her differently when we next meet. For after seeing this… this… woman," the man looked at Leah with gray eyebrows raised in amazement, "our bargain cannot stand."

Her father's response was immediate and hard. "We reached no agreement about my daughter."

Momentary anger flashed on the stranger's face, but he shrugged his shoulders and scoffed. "She is of no significance to me. No loss." His long, embellished robe billowed behind him as he strode away, its rich embroidery a stark contrast to the fine gray dust of Leah's street.

His final words echoed in the beating sun. "Keep her."

"My daughter." A deliberate silence hung in the air, an omen of the greater fury that was yet to come. "My daughter, my daughter, my daughter…"

Each utterance became more clipped, the words no disguise for his fierce anger. He closed his eyes. One would have thought it caused physical pain to wrench his words from some seething inner well of hatred.

"Where have you been?"

Leah stared at the small bundle of wildflowers clutched in her hand, wishing she held almost anything else. Their fragile beauty represented so much that she loved and everything her father despised.

As though he read her mind, his words were a vicious hiss. "What are those?"

The lifeless blossoms felt dirty in her hand.

Leah was mute with dread, a girl lost in the indefinable age somewhere between child and woman, standing at the start of life but not yet ready to survive it. She pressed her white lips together, silence the only refuge before the rage that was her father.

The echo of his words stretched between them. She did not flinch as he pried the wilted bundle from fingers rigid and unmoving. Harsh words began a familiar, ruthless interrogation.

"I asked you a question. Where were you?" He threw the flowers on the ground.

Leah tried to summon a voice but could fine nothing. The imperceptible shake of her head was enough to fuel the fire.

"Answer me! Where. Were. You."

There would be no refuge in silence today. "We... I was with... my friends." The smallness of her voice saddened Leah. She glanced up but looked down at once, startled by the inflamed red face so close to her own. She tried to focus on the sleeve of her father's fine linen tunic, but could not look away from the balled fists of white knuckles disguised as a father's hands.

"Look at me."

Leah raised her head and stared at the spot between her father's bushy eyebrows, for she could not look into his terrible black eyes. She stood perfectly still as he took in her messy hair, dirty clothes and muddy feet. Her desire to flee strong, but the wisdom against such utter foolishness was much stronger. She wilted under his savage stare, just like the flowers scattered in the dirt, his words raining down on her.

"Covered in dust. A filthy tunic. Mud on your feet. Your hair is a tangled mess, your face is disgusting and you smell. Have you been rolling around with some Gentile pigs today?" His voice was like gravel as he counted her faults, delighting in his cruel assessment one jagged word at a time.

Leah shook her head, her gaze shifting to a spot just over his shoulder. She could not bear to look at him.

"I ask you again. Where have you been?"

"At the stream." Her voice sounded small and far away.

"In the stream is more like it. Like a child! And when you returned, I know you did not stroll through town where everyone could see you covered in sweat and mud like some common tramp. Did you?"

Leah had no answer, for the only way to her house was to walk through those streets where indeed, everyone did know her. She had waved or spoken to most of the neighborhood women just a few moments ago, each one returning a smile or nod to the beautiful, sunny girl.

He shook his head, as though words could not describe the terrible sight before him. "What a fine young woman you have become, Leah. Fit for marriage to a shepherd, men that smell just like the sheep they herd."

Leah's father was a trader of linen. He bought the woven cloth and finely-spun thread from the great farms in the area and then sold it at Caesarea Philippi's market or in the bigger cities like Capernaum or Damascus or even the grand city of Caesarea on the Great Sea. He had a particular contempt for the lowly shepherds whose animals produced the dirty gray wool of the poor.

"You heard what the man said. You are of no significance. A dirty shepherd will be the best I can find for someone like you." But Leah heard only one terrifying word: marriage.

"What do you have to say for yourself?"

Leah did not answer, still stunned by the enormity of one thought. Surely her father was not negotiating a marriage for Leah with that old lecherous man. Her father had said there was no agreement.

"I asked you a question. Answer me!" His patience gone, her father's voice roared in the courtyard.

"No more!" The squeaky voice was as fierce as it was shrill. Leah had not heard the soft tread behind her. She did not dare turn around, but so thankful was Leah for the sound of her grandmother's voice, her knees threatened to buckle from under her.

"Savta." Leah's father snorted, his voice mocking his mother-in-law, baiting her.

"No more. Leave. Return to your barns and your work." Savta's anger was equal in its intensity. "Return to your trading and money."

But he was not intimidated by the small woman before him.

"This is no concern of yours, Savta." He tilted his head at his wrinkled, miniscule mother-in-law, seemingly amused at the sight of her.

Her stooped frame was tiny before his towering bulk, but she pushed her granddaughter aside to stand inches from her son-in-law. Faded brown eyes snapped in a wrinkled brown face, chin jutting while a knobby forefinger jabbed the air.

"You may speak like that to your hired men, but you will not speak that way to Leah. No more!"

"Savta, I only am concerned for my daughter's future. What man would marry someone who paraded through the streets looking like this?"

"She is a fine girl. You will not speak to her this way!"

"She is my daughter, Savta. I will speak to her any way I want." Leah heard the menace in her father's measured words, but it took more than words to stop Savta.

"No more. Leave this house, leave us!"

10

It was the wrong thing to say. This had not been Savta's home for many years.

He turned to the trembling Leah, his words a hiss. "Get out of my sight."

Leah did not want to leave Savta with her father. Her moment of hesitation was all it took. He grabbed her arm and shook it fiercely, so strong he lifted Leah off her feet. Leah cried out at the pain of his iron grasp. Her sob only tightened his grip.

"Leave us, Savta." His voice was a hiss.

"No!" Savta jumped up to grab his other arm, his height making her small feet graze the dust of the courtyard. Leah's heart wrenched in fear for her grandmother.

"Leah, Savta! You are both here."

Three set of eyes stared at the woman, Leah held tight in the grip of a painful fist, Savta tugging on the other arm, the man between them a tower of black rage.

Leah's mother stood across the courtyard. Talitha wore a taut smile on a head held high, willing them to believe she was oblivious to the anger in the room. She continued smoothly, as though they did not gawk at her with open mouths. "You are home early, Leah. Did you have fun with your friends today?"

Leah could not have spoken if her life depended on it. Her arm throbbed under the tight pressure of her father's fingers. Even with her mother there, she did not have the courage to pull away.

"Goodness, Leah, your father is right. Please go wash up and change clothes. Then you can walk Savta home before the evening meal. Savta, will you help Leah before you go? You can braid her hair."

Talitha walked up to her husband, her words quiet and respectful. "You will return in an hour or two for the evening meal?" She met her husband's angry face with wide eyes, as though his return would be an unexpected pleasure.

His black eyes narrowed as the silence stretched into an eternity. Then, just as sudden as his rage, he shoved Leah away from him, nearly sending her into a sprawl at his feet, and shook the frail Savta from his arm. Leah crouched in a half-kneel, staring at the big hand suspended in the air, fingers splayed, the palm flat and open. "As though he wants to slap me," thought Leah.

But instead, he shrugged and turned his hand up to casually

wave his daughter away, dismissing her with a mocking flick of his fingers. "Do as your mother says. Now." He ignored Savta.

Leah clambered to her feet and sprinted from the room. She heard Savta's slower steps behind her.

She ran but could not escape her father's words. "She is a disgrace."

"She is not a disgrace, she is only twelve. I told her she could go to the stream with her friends. Soon enough she will be a woman and leave me to be married. Please overlook this. I will speak with her."

Far from her father's sight, Leah could not help but pause to listen. Savta placed an arm around Leah's shoulders. She heard her father's mumbled response but could not understand his words.

"You are right, of course." Her mother sounded pleasant, as though they might be discussing what food she would serve him at the evening meal.

Savta pushed up the sleeve of Leah's tunic. Angry red fingerprints were clearly visible, a bruise already spreading across Leah's forearm. Savta's face was a mask Leah could not read. Her father grumbled something else unintelligible.

"I am sorry things did not work out as you had hoped. But you know what I ask of you."

More jumbled growling, rough and angry.

"I thank you for that."

She could not hear the words but she could feel the fury in his voice.

"Yes, of course. It will be as you say, husband. I will speak with our daughter."

Tears filled Leah's eyes. Why did he hate her so?

"He hates everyone," Savta whispered in her ear, as if she knew what Leah was thinking. "You are a beautiful young woman. He is the abomination."

Leah had no answer. Only Savta dared to say such things of Leah's father. She heard the wooden gate to their courtyard bang once, twice, and be still. Her father was gone.

Great sobs tore at Leah's throat, fear, pain and relief rolled into one.

"Leah." Her mother paused at the door, as though seeing her daughter for the first time that afternoon. She held the wildflowers in her hand. "Are these for me?"

12

Leah looked at the bedraggled flowers, too upset to speak.

"They are beautiful, Leah, thank you." She walked up and wiped away her daughter's tears, Savta's arm still around Leah's shaking shoulders.

Her voice was gentle. "It's all right now, Leah. Your father will not return for several hours. He is just upset about something that happened today. You startled him. Don't cry. You know your father is... difficult."

"Difficult? Pah."

"Mother, please." Talitha's voice was patient but her eyes never left her daughter's face. "Leah, I am sorry your father lost his temper with you. I am."

Leah let out a long, shaky breath. She stared at her mother, her beautiful face wrinkled in worry for her only daughter. At once Leah's words tumbled out in a jumbled rush. "I am sorry I got so dirty, we just... We went down to the stream, and we did wade in the water. It was...is just so beautiful today. And Savta gave us a picnic to take with us..."

"I did! Cakes and figs for my little dove."

"And I, we... just had fun. I did walk through town and people did see me and I am a mess. And then Father was here, he was so angry that I got so dirty, and especially that people saw me. I am sorry. I am."

Her mother was unperturbed by Leah's babbled confession. "It's all right. By the time we eat this evening, your father won't even remember this afternoon. His mind will be busy with other things by then."

"Pah." Savta's aversion to Leah's father edged its way into the conversation, but Leah still had many questions for her mother.

"And why was Father here in the middle of the afternoon? Who was that man? He was horrid, he stared at me so, and then he said something to Father about me being the girl Father was offering. What did that mean, Mother? What?" Her words were a nervous prattle, but the fear of her father was ebbing away in the calm presence of her mother. "Who was that awful man, Mother?"

"Pah."

Talitha's quiet voice matched her expressionless face. "Daughter, do not concern yourself over that man. You will not see him again, I am certain."

13

"But Mother…"

"Do not worry about what you heard today, Leah."

"Pah!"

Leah's mother ignored Savta, and even though Leah was dirty and muddy and, just as her father said, smelled of sweat, kissed her cheek. "Let's put this afternoon behind us, shall we? Let's think about the pleasant day you had with your friends instead."

Savta's eyebrows drew together in a look of pure mutiny, but Leah's tentative nod settled it. Her father was gone and so was the last remnant of his anger. Her mother said not to worry about the stranger. Her father had said there was no agreement. Leah did not want to think of it ever again.

Talitha clasped her daughter's hand on one side and her mother's hand on the other. Three generations of women walked to the large sunlit room where Leah's mother and grandmother worked every afternoon but the Sabbath.

"I have something to show you, Leah. Savta and I finished it while you were gone. We have been working on it for a long time, a surprise for you. Savta came back so we could show it to you together."

How many times had Leah returned home to find her mother and Savta sitting at their looms in this room? She looked at the faded flowers her mother still held. How many times had she crept beside her mother, shyly holding out the same bright but wilted gift? Or climbed into her grandmother's lap to share the adventures of her day? She could not begin to count them.

Talitha stopped her at the door. "Close your eyes, Leah. It is a surprise."

"Close your eyes, my little dove! A surprise for you," Savta echoed.

How many times had Leah run to this room, only to have her mother cry out, "Close your eyes, Leah. I have a surprise!" Leah would stand, expectant and excited, eyes squeezed shut. Her mother would smooth back the sleeve of Leah's workaday wool tunic and fumble at her wrist with strong hands calloused from long hours of weaving.

"Look," her mother would say, and there would be a small colorful bracelet, a neat circle woven with all the colors of the flowers wild in the fields. Happy bracelets, Leah called them. Leah wore them until they frayed into threadbare strands.

"My father would say I am too old for surprises," Leah thought. She pushed him from her mind.

"Open your eyes, Leah."

Leah caught her breath. Savta beamed as she held up a beautiful linen cloth spread out on her old loom, a rich blue expanse woven with the colors of a breaking storm, purple and violet and silver gray. "It is for you, Leah, for your dowry. We will sew a new tunic from it, for when you marry." Her grandmother's brown face wrinkled up in a smile.

"Oh." It was a sigh, for Leah had no words. It was magnificent.

Leah was the seventh generation of women who worked at their looms, weavers of beautiful cloth prized for their even threads and durable strength. It was a skill handed down from mother to daughter to granddaughter, the sturdy fabric of their hands well-known at the markets, sold by fathers and husbands for a good price.

Except for the work of Leah's mother. The weaving of Talitha's hands fetched prices the women before her could not have imagined. Leah's mother was not a weaver; she was an artist. She cared nothing about bleached gray wools or nubby brown cottons. With her hands, Leah's mother unfurled the most beautiful linens of brilliant blue and chalky brown and pure white, like a clear sky shining over the snow on Mount Hermon. From her clacking loom came the lush green and deep gold and earth brown of the nearby fields. Her nimble fingers created the vivid reds and oranges of a Jordan sun setting over the fading silver-pink mountains.

Everyday, Leah's mother and grandmother sat with the sun shining in through open windows, weaving the valuable linen for Leah's father to sell. It was a rare day that Leah did not sit there too, Leah's mother at her large loom, Savta at her ancient one with its creaking pedals, and Leah at the tedious spindle pulling the threads of costly linen or common wool.

The wooden beaters of the two big looms would click in an easy rhythm with each other, clack, clack, shuttles passing back and forth at a steady pace, in, out, in out. Savta's cloth would pile up in a tight sturdy nap while her mother's sprawled out in slow beautiful folds.

Leah looked at the rich blue cloth Savta still held, a gift of beauty for the day she married. She felt the love worked into every thread. "It is amazing. Thank you." She turned to her mother, hesitant. "Are you sure Father will not want to sell it? It is amazing. This would bring a very great price."

"It is not for sale. I made it for my daughter." Talitha was strong like Leah's father, but in a different way, one Leah could not comprehend. Everyone was afraid of Leah's father: her brothers, the workers, their neighbors. Everyone feared him except his wife Talitha. And Savta, of course.

Talitha was still talking. "This is just for your wedding. We will weave more cloth for you, too, in colors you may choose. After all, you will need some new things to wear when you are betrothed."

Leah suddenly remembered what she had forgotten in the moments with her father, her reason for rushing home lost in the terrible events of that afternoon. "Mother! Guess what I found out today? Dorcas is getting married and moving to Damascus! Her father just signed the betrothal contract. Did you know this?"

Savta and Talitha exchanged glances before her mother nodded. "Yes, I heard. That's why I wanted you to go today, so Dorcas could tell you the news herself."

"The first of your friends to marry, my little dove. My granddaughter will soon be a woman, too."

"Before long, your father will enter into negotiations for your betrothal and marriage too, Leah."

Leah plopped down on the bench, her knees as weak as when her father had loomed over her. She thought of the stranger. "He is? To who?"

Her mother smiled. "He will enter into negotiations, Leah, not has. He has not yet started serious conversations with any families. Your father has not picked out any particular young man yet."

"Mother, Dorcas is marrying a cousin she doesn't even know. And she will have to live in Damascus!" The thought of moving to far-off Damascus was much more upsetting to Leah than the idea of marrying a stranger. "I do not want to marry anyone if it means I must move away from you or Savta."

"Damascus is not that far away." But Leah thought her mother did not quite look her in the eye as she said this.

"Pah!" Savta snorted.

Leah remembered the stranger and his sneer, the covetous way he had looked at her, as though she were a mere possession. "Who was that man today, Mother? He said to Father, 'So this is the girl you would offer me?' He was so old, and a stranger! Mother, please, who was that man?"

Talitha gazed at her. Leah could tell she was choosing her words with great care. "Leah, first, you know you must not worry about tomorrow. Tomorrow and the things it will bring are in God's hands. Trust me, you do not need to worry about that man anymore."

She laid a gentle hand on Leah's cheek. "I waited many years for God to bless me with a daughter. You are God's greatest gift to me, all I hoped and prayed for. As Savta said, soon you will be a woman."

"My granddaughter, a beautiful woman."

Leah's face grew warm with pleasure, her father's scornful rage, the sneering stranger, the afternoon's hatred forgotten.

"It is my deepest desire that after you marry, you remain here in Caesarea Philippi, close to me, as I have been able to stay near to Savta all these years. It is what I would choose for you. It is all I ask of your father."

"And you will tell him this?" Leah was as startled at the demand in her words as she knew her mother must be. But she had to know the answer.

"Pah. No one tells him anything." Savta's wrinkled brown smile was gone, her voice bitter.

"Mother, please do not speak so. Leah, I have talked with your father, asking that you be allowed to stay near me. This is a busy little town and there are many opportunities here. I see no reason why your father cannot find a husband for you close to home. A young man might even be given the opportunity to work for your father. Many people do, after all."

She pulled Leah to her feet and stroked her messy hair, smoothing the tangles. "My heart would break if you were to go far away, Leah. For didn't King David say, 'Even the sparrow has found a home, and the swallow a nest for herself, where she may keep her young?'"

"Where the swallow keeps her young, little dove," Savta echoed.

"I have been faithful to Gracious Jehovah for all my years, no matter what hardship life has brought me. Surely my Lord will allow me this one thing, that you might remain close to Savta and me after you marry."

"Close to your mother and close to me, your beloved grandmother!"

Talitha grabbed Leah in a quick hug and then pushed her back to look at her from head to toe, her eyebrows arched high on her smooth forehead. "Now, you must get cleaned up, and quickly. Savta, will you take the evening meal with us?"

"No."

Leah's father loathed his mother-in-law as much as Savta despised him. It was the rarest of occasions that they would break bread together. But in all of Leah's years, her mother never failed to ask Savta to stay.

"Then Leah will walk you home." Talitha looked at her disheveled daughter and shook her head again, this time with a mock sternness. "You must hurry."

"I can walk myself. Leah must be ready before her father returns." Savta waved away her daughter with an unconcerned shrug.

"I will walk you then, while Leah baths."

"Pffth. Get your dinner ready, it is only a few quick steps to my house. Or slow steps for me. But I am not walking through death's door just yet, daughter."

"If you are sure."

"Of course I am sure. I can walk myself home, girl. After all, I am the only one in this room who has climbed all the way to the top of the Old Gray Haired Lady and felt the snow between my toes. That's more than you can say, my dearest daughter."

Leah's mouth fell open. "Savta, you have not been to the top of Mount Hermon!"

The Old Gray-Haired Lady was Savta's pet name for Mount Hermon, for "she's a gray-haired old woman like me." It was a remarkable sight Leah never tired of, the massive mountain looming over Caesarea Philippi, its brown jagged peak covered with dazzling white snow for much of the year. And Savta once felt the mountain's snow between her toes? "You have not!"

"Yes, I have. Years ago, when I was young and strong like you. But perhaps you are not as strong as me, my little dove? You seem a bit puny. Let's see."

At once, Savta clamped Leah's wrist in a grip made strong by decades of weaving, despite bony knuckles swollen with arthritis.

"Savta! Ow! Let go, please!" Leah squirmed to pull away, but one could not escape Savta's strong hand if she did not choose to release you. "Please!"

Her grandmother laughed and loosened her iron grasp. "Hmmm. You are not as strong as your ancient grandmother, but I believe you might be strong enough to climb the Old Lady with me. Wouldn't you like to go to feel the snow between your toes?"

"Savta, it would take days to get to the top, you know that."

"Mother, do not fill Leah's head with nonsense." Leah grinned at the tone of exasperation in Talitha's voice. Only Savta could evoke that reaction.

"Pffth." Savta dismissed her daughter with an airy wave and turned to Leah. "It is only a day's ride by donkey, a long day, that is true. But once you get to the top, you have to spend the night, for you cannot go up and come back down in one day. I guess you will just have to wait and go with your husband like I did."

"What?"

"Why, Leah, have I never told you about the time I went to the top of the Old Gray-Haired Lady? Right up in the snow! It was so much fun. I went with your grandfather when we were first married. He rode to the top, he on his father's donkey and me on ours. We set up our tent with a fire in the snow, just the two of us, snuggled up under our blankets." Her grandmother winked at the memory, one Leah had never heard before. Talitha's lips twitched, not to scold, Leah knew, but with affection for beloved Savta.

"You went to the top, Savta?" Leah could not keep the disbelief from her voice.

"Yes! It was quite shocking to everyone, you see. For we went only for fun, your grandfather and I. Everyone thought we were true sluggards, wasting two whole days going up and down the Old Gray-Haired Lady for no good reason at all!"

Leah had never met her grandfather; he had been dead for many years. Everyone knew Savta still loved him.

"Oh, how everyone was scolded us, especially my mother! Such a scandal. And yet, it was the most wonderful thing…"

"She was right to scold you," Talitha interrupted. "Mother, Leah must get cleaned up before her father comes home."

"Pah!" But Savta fell silent, for it would be a terrible thing for Leah's father to find his daughter still in her disheveled state. Leah's mother could only diffuse moments like today so often. Still, Leah was not ready to let go of the moment.

"Savta, you never told me this before. There is not time today,"

Leah glanced at her mother, "but I can't wait to hear it all about it. Will you tell me tomorrow?"

"Of course, Leah, of course. Tomorrow is as good as today. Goodbye, my favorite granddaughter."

"Savta, I am your only granddaughter." Despite that minor detail, Leah wore a smile to be called Savta's favorite.

"True enough. Kiss me, my little dove."

Leah pecked the wrinkly brown cheek and then turned to stare at her grandmother's loom covered by the beautiful blue linen of her dowry. Talitha knew exactly what Leah was thinking, as usual. "Don't touch that, dearest daughter. Your hands are dirty."

Leah did not argue with her mother when she called her dearest daughter.

Savta added in a stern voice. "'Those who are pure in their own eyes are not cleansed of their filth.' King Solomon spoke wisely, for you are filthy, filthy, filthy, Leah!"

Leah grinned. Her mother might quote the splendid poetry of King David's psalms to her daughter, but Savta preferred the stern proverbs of King Solomon to scold. Leah heard from cranky old Solomon far more often than mighty King David.

"Now go, my granddaughter, before your sweet father returns." Savta raised mischievous eyebrows at Talitha and winked at Leah. "I will tell you all about my stroll up the Old Gray-Haired Lady some other time."

"Tomorrow. You must tell me tomorrow, Savta."

"Tomorrow, tomorrow. Pffth. As good as today, isn't that tomorrow?"

Leah's voice was firm as she spoke to Savta's back.

"Tomorrow, Savta."

Her grandmother turned in the doorway, little and shriveled, and nodded with a knowing smile on her wrinkled face. "Yes, my little dove. Tomorrow is as good as today, my Leah. Tomorrow."

∞

Leah scrubbed herself clean with one thought chasing another in her head.

The beautiful gift from her mother and Savta came to her mind with its vivid colors. Knowing it was something precious to be set aside for the day she took a husband made her shiver. Suddenly that day was not so far away.

Her grandmother had been to the top of Mount Hermon! Leah could not wait to see her grandmother tomorrow, for Savta's story was certain to be full of the laughter of her youth and love for her long-dead husband. Tomorrow Leah would hear about Savta and the Old Gray-Haired Lady.

Who was that awful stranger, who thought the loss of Leah was of no importance? He had been a nasty man. Her father could not possibly choose someone so repulsive to be her husband.

Surely Talitha would not let Leah be married to someone so old, so disgusting. She desperately believed her mother would not allow her only daughter to be sent far away in marriage to a stranger or to some distant city. Her friends might marry and move from Caesarea Philippi, but not Leah. Only Talitha could change the mind of Leah's fearsome father.

Her mother prayed only that Leah could marry and stay near her. "I have been faithful to Gracious Jehovah for all my years, no matter what hardship life has brought me," she had said. Leah's mother had sounded so sad.

Talitha had rescued Leah from the terrible rage of her father today, as she had done so many times before.

Life with Leah's father was surely a hardship for her mother, too. But Talitha never uttered even one disrespectful or angry word about her husband.

When Leah was small and heard her father approach, she would run to the safest place she knew, the lap of her mother. She would climb up and cuddle, listening to her mother sing the gentle psalms of Kind David until he left. When little Leah was certain her father was gone, she would turn to look at her mother until their noses nearly touched, Leah cross-eyed with the effort to not blink.

Her mother would call her silly, but she always smiled. "God has brought me laughter, and her name is Leah," she would say, just like Sarah had said about Isaac.

Leah loved her mother more than anyone in the world, even more than Savta, if that was possible. Savta was fun and joy and love. Leah's mother was... well, she was that and everything else, too.

For who loved Leah like her mother?

As long as Leah could remember, her mother talked to her as

though she were smart, grown up, and most of all, as if she were a friend. Her mother was always at work and while she was working, she always teaching Leah: how to cook lentils with lamb, how to press the oil from the olives, how to grind the wheat into the finest flour possible. She would patiently show Leah how to spin the thread so it was strong and smooth, without knots or flaw. She taught her to prepare the Passover feast with its unleavened bread and bitter herbs, and to recite the evening prayers, even though Leah's father always prayed them.

Most important of all, Leah's mother taught her the Psalms, every beautiful word.

"My mother taught all the Psalms to me," Talitha had said.

"Savta knows all the Psalms? She only talks about Solomon!"

"Never mind that, she knows them all. She taught them to me and now I teach them to you. Never forget a single word, Leah.

> 'I lift my eyes up to the hills –'
> See our beautiful hills, Leah?
> 'Where does my help come from?
> My help comes from the Lord,
> Maker of Heaven and Earth.
> The Lord will keep you from all harm,
> He will watch over your life,
> Your coming and going, Leah, now and forever more.
> Selah.'"

"Selah," Leah would echo. She loved the quiet, unshakeable strength in that final word.

"Selah," Leah whispered in the quiet of her room, coming back to her present dilemma. Why couldn't Leah's father find a husband for Leah here in Caesarea Philippi? Why would he send her off to some foreign city like Damascus? Why should she have to wed some unknown, alien stranger of a man? If only she had the courage, she would beg her father to do as her mother asked and not send her away. The only person he ever listened to – when he listened to anyone - was her mother.

She snickered over her mother's suggestion that Leah's future husband could work for her father. "If a job with him is part of my dowry, I will never get married." She stole a fearful look at that impertinent notion, even though her father could not possibly know her thoughts when he was not even at home.

She could hear the clanking of pots as her mother prepared their evening meal. Her father would soon return with her two older brothers to recite their prayers and eat their quiet evening meal.

Her father would drone on and on about his business and work and deals he had made. Her brothers would nod silent responses, speaking only if asked a direct question. Leah would sit as still as a mouse, eyes fixed on her plate. Her father never asked a question of her.

The only smile to ever be found was on the face of her mother. But even Leah was old enough to recognize the tense set of her mother's jaw that accompanied her polite responses to her husband.

Yes, meals with Leah's father were solemn affairs.

Leah brightened at a sudden thought. Her brothers now both were old enough to work for her father. Better yet, both were recently betrothed to be married, one right after the other. With two weddings in their family's immediate future, perhaps her father wouldn't have the time or the money to find a husband for Leah anytime soon.

Boys were lucky. Her brothers were both in their early twenties. They weren't considered old maids before they were thirteen. Boys had some say in who they married.

Well, some boys did. She didn't think her brothers had any more choice about their intended brides than she would about her husband.

Leah sighed. She did not want to be a young woman, or get married, or leave her mother or Savta. She just wanted to be a girl, like she was right now, forever.

She mulled over the unfairness of her future until another thought crossed her mind.

Her father would be very angry to return home and, clean down to her last toenail or not, find his daughter sitting idly on a stool while her mother worked alone, especially after he had seen her in such a mess that afternoon. Her father's rage was far worse than marrying some ancient, horrid, alien stranger from a faraway city.

Leah jumped up and ran to the hall. "Here I am, Mother!"

Talitha turned at the sound of her daughter, smiling at the laughter that was Leah.

CHAPTER 2

Leah forced her feet to behave as she walked down the dusty street. It seemed wise to appear somewhat dignified, considering how many people had seen her bedraggled state yesterday. She was, after all, almost a young woman.

But not quite.

Besides, after yesterday's joyous romp in the rushing water and gray mud of the stream, chattering and laughing as girls are prone to do, her friends had not looked much better than Leah. Not that her father cared anything about that, of course.

The sun beat down hot and bright. Leah wished she was a young girl with a bare head and loose hair. Instead, she was nearly a woman with a tight braid and heavy veil, even if the veil was a golden shimmer woven by the hands of Talitha.

All the way, Leah greeted the women grinding wheat, spinning thread and stirring pots in their small courtyards. Her cheerful hellos were returned one after another. It was impossible not to smile when they saw Leah.

Privately, those women often questioned how that coltish, giggling girl had grown up to be the sparkling young woman she almost was. Leah had the beauty and wit but none of the elegant reserve of her mother, a woman whose devout fervor for Jehovah was unmatched in their close-knit Jewish neighborhood.

"Be strong, take heart, and wait for the Lord," Talitha was often heard to say. "Selah."

On the other hand, Leah bore no resemblance to her father at all. From her striking looks to her sunny – albeit often giggly – temperament, there was not a single scrap of him to be found in his only daughter.

Thank goodness, those same knowing wags gossiped. The fact that Leah had turned out to be such a laughing - yes, it was true - truly happy young woman was nothing short of a miracle if one thought of her angry, impossible father.

But one could never forget that Leah was not only the daughter of beautiful, unshakeable Talitha but also the only granddaughter of cheerful, irreverent Savta. The two women had rescued little Leah from the travesty that was her father, molding her into the young woman she was today.

Leah was headed to Savta's now, the basket on her arm hiding bread fresh from her mother's oven. She swung it back and forth in time to her quick stride, higher and higher, forgetting her resolve to be a proper young woman as she strolled past the neighbors who knew her so well.

Mount Hermon loomed in the distance, its brown craggy terrain casting an ashen shadow over the lush, green landscape for miles. Smaller gray mountains waited on her, handmaidens stepping down to the luxuriant grassy hills and golden fields of northern Galilee, the least of the kingdoms of Israel. In Hermon's long shadow sat the city of Caesarea Philippi. The grand palace of King Philip with its fortified Roman garrison, the white stone temples to the pagan idols, and the prosperous houses of important people stood on one side. The simple brown homes of the Jews, laborers and poor people lay on the other.

Leah lived in one of the biggest houses on the brown side.

Only a few old people like Savta called the village Panias anymore. As soon as King Herod died, his son Philip renamed it Caesarea Philippi in honor of himself and Caesar.

Whoever Caesar was, Leah would think with a sniff.

King Philip sometimes lived in the beautiful palace he had built in his namesake city, and visited his temples to the foreign gods near the springs that fed the Jordan River.

Since she lived on the brown side of the city, Leah cared nothing for the Romans and their temples or even the soldiers that sometimes passed by on their horses with their glinting swords and helmets.

Leah was born in Caesarea Philippi. She shared her large home with her parents and two brothers, a home larger than most of her friends and neighbors. Except for the sunny workroom of Talitha and Savta, it was a hushed, cold home. Leah spent as little time there as possible, preferring the sunny streets and noisy homes of her friends instead. She knew every street, shop and person in the brown half of her city. Every neighbor young and old knew her just as well. Her mother shopped and worked and visited with the other women here. Her family worshipped in the same synagogue with the same people for all of Leah's short life. The brown side of Caesarea Philippi, Panias, was home.

Leah's pace quickened. With each step she swung the basket a bit higher. She found herself on her toes and, just because the wispy clouds were so white in a sky so shockingly blue, she twirled around in the street. She could not wait to hear about Savta the new bride standing in the snow on top of the Old Gray-Haired Lady.

Perhaps Savta would be sleeping, Leah thought, chuckling at the memory of only a week ago. Leah had stepped into Savta's small house, only to spy her grandmother sitting straight up in her corner chair with her eyes closed and her chin on her chest. Savta was asleep, drowsing in a small patch of warm sunlight. Savta did not like to be caught napping.

"Pah. A little sleep, a little slumber," she would often sniff when awakened. "Let King Solomon and his poverty find me, I don't care."

Leah had not wanted to startle her sleeping grandmother, so she spoke softly, her voice a gentle singsong. "Saav-taah…"

Savta's eyes had flown open. She stared at Leah as though a complete stranger stood before her. Then, she jumped up with a shout.

"Go to the ant, you sluggard!"

Leah had been frightened half to death instead of the other way around.

Savta had stood there with her eyes wide and unblinking, a look of tremendous surprise on her face. They both stood there in the silence, until the quivering of Leah's chin could not be denied. Savta broke into a grin.

"Pffth! I guess I was dreaming about those silly sluggards of old Solomon."

They both laughed so hard, they were crying. "Oh, goodness, go to the ants," Savta said several times, hiccupping. "Sluggards and ants, Leah."

Leah giggled at the memory. Sluggards were excuse-making dullards that lay in bed all day, too lazy to even lift their hands up to their mouths to feed themselves. So ancient King Solomon and Savta claimed, anyway.

When Leah was small, she had asked her beloved grandmother, "But what does a sluggard *look* like, Savta?"

Savta had been most perplexed. "Hmmm. I don't know," she said, frowning. "Solomon tells sluggards to go the ants. Let's find one!"

Together, little Leah and Savta had knelt down on the ground. Their eyes kept close watch on an ant hill, to see if a sluggard would come. Would it look like a butterfly, Leah wondered? A worm, Savta guessed. But no sluggard ever came, only busy ants that scurried about on their little hill. They fed the ants bits of bread from Savta's pocket, admiring the great crumb a single tiny warrior could carry. They watched until they got hot, and then went inside to eat fresh bread and honey themselves.

Leah and Savta laughed a lot that day, too.

Savta's life was a string of stories, one excitement after another. Savta remembered many, many things, and she told them all to her granddaughter Leah.

Savta remembered when Philip's temple was constructed in their then-small village. She told how all the Jews labored on that mighty white building; long, harsh days worked by Jew and Gentile to satisfy the new King's cruel overseers. At least King Philip was not as terrible as his father, Herod the Great, the murderer of baby boys, Savta said. At least King Philip was not as bad as his insane brother Herod Antipas of Jerusalem, whose rule and marriage were abominations to Jehovah.

Savta remembered when the temples to the pagan Roman gods were built near the springs in the cliff side caves. When the Jewish carpenters and craftsmen refused to work at the heathen sites, the rage of the Romans had been terrible. It had been a frightful time, all caused by those false gods whose very presence mocked Jehovah, the One True God of the Chosen People.

Savta remembered when Jews from her childhood had been persecuted, sent to their deaths by a man whose name Savta would only whisper, the evil Varsus, now dead for many years like the evil Roman ruler he obeyed. Savta's eyes still filled with tears when she recounted the names of men, women, even children who lost their lives to that vicious general's reign of terror.

The biggest temple was dedicated, Savta said, to the Roman god named Pan, who was half-man and half-goat. Savta laughed about worshipping a smelly goat. "How can anyone bow down to something you have to milk every morning?" Savta had chortled. "Which half is the man, the head-half or the back-half?"

"Mother!" At such impertinent comments, Talitha would shush her mother with a very real irritation.

Leah would snicker at her grandmother's impudence about the god of the Gentiles. A long life of living behind her, Savta did not take many things seriously any more.

Leah stood at the gate to Savta's tiny courtyard. When Leah's mother married, the widow Savta immediately left her large home and moved into a small house only one street away, leaving the stately home to her only child and new son-in-law. The grandparents of many of Leah's friends lived with their grown children and grandchildren, but not Leah's. Leah thought she knew why, but it was never discussed.

Now, Leah spent her mornings helping Savta, who was not as strong as she once was, and certainly not as strong as she stubbornly claimed to be. Leah would fetch the water from the well, clean Savta's little home, make up her bed, milk the small black goat, gather up clothes to be washed, or match Savta's slow steps to walk arm in arm to the market. It was not a chore, for Leah loved Savta like no other.

Most days, Savta would return to her old home with Leah, where three generations of women would pray and take their lunch. Then, Leah's mother and Savta would seat themselves in the workroom, Leah's mother on her large loom and Savta on her ancient one, their hands flying as the beautiful cloth rolled from their looms.

But before Leah did her grandmother's chores this morning, Savta had to tell her about her trip up the Old Gray-Haired Lady. Leah did not know a single woman who had been to the top before, but she had no doubt that her grandmother had done exactly what she said. Her grandmother was special. Everyone said so.

"Savta!" She stood in the courtyard, but silence answered Leah. "Savta!" She peeked into the door of Savta's home, but did not see her. Where was she? Perhaps she was dressing. Leah moved the curtain to look into Savta's tiny room.

Savta was still in her bed! Leah smiled. Oh, Savta would scold herself when she found out she had slept so late into the morning sunshine. Savta yelled at herself all the time, but she always laughed when she did so.

Leah stood at the bedroom door and watched her beloved Savta sleep.

"Savta," Leah lowered her voice, for she didn't want to startle her grandmother like she did last week, when Savta had jumped up to shout about sluggards and ants. She walked to Savta's bed and looked down. Savta looked so peaceful, happy in her rest.

"She must be having good dreams," thought Leah. Perhaps her dreams this morning were of a beautiful bride and her young husband at the top of the wind-swept mountain, instead the lazy ways of Solomon's sluggards.

"Savta." Leah's voice was soft. Her grandmother did not move.

"Saav-ta." This time Leah gave her grandmother's shoulder a little shake. Her grandmother still did not answer.

"Saaav-taaaa." Leah took Savta's hand to gently pull her awake.

Leah bolted from the bed like a startled deer, staring at Savta as she clutched the curtain at the doorway. Savta had not moved. Her eyes were still closed. Her old, wrinkled hands with their big blue veins and brown spots and knobby knuckles were as cold as the snow on Mount Hermon. The only sound was Leah's loud and ragged breathing in the silent room.

Savta did not move. She would not wake up. She was cold, so terribly cold.

"Savta!" Leah's cry was a shout in the silence.

Leah ran through the streets as fast as she could. She had to get to her mother. Only her mother could help Savta.

"I shook her, she would not move, her hands were so cold, she would not wake up!" Leah was all but incoherent in her urgency over Savta.

"Savta's hands were cold? She would not wake up?" Talitha turned to look at her daughter, her hands motionless at the loom, her gaze steady. She did not jump to her feet as Leah anticipated.

"No! I shook her and shook her again, but she would not move! She is so cold, Mother! Hurry, please, please hurry!" she begged.

But Talitha did not move.

"Mother!" Leah's voice was nearly a shriek. "Please!"

"Oh, Mother." Talitha's eyes filled with tears. "How can I face life without you?" She bowed her head until it nearly touched her lap. "Oh, my mother."

"Please, Mother, please." Leah heard the tears in her voice.

"Sit, Leah." Her mother's voice was muffled. Leah perched on the edge of Savta's stool, every muscle tense. She had only one thought, that her mother would know how to help Savta.

But her mother did not get up. She began to sway back and forth, a low moan the only sound in the room. Leah stared; something was very wrong.

Before Leah could speak, Talitha stood, her posture slumped, her movements as slow and painful as Leah's aged grandmother. Leah watched in bewilderment as her mother began to beat her chest with one hand, a slow, rhythmic pounding. With the other hand, she yanked and tugged at the collar of her tunic, pulling and pulling until finally the cloth gave way. The large tear was right over her heart. Leah's eyes widened at the sight.

"May his great name be exalted and sanctified in the worlds that he created." Leah jumped. Her mother's voice was loud in the silent room. Tears ran down her face.

Leah's mother was praying! Leah was so surprised at her mother's actions, she forgot to close her eyes. What was she doing? Leah tried to listen, but she wanted to drag her mother to Savta.

"May his great name be blessed forever and ever. Blessed, praised, glorified, exalted, extolled, Oh Mighty Jehovah." Her voice trailed off. Leah was afraid to speak; she could not remember ever seeing her mother cry. Why did they not run as fast as they could to help Savta?

"Is it Savta?" Leah's oldest brother had come to stand at the door at the sound of Talitha's loud and plaintive prayers.

Her mother nodded and reached for her veil. "Find your father and tell him to go to Savta's."

Her brother walked away quickly, his backward glance at Leah solemn. Leah did not understand what her mother and brother knew and she did not.

"Come with me, Leah." They walked in silence to Savta's. At the sight of Talitha's tears and torn robe, the neighborhood women straightened from their labors to stand quietly, only their expressive eyes showing any emotion, their heads bowed in respect as Leah and her mother walked by. A few women dabbed at sudden tears, but Leah paid them no attention.

"We need to hurry," Leah thought desperately. "We need to help to Savta."

The house looked just like it had when Leah ran from it only minutes ago, the shutters still closed, the courtyard fire a pile of cold ashes. Savta's little black goat stood tethered to the stone wall, bleating for attention. Talitha walked inside, Leah right on her heels.

"Sit here, Leah, until I call for you." Leah sat down on the low bench by Savta's table.

Leah sat for what seemed to be an eternity. She did not know when she began to cry, but now she could not stop. She wiped her tears on the hem of her veil, once and then again and again. For as she sat alone in the dark room, Leah understood. She had run to her mother for help, but she knew. She had known the moment she touched Savta's icy hand.

Her grandmother was dead.

Leah's father walked in. He did not even glance at Leah but went straight to Savta's bedroom, his rough hands pushing aside the worn cloth that separated the space between Leah and her grandmother.

"She died in her sleep last night, I suppose." Leah heard her mother's voice, but could not understand her father's low, mumbled response.

"Yes, this afternoon, of course, if you would hire the mourners and ready the grave." Her mother sounded sad beyond measure. "I have all I need. Savta was ready."

31

The low rumble answered.

"No. Thank you. Leah will help me."

Her father walked into the room where Leah still sat. She cast her eyes down, hoping he would not see her tears or worse, speak to her.

He paused to look at the shaking, crying huddle that was his only daughter, then left without a word.

☙

Leah wanted to run away, to her home or to her friends or to the stream or even to the top of Mount Hermon. She wanted to be anywhere but here, but she did not move from the spot where her mother had told her to sit. Her mother still was with Savta. Leah wanted her mother in the worst way, as if she were a small girl rather than a young woman, but she was afraid to go into the room where Savta lay dead.

The shuttered room had an eerie darkness, the cracks of sunlight creeping through casting odd shadows. Without Savta's laughter or songs, this room was cold and shadowy. When would her mother come out?

"Leah, come in here please."

Leah did not answer. Perhaps her mother would come out instead.

"Leah, please. I need you."

Leah stood up, but her knees were shaking so hard she could barely make them move. She forced one reluctant foot after another until she stood before the curtain that hid Savta from her sight. She pushed the worn cloth aside.

Her mother knelt on the floor beside Savta's low bed. She looked up at Leah. "Come, sit here beside me and Savta."

Leah shook her head.

Her mother's eyes filled with tears, but her voice was gentler than Leah had ever heard it before. "It will be all right, Leah. Come sit with us."

Leah took the two steps to the bed and cautiously crouched beside her mother and the peaceful form of her grandmother. She wanted to burst into loud sobs, but instead took a deep breath and held it, every muscle in her body as taut as a bowstring. Her mother

32

was not crying anymore, so she would not either. Leah scrunched her eyes shut, as though that could keep her loud and noisy sobs at bay.

With her eyes closed, Leah saw Savta beside an ant hill, looking for a sluggard, feeding bits of bread to the insects that others called pests but Savta called Jehovah's tiniest warriors.

In her mind's eye, she saw Savta at her loom, slowly moving the shuttle back and forth, painfully pulling the heavy beater to her in a clack clack motion, a bright gold cloth under her knobby fingers, the words of King Solomon on her lips.

She could see Savta gesturing with her arms wild in the air, as she told Leah story after story. Tales of the Roman gods and the persecuted Jews, about the young, handsome man she had married and loved and then buried, about the beautiful and sometimes naughty little girl who was her only child.

She saw the face of Savta beaming as she held up a beautiful cloth for her granddaughter, blue folds spread out over her ancient loom. There was Savta sitting on her little stool in the corner under her window, sleeping in the sun with a smile on her wrinkled face. Savta's aching hands were packing a bag of treats for Leah and her friends for a picnic. Savta was standing in the doorway, smiling and waving goodbye.

"Tomorrow is as good as today, Leah!" With her eyes closed, Leah could hear Savta's joyous voice. "As good as today, that is tomorrow, my little dove."

Leah would never, ever know the story of Savta the new bride climbing the Old Gray-Haired Lady.

She let out a long sigh. The moment her breath left her, the sorrow won. Sobs tore at her throat, angry, loud, broken-hearted. She fell over from her tense crouch into a jumble of limbs on the floor, her wails loud in the room.

Her mother pulled her up and laid Leah's head in her lap. "Oh, Leah, it is all right. Don't cry so." She stroked Leah's hair. "Savta was old and terribly frail. She lived a long, long life, much longer than most. She was not afraid of death. Don't cry, my little dove."

At the sound of Savta's pet name for her, Leah cried harder. "I won't ever know the story of Savta climbing the Gray-Haired Lady when she was a bride!" Her mother looked at Leah, listening to her frenzied sorrow, her eyes wide pools of understanding in the shadowy room.

"And now, Savta is gone, and I can't come here anymore to help her or to listen to her stories or to be with her ever again! I didn't come here yesterday and now I can't ever be with her again, ever!" Leah buried her head in her mother's lap, shaking with sobs. "I told Savta I would come tomorrow, and she said tomorrow is as good as today! But it's not, because Savta is…" Leah choked on the words. "Savta is dead!"

Talitha stroked her daughter's hair, silent tears in her own eyes before she spoke. "Don't cry, Leah. Your grandmother knew you loved her."

"But I didn't get to say goodbye!"

Leah hid her face. That was the worst part. Leah never got to say goodbye.

"Well, Leah, we can never know when to say goodbye, can we? We never know when a simple goodbye might be the last one. We can only treasure each moment we have with the people we love." She pulled Leah up to a sitting position, her arm warm and comforting around Leah. "She has gone the way of the earth, as did my father so long ago, and my grandparents and Savta's grandparents before her, and as I will go someday, too."

Leah cried harder at her mother's words. The way of the earth was to die. She most certainly did not want to talk about her mother's death when her beloved grandmother lay dead beside her.

Her mother smiled at Leah's renewed tears. "Why, Leah, you too must go when it is your appointed time. The earth's way is God's way, for we do not live forever. God blessed Savta with a long and happy life, and when it was her time, she did not suffer. She just left the world, her death gentle and peaceful. You have not seen death, and so do not understand what a wonderful gift that is, Leah. It was her time."

Leah's voice trembled. She knew what she was about to say was foolish, but she could not help herself. "I don't want Savta to be dead. Or you, or me either. I want Savta to be alive, here with us now!" Even Leah thought she sounded like an unreasonable six-year-old but she couldn't help herself. Savta was dead.

"Oh, my daughter, how I love you. You surely were the sunshine of Savta's life. Now, look at me, Leah." Her mother's voice would not be denied.

"Savta loved you, and she knew how much you loved her. I

know you will miss her, but Savta could live no longer. Remember how much she hurt sometimes, almost so much she could not walk? Her tired body was worn out. Once she was a little girl, then a young woman just like you, next a wife and a mother just like me, and then Savta was an old woman. Her body was not meant to last forever."

Talitha gave Leah a gentle shake. "But Leah, her spirit lives forever with God, and with us. Forevermore, Savta will have a place in our hearts."

She motioned to a large basket on the floor beside them. "Now, you must help me, Leah. Because no one loved Savta like you and I, together we will honor Savta. We must prepare her for burial."

Leah shook her head. She wanted to help her mother, but she could not touch Savta.

Her mother took her hand, her voice a whisper. "Those who loved her best must honor her. That is you and I. Because you love Savta, will you help me? Will you honor our Savta this last time?"

No one loved Savta like Leah. She sat there for a long time in the silence. No one loved Leah like Savta and her mother, either. No one. Leah sighed. "I will help you, Mother."

But her voice trembled as she spoke.

"Don't be afraid. I will tell you what to do. It is our... joy to do this for the woman we both loved so much." Her voice was strong, but there were new tears running down Talitha's face.

Leah looked at her mother and then nodded, this time with certainty. Her mother needed her.

Talitha opened the basket and removed six new candles. "Please light these, Leah. Put three at the head of Savta's bed and three at the foot."

Leah fetched the lamp and used it to light each candle. She placed them on the floor as her mother instructed while Talitha busied herself with the contents of the basket, removing several cloth-wrapped packages and two large jars. She broke a seal of wax from one, the warm glow from the candles mingling with the heavy aroma of a strong perfume.

"Where did all this come from, Mother?"

"Savta bought it some time ago. She knew her time was near, and she wanted everything to be ready. She showed me where it was every week, as if I might forget. Doesn't that sound just like our Savta?"

Leah's eyes widened, horrified that Savta purchased things for her own burial.

Talitha answered the thoughts Leah could not hide. "Yes, Leah, Savta bought these things herself. I was with her. She even wove her own shroud from the finest linen, saying she did not want me to do it, and she certainly did not want to buy an 'inferior' one from the market. That's our Savta, isn't it?"

Leah nodded. Savta was very particular, this was true. Everyone knew it, particularly Leah. Her grandmother had fussed over the finer points of Leah's chores every day.

"Savta was not afraid, Leah. She wanted to be ready when Jehovah God came for her. And you know Savta. She wanted things to be exactly the way she wanted them. Doesn't that sound like your grandmother?"

Despite her tears, Leah nodded. Her grandmother liked things a certain way and was not afraid to tell anyone what that way was.

"Get me her good green tunic from the chest against the wall."

Leah opened the chest, trying to do what her mother said and not stop to touch Savta's familiar things. She found the tunic neatly folded on one side. "This one?"

Her mother nodded. "Now, bring me several bowls of water and clean cloths, so we can wash Savta."

Leah ran from the room and poured water from the jug she herself had filled up for Savta yesterday before she went to the stream with her friends.

"I should have stayed with Savta yesterday, not gone to the stream," Leah thought. The silence of Savta's house taunted her.

She carried the bowls one after another into the bedroom, careful not to slosh water, and set each one on the ground beside her mother.

"Alright, Leah, this is what we must do for Savta. We will wash her, change her clothes, anoint her with these perfumes and ointments and then wrap her in the shroud. Can you do this with me? For Savta?"

Leah took a deep breath and nodded, afraid to say what was in her heart: she did not want to touch her grandmother.

Mother and daughter washed their own hands in preparation to bury Savta, Leah's mother whispering soft prayers. They pulled Savta up to a slumped sitting position. Leah gritted her teeth to hold back her scream when Savta's head lay limp on Leah's shoulder. She had never thought she would do something as terrible as this.

Except, after a few moments, Leah realized what they were doing was not so dreadful after all. Her mother was very, very careful, and so Leah was too. Leah's mother was tender as she moved Savta's limbs as Leah cradled her grandmother's small shoulders and face. Her mother covered Savta's little shriveled body with a clean, white sheet of cotton and then beneath the privacy of the sheet, removed Savta's clothing. Leah watched her mother's gentle hands without speaking.

Her mother was right. There was no one else in the entire world that could do this for Savta except for her daughter Talitha. And there was no one to help Savta's only child except for her beloved granddaughter Leah.

"Savta would have been proud of me," Leah thought. "Perhaps I am ready to be a woman, after all." The thought pricked her heart.

Her mother carefully placed a clean, white cloth over Savta's face. "A sign of respect," she murmured to Leah. She began to wash Savta, careful to keep the body covered so only what was being washed lay vulnerable and naked. Leah marveled at the sinewy muscles of the thin arms and legs usually hidden beneath Savta's small tunic.

All the while, Leah's mother spoke to Leah in a low tone, words of comfort to strengthen them. "Leah, death is not a tragedy. It is a part of living. Our deaths, like our lives, have meaning. Life and death are both part of Jehovah's plan for us. King David said, 'What man can live and not see death, or save himself from the power of the grave?'"

"Selah," was Leah's husky reply.

Talitha rubbed the heavy, perfumed balm on Savta's arms while Leah massaged the fragrant ointment on the work-worn hands, hands that only yesterday gripped Leah's wrist like an iron shackle. They clothed Savta in the fine robe of dark green linen, Talitha's words a soothing balm to Leah.

"God cares for us in the world to come. Those who have lived a worthy life - and no one has lived a life more worthy than your grandmother - will be rewarded by Almighty Jehovah himself. As we are taught. 'The Lord has rewarded me according to my righteousness.'"

"Selah."

"We will mourn for Savta in the weeks to come. You have never seen this act of formal mourning, Leah, for we have not lost anyone to death in your young life." Leah pulled the comb through Savta's hair and braided it into the neat bun Savta always wore.

"We will mourn as a family to honor Savta. As it is written, 'I bowed my head in grief, as though weeping for my mother.'" Leah wondered about her father mourning for Savta. Savta had not liked her father very much. As a matter of fact, she did not like him at all.

On those rare occasions when Leah's mother mentioned Leah's father, "Pffth!" was Savta's standard reply. Worse, she often said that to his face, much to his great irritation.

Leah forced herself back to her mother's words. "We mourn to find comfort, to assure ourselves that Savta stands now with God." Leah wrapped the beautiful woven belt around Savta's tiny waist as her mother fixed the veil on her head. Leah saw a glint of gold at the neck of Savta's tunic.

"What about Savta's necklace, Mother?"

"No, it stays with Savta."

"But…"

"Mother must be buried with that necklace, as was her mother and grandmother before her."

Leah did not understand. How could Savta be buried with the same necklace her mother and grandmother had been buried with, too? She opened her mouth to ask a question, but her mother silenced her with a shake of her head. "Soon you will understand what I mean about this necklace. Please, leave the necklace on Savta."

Leah tucked the slender gold chain with its single pearl back under Savta's tunic, where it was hidden from sight. Savta never took it off. Lead did not voice what she was thinking: she would like to have that necklace, a precious memento of her beloved grandmother. If Leah were given Savta's necklace, she would never take it off.

But her mother again knew what she was thinking. "Savta must be buried with this necklace. Trust me on this, Leah. That necklace has a special meaning, and it must be buried with her."

Leah sighed. She knew there was more to be told about the single pearl on its golden chain, but she also understood the moment was not now, while her mother's grief was so raw.

They were finished. Leah's mother uncovered Savta's face. The peaceful, contented half-smile Leah had first seen that morning was still there. Savta was ready for burial, and she looked beautiful and peaceful and... happy. Her mother had been right. To prepare Savta for her burial had not been terrible at all.

It had been an act of love.

"This is the last time you will see Savta in this world, Leah. Look long and then say good-bye to your grandmother." Talitha's eyes again filled with tears. Leah put her arms around her mother's shoulders and felt her shuddering silent sobs. They looked down at the tranquil face of Savta for a long, long time, until her mother reached for the burial cloth that would cover her forever.

Leah's mother cried as they tightly wrapped the shroud around Savta's little body, Leah following her mother's stammered directions. Finally, this last thing was done.

Her mother looked at Leah. "'The Lord will lead Savta beside the quiet waters.' Remember how Savta liked to sit by the little stream?" Her voice broke.

Leah had sat by there with Savta many times. She reached out to take her mother's hand, to answer with words she knew would comfort her. "'The Lord will restore her soul, and guide her in the paths of righteousness.'"

"Yes. In death, God has restored her, made her whole and strong again."

"I wish Savta was here with us, even if it was just for one more day."

"Oh, so do I, Leah." Her mother wiped her tears on the corner of her veil. "But Savta is in a better place, a place of no pain, no tears, no crying. God's word to us is clear, Leah. 'Even though I walk though the valley of the shadow of death, I will fear no evil. For God is with me. His rod and staff comfort me. He prepares a table for me, and anoints my head with oil.' Savta was not afraid of anything, not even death. You should not be afraid of anything either, my strong and beautiful daughter."

Leah had no answer, for she was not strong like her mother and grandmother. Leah was afraid of so many things: afraid of death, afraid of her father, afraid of marrying a stranger or moving far away from her mother... Her mother interrupted Leah's silent litany of fears.

"Goodness and mercy will follow Savta all the days of her life. And now, Leah, your grandmother, my mother…" Leah heard the catch in her mother's voice, "Savta will dwell in the House of the Lord forever." Her mother smiled the smallest of smiles. "It makes us feel better to know that Savta was not afraid, that she is free from her pain, and that she is now with God forever and ever, doesn't it?"

Leah nodded again. "Yes, Mother."

"Jehovah, please forgive me for that lie," Leah thought. She would say nothing else for her mother's sake, but Leah did not feel better at all.

She did not want Savta dead, she wanted her alive and laughing. She did not care that Savta now stood with Jehovah. Leah wanted her grandmother to sit in her corner chair smiling in the sunlight. She wanted to hear Savta's rambling stories, watch her bony fingers fly across the ancient loom, see her snapping black eyes lost in a smile on the beloved, wrinkled brown face.

She did not want to hear that Savta and Talitha stood ready to meet Jehovah, that neither one was afraid to die. For no matter what her mother said, Leah was afraid to die. To go the way of the earth, as her mother had called death, terrified her.

Leah heard her mother sigh. Leah put her arm around her mother, consoling her just as she had been comforted so many times before. They sat together beside the silent Savta, Talitha with her head on Leah's shoulder, numb in their grief and silent tears.

"Yes, Savta, I am a woman after today," Leah thought. "Whether I want to be or not."

They sat like that for a long time, waiting for Leah's father and brothers, the other young men who would carry the funeral bier, the paid mourners and flute players, waiting for the sad lamentations that would soon begin. Waiting, waiting, waiting, until it was time to bury Savta.

CHAPTER 3

Leah had almost given up on getting married.

"What are you waiting for? What, what, what!" Leah was annoyed to the point of anger with her father. Well, perhaps she was not angry, just irritated.

"Why won't you finalize my betrothal? Why? What in all of Jehovah's blessed creation are you waiting for?"

She asked these questions every day, exasperated and impatient.

But Leah did not ask the questions out loud. In fact, she would never dare to pose a single thought to her father, especially not that one. Leah never spoke to her stern, forbidding father except to answer him, and then with as few words as possible.

If Leah needed information from her father, she asked her mother. If her mother did not answer, Leah understood there was nothing to know. Only her mother knew how to talk to her father. She did not seem to be afraid of him at all.

Leah's thirteenth birthday had come and gone. Both her brothers had married the previous summer. Both worked for her father. They sometimes came to see her mother, their only notice of Leah a quick smile or a tuck of her chin. But they kept themselves and their wives away from Leah's home anytime her father was there. Leah thought she knew why. She and her mother never spoke about it.

Worse, one after another, all of her friends were now betrothed, married or even mothers. Leah was the only one left, and she would soon be an ancient spinster. She had already participated in the weddings of four different friends. To stand there and watch what she now so desired was torture.

She would not admit how much fun the weeklong celebrations were, or how she preened under the admiration of young eligible men who glanced her way during their games and wild dances and feasting.

"My fate in life, to always be a virgin bridesmaid dressed in white, doomed to hold the lantern for the bride forever, to never be a bride myself," she thought.

All her father would say to Leah's mother was that he was in secret negotiations for a betrothal to a fine young man, and had been for quite some time. He would not say who the family was.

He said nothing at all to Leah.

"Betrothed, schmee-trothed. I am never, ever getting married," she thought. "What is he waiting for?"

The thought that the young man or his family might be the ones dragging their feet was something that never once crossed Leah's mind. After all, Leah was beautiful, and she knew it. Lots of young men eyed her at the synagogue or her friends' weddings, or even as she passed by at the market. They had only looked with the most furtive of glances, however. Leah was not the only one with a fearful respect for her father.

Leah knew the Torah, all the psalms and the ritual prayers. She even knew everyone of those stinky Proverbs her mother now trotted out anytime Leah had a chore to do.

"In honor of Savta," Leah thought glumly. She hated the proverbs.

At any rate, by the strict standards of her faith, Leah was the best of young Jewish women. After all, when her father was not working, he was at their synagogue. He was an elder, and had sat on the ruling council for over two years now. He was very important; by extension, his sons, his wife, and even his daughter were considered significant, too.

And, her family had money. They weren't rich, exactly. They did live in one of the largest homes with lots of nice things, even if it was on the brown side of Caesarea Philippi. Leah's mother did buy flour already ground and oil already pressed. Leah didn't know if that was because they had money, or so her mother could spend more time weaving. The beautiful work of her mother's loom was well-known through the entire region, a valuable contribution to her husband's business transactions.

But, even though her mother bought flour and oil, she still taught Leah how to grind and press anyway, and how to sew and bake and barter at the market. Her mother had taught her everything she needed to know about being a wife.

Leah was ready.

What was her father waiting for?

Every day except the Sabbath, Leah's father and brothers worked from sunrise to late night as traders of the finest linen thread and cloth, stopping only for prayers and meals. With two sons now under his domain, he had purchased a much larger place to buy and sell his many goods. Leah never went there. She didn't give one copper coin about the business of linen, for she was preoccupied learning the business of being a woman.

Leah had many pretty tunics sewn from fine linens of bright colors and the most intricate of patterns from her mother's loom. She had a beautiful dowry of jewelry and the promise of new furniture from her father when she was married. Leah's bridal dower even included a house, a nice house, the one her beloved Savta had lived in for so many years.

Leah was confident that anyone offered the chance to marry her would leap at the opportunity.

"And leap for joy," Leah added for good measure, her face wrinkled up in irritation. The more she thought about it, the more annoyed she became.

"What is he waiting for?" As meek and silent as she was before her father, Leah didn't hesitate to complain to her mother at every opportunity, her voice loud over the two looms clattering in a noisy syncopation. "After all, didn't King Solomon say, 'He who finds a wife finds what is good?' What is my father waiting for?"

Talitha pushed the shuttle in and out, not even glancing at her daughter over her frequent complaint. "Press these words on your heart instead, dearest daughter. 'Many are the plans in a woman's head, but it is God's purpose that prevails.' When the time is right,

God will bless you with a marriage."

Leah pulled the loom's heavy beater towards her, once, twice, the rhythm smooth and familiar to her. "It's 'plans in a man's head,' not a woman's, Mother. You know I know the proverbs, too. King Solomon also said, 'A wife of noble character is her husband's crown.'" Aha!

"Don't forget the second half, Leah. 'A disgraceful wife is decay in his bones.'"

"I am not disgraceful, Mother," Leah said, in the most disdainful tone she could muster. To do this, however, she had to stop weaving, so the full effect of her haughty profile with its nose in the air would not be lost on her mother.

Her mother's loom did not miss a beat, but she laughed at Leah's upturned nose. "No, Leah, you are not disgraceful, only annoying, as in 'a fool shows her annoyance at once.' And why did you quit weaving, your hands can't keep up with your mouth? 'A fool's mouth is her undoing?'"

Leah dissolved into giggles. If there was one thing she knew, it was that you could never one-up her quiet, gentle mother when it came to the wisdom of King Solomon.

Leah turned back to her work to avoid further reprimands from Solomon or Talitha, her complaints clamped down in the face of her unsympathetic mother. But the lack of sympathy for her woebegone state did not temper Leah's impatience. For the question would not leave Leah alone, not for a moment.

When, when, when was Leah getting married?

℆

Leah had worked at Savta's loom every day for six months now, ever since the thirty days of mourning for Savta had ended. The death of Savta was still raw, as painful as though it had just happened.

"This loom is now yours, Leah. That was Savta's wish." Leah had stood with her mother, admiring its ancient, meticulous craftsmanship. Poor Savta, with her aching hands and sore joints. This beautiful old loom had caused Savta so much pain in the last years of her life.

"I spoke to your father. He agrees that you are ready to begin weaving with linen."

"What?"

"You and I will work together every afternoon. I will show you how, teach you what I know."

Leah's father trusted her enough to work with the expensive linen? Until now, she only spun the linen thread or wove the inexpensive wool on the small loom.

Her mother answered the unspoken question. "Yes, he agreed, Leah. I know you will have a talent for it. But you must let me teach you. If you won't listen to me, I cannot let you work with the linen thread. Mistakes cost too much, for it is your father's livelihood."

"You mean you are my father's livelihood," Leah thought. But she was silent, for Leah's father would be most irritated if Leah were to ruin even one scrap of the precious, expensive linen thread. It surprised Leah that he would even let her work with anything but the cheapest wool.

Leah took a deep breath and ran over to sit in front of Savta's loom. "I will listen. I won't let you down, Mother."

Her mother nodded, delighted at Leah's eagerness. "I know you won't. Here, let me show you." She sat down beside Leah. "We will keep the little loom you have been using over in the corner, so it won't feel lonesome." Leah smiled at the small brown loom of Leah's and her mother's childhoods. It was very old.

Her mother read her mind. "Yes, we must take good care of that little loom, for it was Savta's when she was young, just as it was once mine and now is yours and someday – if Jehovah wills it – your daughter's, too."

Leah grinned at the thought of children, forgetting she did not yet have even an inkling of a husband. She squared her shoulders, took a deep breath and picked up the shuttle. For the first time, she was going to weave using the beautiful linen threads, on the loom of her beloved grandmother Savta, with her mother at her side.

"I will never forget this moment," Leah thought.

She pushed shuttle across the loom, just the way she had seen her mother do a thousand times. In and out. She sent it back across the expanse of the loom a second time. In and out. She drew the heavy beater bar to her, trying to make the motion smooth, once, then again a second time. She had done it. Her first row on the loom lay before her.

"Just like that, Leah. Excellent!"

Leah flashed a smile at her mother's praise. She straightened her shoulders and took a deep breath, ready to begin the work in earnest. Her ancestral calling as a weaver was hers to claim.

In and out. In and out. Clack. Clack.

In and out. In and out. Clack. Clack.

It only took Leah two passes to realize that weaving on this great big loom was quite different than working on the small one smiling at her from the corner. This kind of weaving was...

Hard work.

Savta's bigger loom took full command of her muscles. Leah paused to stretch out her arms and catch her breath, just for a moment.

"Why are you stopping, Leah?" Her mother wore the smallest smile.

"I'm not stopping," she huffed and sat up straight, making two more passes with the loom, each one slower than the other.

She stopped again and looked at her mother. "It's kind of hard, harder than I thought it would be." She wrinkled her forehead and took a deep breath. "But I can do it."

"Ah, a true daughter of Solomon! 'You set about your work vigorously; your arms are strong for your tasks!'"

"My arms are strong," Leah crowed. With those words of encouragement, she pushed the shuttle in and out and pulled the beater twice more, as fast as she could.

"Slow down, Leah. You don't need to go fast; you just want a nice even tempo. Watch." Her mother stood and leaned over Leah to demonstrate. "You know how, this is just on a bigger scale. First the shuttle: Push it all the way across, take hold of it and pull it out. In. Out. Push back to the other side. In. Out. Then the beater. Push it out, smooth and easy, and pull it back to you."

Clack answered the loom.

"And again." Clack.

"In and out, in and out. Clack. Clack." Her mother's voice was a singsong as she worked the loom with a smooth and fluid motion.

Leah's mother wasn't even sitting down but instead leaned over Leah's shoulders at an awkward angle. And she had made two quick and even rows with so little effort!

Leah pushed and pulled the shuttle and then yanked the beater once more, puffing with effort and exertion. She looked at her mother. "Does this thing get heavier as the cloth gets bigger?"

Her mother laughed. "No."

Leah soon realized she was not as strong as she thought she was. Working on this loom was difficult, physical work. And her mother did it every afternoon for hours, six days a week. Leah's shoulders ached and she had a stitch in her side. She paused again.

"Why Leah, you cannot stop after so few passes." Her mother was amused.

"This is hard, Mother. I can't believe you do this all day long. I'm already worn out!" Leah sat red-faced and perspiring.

"Leah, you come from a long line of women who, the first time we sat down at our looms, all complained what hard work weaving is. It is difficult at first. But you will get used to it and soon it becomes easy, a second nature to you. My grandmother wove on this loom, and my mother used it right up until she died." She stroked the old wooden contraption, as one might pet a favorite donkey. Under her mother's soft hand, Leah was certain she could hear the bulky wood hum in contentment.

Her mother did not look at her, still feeling the worn loom beneath her calloused fingers. "This loom will come to be something you love. You will get to know its little quirks and idiosyncrasies, like a musician with an instrument he has played for many years."

Leah looked at her mother, curious. Her matter-of-fact mother never spoke like this.

"Together, you and this loom will create beautiful things that will roll out before you like a gift. You cannot do it without each other, for you must pull the thread, move the shuttle, tug the heavy beater, again and again. But you cannot create anything without the loom, either! Some days you will hate it. It will be contrary and uncooperative. Other days, you whisper your secrets to it, for it will feel like your only friend. And always, you will love it, amazed at what the two of you can make together. You will be thankful one day that Savta wanted you to have her loom."

"Savta wanted me to have this?"

"Oh, yes, and it is very valuable. It belonged to Savta's mother and her grandmother before her. If your father were to sell it, it would fetch a great price."

Leah nodded. "Oh, Savta," she thought.

47

"I picked out my own loom years ago when I married, as part of your father's dower to me. But Savta wanted you to have this, her only granddaughter. Isn't it beautiful? Look at all this intricate carving, such a beautiful wood. See the grain of the wood? This is an old loom, straightforward, simple, yet complicated, with a history you can feel under your fingers. I hope you will love it as much as she did."

"I already do." Leah looked up at her mother. "Do you want me to come back and weave some more with you tomorrow?"

"Well, of course, you must come back tomorrow, for that is how you will get better. As a matter of fact… you are not quite done today, my dearest daughter."

This was not what Leah had planned. But when her mother called her dearest daughter, there was nothing to do but obey.

"Weaving is something that takes practice, Leah. You and I will work together every day, and it will soon be easy for you. Remember, 'The sluggard's craving is the death of her. Her hands refuse to work.'"

"Savta and I never saw a sluggard," Leah thought, "even though we watched the ant hill so many times.

"It's his hands, not hers, Mother." But Leah smiled as she picked up the shuttle, ready to get back to work. "Did you weave with Savta when you were my age?"

Her mother nodded. "Oh, and when I was much younger, too. Savta worked at the big loom and I worked at the little one. My mother did not let me work with linen until I was married! We spent many years together, working side by side."

Her mother looked sad, remembering Savta.

"Well, I know you married before you were thirteen. You weren't a spinster like me."

Her mother laughed, her sudden sadness gone at Leah's teasing words. "You are right. Now, let's get some work done. You pay attention and mind me when I tell you what to do. You do not know everything about weaving just yet. This is linen you are using, after all."

"Yes, Mother." Leah lingered over the two words, her voice resigned.

"Daughter, remember what King Solomon said to the complaining Israelites and Savta said to me." Her voice got high and squeaky. "'Do not forsake your mother's teaching.'"

Leah giggled at her mother's spot-on, uncharacteristic imitation of Savta.

Her mother might sing the songs of King David while she worked, but she had the proverbs of good old King Solomon handy in her pocket whenever she felt like scolding her dearest daughter Leah.

CHAPTER 4

Leah was strong to begin with, and working on Savta's loom soon became second nature to her. As the motions grew easy and familiar, Leah's fingers soon could keep pace with her mother's as they sat together at their looms.

Every day but the Sabbath, the two women sat together to work at their looms. Perhaps working was not the best description, for the beauty that rolled out beneath their hands was accompanied by lighthearted chatter or thoughtful conversation, boisterous laughter or silent tears, or, when their own words failed them, the glorious psalms sung in tandem with the clack clacking of their two looms.

Leah wove the simple, cream-colored linen used for everyday utilitarian uses, those times when wool or cotton would not suffice. "Like for shrouds," Leah would think, "Like the shroud Savta wove for herself." The thought never failed to make her shiver. She still trembled at the thought of death, and her heart still hurt at the thought of her grandmother.

Her mother sat next to her, her deft fingers adroitly pulling linen threads of deep, rich jewel tones, a brilliant emerald green and deep sapphire blue. Now that Leah understood how hard the work was, she appreciated more than anyone the true artistry of her mother's work. It was truly amazing, even to Leah's familiar eyes.

Her father not only sold the cloth his wife created, but what his daughter wove, also. The beautiful work of Talitha's hands fetched a great price, but the linen of Leah's hands was strong with even, tight threads, hard-wearing and durable. It too sold well, for people could see the quality of Leah's work.

Only a few people in Caesarea Philippi could afford Talitha's work anyway. More often, Leah's father took it to sell in the larger cities around them, or sold it to the caravans that passed though each season.

Sometimes, Talitha would give Leah some of the precious, brightly-dyed thread and let her create her own simple patterns, work that was so much more satisfying than weaving the simple beige linen day after day.

"See? She has an eye for beauty," Leah's mother said as Leah's father watched her work some soft gold and brown threads into her cloth.

"Humph."

Leah waited to see if her father had anything else to say about her work, or even about her. He never did. Today was no exception to his customary critical silence.

Still, her mother had more to say. "Yes, Leah, you have an eye for beauty; you are a beauty and you are my greatest joy." She smiled with obvious pride, Leah red with embarrassment before her father. "The Lord has brought me laughter, and her name is Leah."

Her father looked at his daughter in what Leah hoped was silent agreement, despite the scowl on his face. But he left without a word to either woman. He seldom came to his wife's workroom, and he never had a word for Leah when he did.

These days were the happiest times Leah had ever known.

ﾟ

One warm afternoon several weeks later, Leah and her mother sat together at their looms, the work of their hands piling up in beautiful folds on the looms.

"'Shout with joy to God, all the earth.
Sing the glory of his name; make his praise glorious.
Say to God, how awesome are your deeds.'"

Talitha's voice was reverent over the clatter of the loom. The shuttles flew back and forth, in and out. In. Out.

Leah answered her mother, trying not to stumble over the words.

> "'So great is your power that your enemies
>   Cringe before you.
> All the earth bows down to you.'"

Leah wrinkled her forehead in concentration. "They... They will... Selah?"

Her mother frowned. "They will sing... "

Leah picked up the refrain.

> "'They sing praise to you; they sing praise to your name.
>   Selah!'"

Mother and daughter tugged the heavy beaters in tandem. Clack. Clack. Talitha arched an eyebrow at her daughter and continued,

> "'Come and see what God has done,
> How awesome his works in man's behalf.'"

In. Out. In. Out.

> "He turned the sea into dry land,
> They passed through the waters on foot.
> Come, let us rejoice in him!'"

Leah wrinkled her nose. "Pffth! You thought I forgot, didn't you?" Clack. Clack.

Her mother did not dignify Leah's question with a response and continued in a quiet voice.

> "'He rules forever by his power, his eyes watch the nations.
> Let not the rebellious rise up against him.'"

In. Out. In Out.

Leah jumped in before her mother could finish. "Selah!" Leah loved the comforting finality of the word Selah, and added one to almost every refrain whether it belonged there or not.

Clack. Clack.

But Leah's mother was pleased. "Good, Leah, very good. Don't you love those words, come let us rejoice in him?"

Leah stole a glance at her mother and began to chant, a tuneless rhyme of nonsense for which she had been scolded for many times before. Her hands did not stop working.

In. Out. "Re-joice!" In. Out. "Re-joice!"

Leah's voice was cheerful, her words as rhythmic as the push and pull of the beaters. Clack. Clack. "Selah! Selah!"

"Leah, hush."

Instead, Leah pushed the shuttle from one side of the loom to the other with a quick motion, faster and faster, grinning, the chant familiar to them both. "Re-joice! Re-joice!"

"Leah, sing the words of King David with reverence."

The muscles in Leah's back flexed, one strong pull, a second strong pull, the beater flying. Clack, clack. "I AM rejoicing, Mother! See-lah!" She winked at her mother, who began to laugh in spite of herself.

Faster and faster. In out, in out. "Re-JOICE! Re-JOICE!"

Clack. Clack. "SEE-LAH!"

"Leah!" The harsh voice silenced the room at once, mother and daughter stunned at the mid-day appearance.

"So this is what you mean when you say you have taught King David's words to your daughter. Is she so dull she only knows one word?"

Her mother flushed at her husband's sneer but remained silent. Her gaze did not waver, even as she pulled her face into a thin smile.

"She sounds like a bawling cow instead of a proper Hebrew girl praising Jehovah."

Leah lowered her eyes, ashamed.

"I could hear her screeching all the way down the street. An embarrassment."

Her mother's expression did not change.

"How terribly proud you must be of your daughter."

Her mother's chin lifted imperceptibly, but her only answer was to nod at her husband's relentless stare.

After a long moment in which Leah did not dare to glance at her father, he cleared his throat and spoke. As surprising as his sudden appearance was the civil composure in his voice. "Talitha, I have something to tell you. Come with me, for I will not sit in a woman's room."

Leah's mother at once went to stand by her husband.

"You too, Leah." The words sounded malicious rather than inviting to Leah. She did not recognize the look on his face. Why did her father want her? He never wanted her.

"Now!" Her father's familiar temper had returned.

Leah's mother held out her hand to Leah, who scampered past her father to take it.

Mother and daughter walked to the low table in the next room and sat down on the floor. Her father loomed over them, silent, and Leah and her mother were forced to look up at him, heads tilted back.

"I have important news." Leah heard a different tone in his voice. She did not know what it was. "It is the best of news for our family. After many months, I have finalized the negotiation of a complicated marriage contract. Start planning now, for in one year, Leah will marry Reuben, the second son of Sheariah."

What? Leah was getting married? Married?

Leah wanted to jump up and dance for joy, but she would never do so in front of her father.

Leah's mother said nothing.

"You know Sheariah. He is a very prosperous landowner whose farms are only an afternoon's travel north of Caesarea Philippi. But Leah will not live in the country with Reuben's family, as is our custom. Reuben and Leah will live in Caesarea Philippi. Just as you asked of me, wife."

Leah would not move away with some stranger that was her husband! She would live close to her mother! Her father's news was getting better and better. Leah could not believe her ears, but she stared straight ahead, careful to not show any emotion.

"Reuben and Leah will live in the home I will provide."

Leah knew he meant Savta's house, the house of her grandmother. Oh, what joyous news!

Leah's mother was still silent.

Her father continued, pleased with himself and his deal. "This young man's family raises huge crops on their many farms just past Mount Hermon. Their farms produce some of the finest flax in all of our kingdom, the most beautiful linen to be found. Reuben will work with me to sell his family's cloth to my contacts. A good percentage of the earnings will go to me, of course. And it is not just the cloth. I will purchase whatever linen Sheariah's workers and women do not weave into cloth and sell it myself. What you weave will cost me far less to produce. The profits could be huge."

Her father's voice droned on. "As the second son, Reuben cannot inherit the lands, the farms and the flocks of his father. Thus, Reuben will instead trade the flax and linen of his family's farms, using my contacts and..." Leah recognized the pompous arrogance in her father's voice, "... my considerable expertise to drive a hard bargain. His family will pay me well in exchange for this excellent opportunity. It is their good fortune that their second son will be part of such a lucrative business opportunity."

He smiled broadly at Talitha. "This marriage between Reuben and Leah promises to be the best business transaction I have ever made, very profitable. Your daughter might turn out to be an even greater financial asset than my two sons. No one is more surprised than me to find that out," he added, as though Leah was not sitting right there.

Leah knew why she had not recognized the tone in her father's voice earlier. He sounded pleased. Her father was happy about her marriage. At last, something about Leah that pleased her father.

Leah's father kept on talking, but she had stopped listening to his words. She cared nothing for the trading of the linen, the flax from this Reuben's farms, being an asset or his family's good fortune or any of the things her father was going on and on about. She cared for only one thing.

She was getting married.

Leah knew who this Reuben was; his family sometimes came to the large synagogue of Caesarea Philippi. He was tall and muscular from the work of their farms, broad shouldered and good looking in a dark, unsmiling sort of way. "Like a man, not a boy," Leah thought with a toss of her head.

This Reuben rarely spoke at synagogue, but when he did he had a pleasant enough tenor to his deep voice. She thought that was true, anyway. Leah had only heard him speak once or twice, and then always in a group. He usually just listened, letting the others talk and laugh. He was quiet and standoffish, but that would change once they were married, Leah was sure.

"He is just shy," Leah decided. "A big man of few words."

For some reason, Reuben's dark face appeared before her, stern and unsmiling. Leah shivered. She had never even spoken to Reuben. But then the best, most wonderful news of her life flooded her mind, erasing Reuben's dour countenance. She was getting married at last, and she would not leave the city she had known for every day of her life.

Leah and Reuben would live right here in Caesarea Philippi, in Savta's little house, almost next door to her mother. Many of her friends did not even have a place of their own, instead starting their marriage sharing the roof of their husbands' families. Leah would have her own home. She would not move away from her mother.

Married. Finally, finally, finally. Leah was getting married!

She looked up, for her father had stopped talking, his brows drawn fiercely together, his eyes narrow slits, his mouth a tight line. He glared first at Talitha and then at Leah.

Just as he had seemed so pleased a few moments ago, he now wore the look Leah knew so well. He was angry.

"Well? Have you nothing to say about what I have done, about my good news?"

Talitha stood up and walked to her husband, her back very straight. "Have you signed the betrothal contract?" Her voice sounded polite, and Leah could hear her nervousness, but her mother did not drop her gaze from her father's ferocious glare.

"No, the terms are still being drawn up. The contract is a very difficult and complex. Much money is at stake. Sheariah and I will sign it tomorrow with the betrothal ceremony to follow."

"Since it is not signed, then, yes. I have something to say about what you have done." Leah's mother took a deep breath. "I cannot believe you chose Reuben as a husband for Leah."

Leah's father looked at her with his mouth gaping open for a moment, his silence as loud as the rush of the flooded Jordan River in the spring. Then he shook his head and made a short snorting sound.

Leah was astonished. She had never heard her mother disagree with her father. Why wasn't her mother happy with this news?

"It is a good match." Her father tried to sound indifferent, as though he were not even really listening to her mother, but Leah heard the edge in his voice. Leah looked down at her lap. She did not like to be in the same room with her father when he was angry, but she could not leave unless he told her to do so.

Talitha's voice was cautious, as though she felt the danger of her words. "I know this young man and his family. This Reuben, I have heard he has a difficult, a... belligerent side. He seems polite, even deferential to his elders... but it is said he also has this... other side, too. An... unpleasant side, one that is... some say... mean."

"You do not know what you are talking about. It is a good match."

"You only have to look at him to see some of these things. He always is irritated, even angry much of the time. He has had... problems with some of the young men from our synagogue, I know this to be true. He has no friends. Ask your sons about him."

Leah glanced up and then down at the sight of her father's clenched jaw and fists. "Stop, Mother," she whispered to herself.

But her mother voice grew more confident in the quiet. "I fear this Reuben will not appreciate or be kind to Leah. I know he will not appreciate her joy and laughter. He is a belligerent young man. My daughter is filled with joy no matter what comes her way, always with a cheerful heart. Reuben is an angry young man, so, so somber..."

"You wrongly confuse Reuben's sober attitude with a bad temper. Typical of you and the other gossiping nags of the synagogue."

"But I have heard many things. No one wants their daughter to marry him."

"You do not know of what you speak. He comes from a fine Jewish family of great wealth."

"They say he is rash in his decisions. Worse, he reacts badly when things do not go his way. These things would be bad for your business."

Leah knew her mother did not care about her father's business. She stared at her lap, afraid of the tension in the room, worried at the words of her mother that continued to antagonize her father. He had picked a husband for Leah, and that was that. Why couldn't her mother just be happy she was getting married at long last?

Her father's voice was dismissive. "Bad for my business? What could you possibly know about that? You know nothing. This

Reuben will bring me great value. I have spent months in negotiation with his father. Leah will marry Reuben. It is a worthy exchange for a man's marriage to your daughter, a good opportunity for my business."

"I don't care about your business!" Leah was startled by the intensity of her mother's voice. "It is not a good match! I fear for Leah's happiness, I would even fear for Leah —"

"It is the best of all possible matches!" Her father was speaking in the loud voice Leah knew best, the one that allowed no response.

Her mother spoke anyway. "I know they are a good family, but this young man, this Reuben, he is not. I must say no to this marriage because…"

Leah stared down at her lap, trying to make herself as small as possible. Her head bowed, she heard but did not see what happened next. The loud crash made her jump to her feet, but she sat back down at once, shocked at the sight.

Her mother lay sprawled on the floor. Her father towered over her, his fists two red balls of flesh with white knuckles.

"The contracts will be signed. It will happen with or without your blessing, woman. Either way, you will prepare Leah for marriage!" He was shouting. "You are thankless ingrate, a nag of a wife! How dare you complain? Leah will only live a few houses away! I could have married her to someone from Jerusalem but you and that nagging Savta begged me not to do that. Yet when I honor your wishes, you still torment me! You are not fit to be my wife!"

He shook his fist in the air. "Before Jehovah, I tell you: the contracts will be signed tomorrow!"

Leah sat like a stone, wanting to help her mother but too terrified to move. What had happened? Had her mother fallen? "Please, Jehovah, do not let him hit her," she thought. "Please, Jehovah, please, please."

As if on cue to Leah's prayer, her mother pushed herself up and stood before her husband, her back straight and her chin high, her jaw set. Leah could hear her mother breathing but she did not speak, unflinching in the face of his rage, her eyes unwavering.

He towered over her, so close that the spittle from his hissed words hit her face. "The contract will be signed. You will prepare *my* daughter for marriage. She is my daughter and this is my will. Do you understand?"

Talitha did not pull back or drop her gaze from the face so close to her own, the expression on her face blank of any expression. A different prayer was on Leah's lips now. "Do not speak, Mother, do not speak. Do not."

"Do you understand?" Leah shuddered at the threat in the voice of her father.

"I will prepare Leah for the betrothal ceremony and marriage."

He narrowed his eyes, his voice low and menacing. "You will not say one bad word - not one! - to Leah about Reuben. My daughter will be a humble, obedient, and…" he spat the last words, "grateful wife."

"As you wish." Talitha's voice quiet, each syllable measured.

He looked her with narrowed eyes and then turned his gaze to Leah, still huddled at the low table on the floor.

"Come, Leah." Talitha's voice was normal, as though she wanted Leah to go with her to the market, interrupting whatever words her husband might have had for her daughter.

Leah jumped up, anxious to leave the presence of her father.

"May we leave you, husband?"

He did not answer, but Leah's mother turned and pulled Leah from the room.

As soon as they were in the workroom, Leah stopped. "Mother," Leah's whisper was urgent. "Mother!"

"Do not speak to me right now, Leah. Please."

They sat down at the looms. Her mother picked up her shuttle but her hands were shaking so hard, it fell to the floor with a clatter.

Leah picked it up and handed it to her mother. Talitha turned to her loom without a word.

In. Out. In. Out. Clack. Clack.

Leah could not stand the silence. "Mother, what happened? Are you all right? Did he… did he…"

Leah's mother kept at their steady work, her eyes straight ahead. "Nothing happened, nothing. I stumbled over my tunic. It was quite clumsy of me." A mottled flush crept up her neck until her face was as red as the scarlet cloth before her.

"Are you all right?"

"Of course, I only stumbled and fell over my own feet. I am fine. Please, be quiet, daughter."

"But why were you so upset about Reuben and…"

"Leah."

Leah was startled by the terse agitation in her mother's voice. She still would not look at Leah, the clack of the loom never faltering. "I do not wish to speak with you now."

Leah was silent, but so many questions were on her mind she could not stay that way. "Mother, about what he said... was he thinking about marrying me to someone from Jerusalem?" She could not hide her fear. "Was he?"

"Nothing came of it."

"Oh." Leah sat for a moment. She remembered the horrible stranger who had leered at Leah and argued with her father. Oh, if she had been forced to marry that old man! Leah could not imagine a worse husband. She was not sure why her mother was so upset over the news of Leah's marriage to Reuben, so much that Talitha would dare to argue with her husband. Leah was happy to be getting married at last. Perhaps her mother did not understand how happy Leah was.

"Mother, I am... I am glad to be getting married, really. And I will live right here, we can still weave together every day. I will be in Savta's little house, so close to you." Leah could not contain her sudden excitement. "It is wonderful, all I hoped for in marriage. I know of this Reuben, I don't think he is so bad. Just think, Mother, I am getting married at last!"

To her surprise, her mother's eyes filled with tears.

"Why are you crying? Please, please don't cry."

"No more talking, Leah. I will not discuss this anymore, my dearest daughter." Her shoulders slumped, weary with effort to wipe away her tears. "Please, I beg you, for once, work and be quiet."

Leah opened her mouth.

"Leah."

She closed it. She picked up the shuttle of her loom, mother and daughter silent with their own thoughts. Leah's mother never took her eyes off her work. Leah could not even look at her own, so much was tumbling through her head.

Her father once wanted her to marry an old man from Jerusalem.

Instead, he picked Reuben. He was signing a betrothal contract tomorrow. He was letting her stay near her mother. He had been happy with Leah, if only for a moment.

Until he lost his temper.

Her father... Why had her mother fallen? Leah had not seen. Her father was often angry, his rages a source of fear to those who knew him. Could she have tripped, as she said? It did not seem possible, but Leah had never known her mother to do anything but speak the truth.

Her mother had disagreed with Leah's father, had argued with him about Leah's future husband. No one argued with Leah's father, but her mother had fought for Leah.

Her mother always talked with Leah, but not today. Her mother was upset. Leah did not know how to help her other than to be quiet as she had asked.

Reuben. Leah had often seen him at the synagogue. He looked all right, with black bushy eyebrows over burning black eyes and a short curly beard. Leah liked those whiskers so much better than the long scraggly ones. He was tall, too, with muscular arms and broad shoulders, strong and brown from hard labor on their farms. Despite his strong physique, Leah and her friends had never whispered about him as they did the other young men. Reuben kept to himself.

With his strapping build and Leah's dark good looks, their sons would be very handsome young men indeed. She blushed at the thought and ducked her head so her mother would not see.

But her mother was still staring straight ahead, her hands working the familiar rhythm of the loom, her lips moving in a silent prayer. She was not paying the least bit of attention to the young woman beside her.

Leah felt her mother's pain. It had been a difficult afternoon. Yet no matter how Leah tried, she could not keep a smile from her face.

For at the ancient age of thirteen, after waiting forever for her father to decide, after being a virgin bridesmaid for one friend and then another and another, after watching and waiting for months, for years, waiting for what seemed like her whole life...

Leah was getting married.

CHAPTER 5

Leah hurt. She huddled in her bed, knees pulled tight against her chest, fighting the stabbing pains in her back and belly bending her in two. Miserable and alone, she tried to stifle her tears. Crying only gave her a headache to add to all her other ailments. She closed her eyes and prayed for relief from her pain and company in her suffering. Since she had neither, Leah went ahead and cried, muffled, choking sobs for her dreadful pain and pitiful condition. No one was there to hear her anyway.

She knew she should get up and change her bandages again, but she was so weak. There was something about losing this much blood for five, six, even seven days that drained the life out of her, leaving her weary and spent.

It was not much fun to be a woman after all, Leah had decided. At least it hadn't been for her so far.

She wished her mother would come to her. For some reason, her pain seemed worse when she was alone. She was alone most of the time when she was sick, ostracized and shunned by her father, who would not permit her to leave her room when she was in her "sinful state," as he called it.

"She carries the sin of Eve, the curse of all mankind, the shame of an unclean, defiled woman," he said pompously to Leah's mother.

He ignored the sad, embarrassed face of his daughter. Her mother had not answered, stoic in the face of his condemnation.

Her father was never there during the day. Still, Leah was not brave enough to go search for her mother. She was too tired to get out of bed, anyway.

The true mark of womanhood had come upon her at last, right after her father signed the betrothal contracts for her marriage to Reuben. It had only been luck, or the hand of Jehovah, that this terrible bleeding started the day after the ceremony. The blood had come so fast and heavy, she would have disgraced herself had she been in any public setting. Leah still shuddered at the thought.

The day her curse first came upon her, she and her mother were sitting at their looms, working and talking. Leah had jumped up to fetch another roll of the unbleached linen thread when she felt a spasm of pain that doubled her over. She jumped to her feet, unsure of what had happened, only certain that it had hurt. "Oh! Mother!"

Talitha looked at her and then at Leah's small stool, covered in blood. "Oh, my goodness, daughter!" Her mother had rushed her to bed, helped her with her bandages and explained to her that what they had discussed so many times was finally happening. She left Leah alone for a long time, scurrying to clean all traces of Leah's shame from the workroom before her father returned home.

"Your father is so strict about the ceremonial laws," her mother had whispered, even though no one else was in the house.

One of Leah's favorite tunics had been ruined, too discolored to ever be rid of the shameful stain that covered its backside.

Then, after questioning his wife as to why his daughter was in her bed, her father had appeared at the door of her small room to condemn her sinful condition and ban her from any life outside of her own room during the time when she was unclean and unworthy.

She had forced herself to lie still during his long tirade, each vicious word as painful as the stabbing cramps. She fought the urge to curl her body up into the smallest ball of pain, instead lying motionless in her bed, her eyes fixed on the wall above her father's head. She would not meet his ferocious gaze, staring instead at her silent mother standing silent beside her husband. The pain on her mother's face was worse than the pain in Leah's belly.

On and on he had droned. He seemed to be waiting for Leah to cry out from pain or break down in tears of shame. "I will not give him the satisfaction," Leah thought, her teeth gritted. "I am sick, and yet he cannot find even one kind word for me." Her mother sat in the corner, silent. The fury on his face for something she could not help steeled Leah's determination. She might bend to this pain, but she would not break before her father.

Leah mustered a small respectful nod, as though agreeing with his tirade against her sinfulness.

At that, her father stopped talking, staring at her through slits of suspicious eyes. When Leah said nothing, he turned to leave room. He paused in the doorway. "Amê." He hissed the final word and walked away.

"Unclean." Her mother whispered her ear before she left to follow her husband. "It's all right, Leah. Amê just means unclean."

When her monthly courses came upon her now, Leah never failed to remember every traumatic moment of that terrible first day.

"All in all, a pretty discouraging welcome to womanhood," Leah thought.

She wished her mother would come.

This time, there was one good thing about the pain of her monthly curse. In ten days, Leah and Reuben were to be married. She had plenty of time to recover and to be pronounced clean by the priest before she stood before so many people to become the wife of Reuben.

"Truly the Lord cares for me, a woman, for His grace in this small thing," she thought.

She wondered if Reuben would be as reviled by this woman's passage as her father seemed to be. For, during her monthly courses she was not only in pain, she was alone. The word of her father kept Leah separate from the world with only her mother for occasional company.

Her mother came to her as much as she could, which, since Leah's father was away all day, was frequent. But Talitha still had to do all the family chores and cook and wash and make some progress on whatever was on her loom. Her husband checked her progress every evening. After all, her weaving was a significant source of income. She could not spend all day holding Leah's hand.

Even though right now that was exactly what Leah wanted.

"Is it like this for everyone?" Leah whispered to her mother one day as she brought a bowl of steaming stew to her room.

"No, my little Leah, it is different for every woman. For some women it is easy, for others a terrible burden."

Leah had thought about that for a moment. "Father will say my bleeding is worse because I am more sinful."

"Your father will not say that, for that is not true." But Leah knew what her mother would not admit, that her father did indeed think that. He had said as much on several occasions. The ways of Leah's father were harsh and difficult.

Talitha knew Leah heard the small stutter of doubt. So she offered her daughter a bright smile and changed the subject.

"Leah, in a few days you will not live under your father's roof. Before you know it, you will be married. And after your marriage ceremony, your husband will want to take you in the secret, loving way that only a husband may take a wife. And your new husband will want you as soon as it is permitted! That is the way of young men."

Leah's smile was no more than a weak grimace. But her mother was determined to cheer her.

"It is true! And when you are first married, Reuben will want you in the way of a man and his wife often, as often as possible, for you are as beautiful as any young woman in our entire city."

Leah wasn't feeling very beautiful, but her mother nodded emphatically.

"Yes, yes, you are. And when you are not sick, you know it, too. So, you must let Reuben take you in the way of a husband, willingly, without complaint, and with joy! If you please your husband in this manner, he will not care one bit about anything else you do as a wife. That will be certainly be true of a strong young man like Reuben."

Her mother laughed and Leah smiled a bit, too.

True to her word, Talitha had never again said anything negative about Reuben to Leah. As a matter of fact, she did not speak of Reuben very often at all. Whatever worries Leah's mother carried so long ago were now secreted in her own heart.

"Most important, Leah, you know this is how your children will come to you. And from the moment you are pregnant, you will not bleed until the child is born. And after the child is born, in either one month or two, you will be pronounced ceremonially clean by the priests. Then, your husband will be able to take you into his bed again, and trust me, he will want to. If it is God's will, another child will come, and this curse will leave you again for another nine months." She smoothed back Leah's hair, tousled from lying in her bed all day.

"And, my daughter, it is quite common that once you start having children, your monthly courses change. Once you had your first child, yours may be much easier. Things will be better, you will see, Leah. You will see."

Leah had thought that over for a moment. Children. She wanted children with all her heart. She loved babies. "I hope Reuben and I have a big, big family, bigger than ours." There was a shred of hopeful anticipation in Leah's tired, thin voice.

Her mother smiled. "I hope you do, too, Leah." They sat for a moment thinking of babies and waiting for a spasm of pain to pass through Leah's thin body.

"What did you mean when you said I would be clean in one month or two, Mother? Which is it?"

Her mother sighed and then cleared her throat. "Well, it is our law. It is as the Lord said to Moses, Leah. 'A woman who gives birth to a son will be ceremonially unclean for seven days, just as she is unclean during her monthly period. On the eighth day the boy is to be circumcised. Then the woman must wait thirty-three days to be purified from the bleeding of childbirth. She must not touch anything sacred or go to the sanctuary until the days of her purification are over. If she gives birth to a daughter, for two weeks the woman will be unclean, as during her period. Then she must wait sixty-six days to be purified from her bleeding.'"

Her mother looked away. "It just takes a little longer to "be clean" if you bear a daughter." Leah heard the rare tone of contempt in her mother's voice. But her bitter look was replaced at once by a wide smile. "So pray for a son first, to appease your husband, and then for daughter after daughter after daughter!"

"Why?"

"With daughters, you get to stay in bed longer! You are free from your chores and daily work for a whole extra month! Hooray!"

As puny as she felt, Leah still laughed out loud. Her mother never said "Hooray."

Her mother laid her hand on Leah's cheek. "And after all, what greater blessing could a woman ever receive from Jehovah than a beautiful treasure of a daughter like you? There is nothing more important to me than you, Leah." They stayed like that for a long time, until Leah's mother at last returned to her work.

The house was completely quiet, the afternoon shadows climbing up the walls of Leah's bedroom. Leah could not hear the noisy beaters of her mother's loom. Perhaps she was preparing the evening meal or had gone to the market. No, she would have told Leah she was leaving if that were so.

In the hushed stillness of the house and the solitude of her pain, Leah felt utterly alone.

Oh, how Leah wished her mother would come.

But she did not. The quiet was broken by the faint clack clack of a loom. Her mother was working after all, as her father demanded. Perhaps in the silence she had been spinning or dying threads, jobs that fell to Leah when she felt well.

Leah thought about the past eleven months. She and her mother had been busy with wedding preparations and readying Savta's little house for the new couple. There was much to do before one could get married.

Leah could not wait for her wedding day to arrive, for her life as a wife to begin. Perhaps, as her mother said, she would be with child at once and this terrible monthly pain would be taken from her.

Because Reuben lived in the country, Leah only saw him on the Sabbath when he came to share dinner with her and her parents, and sometimes her brothers and their quiet wives, too. Most of the meal was spent listening to her father talk about flax crops and his latest linen trade. Reuben rarely said a word to her or anyone else.

Leah didn't care. Soon enough, she would sit alone with Reuben at a dinner table, and then they could talk to her heart's content.

"Reuben doesn't seem bad tempered to me," she thought. "He is just shy. He may not have much to say in front of my father, and who can blame him?" For Leah also had little to say to her father.

Her mother was preoccupied and worried, working at her loom even as she prepared for a celebration and again taught her daughter the household habits of a good Jewish wife. Leah was preoccupied, too, for when she was not sick she was happy, ecstatically and emphatically happy that she was getting married at last.

Leah knew her mother was troubled about Reuben and their approaching marriage, but Leah had seen the way Reuben looked at her. It was a look she did not recognize, and it excited her. Reuben was pleased to be marrying her, too. She could tell by the way he flushed whenever she caught him stealing a glance her way.

"He's like a nervous little animal, waiting to be tamed," Leah laughed to herself. Leah had no doubt that she was the one to tame Reuben.

Unlike Talitha, Leah had no reservations about her marriage. She would live near her mother in Savta's little house, children would come, Jehovah would deliver her from this monthly pain, and Leah would make sure her marriage to Reuben was wonderful.

Reuben would love her. Of this, Leah was certain.

CS

Leah was sitting in her room, working wool at her childhood loom to occupy her time. She felt much better today, her monthly courses all but finished. There would be just enough time for the purification ritual before her marriage to Reuben. The timing had been perfect. Thank you, good and Gracious Jehovah!

She heard a little tap announcing someone's arrival. She smiled, for it could be no one except her mother.

"Guess who?"

"Mother, you know I know it's you."

"You are better today, I can see it." There was relief in her mother's voice.

"Yes, so much better. I am so thankful this happened now, instead of next week. This would have been a disaster in the middle of my wedding."

"Women have been known to marry during their monthly courses, for who can predict them? But yes, I am happy this has come and gone. God's hand is on you."

"As Savta would say, 'Wait for the Lord and he will deliver you!'" Leah giggled.

"I think Solomon was referring to revenge in that passage, but I am glad you know your Proverbs nonetheless." Talitha shook her head.

"Savta's proverbs."

Talitha smiled and sat down on the bed. "Speaking of Savta, I want to talk with you about something important. The last thing I must discuss with you before you leave this house and become a wife."

Her mother held something covered with a beautiful embroidered cloth. Leah had never seen it before. "A surprise, for me?" She opened her eyes wide to tease her mother. "Should I close my eyes? Just like when I was little? No peeking?"

"This is better than a surprise, Leah. This is your legacy."

"A legacy is better than a surprise? Impossible!"

Her mother shook her head. "Be serious, my dearest daughter."

My dearest daughter? Leah pressed her lips together, for those words signaled her mother meant business. She watched her mother unwrap an ornate wooden box from the delicate linen she held. Its lid was inlaid with a yellowing ivory. The box looked very old.

"This is for you, Leah. Open it." Leah ran her hands over the smooth surface of the box, the ivory cool to her touch. She took off the lid and then stared in silence.

The box was lined with what appeared to be a silvery fabric, ancient and fragile. Lying in the center was a necklace, a large, beautiful medallion. It looked like an open flower, its center a handsome round-cut ruby the size of Leah's fingernail, the biggest Leah had ever seen. Eight pear-shaped rubies surrounded the center stone, like petals surrounding the center of a Jordan bloom, silhouetted in elaborate gold filigree. Small diamonds sparkled, clustered in groups of four in between each ruby petal. The entire effect was repeated for a second row of precious gems and small diamonds. Of these, six were round red rubies, the other six large ivory pearls. The entire medallion was almost three inches across, as long as Leah's forefinger.

If you moved the medallion, it looked like a flower in full bloom, rippling in the most graceful breeze. Leah had never seen anything like it. She touched it with a careful finger.

"Oh," was all she could muster, the word no more than a sigh. Her mother smiled.

"This necklace is precious to the women in our family, Leah. I wore it at my wedding years ago, and before that, it was worn at the wedding of my mother, and my mother's mother, and her grandmother, and her grandmother's mother before that."

Talitha lifted the necklace from the box and draped the heavy gold chain over Leah's head. The medallion lay squarely in the middle of Leah's chest, breathtaking in its jeweled beauty. "Leah, since you are a woman about to marry, this medallion now belongs to you.

Someday, you will give this same medallion to your oldest daughter just before she marries. Just as I give it to you today.

"See these rubies? They are of great value. This medallion is the only thing in our family that is passed from mother to daughter, it is written that way in your betrothal contract, as it was written for my marriage and Savta's and her mother's, too. For this necklace is passed on with a special blessing, the same one my mother gave to me and her mother gave to her. Just as I give you this medallion, I give a special blessing to you as you marry. Never part with this medallion and you will never part with the blessing it carries. I bless you just as Savta blessed me and someday, you too will bless your own daughter."

Her mother picked up the heavy medallion and placed it in Leah's hand. She took Leah's other hand and placed it over the medallion, pressing down until Leah could feel every stone, prong and setting rigid against her flesh. Her mother's familiar hands were rough and calloused against Leah's skin.

"The first part of this blessing you will understand, Leah. You come from a long line of women who all taught their daughters the skill of their hands, to spin and weave and work at their looms." She closed her eyes and took a deep breath. Leah did not close her eyes, but instead watched her mother's face to burn this moment into her heart.

"O Holy God, bless this woman. Let her select the finest wool and flax and work with eager hands. Let her set about her work vigorously. Let her trading be profitable. Let her hold the distaff in her hand and grasp the spindle in her fingers. Let her make the best coverings for her bed and be clothed in fine linen and purple. Let her make linens and sell them. Let the work of her hands ever praise you, Almighty Jehovah, Lord of All."

Leah remembered what her mother had once said sitting before her own loom, that she hoped the work of her humble hands would honor God. Surely the magnificent work of her mother's hands praised God.

Talitha opened her eyes and smiled. "Close your eyes and bow your head, Leah, for the blessing I now give you." Leah bowed her head and felt her mother's hand rest there.

"Leah, my precious treasure and the daughter of my heart." Her mother paused, as if to compose herself. "May you be a wife of noble character, for you are worth far more than these rubies. May you have strong arms for your tasks, for your strength is stronger than diamonds. May your lamp never go out at night, but shine as bright as gold. May you be clothed with strength and dignity and speak with wisdom, your words like pearls before God. May you always fear the Lord and receive the reward you have earned. May your days be filled with laughter and with joy. Never forget that you are more precious than rubies or diamonds, gold or pearls. My daughter, my laughter, my life, my love. Leah, my most precious treasure, I bless you."

Talitha's voice was a whisper. "Everlasting Father, I entrust this child of my heart into your almighty hand and everlasting love. Guide her, protect her, never leave her. Selah."

"Selah." Leah whispered.

Leah and Talitha raised their heads at the same time. Leah remembered her impatient claim of only a few months ago, that she was ready to be a wife of noble character. As always, her mother seemed to read her mind.

"Still ready to be the crown of your husband, daughter?"

They laughed together.

The medallion was her mother's most precious possession, and had been her grandmother's, too, Leah thought. She shivered. Now it belonged to her.

Her mother held up the medallion. "There is one more thing I wish to tell you about this necklace, Leah. It is very precious to me and to all the women of your family."

She pulled out a necklace from under her tunic where it was hidden. A single pearl hung from the slender golden chain.

"Savta's necklace." Leah was surprised.

"No, Leah, that necklace was buried with Savta, just as I told you it would be. Just as this one will be buried with me." Her mother pointed to the outside row of rubies and pearls. "Leah, each time a generation marries, the mother passes on the medallion with one more ruby added. See these six pearls and six rubies?" Leah nodded, riveted by the beauty of the medallion and her mother's voice.

"Until just a few weeks ago, this row had seven pearls and five rubies. I had the goldsmith remove a pearl and add a ruby last week, and place that single pearl in this necklace for me. Whenever this medallion is passed from mother to daughter, the mother takes one pearl for herself. From this day forward, I will always wear this necklace, hidden from sight, next to my heart. This was the way of my mother and my grandmother and their mothers before us. It will never leave me, for it will always remind me of the most precious gifts from God, our daughters. Every day when I kneel in prayer, I will touch this pearl and be reminded of how much God has blessed me, to give me such a daughter, you who are the child of my heart."

Talitha laid her hand on Leah's cheek. "Just as the father values the son, the mother treasures the daughter. It has been my privilege to see you grow from a child to a beautiful woman, my daughter and my friend."

Leah covered her mother's hand with her own, unable to speak.

"This pearl is for me and me alone, for no one can share the connection I have with you. When I die, this necklace will be buried with me. Just as the necklace my mother carried for so many years was buried with her."

"Savta showed me her necklace. When we buried Savta, I wanted it so much. Savta once told me it was her most cherished thing. That was all she would say about it."

"Oh, I think Savta's most cherished thing was her granddaughter. For she loved you as I love you, just as my grandmother loved me, too."

"Not just me," Leah whispered. "I know how much you and Savta loved each other."

"Leah, this pearl is only a symbol, but it is something real we can touch and hold, to remind us of the love we have for each other. The love of a mother and a daughter is something no man can ever know."

Talitha dabbed at her eyes. "For Leah, I love you more than anything except for our Abba God. Jehovah blessed me beyond measure when he gave you to me fourteen short years ago."

Almighty Jehovah, her mother's unshakeable, steadfast foundation.

Leah's mother hugged her. "Oh, Jehovah, you have brought me laughter, and her name is Leah. Selah."

They cried together, and then laughed as they wiped away each other's tears, two women, mother and daughter, friends.

Leah was getting married at last. But she would always be her mother's daughter, her beloved, cherished, treasured daughter. Nothing could change that: not growing up, not marriage, not children of her own, not illness, not being parted from her, nothing, not even death.

Nothing would ever separate her from her mother.

CHAPTER 6

Reuben's father was a landowner of vast and prosperous fields, with large barns and dozens of paid workers. As such, the dowry from Reuben's family was great: silver and gold jewelry, expensive perfumes, spices and the finest of fabrics.

Not to be outdone, Leah's father added to her dowry contract in great amounts: carved wooden chests for their home, Savta's house, a beautiful bridal diadem of gold, and even a donkey!

Reuben's family sent a full bolt of beautiful pale blue linen for Leah's wedding gown, fit for a princess. Leah and her mother had embroidered every inch of her wedding tunic and her headdress with threads of an even paler blue and ivory. The cloth shimmered at the touch, like the ripples of a stream reflecting a vast blue sky.

The marriage festivities would take place at the home of Reuben's uncle in Caesarea Philippi instead of his family's large but humbler country home. The uncle's home was large, with a spacious courtyard and floors of tile, the grandest home on the brown side of Caesarea Philippi. Leah and her friends had often admired it, casting sideway glances as they walked past its iron gate. Leah never knew the house belonged to Reuben's family and never dreamt such a fine place would be the site of her wedding. She privately thought having the wedding in such a fine house was a final attempt to outdo her father in the wedding rivalry.

Family and friends came from all of Caesarea Philippi and from many miles away to enjoy the week-long celebration. By the modest standards of the brown side of Caesarea Philippi, Reuben and Leah's wedding would be exceedingly fine, much more elaborate than the weddings of her friends

On the day the wedding celebration was to begin, Leah waited impatiently in her home for Reuben and his friends, tended to by her mother and bridesmaids. The festivities would last for three days, but she was not nervous. At last, Leah would be a wife.

She wore the beautiful blue robe with its intricate embroidery. The sheer veil that covered her face was held in place with the graceful diadem, a circlet of gold. "Like a crown," Leah mused.

Twelve golden coins hung down from the circlet, each with an intricate design worked into the precious metal. Leah's wrists held heavy bracelets of all sizes from Reuben's family, decorated with ornate engraving and small jewels. Her neck was covered with shining rows of gold and silver chains. "The dowry of a princess," she thought, awed that the princess was her.

Most amazing was the medallion, a magnificent piece of art. Leah was astounded every time she touched it. Reuben would be so surprised when he saw this beautiful necklace. Wait until Leah told him the wonderful story of her mother and grandmother and great-grandmother, and the blessing that was handed down from generation to generation.

Or maybe she would not tell him, for this was a sacred and special trust between the generations of women in her family. She thought of her mother's blessing for her and sighed. Her life as a wife, as a woman, was about to begin.

Before she could exhale, Reuben stood before her, dressed in his own splendid tunic, his face red at the sight of his betrothed, his mouth working nervously to greet her. He managed only a single word. "Leah." He glanced at his intended and at once looked nervously around, his eyes finally landing on his own two feet. Reuben's friends stood silently behind him, but their eyes laughed at jumpy unease of the groom.

Leah's laughter broke the moment. "Reuben!"

Reuben escorted her to the wedding litter, a gilded chair covered in flowers, his arm a tight grip on Leah's arm. She sat down gracefully as Talitha arranged her robes around her. "Daughter," she whispered with a small smile.

The four groomsmen bent and picked up the litter by its four ornate poles, one set of strong arms on each corner. They lifted the chair with a smooth, practiced motion, not even grimacing at the added weight of Leah. Reuben stared up at her in silence but then surprised Leah with a nod and a wide smile. She grinned back at him.

Her groom turned to lead bridal procession on its serpentine journey to his uncle's home, the groomsmen carrying the precious cargo that was Leah with her bridesmaids walking behind. Leah wafted through the air past the cheering and smiling faces, alone with her thoughts in the swaying chair of gold.

Although he had not looked at her for more than a moment, Leah knew Reuben was enchanted at the sight of the woman that was his bride. He was proud that his friends were in awe, that they were perhaps even a little envious that Reuben was marrying the beautiful Leah. She could see the delight in his eyes.

Or was it more of a smug pride? Leah did not know and she did not care. Reuben wore a wide smile of white and even teeth and a look of confidence Leah had never before seen on his face.

"He looks handsome," Leah thought, somewhat surprised. "And happy."

As for herself, Leah knew she had never looked more beautiful, her long black hair shining on her shoulders, her eyes sparkling with excitement. As they carried her in the bridal litter though the streets, she heard the approving comments about her dress, her crown, the fabulous medallion, and most of all, her beauty.

Leah tried to look regal and dignified sitting in the golden litter, like a queen, but she kept forgetting and waving at people she knew. She was so excited.

All along the way her family and friends were singing to her, the ancient love songs of King Solomon.

Alone in the litter, jittery and nervous, Leah giggled at most of wise Solomon's words. His Songs were certainly different than his Proverbs.

"Your teeth are like a flock of sheep just shorn." Teeth like those dirty bleating sheep! Her father hated sheep! Ha!

"Your navel is a rounded goblet that never lacks wine." A navel full of wine! Ha! That would be one really big navel on one great big girl! She personally had a tiny belly button.

She blushed in embarrassment at some of the others: "Your breasts are like clusters of fruit. I will climb the palm tree; I will take hold of its fruit." Leah giggled again at the thought of Reuben shimmying up her like a palm tree, groping for her fruit. She hoped he wouldn't fall off and hurt himself! Ha!

Someone else sang, "My lover thrust his hand through the latch opening, my heart began to pound for him." Soon Reuben would be her husband and… her lover. Her lover! Her heart was beating hard with nervous anticipation.

They carried her through one street and then another so all might see her beauty, at last coming to the courtyard of his uncle's house. Reuben and the groomsmen set Leah in her litter down before the bridal platform with the greatest of care. The courtyard was filled with people already eating, drinking and feasting. Her arrival was met with great enthusiasm, cheers from people she knew and many more she did not, complete strangers.

Reuben took Leah's hand to help her stand. She flinched at its unfamiliar hot roughness and then stood before him, beautiful and expectant, radiant with joy. The noisy crowd of well-wishers fell silent at the sight of the beautiful couple.

As was customary, Reuben too began to sing to her from the Songs of Solomon, the words reserved for a husband and his bride. He sang the verses in a somewhat dissonant melody, his deep voice cracking on every other stanza. The words he sang were the most words she had ever heard him string together at the same time.

His face was red as he finished Solomon's amorous refrain. "How beautiful you are, my darling! Oh, how beautiful! Your eyes are doves." Leah was embarrassed for him and yet flattered that he would sing to her in front of all these people, even though Jewish tradition required it.

The end of Reuben's song was met with enthusiastic cheers, as the guests returned to their food, drink and conversations.

Leah ate her dinner seated at a table with the ten virgins all dressed in white. They sat directly across from Reuben and his friends. Bolstered by a goblet of his uncle's best wine, Reuben now stared openly at his bride.

On the other hand, so open was his admiration now, Leah now could barely meet Reuben's eyes. To be stared at so hungrily was an odd and unfamiliar sensation.

That was not the case with her ten attendants, however. They laughed with loud sudden bursts of mirth and looked at the groomsmen from under their darkened lashes, bold and coy at the same time. Their smiles flashed so wide that nearly all their white teeth were on display, and they tossed their heads time after time so their shiny black hair swung free for all the young men to see.

Leah had sat at such a table dressed in white eight times herself. She remembered flirting just like each young girl now did, in hopes that someone would notice and choose her to be the next bride, the next guest of honor, the next princess at the head of the table.

"It was more fun to be the bridesmaid than the princess," Leah thought. She ate and drank little, due in part to her jangling nerves but even more to her very great fear of spilling one drop of food or wine on her beautiful wedding gown before this great throng of people.

As soon as possible, Leah retired to a private chamber in the uncle's home to seclude herself with the ten attendants. Custom required her last night as an unmarried woman be spent in the house of the bridegroom's family. She didn't know any of the girls well, for they were younger, cousins from afar and acquaintances from the synagogue. Her real friends had married long before and were no longer virgins. Most were already mothers! They could not serve as the virgins required to attend her. Instead, they were downstairs having fun at the celebration, secure in their roles of wives and new mothers.

Her mother came to see her at last, shooing the bridesmaids away so she could speak one last time to Leah as a mother speaks to a daughter.

"Leah," she said, and was silent. She placed her hands on Leah's cheeks, just like Leah had done to her mother when she was a little girl.

"Leah," Talitha said again, "Promise me." Leah was surprised to see tears in her mother's eyes.

Her words came in a rush. "Leah, God has given you a special gift of laughter and of love. God has made you a woman of great determination, incredible fortitude! No matter what, Leah, hold tight to these gifts. You must submit to your husband. But never submit your spirit! Never let go of who you are, such a wonderful creation of

God. You are my beautiful, accomplished daughter, and you will be a beautiful, accomplished wife. Never forget your strength. Never lose your joy. Never give up your faith in God. No matter what happens with your husband, no matter what manner of man he is, you must hold tight to who you are and to your faith in Jehovah. Promise me, Leah."

Leah had no idea what her mother was talking about. "Mother, I don't…"

Her mother interrupted her, eyes closed, her face lifted up to her God. "God has brought me laughter, and her name is Leah. Promise me, Leah. Promise!"

Leah stared at her mother. Tears ran down Talitha's face.

"I promise, Mother." She reached up to wipe her mother's face. "Oh, Mother, don't cry. Be happy for me, please, for tomorrow is my wedding day!"

"Yes, tomorrow is your wedding day, the start of your new life. I love you, Leah, more than anything else in this world. I will rejoice and be glad in you."

"Rejoice and be glad, Mother!" She gave her mother's arm a little shake, trying to cheer her. "I am staying here with you, not moving far away. That is cause for celebration! Be happy, I will soon be married. I will live nearby. Everyday, we will work together. You will be part of my children's lives. It is all I ever hoped for."

Talitha nodded.

Leah put her arm around her mother's waist. "Now, Mother, I want to see you rejoice for real. Like I do. Remember, Mother? Re-Joice! Se-lah!" Her mother smiled at Leah's laughing chant. "Re-Joice! Re-Joice! Se-lah! Se-lah!" Her voice was loud in the room.

"Quiet, Leah, your bridegroom will hear you and run off to Egypt."

"I don't think so. I saw how he was looking at me. I think he was thinking, 'Selah! Selah!' too."

Talitha tried to frown at her daughter's habitual sacrilege, but it was impossible. She arched one eyebrow instead. "As Savta would say, 'Pffth!'"

They both grinned at each other, the echo of clattering looms and Savta's laughter faint in the quiet room.

☙

Instead of a wakeful night of nerves and worry, Leah had slept through the eve of her wedding in a stranger's house as though she were dead.

"Leah, my little dove." At the sound of Talitha's voice and Savta's pet name for her only granddaughter, Leah was awake at once. Today was the day. If only Savta was here.

Before Leah could linger on that thought, the incessant chatter of the ten attendants burst into the room. Attended by the watchful eye of her mother, they dressed her in her bridal finery, the delicate diadem, the gold and silver jewelry and the heirloom medallion.

Surrounded by the bridesmaids dressed in white, Leah met Reuben in the courtyard where they were blessed first by the synagogue ruler, then by Reuben's father, and finally by her father. In a strong clear voice, Leah began singing her assigned Song from King Solomon to her betrothed, her husband Reuben.

"'I am a rose of Sharon, a lily of the valleys.'"

In a shaky voice, Reuben responded,

"'Like a lily among thorns is my darling among the maidens.'"

Leah continued in a strong voice, the melody a haunting air:

"'Like an apple tree among the trees of the forest
    is my lover among the young men.
I delight to sit in his shade,
    and his fruit is sweet to my taste.
He has taken me to the banquet hall,
    and his banner over me is love.'"

Leah continued singing the long stanza, asking to be strengthened by raisins, comparing Reuben to a gazelle leaping over the mountains or a stag peering through the lattice, telling them she heard a dove cooing at the gate. She had to work hard not to giggle; if she did, she would embarrass herself and her mother forever.

Leah came to the final refrain at last. "'Until the day breaks and the shadows flee, turn, my lover, and be like a gazelle or like a young stag on the rugged hills.'"

The synagogue ruler stood one last time to bless the union between Reuben and Leah. It was done.

Reuben and Leah were husband and wife. Leah was married at last. Leah blushed as they turned to face the expectant faces.

The gathered guests broke into a cheer of congratulations, throwing seeds on the ground in front of their canopy to ensure the fertility of the bride. As one, the couple and the crowd turned to begin the wedding feast. This celebration Leah could enjoy. She was no longer nervous, only happy.

There was food everywhere: roasted meat, flakey baked fish, fresh bread, fruit and sweet cakes. More wine was served, the best Reuben's family had to offer. The courtyard noise was a constant hum without a quiet moment to intrude; the moment one musician finished a song, another took up a different refrain, with the cover of loud conversation and laughter over it all.

The girls danced, sang and played tambourines, hoping to catch the eye of some future husband of their own. The young men played games of chance and competition, hoping their skill would impress the maidens who watched, some with furtive glances, others with open admiration that invited a response.

Young mothers stood with babies balanced on their hips, talking with other young wives either pregnant or toting their own precious loads. Children wove through the knees of the adults, shrieking as they chased each other in games of tag or hide and seek.

Men stood in small groups to discuss the ever-widening circle of Roman roads, the bountiful harvest of crops in the country, the increasing expense to send items with the caravans that stopped in little Caesarea Philippi, the costly repairs and renovations to Herod Philip's palace on the other side of the city.

Leah's mother was surrounded by women, garnering compliments and congratulations over her daughter's beauty and good fortune in marriage. Her watchful eyes did not leave her daughter's happy face.

Leah and Reuben ruled over it all under the bridal huppah, its embroidered canopy heavy with flower garlands. One guest after another, so many that Leah lost count, stepped forward so Reuben and his bride could acknowledge their gift and the good wishes. Leah's face hurt, she had smiled so much. Reuben had not smiled as much, but he seemed happy, too.

Their wedding night began late. Leah could still hear music and people celebrating in the courtyard down below. Reuben lay beside her, already asleep.

She thought about what had happened to her only a few minutes ago and stretched out her entire body. It had not hurt. Reuben was somewhat hesitant and, Leah thought with a bit of amazement, exceptionally uneasy. Those nerves made him stutter and fumble; he was not quite as eager as Leah had expected. Still, it was all her mother had told her to expect.

"He will get used to me," Leah thought. "He will not be so nervous next time."

She smiled to herself. "Now I am truly a woman. Next come the babies, and Reuben will love me more than anything, love me forever. I am a woman!"

She stretched again, rolled over and shook Reuben awake. "Reuben, awake, awake! How can you sleep? Our lives are beginning right now!"

Groggy in his sleep, Reuben looked at her, uncomprehending. Then he laughed one of his rare laughs. "Leah, you must sleep, we have much to celebrate tomorrow, and the next day and the day after that, too."

"Sleep!" Leah exclaimed. "Aren't you excited, Reuben? For today begins our journey. Today we start on the path that is the rest of our lives. Together we will worship, raise our children, earn our living, and have a home! Today! How can you sleep?" She gave his arm a little shake to wake him.

"Leah, Leah." Reuben shook his head. Leah remembered he had enjoyed a great deal of the wine. "It is not today, it is tonight. Sleep, Leah, sleep."

"Then let us think about tomorrow. Tomorrow is as good as today, Reuben! Tomorrow and all the promise it holds!"

Reuben closed his eyes again and did not answer. Leah propped her head up on an elbow and smiled. "Tomorrow, my husband, let us run away from all these people! Let us jump on our new donkey and ride him all the way to the top of the Old Gray-Haired Lady."

"What?" Reuben opened his eyes.

"The Old Gray-Haired Lady. Mount Hermon! My grandmother Savta rode to the top when she was a bride. She slept in a tent and felt the snow between her toes! I want to do it, too. Let us go up to the snow, to the top of Mount Hermon, Reuben. Let's go tomorrow!"

"Leah, it is late. We must sleep."

"Pffth! Sleep is for the aged, Reuben!"

And before Reuben knew it, sleep escaped him too, in the arms of Leah, his beautiful, passionate, happy bride.

CHAPTER 7

"So, Leah, what are you cooking for me tonight?"

Leah whirled around at the sound of her husband's gruff voice. He stood looking at her with a scowl.

But Leah knew how to cheer up Reuben.

"Lentils and hot bread, my husband." She gazed up at his dark face with a smile and slid her arms around his broad shoulders. He shrugged at the arms encircling his neck, but they both knew his protest was only for show.

A moment later, Leah felt his lips pressed against her own, his beard rough on her cheek, the smell of dust from her father's warehouse clinging to his robe.

"Leah." His voice was a whisper against her hair.

Married less than a month, the first days of marriage came easily to Leah.

"Welcome home, husband," she whispered back. He pressed his muscled body against hers. She buried her face buried in his robe, smiling at the strong expanse that was her husband. As he rested his chin on her head, Leah felt the stress ease out of his body.

Leah loved the memory of their wedding ceremony, three happy days of celebration with the two of them sitting like a king and queen under the bridal huppah, dressed in their finest, the beautiful medallion around her neck. She still smiled at their wedding night and the first touch of the man she would call her beloved for the rest of her life.

But their wedding was nothing compared to the life Leah vowed they would enjoy as husband and wife. She would work every moment of her life to make Reuben happy. Leah would be the best of wives, just like her mother.

Leah refused to acknowledge the small certainty that, while her mother was indeed the best of wives, her father most certainly was not happy.

Leah's marriage would be different. Reuben was not her father. Reuben would love her.

And so, the moment her wedding finery was packed away, Leah began her life as Reuben's wife. She cooked their meals, ground the wheat, smoked the fish and kept her lamps full of oil. All the things her mother had taught her to do as a girl.

Reuben and Leah lived in the little house of beloved Savta. How Leah loved their home. She tended to the housekeeping chores as though Savta herself stood watching.

And, oh, the cloth she would weave from her loom! Leah was learning her mother's art of subtly changing colors, one hue piled up on another, just like the mountain sunsets Savta had taken her granddaughter to see. Reuben's outer cloak was handsome, easily spotted in a crowd, woven with love by Leah's now skillful hands.

Some days, after a hard day of working with Leah's father, Reuben would walk in their door tired and even grumpier than he usually was. But prodded by the company of Leah's laughter and good spirits, it would not take long for Reuben to find a better mood in the embrace of his beautiful wife.

"Leah, what did you do in our little house today?" He would lift her by the waist and spin her around till she was dizzy, her thin frame no match for his brute strength, a rare smile on his face.

"Leah, who taught you to weave such beautiful colors into your cloth?" He would marvel at the work she produced on Savta's loom in the workroom of her mother.

"Leah. Oh, my Leah," he would whisper at night in their bed. "Come closer, sweet Leah." He would hold her close to him all through the night.

Much to her mother's amazement, melancholy, brusque Reuben

seemed happy.

If Reuben was happy, Leah was overjoyed. She loved being a wife. She rose early to make her husband breakfast. Reuben would leave to join Leah's father at his large shop where trade of flax and linen took place. She would walk to the well with the earthenware jug on her head and hurry home to tackle her chores, finding true pleasure in each task her home required of her.

She would join her mother for lunch and then in the afternoon, they would sit and weave together. By now, Leah was an accomplished weaver, just like her mother and before her, like Savta. Leah's father sold the cloth woven by of both his wife and daughter for handsome prices. The work of their hands rolled off the two looms as effortlessly as the sun slid down into darkness.

"Except I don't have my mother's sense of color," Leah thought often. "My mother is not a weaver, she is an artist."

But she was not the least bit jealous, for who could do what her mother did? Her mother's work was breathtaking, magnificent. Everyone knew it except Talitha.

"It is God's will," she would say with a self-conscious smile.

"Oh, Mother, don't be so modest!" Leah teased her unassuming mother. "After all, 'parents are the pride of their children.'"

"Really? Well, you remember this instead: 'When pride comes, then comes disgrace.'"

"Humph," Leah snorted. "Well, I 'do not want to forsake my mother's teaching' for she who scorns her mother will be pecked out by the ravens of the valley and then eaten by the vultures!"

Talitha laughed out loud. "How I have failed you, my dearest daughter. For no one can jumble proverbs together in such a string of nonsense like you. 'A foolish son brings grief to his mother, but a foolish daughter makes her laugh all day!'"

Leah grinned.

Marriage was full of laughter for Leah, too. It did not mystify or challenge her, or make her nervous. Marriage was all she had hoped it would be, indeed, had even expected.

For what Leah loved most was being a wife. She loved calling Savta's little house her own, filled with all the new things from their wedding. She loved her household chores, the familiar routines of daily living. She loved spending afternoons with her mother, time spent in laughter and prayer and productive work at their looms. She loved her quiet evenings with her new husband, trying to get to know and understand him.

She was still getting to know Reuben, and she supposed she would someday love him. She didn't worry about that part of marriage too much. Leah was happy, as happy as she had ever been. Reuben seemed happy, too.

Love was not an important part of her mother's marriage, after all.

Leah refused to consider what her mother's marriage was like. She could not imagine being married to someone like her father.

Leah would never allow her marriage to be anything like her mother and father's life together.

Her marriage would be happy, no matter what.

ᛈ

Leah stretched in her bed, feeling the warmth of her husband beside her. She smiled at his muffled snore, the only sound in the gray light of morning. Would she ever get used to the wonder of a husband lying in bed beside her?

"Everyday he must work with my father," she thought. "How hard that must be for him." She felt a tender affection for Reuben, so solemn and quiet, working with the demanding, angry man that was her father. Poor Reuben.

As Leah reached over to lay her arm on his waist, she felt it: the stab of pain twisting in her mid-section. The cramp was so severe, she cried out with the pain.

"What? What is it?" At once Reuben was awake.

"Oh, Reuben!" Leah could not find any words for the pain. She grabbed her belly and rolled away from him.

"Leah." She heard the shock in his voice. "You are bleeding... What is this?"

At once she knew. Fully awake, she felt the wet pool of cold, dank blood soaked through her nightgown. And at once she was ashamed.

"Reuben, please bring my mother to me."

"You're bleeding! A lot of blood! Are you... are you...dying? What is this?"

"No," she gritted her teeth. Surely Reuben knew what this was. "I will be fine. This is just what every woman goes through each month." A groan of pain escaped her, and Reuben jumped to his feet. "Please, Reuben, my mother."

He stared at the blood on her gown, uncomprehending.

"Reuben, please! My mother…"

Without a word of parting to his wife, Reuben turned and ran, ran away from Leah.

⚘

"It didn't take much to turn Reuben away from me." Leah sighed at this sad thought. She was once again in her bed, alone in the small house she called home, waiting for her mother to come to her.

She remembered that terrible morning, the first time in their marriage that Leah's courses came upon her. Reuben had returned with her mother and at once, Leah saw an unfamiliar look on his face.

Revulsion.

As soon as he could, Reuben left Leah with her mother and bolted for the door. Each night, he would look in on his ailing wife and leave as soon as possible, uncomfortable with the unspoken disgust they both knew he felt. His beautiful bride was not the wife he expected.

After the first month, Reuben waited the prescribed seven days as set forth by the Law of Moses, waiting for his wife to be ceremonially clean in the eyes of the Jewish law. But when the time came for Leah and Reuben to be together as husband and wife, Leah knew at once something was different. Her husband would not look or speak to her, hurrying through the act of marriage as though he were in pain.

"Reuben," she had whispered his name.

"Hush, Leah."

Leah lay silent in the dark for hours.

Leah's bleeding lasted longer each month. The ceremonial seven days of cleansing stretched to nine and then twelve and in the fourth month of their marriage, Reuben lay with his wife only once, a forceful undertaking that left Leah crying silent tears of pain and dejection.

In four short months, her marriage, the one she had sworn would be happy, had crumbled to dust.

Each month, her courses would come upon her, painful, agonizing, difficult. Each month, worse than before. Each month, a longer period of isolation in her unclean state, tended to only by her mother. Reuben was as repulsed by her bleeding as her father had been.

Even more bitter was Leah's failure to conceive. Each month, the mark of shame that Leah was not the wife Reuben so clearly needed left its stain on their marriage.

If only she were with child. Leah wanted to be pregnant so that she might end this cycle of blood and pain, shame and isolation, misery endured month after month.

Reuben cared nothing about her pain. He had wanted an heir. It was as though he had something to prove, and Leah's flaw marked him as a failure, too.

But Leah never even once thought she might be pregnant, that she might carry the babe she so longed for in her womb, the child that Reuben was desperate to father.

"When I get better, then I can be a wife to him. When I conceive, it will change, he will be different," Leah would think in despair. "He will be different. He will love me."

But each month, her bleeding and her marriage got worse.

"Why are you always sick? Why could you not get with child when we were first married?" Leah shrank back from Reuben towering above her. The rage of Reuben that Talitha had dared to speak of so many months ago was a fierce anger that now frightened Leah, too. Reuben was truly fearsome when he was angry, black eyes matched by a fierce scowl.

"People will think it is my fault, they will think I cannot father a child! It is a disgrace. You are a disgrace!"

"I'm sorry, Reuben," Leah whispered, her face turned to the wall. She could find no other answer for her outraged husband. "I'm sorry."

"Sorry! That's all you have to say!" Reuben had finally stormed out of their house, leaving her alone while he went who knew where. He stayed away more and more, returning home at all hours of the night and day.

She would never conceive now, anyway. According to the Law, Reuben could not lay with her while she bled – not that he ever would want to. The required purification stretched out longer each month. To lay with an unclean wife would make him ceremonially unclean. Worse, her condition sickened him. He would not even touch her.

Some of her friends had once joked about their husbands' eagerness to share their beds, no matter the time of the month and regardless of the consequences. "He says it's worth the extra sacrifice," one had once giggled.

Leah was silent. Reuben had trouble even looking at her when she was bleeding.

Worse, soon her father, his parents, her friends, neighbors, all those near to them began to ask, "Where is the babe in your belly?"

Reuben would look away. Neither she nor Reuben had an answer for their insistent questioning.

"I'm sorry," Leah would whisper, eyes downcast. She could not bear to look at the inquisitive stares any more than she could look at the angry man she called her husband.

☙

One month, a period came upon her that did not last for seven or ten days. It lasted for a full two weeks. She was in agony most of the time, despite all the herbal remedies and potions her mother provided from the midwives. Leah bled heavily and with the worst pain she had ever endured.

"Tell no one," her mother had commanded them. Leah did not know why, but both she and the sullen Reuben obeyed.

Leah had no one to tell, but she feared that Reuben would not be able to keep the secret her mother demanded. She worried he would soon cave in to the persistent questions long before Leah might. She rarely saw anyone anyway.

When they were alone, Leah asked her mother about her insistence on their silence. "Why can we not ask for help, for prayers, Mother?"

A look of pain crossed her mother's face. "You must tell no one. No one."

"But why?"

When Talitha answered, her voice was soft but angry. "Why? Let me tell you why, Leah. The men of this world, the men of our world, they set great store by the 'law.'" She spoke the word "law" the way one might say vomit, as though it was vile and disgusting.

"There is no compassion, there is no understanding. There is only the 'law'. And this is what the Law of Moses says."

"'When a woman has a discharge of blood for many days at a time other than her monthly period, she will be unclean as long as she bleeds.' As long as you bleed, Leah, you are unclean, according to the 'law.'"

Leah was shocked at the contempt in her mother's voice.

"The 'law' does not stop there. 'Any bed she lies on while she bleeds will be unclean. Anything she sits on while she bleeds will be unclean.'" Her mother's voice was a mocking singsong. "'Whoever touches these things will be unclean; he must wash his clothes and bathe with water, and he will be unclean till evening.' Anything you touch, Leah! Anything of yours that Reuben touches, that I touch, just a touch makes us unclean. Unclean! So says this 'law.' You are unclean, and we are unclean, too, just by touching you! Are you listening, Leah?"

Leah stared at her mother.

Talitha started pacing. "Oh, there is more, daughter. The 'law' says 'If a man lays with her, and her blood touches him, he will be unclean for seven days.' Seven days, Leah, that's how long the Law says Reuben will be unclean, just for sharing your bed! But it is not just "your bed" for the 'law' goes on to say 'his bed will be unclean, too.'

"And when you are finally cleansed from this disgraceful bleeding, this bleeding that every woman has had since God created Eve from man's rib, then you must count off seven days, too. Seven days, Leah, just to be sure you are really, truly, completely 'clean' or as the priests tell us, 'ceremonially' clean."

Leah had never heard her mother speak in such a way, her voice dripping with bitter sarcasm.

"And then, when you are truly, completely, ceremonially clean, you are to make atonement to the priest so he may make atonement for you before the Lord for the uncleanness of your blood.

"You do not dare approach Jehovah, oh no. Some uncaring priest, lost in his own sin, must do that on your behalf, for after all..." Her mother spat the words out. "You are just an unclean, sinful woman.

"And don't forget the final words of the Law about women and bleeding and their uncleanness. 'You must keep the Israelites, the Chosen People, separate from things that make them unclean, so they will not die in their uncleanness.' Those are the 'regulations,' Leah, the 'law' that man upholds with such arrogant pride today."

Her mother gripped Leah's shoulders and shook them, her fingers tight. "To tell anyone of your illness is to make yourself an outcast, Leah, an outcast! Do you understand? For your uncleanness makes them unclean, and Jewish men fear that more than anything else! It is ludicrous, that the Law would keep me, your own mother away from you because you are unclean! But it is the law of our people and the Law of Moses!"

She released Leah's shoulders from her iron grip. Leah was mesmerized by the look of fierce anger on her mother's face. "Tell no one! Tell no one! For the men of this village, the rulers of our synagogue, the council of the place where we worship will cast you out as though you were infested with a thousand demons! Tell no one! No one!"

"But Mother!" Leah was stunned by her mother's outburst. All she could think of was her mother's last statement. "Father is on the council."

Talitha looked at her daughter with hard, glittering eyes, her voice a whisper. "Leah, my dearest daughter, child that I love. Tell no one. Command this of Reuben. Do not tell him what I told you here today. But tell him, tell him to speak of this to no one. No one!

"And especially, Reuben must not tell your father."

CHAPTER 8

Leah opened her eyes; the small room she shared with Reuben was bright with sunlight. She heard the loud snores of her husband first, and then smelled the faint odor of rancid wine clinging to his disheveled robe. He was curled up on the edge of the pallet they shared. Even in his deep sleep, he was as far away from his wife as possible.

She sighed. Reuben only slept in their bed when he was overcome with wine, never for the comfort of his wife. He had not touched her for weeks. He stayed away from her and their home, returning at odd hours with the slur and smell of wine.

Leah never knew where he went, her timid questions met with a stony silence. But sometimes, she would wake to the smell of drunkenness and defeat at her side, Reuben too weary – or drunk – to make up his usual pallet far away from his wife.

She was always unclean in the eyes of Reuben.

She felt the familiar clench in her gut and at once she knew. The worst had happened in her sleep. She tried to be prepared, but often the bleeding surprised her. She had only been bleeding a few days ago!

She reached down and felt the pool of blood under her. It was bad. Horrified, she stared uneasily at the red smear on her hand.

93

A tremor of fear ran through her.

Reuben must not find out.

Before she could wake him, she heard an unfamiliar shout. "Reuben!"

The sound at her front door was so unfamiliar it took a moment for her to recognize it. But a wave a dread rolled over her. It was the voice of her father.

"Reuben!" She gave her husband a fierce shake. "Reuben, wake up!"

He looked at her with bleary eyes, uncomprehending.

Of course. The bright sunlight meant it was late morning or even mid-day. Reuben had long ago been expected by her father.

"Reuben!" This time, the man's voice was a roar. Before he or Leah could do anything, her father stood at the side of their bed. Reuben threw off the blanket and sprang to his feet. Leah snatched the blanket up to cover her, but it was too late.

Her father walked up to the bed and stared down at his only daughter. "He's never set foot here since Savta died," Leah thought. She wanted to laugh at the absurdity of it.

"My daughter, what is that on your hand?"

Leah remembered another day a lifetime ago. "What are those?" he had asked, even as he pried the wildflowers from her fingers.

"I asked you a question. What is that on your hand?"

She stretched out a hand shaking so badly she could hardly keep it raised.

"Blood. An unclean, defiled woman." His voice was a terrible whisper.

"And you." Her father turned to Reuben. Reuben shrank before his malevolent glare. "After all I have done for you, you do not come to work. Is it not enough that you shirk your duties as a son-in-law? You cannot even do your work as we once agreed? As your father promised you would? And then, I find you at this late hour lying with a woman during her time of uncleanness?"

Her father turned away from Reuben to stare at Leah. "Look at her! She is an abomination!"

Leah huddled in terror before his temper.

He turned back to Reuben. "You are not a man at all."

"I did not sleep with her!" The furious words burst from Reuben, who at once stood toe-to-toe with the rage of Leah's father.

"It is not what you think! I would never lay with her when she is bleeding! I never lay with her at all! She disgusts me! She is unclean! You are wrong, wrong!"

Leah watched the scene as though in a trance, too afraid, too sick to move.

The smack of her father's fist hitting Reuben's cheek.

Reuben reeling against the wall and sliding to the floor.

The trickle of blood from Reuben's mouth, one eye swelling shut.

Reuben crying, his words a murmur over and over, "She disgusts me, she disgusts me…"

Her father turned from Reuben to stare at Leah. He looked down on her for so long, she thought he surely would drag her from her bed and beat her, drag her away, do anything to be rid of her.

But he turned to face Reuben, his voice as hard as the stone pavers in the streets. He shoved Reuben with his toe.

"Listen well, Reuben. You were the worthless second son of a family who was glad to be rid of you. I bought and paid for you to do my bidding, for your connections to grow my business. You are part of a business transaction and I will not be cheated.

"You will never be late for work again. You will live up to the bargain I made with your father through this marriage, or I will shame you and your family for generations to come.

"You will never again walk into my place of business, or even this house, stinking of wine. I know what you do. I hear the talk. Wine will loosen your tongue and that is unacceptable. Her shame will not tarnish our family because you yammer like a whining woman deep in your cup of wine. You will stop the drinking and behave like a man."

Reuben's stared at the man towering over him, his expression unfathomable, blood tricking down his chin. But Leah recognized the angry set of his jaw.

Her father continued. "You will speak to no one about your wife. No one! The shame of your wife is the secret of this family.

"You will behave like a good and respectable husband. If she needs doctors, you will find doctors. If she is dying, then those we know will watch us mourn.

"The world must never know what goes on behind our family doors. No one must know the shame that is Leah!

"Pack your things. We leave at once for Jerusalem to make the required sacrifices for your purification. I will not risk a careless, unclean, drunken Jew undermining my business. If our customers were to find out. You foolish cur!

"Meet me at the warehouse with your things. Bring money for the sacrifices. You have one hour."

He stopped to look at the shaking woman that was his only daughter, and then, just as he ignored her tears over Savta in this house so many years ago, left her without a word.

She heard him shout in her small courtyard. "Say nothing, woman! Nothing!"

Her father might not want the world to know about his vile daughter, but surely everyone in her neighborhood had heard.

Her mother stepped through her bedroom door, and with a swift look understood. Talitha's voice was gentle. "Reuben."

He leapt to his feet as though his robe was on fire. He strode to the small chest and grabbed two robes, wadding them into a ball.

"Reuben." Leah's voice was a whisper.

He whirled around and strode to the bed, staring down at her.

"I hate you." His voice was a hiss rising in intensity. "I hate you. I hate you, I hate you!"

Talitha laid her hand on his arm. "Reuben, I…"

Reuben jumped at her touch. "Say nothing, woman! Say nothing!" He rushed from the house with only the two robes balled up under his arm

Leah trembled. If there was one thing she had never thought to hear, it was the words of the man she feared most coming from the lips of her husband.

CHAPTER 9

Leah lay on her bed, pretending to be asleep.

Her mother sat at her side, waiting with her for Reuben. For some reason, Leah did not want her mother to know she was awake. To be awake was to invite conversation. She slowed her breathing, trying to make it even and steady.

"I wonder if I am dying?" Leah thought.

If she was dying, she didn't want her mother to know. It would hurt her mother if Leah were to die. She sighed, forgetting she was pretending to be asleep.

Reuben would soon arrive with yet another doctor. Another futile attempt on Reuben's part to find out what was wrong with his wife. The wife he had grown to hate.

Leah had been sick now for four years.

"I have been sick forever," she thought miserably. "For as long as I have been married, I have been sick."

As though she could read Leah's mind, her mother laid a soft and gentle hand on Leah's forehead. Leah could never fool her mother.

Leah sighed again, her eyes still closed, wondering when her husband and the doctor would arrive.

After that terrible morning with her father, Leah worsened in each month of the first year of their marriage. She spent much of her time hidden in her bed, afraid to leave her house.

Reuben, however, changed. He never again came home smelling of wine. If Leah asked a question, he would answer, although the curt words from his mouth usually pained Leah. He was away most of the time, but Leah understood from her mother he worked long hours for her father, even to the point of her father's terse praise about his son-in-law to Talitha.

Reuben was apparently holding up his end of the business transaction that he was. His attitude to Leah also changed: it was soon apparent Reuben believed that his once-beautiful wife would die from this dreadful affliction.

So in the second year of their marriage, Reuben started the parade of learned physicians and men of healing.

Leah was not sure why Reuben did this for her. He seemed to despise her, he thought she was dying. But perhaps there was still hope for her marriage.

She remembered her father's brusque command to Reuben, "If she needs doctors, you will find doctors."

But perhaps that was not the only reason. Perhaps Reuben might learn to love his wife if only she were healed.

She asked her mother.

Talitha hesitated. "Many people now know or suspect you are sick. To not bring in the doctors would appear... wrong to others. As if Reuben was not doing the things a husband should do. Both Reuben and... your father... set great store by the opinions of others..."

The comment saddened Leah. Every night, she prayed to be well, that she might be healed, that she might once again be a wife, that God might give her children. Somewhere in her heart she still harbored the hope that Reuben might want that, too.

Perhaps her mother was wrong.

Leah had lost count of the number of doctors she had seen. She had seen so many. None could help, and each one seemed to know less than the one before. But not one of them could find any remedy that helped her at all.

"A vitiated body is the sign of a vicious soul," one had sonorously proclaimed. Leah, a vicious soul? And what did vitiated mean? When Leah found out, she was angry. Disgraced and decaying, indeed! And what was this doctor's advice? More prayers and sacrifices, plus, of course, his fee. Pah.

Another doctor, another diagnosis. "Hyssop and rue in water, morning, noon and night for seven days. Fasting for seven days, only the herbs are to be taken. During these seven days, you must also offer sacrifices in the Temple every day at sunrise and at dusk, two sacrifices of two doves every day for seven days." This doctor left them with the prescribed herbs, collected a hefty fee and left.

A few days later, Leah and Reuben had made the one hundred-twenty mile trip to the Temple in Jerusalem with the begrudging consent of Leah's father. Leah rode the donkey the entire weary trip. Reuben purchased the daily sacrifices of doves while she fasted and drank the daily herbs. The results? If anything, the travel made Leah's bleeding worse. And, because she was already so frail, seven days of fasting left her so weak she could not stand up for more than a few minutes.

The doctors prescribed potions, ointments, and herbal remedies. These she drank, rubbed on her body, inhaled, wore around her neck, or hid under her pillow. Leah tried them all to no avail.

As the doctors came and went, it was becoming more and more difficult to keep their secret. Especially for Reuben.

Twice she had sat at the fork of the road outside Caesarea Philippi. From there a traveler went to the city of Dan or followed the Jordan River, depending on whether one turned to the left or to the right. She preferred the road to the right, for the road along the Jordan was beautiful, the silvery meandering river lined with rustling rushes and reeds, stands of trees with their quaking golden leaves, God's gentle creatures startled into stillness at the sight of a fellow creature standing on two legs. Such a peaceful place.

She sat there alone at the fork of the road, waiting and wondering why Reuben had left her there. The loud clang of cymbals and bellowing yell right behind her frightened her so badly she fell over backwards.

"If a woman suffers a sudden fright at the fork of a road, the bloody flux she suffers shall cease, thanks be to Almighty, All-Knowing Yahweh."

Oh, indeed!

The sudden fright did not stop the bloody flux. However, she did start bleeding at the other end since she hit her head on a rock when she fell. This truly was a remedy developed by a man; no woman would ever think such a ridiculous plan would work.

To the doctor's professed surprise - but not to Leah's - this remedy did not cure her. To the doctor's good fortune, they paid him not only for this foolish advice but also to attend to Leah's bleeding head.

However, Reuben seemed encouraged by the flow of blood moving to another part of her body. He later paid a different physician for the same treatment, again to no avail. It was hard to be surprised when Reuben again mysteriously left her alone at the fork of the same road, sitting and waiting for what?

"He isn't even smart enough to pick a different place," Leah thought, cross.

Although the anticipation of the loud noise was almost as bad as the actual hollering and clanging, the second time Leah was prepared enough to at least not topple over and crack open her head.

Reuben's slow burning anger increased with each weary month. To placate him, Leah went along with the prescribed remedies, no matter how absurd, futile or idiotic they seemed. A traveling physician - Leah thought she knew why he didn't stay too long in any one town - had Leah eat a single barley corn picked out from the dung of his white mule. Rumor had it that this was a very famous white mule. After Reuben left with the doctor, and when she was certain he could not hear her, she said it out loud.

"Barley corn from the dung of a white mule! Pah! Men! Pah! As if eating a crumb of dung could ever cure me." Distraught people would believe any sort of feeble magic trick and exchange their money for the smallest glimmer of hope.

"If I was a man and I wanted to be rich, I would be a doctor." The words were loud in her bedroom. But she knew she could never be a physician, someone who traded on people's fears for money. Leah knew too well that the desolation of shattered hope was worse than the desperation of a sickened body.

In the early years, Leah placed hope after hope in these doctors, praying that one might find the cure that would heal her bleeding body and mend the ever-worsening relationship between her and

Reuben. Later, as the years and doctors went by, Leah's hopes vanished. None but God could help her, and he did not answer her prayers.

So here she lay again, pretending to be asleep, her mother at her side, waiting for yet another doctor that Reuben had found. He no longer told her when or how he found the doctors, only when to expect them.

Today was a bad day. Her bleeding was heavy, her heart heavier still. She felt isolated in her illness. No one could really understand what she was going through, to feel her life ebb away one slow day at a time.

The thought she fought so often as of late came to her again. Was she dying? She felt her mother by her side. She did not want her mother to know what she was thinking. Leah was afraid to die.

Her mother took Leah's hand, caressing her face, wiping the tears that trickled from Leah's eyes. She began to pray out loud to her God, asking for mercy for her daughter who suffered so. She prayed the only way she knew how, through the words of the psalmist.

"'Listen to my prayer, O God. Do not ignore my pleas.
Hear me. Answer me. My thoughts trouble me.
I am distraught.'"

Talitha's voice broke and she fell silent. Leah squeezed her mother's hand. Without opening her eyes, Leah whispered the next words of the psalm she knew so well.

"'The voice of the enemy, the stares of the wicked,
They bring down suffering on me
        and revile me with their anger.
My heart is in anguish. The terrors of death assail me.'"

At the sound of a single sob, Leah opened her eyes. Her mother was crying. Her mother, who was always strong for her weak daughter, was crying. Leah closed her eyes again. She needed her mother to be strong. She continued in a faint voice.

"'Fear and trembling have beset me;
Horror... has overwhelmed me.'"

The words caught in Leah's throat, but she forced herself to finish. The words came out in a rush.

"'Horror has overwhelmed me...
Oh that I had the wings of a dove.
Oh, Jehovah! If only I had the wings of a dove,
That I could fly away... and be at rest. Selah.'"

As she whispered the last word, Leah started crying, too.

"That you would be at rest, my little dove. That you would be at rest." Her mother took Leah's hand and smoothed her hair. "Selah."

They sat like this, unmoving and silent, until a sullen Reuben ushered the doctor through the door.

This doctor was different. At once, he began to examine Leah, but in a way no other doctor had. She turned her head in shame. She had seen many doctors, but never had one examined her before in the most secret and private of places. She was naked from the waist down, naked and bleeding and defiled and shamed. He shoved her legs apart and poked and prodded.

Tear streamed down Leah's face but she did not make a sound.

Her mother stood in the corner, determinedly resolute, every cord in her neck standing out with tension. Her eyes never left Leah's, willing her to be strong. Reuben stood in the other corner and would not look at her. His horrified shame of her worsened each day. Today, his revolted humiliation of her unclean nakedness before another man was palatable. Oh, that her father would never learn of this dishonor!

Leah fixed her eyes on her mother's headdress, a beautifully woven piece of many shades of green. Beautiful, she thought. She wondered when her mother had made it.

This doctor was no different than the other doctors before him. She tried to listen as the doctor covered her and spoke to Reuben. "She has been like this for how many years?"

"Four. Ever since we were married."

The doctor was silent for a few minutes.

"Wondering how much money he can get out of Reuben," Leah thought cynically. "Mother should have worn an old brown cotton veil, not that beautiful linen one with all those colors of green."

The doctor busied himself with his bag, pulling out small pouches and setting them on the table in a neat row.

"Every evening for seven days, she is to drink this remedy I leave you. Stir the powder in hot water with great vigor until you can no longer see the drugs. Do not miss a day. After one week, the bleeding will abate. Do not miss a day! But make certain you do not use the remedy more than once a day, and only at night. It will make her sleepy; she will always fall asleep at once. Remember, only once a day and only in the prescribed amounts. More often, even just a little bit too much, could lead to her falling into the sleep from which she will not awaken."

At that, Leah's mother walked to the table and picked up the seven small pouches, a sharp look on her features. "My son-in-law Reuben is a busy man." Her tone was soft and measured. "I will be certain my daughter takes this medicine in the exact manner you have prescribed."

"My mother," Leah thought. "What would we do without her help?" She closed her eyes, trying to forget the shameful examination she had just endured at the hands of a stranger.

Reuben walked the doctor to the door. She listened as he paid the fees. They had little money, she knew. Her mother gave all she could. Her father no longer saw her, not wanting to be contaminated by her sinful uncleanness, shocked and appalled and secretive about the sin that had wedged itself in his own family.

They had already spent so much money on the doctors, all they had, really. All that remained for the doctors was the jewelry of her dower, her security in the unlikely event Reuben were to leave her a widow.

Or divorce her.

When the doctor of the seven pouches left, so did Reuben. Her mother sat on the bed and took the shaken and sad Leah in her arms, comforting her with a gentle rocking motion. Leah's mother did not care that her daughter was unclean and untouchable and forever defiled at the prodding hands of a stranger.

Once again, they sat in silence, for there was nothing to say.

CHAPTER 10

"Amê!" Leah heard the loud, echoing pronouncement echoing in the spacious room. How could this be happening to her? Unclean. Amê.

An abomination, an outcast. The same synagogue ruler who had known her for every day of her childhood in little Caesarea Philippi, the man who had blessed her wedding, was now banishing her from the synagogue, from worship, from all she knew. How could this be?

Beautiful Leah, who could recite the Torah and sing every psalm, cast from the synagogue like a leper. Faithful Leah, banned from worshipping her God with her husband and her mother. Joyous Leah, forced by law to remain out of sight to all. Amê. Unclean. Untouchable. And until God chose to remove this curse from her, unforgivable.

For almost five years, Reuben and Leah hid her condition from those around her. Her father knew, but pretended his daughter did not exist. Only her mother cared that she suffered, and helped Leah hide her constant bleeding. "Tell no one," was her constant refrain, her relentless warning to Leah and Reuben.

Reuben obeyed, with little to say and little time to spend with Leah. He came home only to sleep alone on a couch. Leah never asked where he had been, or what he told their friends. She cried often that she would never bear children. Reuben had not touched her for three years, not even to hold her hand when she was at her sickest.

Their great secret covered them, suffocating their every action, word and thought. Leah went out less and less, aware of the curious stares. Her fear of exposure, coupled with longer and longer bouts of illness, drove her to the solitude of her home. If it had been up to Leah, she would have never left her bed.

But her mother would not hear of it.

Talitha came every morning, forcing Leah to get up and dress herself. She would comb Leah's long hair and fix a meal, coaxing Leah to eat at least a few bites.

Talitha would take her daughter's arm and together they would make the short walk to Leah's childhood home, Talitha smiling and nodding – but not talking – to the neighborhood women with their sly glances or overt stares. Talitha would lead Leah to the sunny workroom, if only for her daughter to sit and to watch her mother weave, even at those times when Leah was "unclean."

"Come!" Talitha would clap her hands together. "Come, no one knows anything but you and I! Come, my dearest daughter!"

Her mother would not let Leah wither away in her bed. And one did not say no to Leah's mother.

"Up, up!" She would sweep into Leah's room with a smile. "There is much we can do today, daughter, much we can enjoy. 'Worship the Lord with gladness; come before him with joyful songs. Know that the Lord is God. It is he who made us, and we are his!' We are his, Leah! Up!"

Under the unwavering enthusiasm of King David and her mother, Leah would arise. And despite herself, she did feel better when she got up, got dressed and kept busy. She was too weak to weave, really, but she loved to sit beside her mother and watch the beautiful work of her hands unfurl, listen to her singing words of praise to Almighty Jehovah. To be around her mother was to live with gladness.

But it was not the same for Reuben. He was increasingly withdrawn. He was afraid, afraid others would find out and blame him, or mock him, or worse, consider him guilty of her sin, too.

Most of all, he was afraid Leah's father would condemn him.

Leah was not angry with him. She was no longer afraid of him. Since that morning with her father, Reuben's angry outbursts had

105

been replaced with the stifling silence Leah knew too well.

Leah knew he did not love her, but her heart refused to give up on her husband. So why were they at the synagogue today? Why was she standing here? No one need have known about her horrible illness, if not for Reuben.

But perhaps he truly thought it was time to confess that there was something horribly wrong with his wife Leah.

Perhaps he thought it was time to confess her sin of uncleanness.

So, in the fifth year of their marriage, Reuben went to the synagogue council and told them everything. Everything! Her shame was too great to bear. Her father had now sat on the council for many years, a respected and feared elder member of this intimidating, unapproachable body of men.

The council had summoned her to appear with Reuben at once.

"Her monthly impurity lasts for how long?" The aged synagogue ruler's voice echoed in the large room.

"It never stops. It... it does not stop after the usual... the prescribed seven days. She is always... bleeding." Red-faced and hesitant, Reuben stood before men seated at the council table, the elders flanking the synagogue ruler in his large raised chair in the center. Her father sat with them, staring at Reuben.

Leah sat off to the side, her veil hiding her face. Other members of the synagogue sat on the benches, here to see the spectacle of a public humiliation. Talitha sat alone in the women's gallery, her back straight, her face a mask that hid her anger.

"Then is everything in your home unclean?"

"Leah stays on her stool before her loom and she has her own bed. We do not share a bed any longer."

"The table? The dishes?"

"I do not take my meals ...with Leah."

"Her clothing?"

"She has many gowns. And, I have purchased more... extra... because she is often too tired to wash the unclean clothing."

"My mother bought them for me," Leah thought, already weary with the work of sitting for so long. "Not you."

"Do you wash the bandages for her?"

Leah could see this question about Reuben taking on the work of a woman pained him as much as the admission that her clothing was unclean.

"No, her mother and she wash everything!" His voice was loud. After a moment Reuben added in a quieter voice, "I am careful... very careful to touch nothing of hers."

"After five years of living with my illness, Reuben is not as careful as he wants this council to think he is," thought Leah. But she was not permitted to speak, of course. Nor would she have done so if given the opportunity.

The men on the council turned to look at her father. Her father looked at Leah as though she were some stranger, his gaze impassive. But his face was a mottled red, a certain sign of the forthcoming anger Leah knew all too well.

"I did not know this woman suffered from this ailment. Neither she nor her mother shared anything of this sin with me."

"This woman?" Leah thought. "This woman? I am your daughter, not some woman." She was as shocked at his words as she was at his lie, that he knew nothing of her illness.

"Neither my wife or my daughter have shared anything of this sin with me!" Leah's father looked at Reuben as he said this, challenging him to contradict this assertion of truth.

Reuben nodded at his father-in-law. Their shared secret was safe.

"Reuben," asked another council member, "when was the last time you offered the two doves for sacrifice for your wife's uncleanness?"

"It has been two years." Reuben voice was strong now. The anger of his father-in-law bolstered his confidence. Or perhaps it was the lies of Leah's father. Sensing an ally in his father-in-law, he plowed ahead, bolder. "But I can never count off the seven days to offer the sacrifice. She does not stop bleeding."

"Do you lay with her?" The synagogue ruler's voice resonated in the room.

Leah's face burned with shame. Her mother sat tall in the galley, her chin high, her stare at the ruler direct and unrelenting.

Reuben raised his head and looked one by one into the eyes of every man on the council, locking eyes with Leah's father last. "No. The law is clear. I have not lain with Leah in almost five years."

The decision was unanimous. Levitican Law could not be circumvented. The synagogue ruler stood, his words a toneless monologue, casting Leah from the synagogue until her sin could be cast from her, until she could again be ceremonially clean before the council and their God. Amê.

Leah sat there unmoving, listening to her judgment, unsure of what to do next. She turned to look at her mother in the silent room.

Leah was shocked by the look of blazing hatred on Talitha's face, her gaze a scathing rebuke of the ruler, of the council, of her husband. She rose to her feet, her head high, her back straight.

The old ruler raised his gnarled hand and pointed at Leah.

"Amê," he roared. "Amê. Leave this house of worship at once!" Unclean. The word had echoed in the chamber. The council all stood at the table. The ruler's sudden rage that his synagogue had been so defiled by such a cursed, unclean woman was contagious.

"Amê!" The entire council was shouting. "Amê!"

Her father shouted with them. He walked out of the synagogue with the other men, never turning to look at his only daughter.

Leah ran to her home, clutching her veil tightly around her, shamed and humiliated. She did not wait for her mother. Reuben did not follow. She knew he would not. She stole into the safety of her home, alone. She waited and waited. Why did her mother not come to her?

As night approached, Leah started to cry. Her mother had known of her illness almost from the beginning. After Leah's first months of marriage when the bleeding began, she was the one who told Leah and Reuben to tell no one, no friends, no family, no one. Her mother had known then what Leah would not believe until now: that her father would see her illness, her unclean state, as an unforgivable sin. But she was his daughter. How could a father cast aside his daughter for something that was no fault of her own?

Leah cried all night long, until she finally fell into an exhausted sleep.

And what she cried harder over was this: Why did her mother not come?

ℭ

The next day, Leah forced herself from her bed and dressed with haste. With no one to help her, it was hard to hurry. She stole to her childhood home, her face covered with a veil, scared of what might happen if met anyone.

She stood at the door, afraid to knock. Before she could, however, the door swung open. Her mother stood there, silent and weeping. One look at her mother's face told Leah why her mother had not come to her yesterday. Fear for her mother struck deep within her heart. "Mother!"

Before her mother could say a word, Leah's father wrenched the door from her mother's hand. "Amê! Unclean! Stay away! You are no daughter of mine. Your sin has brought me the greatest shame. You alone shall bear that shame, not I, not your brothers or their families and not my wife. You have lied to me for years about your filth. Your mother has lied! You are a child possessed of sin, of demons! How many times have I touched you in your defilement and broken the laws of Moses? You are worse than any leper, for a leper hides himself away. You are a curse! An abomination! Amê! Away!"

In disbelief, Leah fell to her knees, her forehead in the dust. He could not banish her from his home, from her mother! He could not! She groped blindly to clutch the hem of her father's robe, her sobs loud in the courtyard.

For the first time in all her life, Leah felt a physical blow. Her father struck her, hitting the back of the head bowed before him hard, with his fist.

"Leah!" Her mother's scream sounded far away, even though she clutched at Leah's shoulder "Leah!"

"Away!" The rage in his voice was fierce. "Away! You are not my daughter. You will not defile my name with your sin and shame and amê. Away!"

As Leah looked up at her father, his hand fell for a second blow across her face that sent her sprawling in the dirt. "Amê!"

Leah could not believe what was happening to her. Her father was shouting at her, hitting her, grabbing her mother in a terrible grip.

He towered above her, one arm raised with its hand clenched in a fist, as though to strike her again, the other wrapped around the neck of her bent mother who still struggled to get to her daughter, tears running down her face. He was hurting her mother. Leah looked up at him, this man who was her father. His eyes met hers, full of a rage she could not comprehend.

He spat on his daughter lying in the dirt. "Amê." His voice was a terrible whisper.

He dragged his wife inside.

The door closed.

Leah lay alone in the dirt, alone with her father's spittle and frenzied hatred.

He had disowned his only daughter.

For the second time, Leah ran all the way home. She bolted the door and hid in her bed. Reuben did not return. She was bleeding her terrible, sinful blood, she wondered if her jaw was broken, and she was terribly afraid for her mother. She could not stop crying. No one came to her, no one.

Leah was alone.

☙

The next day, Leah waited until mid-morning when she felt her father would be at his work. Her veil pulled tight over her face, she snuck to her childhood home, hidden beneath a window, listening for any sound of her father's voice. After an eternity, she crept through the courtyard to the door and knocked the smallest, quietest of taps. She had never before knocked on the door of her home.

Leah heard the quick footsteps and then a pause; she knew her mother was on the other side of the door.

"Mother!" Leah whispered. Her mother pulled the door open and gathered Leah into her arms, closing the door behind them.

Leah clung to her mother as though she would never see her again, both women holding each other tight. At last, Leah stepped back and cupped her hands on either side of her mother's face, to see in full force what she had glimpsed yesterday. Her face! Her beautiful, gentle mother's face.

The lingering red mark of a slap, perhaps more than one, across her face. A harsh bruise gathering on her cheekbone. Terrible red marks, as distinct as the prints of fingers in dough, lined her throat. A blackened eye, already purple and swollen shut. The other eye red and almost swollen shut too, but from weeping. Not for her pain, Leah knew, but for her daughter. Who knew what other marks of pain were hidden under her mother's tunic?

Leah closed her eyes and sank to her knees, unable to stand. Her mother, her beautiful, gentle mother.

Her mother knelt by her side. "Oh Leah, are you all right?"

110

"Oh, Mother. What has he done to you because of me?"

"I will be fine. It is over."

"Oh, Mother."

"Leah, I am sorry I did not come to you. I could not... leave last night. Your father, he will return soon, I think." She wiped the tears from her swollen and blackened eyes.

"Leah, my daughter, you cannot come here. He... your father will hurt you. I did not come this morning for I was afraid your father might look for me, find me with you... and hurt you. I will come to you as soon as I can. I do not want your father to see you."

"Oh, Mother... your face." Leah reached out an uncertain hand.

Talitha shook her head. "It is of no matter."

"But..."

Talitha placed a gentle finger on Leah's lips. "I love you Leah, you are the light of my life. I love you than anything else in this world!"

"How can you love me, Mother?" Leah's eyes were brimming with tears. "Father hurt you over me! I have been expelled, publicly denounced, disowned by your own husband! By my husband, too! Mother, why, why is God doing this to me?" Leah could not hold back the anger in her voice.

"I have not sinned, yet for many years I have suffered. I have no child. I have no husband. And now, my own father has cursed me, beat me, cast me out because of my uncleanness, my sin! And to punish me even more, he has hurt you! Why, Mother?"

Her mother grabbed her shoulders, and held her tight. "Leah, Leah, no sin has caused your illness. I do not know why you are sick, but I know in my heart that that your sickness is not caused by sin! That is not the way of Yahweh! As for your husband and father," Leah saw the sudden hatred on her mother's face, "these are the ways of men! These are not the ways of God!"

"But the ways of God are the ways of men! And my faith, my father, even my husband condemns me for my sin. They say it is my sin that makes me sick! Father said I was worse than a leper, a curse!"

Her mother looked at her for a moment and then released her. "The ways of men are not the ways of God! Your father thinks only of his own business, the money your marriage will bring to him, his precious standing in the synagogue. Your husband thinks only of the pleasure of his bed, the comfort of a home, children to carry on his name, what money he will make with your father. And the synagogue! Pah! The synagogue is filled with men, but it is not filled with God." Her eyes glittered with anger.

"Remember, Leah! God is a God who forgives all sin and heals all diseases. He will mend our broken hearts. He will crown you with love and compassion. From everlasting to everlasting, the Lord's love is with those who fear him. Those who fear him, Leah!" Leah couldn't tell where her mother's words began and King David's left off.

"This world is sometimes harsh and unfair," her mother said, looking hard at Leah, "so you must promise me, no matter what, you will never lose faith in the God that loves you. Promise me, Leah."

After a long silence, Leah said, " How can I, Mother?"

Her mother took her shoulders and shook them. "You can never, ever forget our God or your faith, Leah. To lose faith is to be lost! And if you promise me, I know you will honor that promise to God. Promise me, Leah!"

Her fingers were tight on Leah's thin frame. "Promise me!"

After a long pause, Leah nodded. "Yes, Mother." Leah could not refuse her mother.

"Remember all I have taught you, Leah. Promise you will never lose faith in God! Promise me. Say the words!"

"I promise."

And she knew as she said it, she meant it. For all of Leah's nineteen years, she had seen her mother hide herself in her faith. Leah knew now that faith had sustained her mother, no matter what she had endured at the hands of her husband. How ignorant Leah had been of her mother's life.

Leah would not abandon the God her mother loved and the God that loved them. Her mother was right. The world had done this to Leah, not God. Leah would honor the promise to her mother and in doing so, would always honor God, no matter how hard this world might be.

Her mother held Leah tight in her arms. "Now, go hide yourself at home. I will come as soon and as often as I can. Leah… I love you."

At that moment, Leah's love for her mother had never been greater.

And in the same instant, Leah's hatred of her father was born.

"His heart is as unclean as he thinks my body is." Leah thought angrily to herself. The things that had happened that day to her and her mother at the hand of her father had changed her.

Leah knew she would never forgive her father.

ℭℨ

Leah's mother came to see her several times each week at first. Soon, she came every day except the Sabbath. At some point, Leah realized her father must know of these visits. However, as long he did not acknowledge the visits, he could act as though his daughter did not exist. Leah's mother never spoke of him.

Talitha would bring her gifts: a new tunic she had sewn, the whimsical woven bracelets to remind her of her childhood, meat cooked with vegetables, which always strengthened Leah, perfume and little luxuries, and sometimes, even a little money for doctors. Leah's mother could not afford these things without knowledge of her husband. The one thing she never brought was any word from her father.

Leah wanted to ask her mother about it. "Will he ever forgive me? How can he think that sin has made me ill? Does he not remember me as a little girl, his child who was obedient to him in all things? Does he hate me? Does he hate you for loving me?"

But to voice those questions was to lay herself bare to the answers, answers that were too terrible for her to know.

As time went by, Reuben came home only to sleep, and sometimes not even that. He never ate with Leah, never touched her, and rarely even spoke to her. He traveled often to other cities, serving as a representative of her father's flourishing business.

If not for the money, the business alliance Reuben and her father shared, Leah was certain Reuben would divorce her. Leah thought her father would probably be the first to encourage Reuben to divorce his unclean, unfit wife as soon as possible, if not for the terrible vengeance of her mother.

Three years later, just after her twenty-second birthday, Talitha stood in Leah's door. Her father had died that morning. He had been found alone, dead at his barns for several hours. She carried no trace of any tears.

"Do not come to mourn," she said. "Do not come to the burial tonight. Your father would not have wanted it. I only go because I must."

Leah barked a short, bitter laugh. "Do not worry, Mother. I will not come to mourn. I am unclean, remember?" She shook her head emphatically, her eyes slits of anger. "Anyway, he would not want it because even in death I would shame him. Even as he lays there, dead and unclean himself."

Her mother had not answered.

Leah felt no pain that her father was dead, simply an incredulous grief that he died hating her. The anger that a father could so carelessly cast aside his only daughter still burned within her, but she was relieved. Her father could never hurt her mother again.

Leah was glad he was dead.

She would ask Jehovah to forgive her for her anger and for her disrespect of her father and of the finality of death, but she would not mourn him.

Her mother's voice had been harsh. "Your father is not worthy of your grief or your anger, Leah." Leah knew these fierce emotions were not directed at her, but at the man her mother had been married to for almost thirty years.

Her mother would not mourn her father, either.

After her mother left, Leah spoke the words aloud. It felt good to use these words to describe the man who had disowned her, shunned her, and wished her dead. The man who, for all of Leah's life, had hated her. He was dead and soon would rot away in his grave.

"Dead. Unclean. Amê."

Leah would not grieve for her father.

CHAPTER 11

Leah had been married for nine years, nine terrible years of agony and suffering. Her bleeding was always with her, nine years of pain that often left her too frail to leave her bed. Her mother and husband did not desert her. But one loved her, the other did not. One nursed her and kept her alive, the other stayed as far away as possible.

It had been five years since Leah had been cast out from the synagogue. Amê, unclean, she had dirtied the sacred ground of the synagogue and publicly shamed her husband, her father and her family name.

It had been a year since Leah's father had died, old, angry, vicious to the end of his days. If someone mourned for her father, Leah did not know who it was. Certainly her brothers and husband did not grieve his passing. Through her mother, Leah learned the once prosperous trading business no longer fared as well as under her father's malevolent eye and malicious tongue. But they got by, glad to be free of the yoke of his heartless cruelty and violent temper.

Leah was glad he was dead. He could never again hurt her mother.

It had been six months since Leah had seen her last doctor. That doctor had proposed a cure that was so peculiar, so dangerous, her mother had thrown both the doctor and Reuben out into the street.   "Murderer," her mother had screamed at the foreign doctor.

"It is the only cure for your daughter," his reply broken with the accent of one native to Egypt.

"Murderer," Talitha had hissed.

Rueben had slunk off after the doctor, but his rage at his mother-in-law over the incident simmered for days. He was so angry. Leah did not know if what the foreigner proposed was murder or not. She no longer cared. For wasn't she almost dead anyway?

Perhaps this doctor's treatment would be an act of mercy instead, one to end the misery of one so wretched and pitiful, so weary.

For after nine terrible, long years, Leah was beyond weary. She was ready for this illness that gripped her to be done, no matter what that meant.

And yet, even the smallest flicker of hope can survive. It will revive the weakest spirit. Even the smallest ember will eventually spark a consuming fire in a bed of sodden leaves thought to be nothing but wet decay. The strongest dam, built to hold back the worst of the flood, will give way to the smallest trickle slowly but persistently wearing its mortar away. So it was with hope. And of all people, it was Reuben that gave Leah that small shred that flickered to life.

They sat alone in their home, Reuben eating his breakfast, Leah picking at hers.

"We are leaving, Leah, to go to Caesarea. I have already made the arrangements."

Since Reuben had not spoken to her in several days, Leah instinctively looked around the room to see if he was talking to someone else. She replied to his unblinking stare, her voice faint. "What?"

"We are going to Caesarea, the Roman port on the Mediterranean. It is the entry point for people from all over the world. Perhaps... maybe we can find a new medical treatment or remedy there."

"What?"

"We are going to Caesarea."

"We are going to Caesarea?" Leah could not believe what she was hearing.

"Maybe there is a chance that some foreign doctor might hold a cure for your disease and unclean state."

"Going to see a doctor?"

"Yes."

"You are taking me to Caesarea to find a doctor for me?"

"Yes." He stood and walked to the door, apparently worn out by the conversation with his slow-witted, uncomprehending wife.

"Tell your mother and prepare your things. We leave in three days." He left Leah sitting there too shocked to move. She crawled back into her bed, tears of thanksgiving sliding down her cheeks. Reuben wanted to help her again. He wanted to help his wife.

She was grateful beyond words. She wanted to be rid of this disease once and for all. She was willing to try anything.

Her mother was not so sure.

"Why can we not send for a doctor?" Her mother paced Leah's bedroom that evening when Reuben returned at the day's end. "Why can't we bring a doctor here?"

Reuben shook his head. "Caesarea is huge. Why would the doctors leave such a large population, so many of whom need doctors, to come here?" Now that her father was dead, Reuben had more to say to his mother-in-law.

"I will travel with you. I will help you care for Leah."

"No."

"I will care for Leah! I have cared for her these many years. I want to hear what the doctors have to say."

"No."

"Yes, Reuben, I insist! I must go with you and Leah!"

"No."

Leah lay in her bed, listening to her husband and mother argue. She was so tired. Her mother's anger was with her husband was not right. Reuben wanted to help her.

"Mother." At the sound of Leah's voice, her mother was at her bedside in two steps. "Mother, it will be all right. Perhaps there is something new, someone Reuben can find to take care of me. He cannot afford to take all three of us."

This was hard to argue, her mother knew. The years of doctors had sapped the money Reuben had earned working with her father. With Leah's father dead, her mother's income was limited, too. Her brothers helped, but both had families of their own by now. Her father's ruthless business tactics had died with him, and their income was far less than it once had been.

"Mother will be a beggar because of me," Leah thought despondently. It was time for her husband to take care of her. He wanted to take her to find a cure. She forced herself to speak.

"It will be all right. My oldest brother travels to Caesarea at least once each month. He can join us when he is there; he will bring news of me back to you. It will be all right."

Talitha shook her head, uncertain and surprised at the usually meek Leah's words.

"We will trust God, just as you have taught me. Remember?

'I trust in you, O Lord. You are my God.
My times are in your hands.'"

Her mother was crying as she answered with the next words of the psalmist's plea.

"'Deliver me from my enemies,
From those who pursue me.
Let your face shine on your servant.'" She sighed. "Your faithful servant, Jehovah." She wiped her eyes.

It was settled with Talitha's fearful consent. In only two days, Reuben would take Leah to the mighty seaport of Caesarea, to search for someone who might know how to heal her, to save her.

There was still hope for Leah.

ॐ

"Leah." Her mother stood at the door. "Leah, where is Reuben?"

Leah no longer slept well at night. Although the bright noonday sun shone through her small window, without her mother to rouse her, she had been sleeping. She rubbed her eyes and rose to a half-sitting position in her bed, trying to remember. "I am not sure, Mother."

Her mother returned to the front door of Savta's little house to latch and bolt it. She pulled Leah up from her bed and helped her walk to the couch near the window. But she did not let Leah sit down.

"Here, Leah, lean against the wall. You cannot sit. Stand here for just for a few minutes. I need you to watch out this window for Reuben. If you see him coming, unlatch the door so he can come in, but make certain you let me know first. Do not let him in if I do not know he is coming."

"What? Mother, I don't understand."

"Do as I ask. There is something that I must do before you leave tomorrow." She disappeared into Leah's room, the woven cloth separating the space waving at her brisk step. "Tell me if you see Reuben coming."

Leah stared into the street, dusty and empty in the sunshine. What was her mother doing?

Leah called out to her mother only once.

"Is it Reuben? Is he coming?" Her mother's response was an agitated, hissed whisper.

"No."

"Then hush, Leah! Watch!" Leah had resumed her vigil out the window, chastised. There was no sign of Reuben.

There was no one in the street. Leah waited until she could stand the silence no longer. "I think Reuben went to the country today to say goodbye to the rest of his family."

"Keep watching!"

Leah was tired. Reuben had gone to the country, but Leah did not know how long she had slept in her bed. He might have left hours ago, actually.

At that thought, she saw him striding down the street.

"Mother, Reuben is coming. He is a few houses away."

Her mother came out at once, unlatched the door and swung it open. "Good. I am finished. Listen, Leah. There is something I must tell you, but there is no time to tell you right now. I am going to tell your husband something, but I do not want you to be concerned. Things will not be as they sound. Don't worry about what I am about to tell Reuben, do you hear me? Do not worry."

"What are you talking about?"

"Do you trust me?"

Leah looked at her mother and ducked her head. "More than anything, more than anyone, Mother."

"Then do not worry about what I tell your husband. And do not ask any questions, not any! I wanted to speak to you first, but there is no time. There is more to the story than you will hear today. Say nothing! Do you understand?"

Leah nodded.

"Just trust me."

Reuben walked through the door. There was no mistaking the rage on his face. At the sight of his mother-in-law, he looked even angrier. But he said nothing.

"I see as I pack Leah's things you took all her dowry. I assume you took it to your family's home in the country for safekeeping until you return from Caesarea. Is this where you have been?"

Leah was surprised. Where was her dowry, the jewelry and gold from her wedding that she kept hidden in her trunk? But she was silent, remembering her mother's hissed words of warning only a moment ago.

He looked at his mother-in-law, defiant. But soon, unable to stand her unyielding silence any longer, he nodded.

"Reuben, it is appropriate that Leah's dowry stay with me, as her parent. By law, what you have done is wrong. The dowry belongs to Leah."

"No. By law, what my wife owns belongs to me. She is not widowed, she is not divorced, she is my wife. Her dowry will be safe with my family. She is still married to me, after all." He glared at Leah's mother, his voice like gravel. "Where is the medallion?"

The words hung in the room. Leah's mouth dropped open. She turned to start at her mother. "The medallion is gone, put away somewhere safe." Her mother lifted her chin, her jaw set. Her voice was like a stabbing dagger, each word a deeper stab in Leah's heart.

"I took the medallion yesterday when you said you were leaving and I would not be allowed to go with you. You can look in my home, in the shop, in this house, with my sons, but you will not find it."

"Give me the medallion!"

"No, for I fear you will sell it in Caesarea. It is very valuable, as I know that you know. But it has been in my family for many years. I will not allow you to take it."

"That medallion belongs to Leah!" Reuben was shouting at her mother.

Leah was confused and scared. What was happening? Where had the medallion gone?

"Yes, it does. But the medallion has been in my family for six generations. It will not go to your family. I do not know what will happen to it yet, but it is not yours for the taking." Her mother's voice was calm.

The only time Leah had ever seen anyone look so angry was the day that her father had struck her and beat her mother. The day after Leah had been publicly denounced and cast out from the synagogue. Now, Reuben loomed over her mother with an enraged face and the same clenched fists of her father.

With difficulty, Leah stood up.

"Mother, where is the medallion?"

His quick glance at Leah was one of disbelief, surprise that his wife did not know the necklace was gone. He took a step towards her mother, who resolutely refused to meet Leah's eyes. She instead lifted her chin and turned again to her red-faced son-in-law, silent.

"I want the medallion. It is part of my... wife's... dowry." Reuben spoke the last three words through clenched teeth.

"No, as you and Leah know, when I gave it to her it was with the command that it was not hers to keep, it was to be handed down to her daughter. Since you have been unable to give my daughter a child..." Leah thought Reuben's eyes would pop out of his head at her mother's veiled accusation of his failed manhood, "...the medallion will remain here until you return. If Leah returns cured, perhaps you will be able to perform your duty, to give her a child, a daughter. Then, the medallion will go to the daughter of Leah, the daughter you will someday perhaps be able to father. But until you can make that happen, the medallion stays with me."

Reuben's hands were shaking with anger, his face red and large as he glared at her mother. But she no longer cared about the exchange between Reuben and her mother.

Her mother was taking the medallion away from her.

Leah remembered the moment just days before her marriage to Reuben. "Just as I give this medallion to you, I give you a special blessing," her mother had said, holding Leah close. "Never part with this medallion and you will never part with the blessing it carries."

Now her mother was taking the medallion and its blessing away. She no longer thought Leah would live. She was taking it away.

Leah was heartbroken. Tears came to her eyes and she opened her mouth to speak.

Her mother's eyes bore into her.

"Do you trust me?" her mother had said.

"Say nothing," she had commanded. "Nothing!"

Leah closed her mouth and looked at the ground, silent.

Reuben's voice was so low, Leah almost could not understand his words. "I curse the day I ever laid eyes on Leah and you, the wicked woman that is my wife's mother."

Her mother smiled sweetly at Reuben and lifted her chin. "I will look forward to restoring both the medallion and our relationship when you return with my daughter, healed or not."

There was no mistaking the tone of her voice. "For you will return with my daughter, Reuben. You will return her to me, and soon."

❃

That night, neither Reuben nor Leah's mother would leave Leah alone. Leah's mother claimed she wanted to spend every last moment with Leah. Reuben seemed afraid if he left, his mother-in-law would abscond with other things that were lawfully his. Not that there was anything else to take.

Leah's mother sat by Leah's bed all night, stroking her hair. Reuben pulled the couch into the room and slept right next to mother and daughter. The standoff lasted all night.

And Leah?

Leah wanted to trust her mother, but in her heart she was afraid. Her mother had taken away the medallion because she thought Leah was dying and would never return. Her mother did not want the medallion to be lost forever.

Every time Leah awoke from her fitful tossing and turning, she would cry herself back to sleep. Her mother thought she was dying. Why else would she take the medallion?

The specter of Caesarea loomed before her, no longer a beacon of hope. Caesarea was an ill omen of the future, the medallion a sad symbol of Leah's shattered dreams.

❃

The three of them ate the morning meal at the small table in Leah's home, an uncomfortable silence noisy between them. Reuben stood.

"I will load our things on the donkey."

Leah's mother nodded. "I will help Leah get ready."

The moment he left the house, she grabbed Leah and pulled her into the small bedroom. She whispered quick words in Leah's ear. "Listen, and do not speak."

Leah's eyes were wide. What was wrong with her mother? "What?"

"Hush, Leah! Listen! I have sewn the medallion into the hem of your bridal veil. It is in a padded hem, I made one for each end and added a fringe to disguise the work. Reuben will not remember how your bridal veil looked so many years ago."

Leah pulled away from her mother, her mouth forming the words. Her mother clapped her hand over Leah's mouth, her lips at Leah's ear.

"The veil is hidden with your clothes and hidden in the veil is the medallion! Never, never tell Reuben you have it, Leah! Promise me!" Leah nodded slowly, her eyes wide, her mother's callused hand still pressing against her mouth.

"Even if he says he needs money for a doctor, do not tell him about the medallion."

Why not, Leah wondered.

"That medallion is very, very valuable, worth a great deal of money. It is all I have to give you. If you need money to make your way back home to me, sell the medallion, sell it for any price, sell it to save yourself."

"I cannot!" Leah whispered against her mother's hand, shaking her head. Her mother pressed her hand on Leah's mouth even tighter.

"You must. It is all I can give you, and I and Savta and all our mothers before beg you to do this. Use the medallion to keep yourself alive and bring yourself home to me! If you must sell it, sell it! I do not care! Sell it, it is nothing compared to your safety and your life! But do not trust Reuben and never, ever entrust the medallion to Reuben. He knows its worth. He values it far above you or your life. Promise me!"

Leah looked at her mother's face, bereft at the hard words. Reuben valued the medallion more than his own wife. How could that be?

But Leah's father had not valued her at all. A great sadness welled up within her chest.

Her mother looked desperate, her eyes wild, her words almost a sob. "Promise me, Leah…"

Leah nodded.

"Say it!" Her mother loosened the iron grip of her hand over Leah's mouth. "Say it!"

"I promise." Leah's hesitant whisper was almost inaudible.

Her mother jumped to her feet and ran to the table, clearing their few dishes as Reuben walked back in the door. He looked at them with suspicion, her mother so brisk and busy, Leah unmoving, both of them silent.

"Come, Leah. It is time to leave."

Tears filled Leah's eyes. She still stood there, looking at her husband and her mother.

Leah's mother walked over to her and gently hugged her.

"It is time to leave! Now, Leah!"

Her mother wiped away her tears and smiled at her. "'My times are in your hands, Jehovah.' It is time, Leah." She pulled Leah to the door, Leah's hand clenched in her own.

Oh, how Leah, sad and broken, clung to her mother before she left. They knelt together in the dust at the feet of the donkey, Leah weeping, her mother praying, Reuben watching and waiting impatiently. Her mother prayed for safe travel, a hedge of protection from the bandits and vagabonds of the rough country. She asked that the trip not be too hard on Leah, that Leah be free from the pain. For the day that Leah's health would be restored. That soon the Lord would reunite Leah to her mother. That the Lord keep his hand on his daughter Leah. Amen.

By the end of the prayer, they were both crying again, frail, sickly Leah and her strong, beautiful mother. They smiled at each other, a shred of hope in one who was dying and the fatigue of worry in the other whose heart was breaking. Then they laughed, just a little, at their shared tears.

Talitha took her daughter's face in her hands. "Oh, Solomon is so wise, for did he not say, 'Even in laughter the heart may ache.' Leah, Leah…. never forget the promises you have made to me and to our God." She gave Leah a final, tight hug, whispering in her ear. "Don't forget what I told you. Never tell him. Come home to me.

Always remember what I have taught you: Never abandon your faith in Jehovah. Never."

She pushed Leah back to take one last look at her daughter's pinched face. "I love you, Leah. Never forget."

She waved goodbye until Leah and Reuben were far from sight. Leah turned around again and again to look at her mother, oblivious to the judging eyes of strangers, once-friends and passers-by from the brown side of Caesarea Philippi, staring instead at the one who loved her, staring until she could see her mother no more.

CHAPTER 12

Leah and Reuben were both walking, their little donkey loaded down with supplies. Because Leah was so weak, their progress was slow. Her halting steps made Reuben angrier every hour. The donkey could scarcely walk either, so great was the small beast's burden.

"If only I could ride for just a few minutes." Leah did not say this aloud, for she knew this was impossible. Reuben had packed many, many provisions for their trip to Caesarea on the Sea, even the small loom of Leah's childhood.

"Who knows when we will return, how long before a doctor heals her?" was Reuben's brusque reply to Talitha's questions.

Leah knew her mother agreed to send the loom as a reminder of precious Savta instead of any weaving Leah might do. She remembered her mother's comment about the tools of their hands so many years ago. "Some days, you will whisper your secrets to your loom, for it will feel like your only friend."

It's like we are moving, Leah thought. At least she would have her loom to keep her company, a much friendlier companion than her husband.

Why hadn't Reuben borrowed another donkey? Perhaps no one who would lend one to them because of her sickness. There wasn't any money to buy another donkey anyway, and she knew Reuben would not suffer such an extravagance just so his diseased wife could ride.

Leah walked as fast as she could, trying to keep up. She had to force herself not to turn around to look at the beautiful Old Gray-Haired Lady growing smaller behind her, the mountain of her childhood.

"I never got to feel the snow between my toes, Savta," Leah thought sadly.

Reuben had to halt his progress many times to wait for the feeble woman falling farther and farther behind. The first long day did not end until darkness had fallen. Reuben set up camp near the shores of Lake Hula. They had covered almost ten miles, walking the entire day.

After the first few miles, Leah became conscious of a terrible but possible thought: at Reuben's relentless pace, she might die just making the trip.

It took every bit of Leah's strength to set out some provisions for the meager cold meal, but she would have to do the work if she wanted to eat. Reuben would never stoop to this woman's task. Leah realized how much she had depended on her mother the past years. Finally, a small meal was set before them.

Like the last years of their marriage, Reuben said nothing to Leah. He sat by the fire, stoically chewing on the bread her mother had packed.

Despite Talitha's desperate worry over Reuben taking Leah away, Leah still harbored the smallest, most fragile hope. She could not help herself. Could it be true? Did her husband have a plan? Did he too long for her to be made well?

In the year since her father had died, perhaps Reuben's resentment of Leah and her illness had died, too. She remembered the first weeks of their marriage. Reuben had been happy. Reuben had loved her.

Why else would they be leaving Caesarea Philippi, Reuben with a sick wife and spending money they did not have to travel, unless he wanted her to get well, too?

Leah gathered all her courage to look at Reuben and speak. "Do you know anything about the doctors we will see in Caesarea?" Her voice was so timid and soft! Impatient with herself, Leah looked at Reuben and asked in a louder voice, "Has someone told you about a new medicine that we may find when we arrive?"

But when Reuben turned to her, Leah recoiled at the look etched on his face by the shadows of the small fire. It was pure hatred. Leah shivered. Reuben was her husband! He did not hate her! He couldn't!

Instantly Reuben's face changed. Leah knew she had caught him at an unguarded moment. But the extreme loathing twisted on his face still shocked her.

"There will be many more opportunities than in Caesarea Philippi," he said in a low voice.

Leah was afraid. Surely the fire was making her imagine things! She took a deep breath for courage. "What... What will happen when we arrive? Do you know how to find these doctors?"

"No. But we will find a synagogue, a Jewish neighborhood where no one knows about you, and they will direct us." The finality in his tone made Leah afraid to ask anything else.

"Thank you, Reuben, for all you have done, for... for this. I am sorry... sorry for everything."

Reuben did not answer.

ೞ

They traveled for four more long and hard days, covering less ground every day. Leah only managed to walk three miles the last day, but at least they made it to the edge of a town. She had been surprised to see it, for she had spent the last hour focused on her dusty feet, willing them to take just one more step, over and over and over again.

"Where are we, Reuben?" Her voice cracked from three days' of disuse.

"Capernaum."

"Capernaum!" How odd. She had passed through the city as a girl, but could not remember anything about it. She thought they were going to Caesarea on the Sea? Perhaps this was on the way. Her mind teemed with questions she could not bring herself to ask.

The deserted little street was lined with shabby houses. Leah sat down by a well, exhausted and dirty.

"Stay here, "Reuben said.

"Reuben, please... can you please give me some water?"

128

He looked at her as though she had asked him to rebuild the Temple. Water from a well was woman's work. But he took a dipper from a bundle on the donkey, dropped the bucket down to the water, pulled it back up with a grunt and handed it to her. A deep drink barely wet her parched throat.

"Thank you," Leah whispered.

He shrugged. "Stay here."

"As though I have the strength to go one step further without you," Leah thought as he walked away, the donkey on its tether plodding behind him.

It had been a difficult journey, made harder by Reuben's unwillingness to stay at an inn.

"An inn? What if someone finds out about your uncleanness?" he responded harshly to Leah's timid question about lodging at night. They had bedded down in fields, last night nowhere near a well. Leah had not been able to clean herself from the hard day's journey, or replace the bloody rags that hid her shameful state.

Today, Leah felt as unclean as the law said she was. Today or tomorrow, Leah thought, she would have to somehow wash out her bandages. How could she accomplish that? There were complexities of travel she had never before imagined or encountered.

Perhaps tonight they would find an inn here in Capernaum where she could wash and rest before they resumed long their journey to great Caesarea on the Sea. "Perhaps a day or two of rest in Capernaum is part of Reuben's plan," Leah thought. "Surely that is why he pushed me so hard to get to this city today."

She saw Reuben coming down the street. It was getting dark; he had been gone for at least an hour. As she saw him returning, hope filled her heart. Reuben did not hate her; he hated her illness. After all, wasn't Reuben taking her somewhere so she could be cured, so she could be whole and they could enjoy a life together?

Where was the donkey? A flicker of unease crossed her mind.

"Get up," he said, and Leah stood, bent slightly from the constant pain and weariness, still clutching the small dipper.

"Come." His tone was abrupt. Leah followed behind him, trying to keep up.

In a few minutes, she saw their donkey tied up in the tiny courtyard of a small, abandoned house. He no longer carried his heavy burden of their possessions on his back. Where were their things?

The house was in the poorest of repair. Tall weeds lined the foundation, there were large cracks in the walls, and the shutter at the only window hung on one hinge. It had an eerie sense of lonely disuse. Reuben walked up to the open door and turned to her.

"Go in."

Leah obeyed. A single dark lantern was set into the wall, unlit. The dark house was sparsely furnished. A small low table stood in the center of the single room, a stool pushed up in the corner by the window. Rickety wooden steps lined the back wall, leading to a door at the top. The roof, Leah supposed.

A narrow, worn mat for sleeping was tucked under the steps. Two chests, one on each of the opposite walls, stood open. A dirty, unlit oven stood in one corner with a small pile of wood; two water jars stood in the other. Several unopened parcels sat next to them. A small spindle and the loom of her childhood stood near the window with several bags of wool.

The place felt dirty and neglected. "Just like me," thought Leah. Then a thought came to her.

"Reuben, are we staying here for a few days?"

At once, she understood Reuben's plan. She was so relieved she nearly burst into tears. Reuben knew how terrible the long days of walking were on Leah. He planned to break their travel here and let her rest. Why else would they be in this house? Because of her illness, Reuben did not want to stay at an inn. No matter how humble, she could rest here. Her real fear that she might not survive the remaining eighty mile journey to Caesarea was replaced with gratitude to Reuben. Her husband had found a place for her to rest.

"Leah." There was an edge to Reuben's voice. Remembering the look of hatred on Reuben's face she had seen the first night of their trip, Leah was suddenly afraid. Standing in the doorway, Reuben was only a dark silhouette against the setting sun. She could not see his face, only his considerable hulk and broad shoulders outlined in the waning light.

"This is your home now." She heard the stiffness in his voice. She knew that hardness. She had heard it years ago, in her father.

Her home? Leah was silent. She did not understand.

"Leah, I do not know what sin you have in you. I do not know if your sin is from your mother or from somewhere deep inside you.

I cannot understand it, for your father was a good Jewish man."

Her father, a good man? Leah's confusion deepened even as a spasm of fear clenched her heart.

"If your father were alive, he would understand. I cannot live with a woman who has been unclean, untouchable for nine years, for all of our marriage. I cannot live with you any more."

She heard a roaring sound in her head. What was that noise? She felt as though she had to shout to hear her own voice, but it came out as a whisper. "Reuben, are you leaving me here?"

"Yes."

There was a long silence as Leah tried to digest that single word. Surely she did not understand.

"Reuben, you are... are you leaving me here... alone?"

"Yes." He was smug in the defiance of his answer.

There was another pause as Leah tried to understand what was happening. The roar in her head was deafening.

"Reuben, please!" Leah felt as though she was screaming, but instead her voice sounded tiny and desperate, begging. "Please, Reuben, do not leave me here. Do not leave me alone."

"Leave you alone! Leave you alone!"

Leah shrank before his rage, but she could not give up. "Please, Reuben."

"Please? Please? For once I please me, Leah! Because for years, Leah, I have been alone, alone in my suffering and disgrace for sin that belongs to you! It is with thanksgiving I leave you alone!"

"Reuben, please, then let me go home to my mother."

"Take you to your mother, in the town where your disgrace is known to all! If I leave you with your mother, your mother will bring disgrace on me. Disgrace I do not deserve! Your shame has brought me shame. Shame to me!" Reuben stepped out of the doorway into the dark house.

"Leah, you will only bring shame to your brothers and your dead father and, even though she is too dull to know it, to your mother! For every day of our marriage, Leah, you have shamed me! But no more!

"For God has punished me!" Reuben's voice had risen to a shout. "No children, a wife who cannot share my bed, only doctors to pay until all our money is spent! No more! Not one day more!"

"Reuben, then take me home and divorce me. Do not leave me

here alone!"

Reuben walked over to tower in front of her. Every feature on his angry face was clear, and at once Leah was more afraid of the man towering over her than of the things she had just heard him say. He could break her neck or throw her down the stairs to her death. He could return home and tell her mother that Leah had died along the way, that the trip was too hard for her. Who here in this strange city would know but God?

He wanted her dead. He had brought her here to die.

But when Reuben spoke, his voice was sounded normal, as though he was telling her about their plans for travel on the morrow. He sounded almost happy.

"No more, Leah. I will not be shamed any more. I will do the right thing, and provide for you as a husband should. There is food here already. You saw where the well was. Your clothes and your, your ...rags..." he said this as though he had the dung of the white donkey in his own mouth, "your ...bandages are in the chest. Your mother packed all your things. Everything else you will need I have already purchased, barley, oil, wool and more. All you need.

"I bought you this home, where you will live alone in your unclean state as the law dictates. Your shame killed your father, but it will not kill me. No, I will care for you as God requires a husband to do. I will not divorce you. I will do my duty before God. May that same God rid you of your terrible evil and have mercy on your sinful soul."

"Reuben," she whispered.

There was relief in his voice, she heard it. He had finally made a decision and he would not be swayed. "I will return each month to bring you food. I brought your spindle so you can make thread, your loom so you can weave wool. What you weave I will sell to support you here. I will return only once each month, so make good use of the food, and the wine, the wood and the other things I will so generously bring to you."

Leah felt the fear well up around her, an intense terror that smothered her with its weight. In all of her life, she had never ever been alone. She sank to the dirt floor and pressed her face to the dirt. The floor smelled faintly of the decayed manure of animals. As she lay there, unable to breath, an even worse thought came to her, terrible in its enormity. The words choked her.

"Reuben. My mother. Please send her a message. She waits to hear of our arrival in Caesarea. She is so worried. How will she know?"

He looked down at her, a sneer on his face at the mention of the woman he hated.

"I am not returning to Caesarea Philippi." He turned and left. Leah lay alone, face down in the dirt.

CHAPTER 13

Three Years Later

Leah would hear the women approaching long before they walked by. Huddled on her small stool beneath the open window, she could close her eyes and picture them. Tirzah, the tall, serious girl, would pass closest to Leah's dilapidated little house in Capernaum; Tirzah's small laughing friend would be at her side. Both would balance large water jars on their heads, their footsteps sure and steady in the dirt.

The small laughing friend would have on one of her new tunics. She had been married less than a year, and as befitted a beloved only daughter, had many new gowns. Her daily household chores had not yet taken their toll on her new clothing. A bright veil would cover her head and a matching woven belt would accent her small waist. A plain girl with round eyes in a round face, she was not beautiful. But she had a wide smile that that crinkled her eyes, a joyous expression that drew people to her. She looked like someone you would want for your friend. She looked happy.

Leah loved her.

Leah listened carefully but still did not hear the two voices so familiar to her. There was only the chatter of the other women and children walking to and from the well. Leah's two friends were always last.

"I wonder where they live." Leah thought for the hundredth time. It could not be too far, or they would not walk every day to the well at the end of Leah's small, tired street.

Sometimes, Tirzah's daughter toddled along. But the little one slowed them down and didn't accompany her young mother very often. There was both a neighbor and two grandmothers nearby who loved to watch the little girl for the hour she spent on this daily chore.

The small laughing friend did not yet have any children.

Careful to stay out of sight, Leah pulled herself up to peer over the window ledge into the street. Soon her two friends would come with their water jars. They would go to the well and then return to their own homes. Only after they passed by the second time, their sloshing jugs full, voices and laughter growing faint, only then would Leah slip out unnoticed to walk to the well alone.

She waited with anticipation, wondering what they would talk about today, even though eavesdropping on these daily conversations saddened her.

Leah sat back down on the small stool under the window of her ramshackle little house. Her loom somberly faced her with its half-finished weaving. She should work while she waited, but it was not even noon and she was already so weary. This probably would not be a good day.

She had slept very little the night before, for one of her terrible headaches had plagued her for hours. But that fierce pain was still not as bad as the suffocating, oppressive nightmares that haunted her, night terrors she could not escape in her fitful sleep. She remembered Savta's swollen hands as they labored over the shuttle, the whisper of her mother's admonitions to attend to the work of a woman. Leah shivered as a trickle of sweat ran down her back, the loom unsympathetic in its silence.

Maybe she would just rest while she waited.

Leah remembered walking to the well with her own her friends years ago. They would giggle over the daily eccentricities of their new marriages, their shy husbands who were still strangers, their tiny squirmy babies, their dreams of children and a life to come. A brief respite from their small, new households. Husbands, homes, children: all were cause for amused conversations.

Leah was once the favored daughter, just like Tirzah's small laughing friend. Leah too was the youngest, much loved by a mother who adored and spoiled her. Not anymore. She had not seen or had any word of her mother for a long time.

She missed her.

Leah crouched under the window, unseen as she waited. She hungered for their conversation, craving the laughter of her two friends. She ached for this human contact, as one-sided as it was.

For Leah was alone. There was no one to call her name or hear her cry at night. No one to help her, hold her, console her. No one. She was cut off from the world, isolated by her husband and her disease.

Leah had been alone in this strange city with her dreadful bleeding and her terrible secret for three interminable years. Her furtive shame had become as painful as her illness.

She grunted at the sharp stab deep in her belly and back. She stretched her arms and tried to flex her hands; the stiffness of her joints was excruciating. She startled at the sight of her hands with their swollen knuckles: Savta's hands.

Leah knew she was much sicker. Thin to the point of emaciation, she could count every one of her ribs, a skeletal frame. Her meager meals were an ordeal anyway, for she could barely swallow past the sores that festered in her mouth and throat. And the pain! Some days she did not know what to do about it but pray. Her will to survive was all that kept her alive, and it was all but gone.

Only three things kept Leah alive: the promise she made years ago to be faithful to Jehovah no matter how much she hurt, no matter how bleak her world was; the overwhelming desire to once again see what she loved most, her mother; and finally, a stubborn determination to not let Reuben win by dying.

Leah was no longer distressed by the inevitable seep of blood between her legs. It was part of her life now, part of who she had been for twelve years. Twelve long years ago the blood had started, and in twelve years, it had never left her, really. How was that even possible?

She could always feel it. It was there when she sat or stood or laid down to her fitful, restless sleep. Some days heavy, other days a slow, degrading ooze. Always with her, never a day when she did not suffer from this filth, this affliction that had ruined her life. This shameful blood that made her unclean to the world and to her God.

She lived in constant fear: fear of discovery, fear of being alone, fear of death. How had this life come to be hers? She tried to remember, but could not. Or perhaps would not. Either way, she did not know this life that was her own.

Leah listened again for her two friends. They seldom went to the well when the noisy crowd of women was gathered there. Instead, they waited until it was almost deserted, stolen time to spend with each other. The sound of their voices meant Leah would soon be able to make her own way to the well, alone and unhindered by the condescending stares of others.

She waited, certain of only one thing: her two friends would come.

Leah knew when they worshipped and about their synagogue, newly-built with massive gray columns and floors of black stone. She heard all about the birth of Tirzah's little two-year-old girl, and about the small laughing girl's marriage celebration just twelve months past. She cried for days when she learned that Tirzah's mother finally died, and shed bitter tears when she heard the small laughing girl's first pregnancy had ended in a painful miscarriage.

Leah knew the names of their husbands, what furniture they had in their homes, what they purchased at the market and what they cooked for their evening meals. She had been part of their conversations for three long years. When they did not walk by on the Sabbath, Leah missed them.

For although Leah had never spoken to the women... they were her only friends.

CHAPTER 14

The conversation of the two women walking to the well was clear in the hot, still air and noontide quiet of the dusty street.

"So how is your mother today? She was so sick last week."

"Oh, Tirzah, I don't know. She is better, I think."

"I'm so glad."

"We walked to the market yesterday afternoon, not even for an hour. She was so tired when we got home."

"I'm sure the walking did her some good."

"I don't know, Tirzah." Tirzah's friend, the small laughing girl with the wide smile, sounded discouraged. "Her cough just seems to linger on forever. It tires her so much." The small laughing woman sounded worried. "Thank you for always asking. I know you understand why I worry. Your mother was so precious to me, too. You know you are like another daughter to my mother."

They walked in silence for a few moments, the small laughing girl somber. "We purchased some fruit and a little oil." She cleared her throat and spoke in a more mischievous tone. "And we spent a lot of time looking at cloth. Mother bought some cloth for a new tunic."

"Your mother needs a new tunic? Why, for goodness sake? She is too tired these days to sew one stitch!"

"Well, the tunic is not for her."

There was a long pause.

"If your mother is not making a new tunic for herself, might I ask who she bought cloth for?"

"Well, for me."

Peeking out the window, Leah could see the small woman's face break into a sheepish grin.

"Oh, you are something else! Another new gown! And you have so many from when you got married. What did your husband say?"

"Well, he doesn't know about it just yet. But when he asks me if I am getting a new tunic, I shall tell him 'Yes, by the way, I am!'" There was laughter. "Fortunately, he hasn't asked me just yet."

"Why do you need another tunic? Is it for something special?"

"These colors are so beautiful, Tirzah, scarlet with bright bands of orange and yellow and pink woven all through it. It is so lovely, like a sunset."

It sounds like something my mother might weave, thought Leah.

"Besides," the young woman tried to adopt a serious tone in her voice, "Mother wanted to buy it. She thought the dark red would look good on me. It seemed to... cheer her."

"Oh, to be the only girl in a family of boys," replied her friend in mock disgust. "To be fifteen, newly-married and still spoiled by your mother. She will spoil her baby girl forever, you... princess!"

"Someday to be a queen, with princesses of my own, right, Tirzah? Besides, if I am a princess, don't I need a gown for every day of the month?" The small laughing woman danced a few steps on her toes, her voice loud and pompous. "'The princess is glorious, her gown is woven with gold!'" Her sideways glance was sly but mischievous. "If I can't have a gold one like King David, how about a plain old red one instead?"

Both women burst into laughter, their voices fading as they continued on their way to the well.

"All glorious is the princess in her chamber; her gown is interwoven with gold," Leah whispered, "In embroidered garments she is led to the king." Tears came to Leah's eyes. How well she knew the words of this psalm. Her mother sang those same words to Leah on her wedding day.

Careful to stay hidden from sight, Leah stared out the window at the women walking away. Tirzah and her small laughing friend would soon return, walking past Leah's house for the second time with their water jars full. Then it would then be her turn to make the long walk to the well. If only it were not already so hot, the sun so high in the sky. Her friends were late today. Leah could already feel the sun's heat through the thick walls of her small house.

She could no longer hear their voices. The street now deserted, Leah walked to the doorway of her small house. She often stood there in the shadows, looking at the quiet street in this strange city. Leah's days were as routine and monotonous as the waves of the Sea of Galilee where busy Capernaum lay anchored. Not that Leah had any part in the daily hum of this foreign city.

Leah was very sick. She was dying, as lifeless as a dead tree floating on Galilee's shore, moving only where the tide chose to take it, bearing no leaves or fruit, rotting away as the water washed up around it and then away, continuous and unrelenting. When the tree finally succumbed to its decay, no one would miss its presence. Just like Leah.

She stood there for a moment, her hands on her hips, frowning as she thought over those mournful thoughts.

"Pffth!" She spoke loudly to no one in particular but herself, the exasperated shake of her head giving full vent to her impatience. "A dead tree! Pah! You're not dead yet, Leah. Why don't we get going and do some work while we wait?" She shook her head again. "A dead tree indeed. King David's somber poetry has nothing on you, silly girl."

Leah only spoke to three people: herself, God, and, on his infrequent visits, Reuben. She wondered if it was sacrilegious to talk to Almighty God as though he was a person.

"Better God than Reuben, Leah." was her immediate and loud response. She smiled at the sound of her own voice in the empty dark room.

She often used her own name, speaking it out loud, secretly fearing if she did not, her voice would rust away from disuse, fading away like smoke on the wind.

There wasn't anyone else to talk to anyway. When Leah talked out loud to herself, she was usually scolding or nagging or giving direction, bossing herself around with strength and persistence and confidence. She had to talk that way to silent Leah, the quiet, puny

Leah that was weak and sick and scared. Silent Leah harbored frightening unspoken thoughts of pain and loneliness and dying alone, secret fears that loud and cantankerous Leah fought to keep away.

"Sit down and weave, Leah," she said in a loud voice. "As Savta and good old King Solomon used to say, 'Don't eat the bread of idleness.'"

She did not utter the rebellious thought that crossed her mind: The bread of idleness might be a nice change from barley bread, barley bread and more barley bread. Silent Leah had a stubborn streak too.

Leah was passing time that morning as she always did, watching for her two friends and waiting for her turn to go to the well. Leah always waited until the sun was hot, for the heat of the day and stillness of the noonday meal, waited so she could go alone, hidden from the eyes of the women on her street. Her two friends were always the last to complete this daily chore of all Jewish women. When at last her friends walked by the second time, Leah knew she could finally make her lonely trek to the deserted well unnoticed and ignored.

Knowing it would be a bit before the women returned, Leah plopped down on the stool under the window at her loom. She was painfully thin. Her ribs almost poked though the old linen tunic she wore. It was far too large for her shriveled frame. Sitting down jarred her bones, making her back and hips and belly cramp in the old familiar way. She grimaced, pain etched on her weary face.

Ow, she thought, miserable in her pain and loneliness. Will I even be able to stand back up when it's time to fetch the water? Can I even stand the walk to the well, carrying my small jar only half full, not even enough water for one day?

She heard her own belligerent voice again. "You went to the well yesterday, and the day before and the day before that. Today is no different. If you don't go to the well, who will? No one will go for you, Leah, no one."

Could that unkind voice really be her own, Leah wondered. That voice sounded so mean. She pushed away the silent worry: What would happen when she could not walk to the well anymore? She was afraid how the mean voice might answer that question.

Leah felt older than Methuselah just before he breathed his last at age 969. 969! She smiled. After living twenty-five years on this earth, even the hairs on Leah's head felt old. She couldn't imagine one more year, much less nine hundred.

Often, she couldn't imagine even one more day.

Leah looked at the loom before her and tried to force her hands to move at the loom, to accomplish something, anything. She remembered her mother's words from so long ago, "You will even talk to your loom, for some days, it may feel like your only friend."

"Help me work today, old friend," she whispered to the silent loom.

Leah rested her hands on the loom, feeling the familiar work beneath her fingers. She thought of her mother, remembering the times they sat together weaving.

In and Out. In and Out. Clack. Clack.

Leah closed her eyes and saw her mother's beautiful hands at work, laying out the bright threads in a complex pattern on her loom. She remembered a conversation from so many years ago.

"Mother, how did you learn to make your cloth so beautiful, to make the colors work together just so?"

How many years ago had it been when she asked her mother that question? Leah had not thought of it for years.

Talitha had laughed. "Oh, I don't know, Leah. It just turns out the way it turns out. Sometimes I use four threads, sometimes six. Sometimes I know what I want, other times I just make it up as I go."

"But how? How do you know what colors go with what, and how to pick an order that turns out to be so... so... wonderful?"

"I don't know." Her mother had not been paying attention to her, Leah knew.

"Mother, really, I want to know."

Talitha had stopped weaving to cock her head at her precocious daughter. "We have work to do, Leah."

"Please, Mother, just for a moment. Tell me how you do it."

Her mother shrugged. "I suppose I just close my eyes and think of all the colors I love and try to imagine them spread out on the loom beneath my fingers."

Leah nodded, encouraging her mother to say more. Her mother seldom spoke of her own work, and then in the most deprecating tone. "Like what, Mother?"

"Oh, I don't know, really. I suppose…" But suddenly her mother's words had come in a rush.

"Leah, I see colors and patterns all around me in this beautiful world Jehovah has created. The shadows of the gray olive tree spotted on green moss beneath a tree. The bright white and rich brown fur of a baby goat nestled against the soft pink of its mother's belly. The streaks of orange and red and gold when the sun sets above Mount Hermon. How the fields change from green to gold to gray as they creep up the side of the mountain."

Her mother had seemed entranced, as though all that beauty were right in the room with her.

"Wherever I go, I see beauty. You can, too, Leah, if only you look with fresh eyes everyday! The rough wood of our door, so many aged shades of brown. Something so simple, still so beautiful! A fallen stone wall, tumbled rocks of faded gray piled on those that are black as ebony. A burning fire." She looked at Leah.

"I don't see a fire, Leah. I see so much more! Blackened charcoal, hot red coals on the brown, gnarled wood, glowing orange embers, gray ashes. All the tiny, intricate details God created. Everything in this world is beautiful, Leah, God's hands at work. Everything. If you look hard enough, you will see that this world God's creation is so very lovely." She had looked down at her hands.

"I believe… I think I am fortunate that God has blessed me with hands that create what I see with my eyes. I only hope that my humble work honors my Holy God. What I weave on my loom, well… It is his doing, not my own."

Leah remembered her words to her mother. "I think what you weave, what you… create is incredible, Mother," Leah said softly. "As beautiful as anything God has created in this world."

Talitha had ducked her head, shy at her daughter's praise. She had returned to her loom, smiling as her hands resumed their work.

Sitting beside her mother, Leah had started weaving again, too, weaving now, too, weaving and chattering and laughing. "Re-joice! Re-joice! See-Lah! See-Lah!" Leah had chanted, over and over, while her mother laughed at her vibrant daughter's unbridled, exuberant joy.

Oh, that was so long ago. This Leah was so tired.

Leah's bleeding was heavier today, the pain more intense. She pressed her forehead to the clay wall, rubbing its roughness on her smooth face. She closed her eyes as she waited for the women to walk by, women with daughters and mothers and grandmothers and husbands and homes. Women who were healthy and happy, loved and alive.

"Not like me," she muttered.

"Not like Leah," the loom hummed beneath her fingers.

❣

If little four-year-old Leah did not come home when her mother called, she might be found playing hide and seek with her aged grandmother. "Oh, like an Israelite, Leah is lost," Savta would explain to her daughter. Savta would look everywhere for her little granddaughter but not be able to find her, even though Leah was standing behind Savta's loom in the corner, practically in plain sight.

If Leah's mother caught Savta and Leah eating sweets in the middle of the morning, Savta would scratch her gray head and ask her daughter, "Doesn't King Solomon say there is nothing better for a man to do than to eat and to drink?" Leah would nod her head in solemn agreement.

If Leah's mother scolded Savta for buying Leah a wonderful, shiny red apple instead of the food she needed for herself, Savta would open her eyes wide in surprise and say, "But children's children are a crown for the aged!"

If the glares of Leah's mother interrupted the whispered giggles of Savta and Leah at the synagogue, afterwards Savta would loudly proclaim: "Teach me and I will be quiet!" Leah would giggle again that her mother was frowning at Savta.

Little Leah had one grandparent, and that was Savta. Better yet, Savta had a single granddaughter, and that was Leah, precious, smiling, beautiful Leah.

Like her mother before her, Savta was a weaver, a worker of the loom. As her mother taught her, she taught Leah's mother. But even when Leah was small, Savta was often betrayed by the ache in her fingers and hands. Some days, her knuckles were huge, swollen and painful, her hand curled into painful claws. She would heat up a little water and dip a rag into it, wrapping her hands with one warm cloth after another, singing as she sat in her corner chair in the sun.

Leah would touch those hands with eyes large and mouth

144

turned down in a petulant frown. She did not like to see Savta hurt. But Savta would just laugh. "A cheerful look brings joy to my heart, my little Leah!" So Leah would paste a reluctant smile on her face and try to be brave like Savta, even though her four-year-old heart ached at her grandmother's pain.

One day, Leah's mother came looking for Leah and found her right where she expected. "Mother, Leah should not be eating!" Talitha scolded Savta. "In just an hour she will eat with her father and brothers, for goodness sake!"

"Pffth." Leah tried not to giggle at Savta's response. Savta motioned for Leah with a bony, crooked finger. Leah crawled into her lap, looking guiltily at her mother, who stood with her hands on her hips in the door of Savta's house.

"Leah, do you know what your mother used to do when she was little?"

Leah shook her head, for she couldn't even imagine her mother being little.

"Your mother would go to see my mother everyday so they could play! Can you imagine, a tiny little girl and an old, old woman, playing? Such nonsense, yes, Leah?"

At this Leah did not shake her head, because that's what she and Savta did every day. Leah didn't know if she wanted her mother to know Savta and she played quite so much. Sometimes she was supposed to be helping Savta.

"Guess what happened one day when I called for your mother?" Savta's voice was soft and dramatic. Leah's mother shook her head.

Wide brown eyes looked up at her wrinkly grandmother. "What, Savta?"

"She did not come! Your mother was not anywhere to be found. I knew that she was hiding. Where do you think she was hiding, my little Leah?

"Where, Savta?" Where had Leah's mother hidden?

"At my mother's house, of course! She only lived just a little ways away, just like you and me. I had such a naughty girl and such a naughty mother!"

Leah couldn't imagine her perfect mother ever being a naughty little girl. But she laughed at the thought of a naughty mother anyway.

"And when I found her, guess what else I found?"

Leah leaned forward in anticipation.

Savta leaned close to Leah and said in a loud whisper, "My mother and my daughter were hiding in my mother's kitchen because... They had a knife!"

Leah gave a little gasp. She was never, ever to touch a knife. She had done so once, and her mother had spanked her for it. Hard.

Savta continued. "Yes, there sat my mother, holding her long, sharp knife. You remember that only very old women can hold knives, right, Leah?"

"Yes, Savta."

"So here sat my mother with a knife. Then what do you suppose she did?"

Leah could not even guess what anyone would do with a dangerous knife, much less Savta's mother.

"My mother took the knife and raised it." Savta demonstrated, her hand hanging in the air. "Then in one quick WHACK, she swung the knife like this!"

"Oh, Mother!" Leah's mother was laughing. Leah's eyes were like saucers.

"Yes, she chopped and chopped something on the table!" Her grandmother was flailing her arms all over, as though an army of Philistines were upon her. "What do you suppose she was chopping, Leah?" Savta stopped her imaginary chopping and looked at Leah, her gaze fierce and wild-eyed, her hand held high in the air.

"What, Savta, what?"

My mother chopped..." Savta paused dramatically, Leah holding her breath. "A great big hunk of a honeycomb sitting right in the middle of her table!" Leah heard her mother chuckle. "And then my mother raised the knife again, and chopped off another hunk of the honeycomb!" Savta was demonstrating again, waving her arm madly in the air. "Hunks and hunks of honeycomb! Honey all over the place!"

Leah giggled. "Then what, Savta, then what?"

"Well, they ate it, of course, my little pigeon! Honey was running everywhere, it was not even in a bowl! Before I could stop them, they were taking big bites, like two greedy, dirty baby goats! Great big hunks of honeycomb and wax with that drippy, sticky honey all over the place. Your mother was a mess, covered in honey from head to toe, and so was my mother!"

"Now, Mother, don't give Leah any ideas," Leah's mother interrupted, smiling.

"If I want to give my only granddaughter ideas, then I shall, my dearest daughter." She turned her attention back to Leah. "Then do you know what happened?"

Leah shook her head, smiling.

"I took both of those two big sticky messes home," she looked at her only daughter, who shook her head in amusement, "and I plopped your mother in a big tub of water. Cold, right from the cistern. I scrubbed my own ancient mother with lots of cold, cold water, too."

"It was really cold, I might add." Leah's mother still sounded a bit disgusted.

"Pffth!" said Savta.

Leah started to giggle, and her mother and Savta started laughing too. Then, even though they were going to eat with Leah's father and brothers in less than an hour, they sat down to eat big hunks of Savta's sweet almond cake drizzled with honey. Lots and lots and lots of honey.

"For revenge," Savta had laughed.

୯୫

"For revenge!" Leah heard her voice and laughter in the silent room. She heard other voices. Who was that? She shook her head, confused. Where was she?

Asleep! Leah had been sleeping sitting straight up in her chair, her face pressed to the rough wall, dreaming forgotten dreams of her mother and Savta and her childhood, dreams that were of no use to her now.

Leah was disgusted with herself. Sleeping again! Just like poor Savta napping in her corner chair with her chin on her chest. She directed a stern "Tsk!" to herself and spoke out loud. "Look to the ants, you sluggard!"

Leah couldn't help but smile. Savta's startled cry when Leah woke her those many years ago still made her laugh.

She shook her head at the memory of Savta, now gone these many years. Her mother hadn't known anything about Savta going to the top of Mount Hermon when she was a new bride. Leah always wished she had heard the story.

Leah heard the women's voices again and peeked over the window sill. Her two friends were returning from the well, passing by her small house with their full water jars.

"So, it's settled for sure? He is going to join your father at the shop?"

"Yes, and I am so relieved! I did not want to leave my home or my family. I've lived here all my life. I never want to leave."

That's how I felt about my home, too, Leah thought.

"And haven't we talked almost every day of our lives since we were old enough to walk? What would I do without you, Tirzah?" Leah heard the voice of the small laughing friend.

"I don't know what I would do without you either!" Tirzah said. "But so many of the tentmakers are leaving Capernaum to work as a group in Corinth. If my father had not asked him to work in our shop, we would have left, too. And tent making is just not his calling. I know his father was a tentmaker, and his father's father, and his father's father's father, but..."

"The babe in your belly is probably going to be a tentmaker too!" the small laughing girl interrupted.

"Not anymore! This baby is going to be born right here! My grandmother is the only reason my father found my husband a place to work here. Oh, my grandmother crying day and night. "First my only daughter-in-law, now my only granddaughter,"

The small woman burst into laughter at Tirzah's high pitched, squeaky voice.

"My granddaughter, my only granddaughter and her little girl, my great-granddaughter stolen, all stolen from me. Like the psalmist, God does not hear my prayers! Ashes are in my mouth, tears are in my eyes!"

"'Enough!'" Tirzah's face was still serious, but her voice took on a deep tenor. "'Enough, woman! They are not going! He will work with me. Tirzah will stay! Say no more! Enough!'"

"Grandmother told me later to always remember, 'The man is the rock, but the woman is the water that wears away the stone.'"

"Really? That's not what your mother said, remember? 'A quarrelsome wife is like dripping water.' Remember?" Both women laughed and then fell silent.

"Oh, Tirzah." The small laughing girl put her hand on her

friend's shoulder. Tirzah's mother had died not even a year ago. Leah had wept bitter tears when she heard the news, grieving for Tirzah's loss. Grieving for the loss of her own mother.

"Anyway, the reason your grandmother wore your father down was so you could stay here. You, Tirzah. She loves you, loves you just as your own mother did."

Leah stood to watch their disappearing backs. She saw the taller woman wrap her arm around her small friend's shoulders and heard her faint words, "You who are more than any sister, you know every secret of my heart. What would I do without you?"

"Well, now we do not have to find out, do we?"

Leah stood to peer out her window, watching the women until they were out of sight. Tears streamed down her face, sadness and relief mingled together. Tirzah was not moving away after all, her grandmother made sure she would stay.

"Your grandmother loves you, loves you just as your mother did," the small laughing girl said. Just like Leah's mother and grandmother had loved her.

"What would I do without you?" Tirzah replied to her dearest friend, she who was more than any sister. Oh, what would Leah do without these two friends?

Leah knew everything about them, but they knew nothing of her.

She listened hungrily for every word they spoke, but had never once said one word to them.

Their faces were as familiar to her as her own mother's, yet she was careful to make sure that they never laid eyes on her.

She waited for them every day, desperate with worry if one or both did not walk by, praying for their happiness, their health, their safety and please Jehovah God, for their return. "Please let them return, O Mighty God, let them walk past my sad little window once more. Please." It was an odd prayer she never failed to whisper each day.

Two women who were complete strangers… they were her only friends.

Leah stared down the street, the women now long gone to their own homes and families. "You who are more than any sister," Leah whispered softly to herself.

She was sad to see them go.

CHAPTER 15

Leah was weary. She did not recall her slow steps to the well. She didn't remember tying the rope and lowering her jar, pulling it up with all her strength or making the slow walk back to her house. She knew she had gone because her jar had water in it. Her shoulder was wet from where she had shakily lifted the jar to her head, water sloshing down. Her face was hot and her body drenched in sweat from the effort, but she was too tired to remember her actual steps.

She vaguely remembered hearing her friends' conversation as they returned from the well. Had that been only a few hours ago? It felt like some old, vague memory.

Leah walked into her small dark house, leaving the door open to catch whatever breeze might come. Her window remained unshuttered too. She set the water jar in the corner. There was much to do today but Leah had little energy or will left to do it.

"I would really like to lie down and rest, just for a few moments," Leah thought.

She heard her mother's voice echo in her head and so spoke the words to herself in a firm, loud voice: "Leah, as a door turns on its hinges, so a sluggard turns to her bed."

What exactly was a sluggard, anyway?

Squaring her boney shoulders, Leah opened the kitchen chest

and removed the large iron pot within. It was her most precious possession, for she used this pot every day. Pouring only enough water needed to do the work, she grunted as she carried the pot to the small stove in the corner. Setting the pot down, Leah stirred up the embers until a small spark returned. She added two pieces of wood, and soon a fire started to warm the water.

Most women kept their small ovens outside their homes in their courtyards. But Leah never ventured outside where any neighbor or passer-by might see her. Better the smoke of the fire and its heat in her house than the judging eyes of others outside.

Sighing, she removed the oil from the chest. Such a small amount remained. When would Reuben return? Leah filled the lamp so it would not run out and cast her into darkness. Leah hated the darkness, for it only added to the aloneness of her life. She whispered Solomon's words,

"'The light of the righteous rejoices,
But the lamp of the wicked shall be put out.'

"Do not let my lamp be put out, Lord, do not leave me alone in my darkness." Her hand shook as she trimmed the wick in preparation for the night, only a few hours away.

She returned to the pot of water now shimmering with the steam. With a practiced eye, Leah emptied one-third of the water into a large clay bowl and one-third into a second just like it. She turned to the second chest that held her clothing. Deep inside, hidden away, she pulled out the basket where she kept her blood-soaked, dirty bandages along with the harsh soap. It was almost full of bloody, unclean rags. When she lifted the lid, the coppery smell of her sickness hit her. Leah sighed. To wash these would use so much of the precious water, yet her shame was too great to carry them to the river for washing.

Who was she kidding? She couldn't walk that far hauling a basket of dirty robes. In the three years that she had lived in Capernaum, she had never gone to wash her clothes in a river or stream. Other women would be there, washing, talking and laughing. Leah could not possibly go there.

The truth was, she didn't even know where Capernaum women went to wash their clothes.

In the clay bowl, careful not to spill even one drop of her precious water, Leah rinsed out one of her three faded tunics, old and shabby and far too large for her gaunt wasted body. Then, she scrubbed each bandage in the same water with the strong soap, diligently trying to remove the stains that never faded away. The simple exertion of scrubbing left Leah breathless. Once the yellowed cloths were as clean as she could get them, she rinsed them in the second bowl of warm water. Wringing each cloth out, Leah sat a few moments to prepare herself for the next ordeal.

Leah climbed up the narrow steps to her roof with great difficulty, legs burning and pain shooting up her back. Step. Pause. Step. Pause. She carried the small bundle of wet clothing in her arms so weak with the small load.

The last three steps were endless. She thought her heart would beat out of her chest, it was pounding so hard. Finally, she made it to the top step and pushed open the door to her rooftop. Hot as she was, the sun felt good on her face. How tempting to lie down and rest in the warm sunshine! But no, this surely would be a sin just because she had much left to do.

One at a time, she stretched the stained cloths and her tunic out to dry. Panting, she sat down in the sun to catch her breath before she set out the stones. They would keep everything from blowing away in the unlikely event that any wind would come up. She set the stones down one at a time, careful to weight down the wet bandages. As hard as this was for Leah, she always put the stones out, even on the stillest of days. What if one of these yellowed, blood-stained cloths were to blow to the ground? Leah was shamed by the thought.

She sat down again to rest for just a moment, looking down at her tiny courtyard below. Every house around hers had two stories, so she had the privacy of clay walls on three sides. Her only view was the sky above, the street below and a small brown house across the way. All the buildings on this street were modest, but hers was by far the most humble. Leah was convinced her house was no more than a former stable for one of these other homes, and her "courtyard" nothing more than an old sheep pen. Indeed, the door to the house was certainly wide and tall enough for a cow or an ass to walk through.

"Or Reuben," she thought. She shook the sarcastic thought from her mind. She needed Reuben.

Leah saw her neighbor bent over the oven in her courtyard across the dusty street. The woman never raised a hand in greeting or even looked up at her.

Long ago Leah guessed what her neighbors thought of her, a woman living alone, visited once a month by a man who only stayed for a few hours. She scrambled to her feet, gasped at the pain that caused and then, clutching the wall for balance, picked her way down the narrow steps from the roof. Down was so much better than up.

Leah peeked cautiously into the deserted street and saw her neighbor had gone inside. She looked both ways to check for passers-by, but there were none. She dumped the soiled water from the two clay bowls at the foot of the house's foundation. A tamarisk bush bloomed there in profusion all year long, spilling pink petals in the dirt from the luxuriant flowers with their strong dark fragrance. Jewish women never washed clothing in their homes, so few bushes on this street bloomed with the glory of Leah's tamarisk. Leah's tamarisk got all her dirty laundry water.

Finally, Leah took the remaining water from the iron pot and poured it into one of the clay bowls. It was still warm. She carried it behind the worn curtain she had hung in the corner for privacy, not that anyone was there to see her. She used the water to clean herself, first her face, neck and hands, and then her body. Leah washed herself slowly, savoring the warm water as it washed away the dust of the day, the sweat from her face, the dirt from her feet, the odor from her body, and finally, the blood that never stopped.

On Sunday, if the bleeding was not too bad, maybe she would try to go to the public bath. The effort to go to the bath would almost overcome her, but to soak her entire body in the warm water was one of Leah's few pleasures. There was a bath right here on her street, closer than the well. No Jewish women went on Sundays; they all went on Thursday and Friday, right before the Sabbath. If she were lucky, she could find an unattended bath and slip into the water unnoticed, her disease hidden from the others who might be there.

Leah was tired from doing the laundry and the trip to the roof. She looked at her loom, knowing she needed to finish this weaving before Reuben came next week. Instead, Leah walked over to her mat.

I will rest, but only for a minute, she thought. Then I will weave for the rest of the day, so Reuben will have something to sell for me

153

when he returns.

She sat on her bed on the floor and leaned against the wall.

Reuben. She thought again of her dwindling supplies. Her husband came once a month, never more often, sometimes a little less. No matter how frugal she was with the wine or barley or wood, by the fourth week the meanest of supplies remained. It didn't seem as though Reuben brought the same amounts each month, which made it hard for her to know how much to allow herself each day.

Leah had run out of supplies the first few months, frightened and famished when Reuben darkened her door, thankful not to see him but falling on the supplies he brought like a beggar. Now, she lived like a pauper, frightened of running out of food, afraid to use more than the barest necessities each day. She was not sure she was strong enough to last three or four days without food now.

"I started this marriage like a princess," Leah murmured to the shadows. "I will end it like Elisha's widow, with nothing but a little oil."

The cramping in her belly was painful right now, excruciating spasms that took her breath away. Coupled with the work of washing today, Leah was tired, even more so than her usual weariness. She was so tired.

"I am going to lie down for a moment. Just for the smallest rest," Leah said out loud to no one in particular. No one answered her, either, not even the tough nagging Leah who made sure puny Leah did not quit or give up. For once, she was tired, too.

Just lowering her body to the thin mattress was an effort. She stretched out at last, grateful for the rest and a momentary respite from her pain. But there was no relief from her memories, disturbing her solitude like gnats in the heat. She could not stop her thoughts from tormenting her.

How wonderful her wedding had been. She hated thinking about it, for it was the start of her life with Reuben. But she could not help herself.

She had been a beautiful bride, treated like a princess by all. Who could have imagined that twelve years later, Leah would live in ramshackle house, destitute, sick, outcast and alone?

Leah sighed at the thought of the beautiful bridal medallion. Worn by her mother and grandmother and the generations before them. Leah had been so stunned when she opened the small wooden box. It was fit for a royal princess, not for simple, humble Leah.

Now that medallion was hidden here in her tiny impoverished house, concealed in the hem of the same bridal veil she had worn so many years ago.

She remembered her mother's frenzied whisper the morning Leah and Reuben left Caesarea Philippi. "If you need money to make your way back home to me, sell the medallion, sell it for any price, sell it to save yourself," Talitha had hissed in Leah's ear.

But Leah could not bring herself to part with the medallion. She remembered another conversation on a happy day so many lifetimes ago.

"Just as I give you this medallion, I give a special blessing to you as you marry," Talitha had whispered in the weeks before Leah's wedding. "Never part with this medallion and you will never part with the blessing it carries."

No matter how sick she was, Leah could not bring herself to sell the medallion. No matter what her mother had said the morning Leah left her small brown city, Leah knew in her heart to sell the medallion was to lose her mother's blessing.

Leah wondered for the hundredth time how much the medallion was worth. She had kept her whispered promise to her mother and had never, ever mentioned the medallion to Reuben. But she also promised her mother she would use the medallion to make her way back to Caesarea Philippi.

No matter. She could not sell it, it was too precious. She would rather be dead than sell her mother's blessing. At least that's what selling the medallion would feel like to Leah.

She had no one to sell it to anyway.

Leah could hear her mother's gentle voice. "This medallion has been passed down in our family for generations, Leah, from grandmother to mother to daughter." Leah did not like to think what would happen to the medallion now. In all these generations, the blessing stopped with her, alone and childless.

Her mother's voice continued. "You will cherish this until the day comes when you give this medallion to your own daughter when she marries." Leah had no daughter to bless.

"Whenever this medallion is passed from mother to daughter, the mother sets one of the pearls in her own necklace to wear next to her heart forever, a constant reminder of the love she has for her daughter." Leah remembered her mother pulling out the necklace hidden behind her tunic, the single pearl suspended on its slender golden chain. Just like the necklace they had buried with Savta so many years ago.

"Every day I will place my hand on my heart to feel the empty spot that was once filled by you as a child."

Did her mother still have an empty spot in her heart?

"I will feel the pearl and be reminded of how greatly God has blessed me, to give me such a daughter, one who is now a woman and a friend." Or was her mother's heart just broken, shattered by the treachery of Reuben and the tragedy of Leah's illness?

Leah found tears welling up in her eyes.

She could still hear her mother's soft voice. "When I die, this pearl, this reminder of my daughter, will be buried with me. I will wear it forever." Did her mother wear the necklace today in life or in death?

"For Leah, I love you more than anything on this earth."

Except for God. My mother loved only God more than me, for God gave me to her. That's what she said.

"For Jehovah truly blessed me when he gave me you."

Leah's laugh was bitter as she recalled her mother's words. It seemed to her that she was far more of a punishment than any kind of blessing from God.

CR

When Leah awoke, she was not a happy bride-to-be sitting by her mother, dressed in all her wedding finery with a beautiful medallion around her neck. She was alone and sick in a strange city, abandoned by her husband, a recluse from the world. She rubbed the sleep from her eyes.

Instead of resting for a few moments, she had slept for who knew how long, dreaming of things that no longer mattered, like her wedding.

Leah's marriage had been celebrated by all the same people who later gathered to condemn her sinful, unclean state. Even friends that were dear to her would not dare to break the uncompromising Laws of Moses. Perhaps, they had not really been her friends after all.

Oh, that was such a lifetime ago. Some things were better

forgotten.

Through the window, she could tell the sun was setting and the day was done. She had slept all afternoon. Another day wasted. Disgusted, she nonetheless refrained from calling herself a sluggard for the third time in one day. King Solomon never had to do his own laundry.

Leah prepared her paltry evening dinner, her hands and heart weary. She pulled out the barley bread, noting that she still had ample ground barley to bake another loaf on Monday, if only she did not run out of oil. "Oil for light or oil for bread? What a choice," she muttered. "Perhaps only a little of both." After this flour was gone, there was no more barley for her to grind.

She cut the bread, pulled out one piece of dried fish and set both on a plate. She poured just the smallest bit of wine in a glass. Closing her eyes to recite her prayers, Leah sat down alone to her meager meal.

The entire day was spent. All Leah had accomplished was a small bit of spinning in the morning, her trip to the well, the washing of her bloody rags, her cursory bath and eating her small dinner.

"The sluggard's craving will be the death of her," Leah mocked herself in the dark room, "for her hands refuse to work."

She scowled. I really hate the Proverbs, she thought.

Leah knelt to pray to her God, asking for restored health and that He, Almighty Jehovah, would save her from death. She prayed for her mother, that the Lord of Heaven and Earth would keep her safe and well. Her final words were the prayer she prayed every night; that Leah would - please, Father God, Jehovah and Redeemer, O Holiest of Holy, please - be allowed to see her mother again.

She lay down on her bed with her eyes closed, but now sleep would not come. She had slept too long that afternoon. Maybe if she lay perfectly still, she could fool herself into falling asleep.

Leah remembered another time when she lay on her bed, pretending to be asleep, waiting with her mother for Reuben and yet another doctor he had found. The doctor of the seven potions that, if administered without the greatest of care, would deliver Leah into the sleep from which she would never awaken. Leah shivered. As sick as she was, she was still afraid to die. She shook off death's meddling and returned to the memory of all the remedies she had tried.

They had spent all their money on herbs and potions, sacrifices and special prayers, clanging cymbals and the dung of a mule. They had tried everything. Well, almost everything.

She thought of the last doctor she had seen, just before Reuben moved her from Caesarea Philippi to Capernaum. Not to the great Caesarea on the Sea, as he had told Leah and her mother. That awful day of the last doctor, the day of her mother's terrible rage at Reuben, at the doctor, even, perhaps, at Leah and her dreadful illness.

The last doctor had examined Leah for some time, asking Reuben the same questions they had answered so many times. Her mother sat in the corner, watching.

Leah had known Reuben was desperate, for this doctor was an Ethiopian from Memphis, that great unknown city in Egypt. Even more unsettling, this doctor was not a Jew.

"She has bled for nine years now? Is this correct?" His voice was matter-of-fact rather than incredulous like the doctors before him.

"About, maybe more," Reuben had answered. "As long as we have been married. Over the years, the bleeding has gotten worse. She becomes more and more frail as time goes by."

"Hmmm." The doctor continued examining Leah for some time, deep in thought, listening to Leah's heart, peering into her mouth, pulling her eyelids up to stare at her eyes, and bending her arms and legs and fingers. For a long time he pressed down hard on Leah's painful belly, poking and prodding until she thought she would scream with pain. "He certainly is trying to earn his fee," Leah had thought crossly.

After examining her for at least an eternity, the doctor stopped his physical inspection and spoke. "I believe your wife has a growth in her belly that will never heal. Most likely, the growth has a small rupture. This is why your wife continually oozes blood. The blood is heavier when it is her time of month. As long as this growth exists, your wife will never have children. This constant bleeding will weaken your wife, for the blood is the life of the body. At some point, she will die from the continued bleeding."

There was a shocked silence in the room. Never before had a doctor said Leah was dying. Doctors got paid for hope, not death sentences.

Reuben broke the long silence. "She cannot be cured."

The doctor hesitated. "There is a way, yes... there is a cure."

Leah was not surprised, every doctor had a cure. No cure, no money.

"The growth... it must be removed. If your wife does not die from the bleeding, at some point this growth may burst. If that were to happen, your wife would bleed to death, almost at once. No one could save her if that were to happen."

Reuben did not look at Leah. "How is it possible to remove the growth?"

"Through an incision in the abdomen. I would actually cut it out, remove the growth for good. I would make an incision at the place where I believe the growth originates. I would pull the skin aside and with great care move her organs – "

"No." Leah's mother was at the side of the bed in one step. "No."

The physician looked at her and turned back to Reuben. "It is your decision, of course. But without it, your wife will die."

"No!" Leah's mother spoke again and this time there was no mistaking her anger. "She may die from this growth - tomorrow, next year, ten years. But Leah will not submit to your knife, your surgery. Can you not see? She cannot stand this, her body is worn out! How could she stand such pain? This cure would kill Leah!"

She turned to Reuben and said in a voice of iron, "No."

Leah did not remember the rest of the conversation, only her profound relief that her mother was there. Her mother had physically thrown the two men out of the room, shoving the doctor out first and then Reuben behind him. "Murderers!" she had screamed, not caring what the neighbors might think. "Murderers, murderers!"

Her rage was great, like none Leah had ever seen in her mother or any other woman. A rage like her father's.

"Murderer," she had hissed at Reuben.

Leah's mother understood how fragile Leah was, and would fight to keep her alive at any cost.

Reuben only wanted her illness to go away, even if the cost was Leah's life.

For hope had abandoned Reuben long ago, long before the last doctor announced she would die.

Reuben wanted his wife dead. She knew this was the terrible truth. He no longer wanted her to live. The Leah he married - bright, beautiful, laughing Leah - had died long ago. Reuben could no longer bear to even look at the Leah that remained.

When he arrived each month with her paltry supplies, Leah saw it in the slump of his shoulders. He refused to look at her when he spoke. After nine long years, numerous doctors, no children and no cure in sight, and now three long years of her dreadful isolation in a foreign city, Reuben no longer had any hope that he could rid himself of wife's dreadful disease. Worse yet, despite all his hopes and inattention, it appeared his frail wife would not die as he had planned, either.

Leah often thought at some point Reuben would just divorce her, divorce and leave her, despite all his claims of doing everything a good husband should do for a wife like Leah. He would divorce her and at last find a woman who would truly be a wife, one who could cook for him, care for him, wash his clothes, be his companion, share his bed. A wife who would bear his children and carry on his name through a fine, strong son. Not some ghost of a woman God was allowing to gradually diminish from this world. Not like hopeless, useless, lifeless Leah: a lifeless shell of a wife who refused to actually die.

However, he had not divorced her, not yet. Instead, he had left her here in this lonely, alien house, in this foreign city where she knew no one. He had abandoned her here alone, hoping that death would soon find her and free him of the burden that was Leah.

She lay on her bed, certain of one thing. She was not going to give her husband the satisfaction of dying alone here in Capernaum. Not if she could help it.

Not tonight, anyway.

"Pah." Her voice was loud in the darkness.

Leah closed her eyes and went to sleep.

CHAPTER 16

Leah awoke the next morning confused and foggy. She had been plagued part of the night by haunting, odd dreams of doctors and imaginary cures, white donkeys and barley corn, the sullen scowl of Reuben and worried face of her mother. "Murderer," she heard her mother shout in her dreams. "Murderer!"

The rest of the night she lay awake with one of the painful headaches that had so often afflicted her. She had much to do today, but she was already tired, too tired.

"It's nights like this that make me sleep all day," Leah said aloud.

And my good days are fewer and fewer, she thought to herself.

Her terse voice echoed in the room, the hard voice that was strong Leah echoing in the morning stillness. "How long will you lie there, you sluggard? Get up from your sleep!"

Obediently, puny Leah sat up, but she allowed herself to mutter a crabby thought. "I *really* hate the Proverbs."

It was the outspoken, uncompromising attitude of strong Leah that forced her silent, sluggardly side to get out of bed. She washed her face, combed her hair, changed her bandages and dressed. She ate some bread for breakfast along with a fig; it was so sweet, a rare treat. She ate it in small, lingering bites. It was the last one.

She sat and spun thread, pausing every few moments to see if she could hear the two women's voices. Finally, she gave up and went outside to look for them, only to scurry right back in when she saw they were just a few houses away.

"Ow," she griped crabbily, once she was back inside. "That hurt."

She peeked through her window to watch them approach. Their heads were close together in a quiet conversation. Oh, if only she had someone to talk to like Tirzah and the other woman! The small laughing friend was earnestly talking, telling Tirzah something Leah could not hear. Tirzah listened with a puzzled look on her face, her brow knitted in confusion.

"Oh, no," Leah wondered aloud. "Such a serious conversation. What has happened?"

She thought about the possibilities. Was the small laughing girl expecting a baby again? Perhaps her mother took a turn for the worse? What was she so urgently telling Tirzah?

Even though she could not hear their conversation, she watched them until they were out of sight, the small girl still gesturing as she whispered, Tirzah still listening.

Hmmm. Puzzled, Leah sat down at the small loom to weave until they returned. She needed to finish this piece soon, because if she had counted the days right - the days were so often so blurred, lately - Reuben would be here next week, just before the Sabbath.

Each month, Reuben said he sold the cloth she wove and used the money to purchase her supplies. "Or at least some of the money," she thought.

Her weavings were not as big as those she had woven years ago. She did not have a large enough loom. They were not as beautiful as those her mother made, for Leah only spun thread of workaday brown wool. Reuben either could not afford or would not bring her any of the dyes needed to create her mother's vibrant colors. After all this time, Leah was too weak to dye wool anyway.

But even if she no longer spun the finest linens, Leah's weaving still had a smooth, graceful art to it. The small loom was easy to operate, too, nothing like the big loom of Savta's. If Leah worked on the loom first, she would still have some energy left for the rest of her chores. It was simple, peaceful work. Push and Pull.

There was only one thing Leah hated about weaving.

The small shuttle passed back and forth in a steady rhythm. In and out.

It was impossible to sit there without losing herself to her memories. Clack. Clack.

She shook off the memories and began to sing, just as her mother taught her many years ago.

"'The Lord is my light and my salvation, who shall I fear?'"

In and out. Clack, clack, answered the loom.

"'The Lord is the stronghold of my life,
    of whom shall I be afraid?'"

She tried to silence the list of fears that crowded her mind, but could not. I am afraid of Reuben when he comes to this house, she thought. I am even more afraid that he will not come.

In and out.

I am afraid of my disease. I am afraid my sin has caused my sickness.

Re-joice, re-joice.

I am afraid of the pain, that others will learn of my shame.

Clack, clack.

I am afraid of dying alone in this house. I am afraid of never seeing my mother again.

Selah.

Poor Leah had so many fears.

She listened to her own voice as if a stranger sat next to her reciting King David's words.

"'Hear my voice when I call, O Lord;
Be merciful and answer me.
Do not hide your face from me.
Do not reject me or forsake me, O God my Savior.'"

Rejected and forsaken. In and out. That's what she was. Clack, clack.

"'Though my father and mother forsake me,

163

The Lord will receive me.'"

David was right; her father had forsaken her. Disowned her and rejected her.

But not her mother! Never had her mother forsaken her, even though today they were so far apart. In her mind, she could hear her mother's cheerful voice take up the psalmist's refrain:

> "'I am confident of this!
> I will see the goodness of the Lord in the land of the living.
> Wait for the Lord, Leah!
> Be strong, take heart, and wait for the Lord.'"

"Take heart and wait for the Lord," Talitha once sang to her daughter. But Leah had so little heart left, she could not even muster a final Selah.

"Wait for the Lord, indeed," she mumbled, bitter and discouraged.

Leah could not find confidence in the goodness of the Lord this morning.

ఆ

Leah supposed she would never again see the synagogue of her childhood. But that did not stop her from wistfully remembering the many hours she had spent there with her mother and grandmother. A small giggly girl sitting in the women's gallery beside them, Leah would close her eyes and listen to the words the men recited in unison.

> "'Hear, O Israel! Love the Lord
> your God with all your heart,
> And with all your soul and with all your strength.'"

"Amen," all would say and then be seated to listen to the reading of the law. Leah loved to hear the words, some readers far better than others. The beautiful words of Jacob recited first in Hebrew and then in Aramaic:

"'O Father, I am unworthy of all the kindness and Faithfulness you have shown your servant.'"

Then, the reader would stand to pontificate on the law. Sometimes this was interesting but usually it was not.

As the reader droned in a loud, sonorous tone about some finer point of the Law - more interested in the sound of his own voice than the actual Law itself - Leah would happily lose herself to daydreams. She would think about the beautiful countryside, the young men who might someday be her husband, and the amazing stories of the women of old.

Women like Deborah, a prophetess and judge who went into battle against the Canaanites and cut off the head of her enemy! Or Sarah, who laughed at angels and bore a son at age ninety. She was older than Savta! Esther, who faced a murderous king armed only with her beauty and her wits to save her people.

Or her namesake, Leah. Leah, the first wife with weak eyes, unloved by her husband, cast aside for her beautiful younger sister.

But who had the last laugh? For God blessed Leah of old. She was buried by her husband Jacob's side, her younger sister Rachel buried alone somewhere under a great tree. From Leah came Judah; from the tribe of Judah came the House of King David. From ancient Leah's lineage, someday the promised Messiah would come. Poor Leah with the weak eyes never gave up, and so found the favor of God. Leah never gave up.

At some point in Leah's reverie, all those around her in the synagogue would stand and so would she. Time for her favorite part, the singing of the Psalms! Oh, and she would sing with gusto, just like Savta:

> "Give thanks to the Lord, for he is good;
> His love endures forever!
> Give thanks to the God of gods;
> Give thanks to the Lord of lords;
>   His love endures forever!
> To him who alone does great wonders,
> Who by his understanding made the heavens,
> Who spread out the earth upon the waters,
> Who made the great lights, the sun to govern the day,

The moon and stars to govern the night:
His love endures forever!"

"What a great God, to make the sun rule the day and the moon and stars rule the night," Leah would think. Her voice would be the loudest on the refrain, "His love endures forever!" As Leah noisily sang along with every word, her mother would hush her. But Savta would lean over with a sly wink and a smile.

Leah missed the words of the law, the prayers, the singing and the reverent worship. Would she ever rejoin the land of the living, those who gathered to worship God? But in her heart, she knew she would probably never worship in a synagogue again.

ભ

Resting with her head on her loom, Leah was startled by the approaching voices. Her friends were returning from the well! She had been sleeping again!

Scrambling to her feet with a deep breath, she felt the claw of pain grasp her lower back and reach around to her belly. "Oy!" she grunted. But she was so hungry for the sound of the women's voices, the pain was forgotten at once.

Leah tilted her head up towards the window to better hear. But unlike their quiet conversation a short time before, the small laughing friend was now animated, her words emphatic and loud. Leah could hear every word long before they reached her house.

"I know you don't understand my story, Tirzah, but you have to believe me."

"Tell me again what happened. There has to be something missing. I don't even understand what you are saying. You have talked of nothing else, but it still makes no sense to me."

"I am telling you, it is like nothing you have ever seen."

"But you did not see anything either! You were outside, you said so."

"Yes, but I saw this: the man who went into the house was a cripple on his bed, but he came out of the house walking!" The small laughing woman danced on her toes, the full jug balanced on her head sloshing droplets of water on her shoulders. She was undeterred by Tirzah's skepticism.

"No one could get into the house where the prophet was. There were people everywhere! Then, here came the four men carrying the cripple on his bed, the other men around them pushing and shoving everyone out of their way. Four men carrying their crippled friend to see the prophet."

"And we know this man? Who is he again?"

"He is like no one you have ever heard, Tirzah. He is like no one I have ever heard! And he is here, right here in Capernaum. Can you believe it? A Galilean! When he returned to Capernaum yesterday, and his followers found out where he was, they just went to the house uninvited, hoping to see or hear the prophet..."

"I know who this so-called prophet is! You have told me again and again about him. Who is the man who is lame?"

"Was lame, was lame, not is!" Tirzah's friend laughed with excitement. Not wanting to miss the end of her story, Leah hoisted herself up to the window's edge so she might better hear as the two women passed by her house.

"You know who he is. When were we younger, four or five years ago, he was repairing one of the boats in the harbor and fell from the mast to the deck. He did not fall far, but ever since he has been unable to walk. His legs just lay there limp, like they are dead. The rest of him is fine. He talks, he eats, he mends nets, his friends still come to see him. But he is forced to lie in bed all day in the home of his mother and father."

"I do know of this man. His mother is Rebecca, the wife of Mattius ben Ralahoth! Such a tragedy, their oldest son..."

"Not a tragedy, a miracle, Tirzah. A miracle! The prophet healed him."

"Impossible, you must have heard the story wrong. Besides, you said no one could enter the house, the crowds were too great."

"I did not hear the story wrong. I saw the story with my own two eyes, even though I was not in the house! The men pushed everyone aside, but no one would let them in. So, they climbed to the roof and broke through the tiles. They just threw them down to the ground, such a noise, tiles shattering everywhere! People running around, trying not to get hit in the head! Then they would have needed healing too." She threw back her head and laughed, excited by her own story.

"Then, the four men lowered the crippled man's mat right

through the opening of the roof. They were so careful! What if they had dropped him? Think how strong they had to be, Tirzah! But they were determined. Once the mat disappeared, no one could see what was happening."

"Then how do you know what happened?"

"Because a few minutes later, the man who was crippled walked from the house, waving at his friends on the roof! Walked! No one could believe it. The men on the roof, the man's friends... Oh Tirzah, they wept! The man was running from person to person, jumping, smiling, telling anyone who would listen he was healed by the Son of Man, the one who forgives the sins of sinners! Tirzah, it is true!"

Tirzah shook her head as though she knew what the woman would say next.

"He is the Messiah." Leah could hear the awe in the small woman's voice.

Silence followed those final words. The two women stood right outside Leah's small courtyard in the dusty street, staring at each other, oblivious to the gaunt woman peering over the edge of the square window.

"That's right, Tirzah." The small laughing woman's words were soft. "They say this man is the Messiah, come to save the Jews, the King of Israel. That's who they say he is." As her excitement grew, so did the volume of her voice. "The Messiah, Tirzah! I cannot explain what it means to sit and listen to the man speak! The words he speaks... And wherever he goes, he heals the people. The sick, the lame, the blind... he heals them."

Leah froze at her words.

Tirzah turned and walked away from the first woman in silence, her shoulders stiff.

"Come back," Leah begged, her plea a whisper in the shadow. "Come back. Say more about this man who heals people. Come back, please stop."

But the small woman ran to catch up with Tirzah. Their words grew fainter as they walked away.

"Wait..." It was a whisper in the shadows. Leah stared at their backs. Come back...

Then, using every bit of strength she possessed, Leah pushed herself away from the window, her back screaming in agony at the sudden movement. She picked up her empty water jar and rushed through the door, turning to follow the women, every step a jolt of pain. She hurried until she was only a few paces behind, straining to hear their conversation even as she pretended she too was walking from the well, the jar on her head bone dry.

"Tirzah, how can it not be true? Jesus of Nazareth, the Galilean, they call him. They say he is the Messiah. And why not? Do we not pray every day to Yahweh that the Messiah would come? It is the Messiah."

Leah was a few short steps behind the women.

"I saw a lame man walking, carrying his mat. I saw his friends on the roof, the ropes in their hands. I saw, Tirzah, I saw. And I believe. Do you know what else? They say he healed a leper! A leper, Tirzah. Jesus touched a leper and made him a new man. Jesus makes the lame walk, the blind see and the leper whole! An unclean leper amê no more!"

Leah froze. Though she knew the small woman was not talking about her, she was paralyzed at the sound of the word. Amê.

The woman's voice carried in the hot still air. "Come with me, Tirzah! Our Capernaum is the home of this great teacher from Nazareth now. Come with me to see Jesus!"

But all Leah heard was unclean. Amê.

CHAPTER 17

"Amê." The word was a like physical blow. Leah stood swaying in the street, her eyes closed. She could not stem the flood of sadness the word evoked. Amê.

She was no longer on a dusty street in Capernaum. She was a sad young wife, living in Caesarea Philippi, frail and sick. She could see the council of old men seated on the raised platform in her synagogue towering over her like the ancient gray stones of Jerusalem's walls. All scowled at the unclean woman before them, the immoral filth that corrupted the holy sanctity of their house of worship.

Reuben, her husband and accuser, stood as far away from the vile presence of his wife as he possibly could. She stood apart and alone.

The synagogue ruler's voice started as a low rumble. "You will be deemed unclean as long as you have the discharge of blood. Anyone who touches you will be unclean until evening. Anything you lay on, anything you sit on, will be unclean. Whoever touches your bed or anything you sit on will be unclean. Amê!"

The grumbled assents of the other men in the synagogue echoed in her mind. Amê.

The ruler's voice grew in intensity and in volume. "When you are cleansed from your discharge, your uncleanness, you will wait seven days." The grumbling grew louder. Amê, amê.

"On the eighth day you will take two doves to the priest, who will sacrifice one as an offering for your sin and the other as a burnt offering. In this way he will make atonement for you before the Lord, atonement and penance for your uncleanness. Only then will you be ceremonially clean! Amê!"

Violent tremors of fear racked Leah's frail body. She prayed she would not fall down before this sacred council. The ruler continued, his rage intensifying. "The Israelites must be kept separate from the unclean! Those who are unclean before the Lord will die, die in their uncleanness, the uncleanness that defiles the Lord! The Lord dwells among his Chosen People that are clean. He will not come near those who are defiled, unclean in his holy eyes. Amê!"

"Amê! Amê!" The other council members answered, loud in their mindless agreement. The ruler held out his hands for silence.

"These are the regulations for a woman with a discharge," The ruler spat out the last words. "An unclean... bleeding... woman."

He motioned, and as one, every man on the council stood up. The ruler's voice was nearly a whisper. "This is the Law of Moses." The ruler fell silent, letting this sacred pronouncement echo in the cold synagogue. He lifted his hand and pointed a long yellowed nail at Leah, his voice a keening, high-pitched wail of anguish. "Ahhh-meeee."

Silence.

Leah had never been so frightened.

Suddenly, he was shouting. "Amê!" he roared. "Amê. Leave this holy house at once! Amê! Amê! Amê!" He was screaming hysterically, spittle flying from his lips, his eyes bulging with revulsion.

"Amê! Amê!" The entire council stood and started shouting, pointing at Leah standing in the middle of the synagogue alone. Her father was the loudest of all.

Only her mother stood to stand for Leah. But Leah had been rushed from the synagogue by the men, without her mother at her side, cast out by the anger of the council. Leah had run to her home in shame, alone and reviled by all.

And for her sin, her uncleanness, her father had struck his daughter, threw her from his home, and disowned her. He beat his wife, Leah's beautiful, faithful mother, beat her till her body was bruised, her eyes blackened, her face swollen and red.

Now, Leah's father lay dead his grave, his own body decaying and decomposed, unclean. Leah hated him still. She would never forgive him. He lay rotting in his whitewashed grave, and Leah would never forgive him. Amê.

ೞ

Leah stood alone in the street, her empty water jar on her head, watching the two women walk away. She stood there alone for a long time, unable to move, the unspoken horror of her own uncleanness overwhelming her with shame. Amê.

Oh, if her two friends, the two women who walked past Leah's small house every day were to learn of Leah's shame, she would not be able to stand it. Here in Capernaum, Leah's secret shame was hers alone.

But even as the dreadful memories twisted her tender heart, the smallest hope crept in. The man from Nazareth healed a leper. He healed someone unclean.

Someone like her.

Leah turned and made her slow trip to the well, finishing an hour later with the jar only half-full, sweaty, tired and hot. Her body ached, but something had sparked in Leah's tender heart.

She swept the dirt floor of her small house, retrieved yesterday's washed bandages from the roof, spun several spools of thread, and baked a loaf of bread from the last of the flour in her small oven. She completed a smooth even cloth that had been sitting on her loom for a week, row upon neat row without flaw or snag. She used some of the precious water to wash her hair and bathe her body. She did all these things mindlessly, without conscious thought about the work her weary hands performed. For once, Leah's day flew by.

For today, Leah's mind was racing, but not with thoughts of fear or pain. New thoughts clattered around in her head like the noisy shuttles on her loom. Her humiliation before the synagogue council. Her mother's courage. Her father's hatred and welcome death. The oldest son of the unknown Rebecca. A lame man and a leper. And the joy - yes, joy was the only word Leah had to describe it - the joy in the small laughing woman's voice as she talked about a man from

172

Nazareth, a Messiah. A Messiah! Could it be?

Leah could not stop thinking about the conversation in the street. A teacher healed a lame man! With a touch, he healed a leper, an unclean leper!

"He's probably just another so-called healer. Haven't you yourself seen many, each one more worthless than the last?" Always ready with an answer, practical Leah spoke out loud.

Puny Leah was not deterred. The small laughing friend, the friend I have known for three years... She saw the lame man walk. She saw it with her own eyes, and she heard about the leper. This man from Nazareth healed a leper, too. Leah could not comprehend such a thing. A leper!

"Now when have you ever heard of such a thing as that?"

But it happened, Leah thought. Our friend would not say it if it were not so.

"No one ever touches a leper, Leah, a leper is unclean! It is forbidden, just as everyone is forbidden to touch you."

Everyone is forbidden but not everyone is afraid. No matter what the law said... Mother was never afraid to touch me. Ever.

"Well..." Strong, wise Leah was wavering. It was hard not to, for the excitement of puny Leah could not be contained.

After a moment, sensible Leah spoke up, for once agreeing with sickly Leah, her words clear and firm in Leah's little house. "Well, Leah, you are unclean. If this man touched a leper, then maybe, perhaps, he could touch ..."

No! Not yet! Not yet....

"Yes, too soon, too soon..." For once, strong Leah was in agreement with puny Leah. It was too soon to speak of the small hope growing inside her.

Oh, the things the small laughing girl had said. A Messiah in Capernaum! People gathering just to hear him speak. Such a crowd that the lame man had to be lowered through the roof. A Messiah from the line of Judah, the fourth son of her namesake Leah, the wife of the patriarch Jacob. After all this time, and in this alien city where she now lived, a Messiah. Could it be?

Her father and all the other Jewish men she had ever known had prayed fervent prayers for the Messiah. But unlike some places, life was quite comfortable on the brown side of Caesarea Philippi. Not like life for the Jews in the Holy City, where Roman rule could force a man to take on the most demeaning of tasks at the whim of a soldier. Hated Romans with their own temples and gods and unclean food ruled the land of the Jewish people.

Jewish girls often whispered about Roman women, women who did not cover their arms or their heads, and who spoke freely in public.

Romans could whip a wrongdoer for hours, his back bleeding until the ground was red. They could even put a man to death in the most vicious of ways. Leah shivered, remembering the horrible sight she had seen as a young girl on the family Passover pilgrimage to Jerusalem. Her mother had tried to shield her eyes, but they passed by cross after cross, decaying bodies picked clean by the vultures and the newly-dead still oozing blood with lolling eyes staring at nothing. Worst of all were the men still living, screaming in agony, begging for death. Roman soldiers stood at their feet, keeping weeping wives or mothers at bay with their swords and their sneers. She had never forgotten the sight as they left Jerusalem.

Leah had been glad to return to Caesarea Philippi, where life was simple and men did not die on crosses.

The promised Messiah was always part of their prayers but not really part of their life in her small town. The Messiah was something prayed for, but not yearned for by Leah's mother, whose days were filled with David's praise and Solomon's wisdom.

Even now, Leah did not pray for a Messiah. She prayed to see her mother again, for the strength to get through the day, and that she might get better. She prayed to survive, not for a Holy King to rule the Jews. She needed strength, not a Messiah.

She prayed for God's forgiveness, just in case it was her sin that caused her illness as her father, the elders and even Reuben claimed. When she died, Leah did not want God to leave her to the agonies of hell. Just in case those old vindictive men and Reuben were right.

At the thought of her husband, Leah wondered for the hundredth time where he lived. He was careful to reveal nothing of his life now. She did not think he lived here. From the little she had seen of Capernaum, and what she had heard of it before, she thought it was a city of some size, bigger than Caesarea Philippi. Could Reuben live here and she not know it?

"Who are you fooling?" Leah said aloud. "He could live five houses away the opposite direction from the well and you would never know it."

It was unsettling to think that if Reuben lived right here in this city, he only came to see her once a month.

If Reuben lived here, had he heard of a Messiah who healed the sick?

Leah shook her head to rid herself of the thoughts of her husband. Better to wonder about the Galilean and the short conversation she had overheard that day. Neither girl seemed to know the leper. Indeed, they scarcely talked about him! But they both knew the man who had fallen and was lame. "The son of Rebecca," Leah whispered.

Did the crippled man's mother grieve for him as Leah's mother surely had grieved for her? Leah imagined a young man, a first-born son, working with his father in the bright sunshine by the sea, making repairs to the highest mast until he fell, his arms clutching at the nothingness of air until he crumpled on the deck below, never to walk again. Surely Rebecca had wept over her beloved son's tragic misfortune.

"But not anymore," Leah said out loud. "Her son walks now."

Leah imagined a handsome young man, his eyes darting and eager, his legs lying useless on a pallet, carried by his loyal friends to the house where this Messiah was. Did Rebecca follow behind, her hand covering a heart filled with hope? When he ran from the house, did he run to his mother and pick her up in the tightest embrace as they cried tears of joy together?

For in her heart, Leah knew that no matter who else might have abandoned the young man in his darkest hour, his mother did not. And when he came leaping from the house on legs made whole by a stranger from Galilee, no one would be louder in their praise of Jehovah than his mother.

∞

The sun had set; shadows crept up the wall of Leah's small house. She sat on her narrow bed on the floor of her lonely dilapidated house in Capernaum, thinking of the unknown Rebecca and her own mother. She wiped away her tears. No wonder she needed so much water; she was always crying. Water leaked out of her like a sieve.

Tonight she cried because of her grief. To have hope reborn in her shriveled heart was to be reminded of all she had lost. What Leah mourned the most was her mother. She no longer cared about her husband or father, or even her own failing body. She grieved for her mother.

Was her mother healthy? She did not know.

Did Talitha still live in Caesarea Philippi? She did not know.

Were her brothers taking care of her mother? She did not know. Surely her mother was not alone, penniless like so many widows, reduced to begging at the synagogue, or worse, in the streets.

Where did her mother live? She did not know.

Leah would not even give voice to this thought. Was her mother still alive? Surely her mother was not dead.

She thought again about the women's conversation about the Messiah, the cripple who now walked, and Rebecca, the mother that loved him.

If Leah were ever healed, she would go at once to Caesarea Philippi, run every step of the way to see her mother. The only pain greater than that in her body was the pain Leah felt when she thought of her mother. The suffering of her body was nothing compared to the agony in her tender heart.

Leah missed her mother.

CHAPTER 18

"Who will bury Leah?"

Leah could hear the tears in the woman's voice. She knew this voice and yet it was foreign to her.

"Who will wash her body? Who will anoint her with sacred oil and spices? Who will wrap her body in the shroud and place the veil over her face?"

A man answered, but his words were muddled and indistinguishable, as though through a thick wall or muffled behind a cloth.

Leah could not open her eyes. Was she dead? She felt as though a heavy weight lay on her chest. She could not move, her arms and legs lifeless on a hard surface. She was cold as she had ever been. If she had not been gripped by this terrifying paralysis, she knew her body would shiver so hard she would fall from the freezing surface where she lay. Was it a bed? She felt as though she lay on stone. She struggled to move but could not.

"Who will cry for Leah? Who will pay for the flute player and for the mourners to wail? Who will carry her funeral bier to the grave?" Sorrow marked the woman's every syllable.

Leah struggled on the cold stone, but her body lay limp and unmoving. She felt as though she were suffocating, smothered by some black presence pushing the life from her. She heard the voice of the man again, distant, unintelligible. She strained to hear what he said.

But the woman continued, her voice rising in pitch. "Who will find Leah a grave? Who will roll the stone across her tomb to keep the animals and scavengers and evil ones away? Who will whitewash the tomb to hide her filth and decay from the world? Who will cry for Leah?"

The woman's questions were covered in her tears. She heard the growling low voice answer her, his words a brusque muttering she could not comprehend. Who was this angry man? Who was this heartbroken woman who cried for Leah?

Horrified, Leah knew. It was her mother! Her mother was asking these questions about her poor daughter.

Her mother's cries were anguished. "Who will cry for my daughter? Who will cry for my Leah?"

And then the man's voice was clear and she knew it at once. It was the voice of her father, now dead these many years. "Amê! Unclean! No one mourns for Leah!"

With a sharp moan, Leah sat bolt upright in her bed, alone in the darkness, gasping but unable to breathe. Oh, such a nightmare! Her chest was squeezed shut, her legs were paralyzed, she was shaking from the cold. She could not even raise her hand to wipe the tears from her face. She sat unmoving in the dark, panting. Oh, what a horrible, horrible dream.

Finally, Leah's breathing slowed, her shallow gasps the only sound in the silent darkness. She rolled from her mat and crawled on the dirt floor to the water jar. Leah dipped her cup into the water, scraping the bottom and then heavily turned the jar over, drinking the little that remained. She knew she would regret this, but her thirst was unquenchable. If only she could catch a deep breath!

Leah lay in the dirt, her prayer only a whisper in the darkness. For the truth was suddenly clear to her: she would soon die from her bleeding. But before Leah died from her horrible disease, she wanted to see her mother again.

Who would cry for Leah indeed? Only her mother. Who would mourn for Leah? Only her mother.

"If Mother were to die," she thought dully, "would I even know? If I were to die, Mother would never know, either. No one mourns for Leah, not today, not ever.

"But what does it matter? After I die, will I know the difference anyway? I will be gone. God has left me to suffer here on earth. I cannot suffer more when I am dead than what I have suffered here, can I?"

Leah silently thought this over but then acknowledged what she had admitted many times before: even as much as she hated to live, she was afraid to die.

For even in death, she would be unclean. No one would touch her. No one would wash her, hold her, mourn her. She would be as alone in death as she was in life.

Leah crawled back to her bed and lay down. The pounding of her heart was so loud, surely it echoed off the clay walls of her house. Her body throbbed in pain, the blood hot on her bandages.

Oh, what a dream.

"'You will not abandon me to the grave,
Nor will you let your Holy One see decay.'"

Leah whispered the psalm in the darkness.

"'You have made known to me the path of life.
You will fill me with joy in your presence.'"

Joy in his presence. Leah was afraid to die, but perhaps she might soon be ready to face the joy of his presence after all. For her life here alone, far from her mother, separated from anyone who loved her or even cared about her, was surely one of abandonment and certain decay, a life of slow measured steps to her grave.

❧

Leah woke to a bright sunshine the next morning. Was last night the truth and this cheerful morning the dream? Perhaps she really was dead and had passed on to the House of the Lord. Either way, she could not remember ever having such a terrible nightmare.

After some reflection, Leah determined she was not dead, but very much alive. She knew this because she was so thirsty she could barely swallow. Perhaps Sheol was a place of eternal thirst, but right now Leah was a living, breathing sort of alive, for she needed a drink in the worst way.

There was nothing left in the water jar. Leah drank it all after her horrifying nightmare. Her thirst was so pressing, she knew she would not be able to wait until her mid-day trip to the well. If only she could carry a jar sloshing over with water instead of only half-full!

Well, no time to fret about that. She had to have something to drink, and soon.

She went to her chest with its dwindling provisions and pulled out the wine flask. Leah was so frugal with wine, the flask was nearly half full. Leah filled her clay cup up to the brim, rare for her, and tore off a piece of bread. As she sat down to eat, she realized she was not only thirsty but hungry, too. Leah was never hungry, often struggling to force the smallest of meals down. The bread tasted rich in her mouth, the wine rich with a sharp tang. She felt strengthened despite the horrible night she had just had.

"It's the wine," she said aloud. "I never drink wine in the morning. The wine always strengthens me."

"It's not the wine," puny Leah answered right back, her voice unwavering. Leah recognized a stubborn strength in her own words. "It's not the wine making you stronger. You know what it is. You remember. It's hope."

Leah shook her head and finished her meal.

She gave thanks for her food after she finished eating, along with asking forgiveness that she ate without seeking the Lord's blessing first. Behind the privacy of her small curtain hung in the corner, she started her morning ritual as best as she could without water. She scrubbed her face on a dry cloth and combed her hair. To change her bandages without water was misery but she had done it many times before. If only she had gone to the public baths last night instead of her cursory bath from a bowl. It had been several weeks since she had last been there, perhaps months. But she did not like to go too close to the Sabbath; too many other Jewish women went then and might find out her secret.

She pulled on her last clean tunic. Instead of the usual brown belt, she pulled a wide woven cloth from the chest and tied it around her narrow waist.

The sash was beautiful, a sky blue linen with ribbons of purple, violet and navy running through it. Leah rarely wore it. She remembered so the day Savta and her mother showed the cloth to her, something special made by their own hands for the day she married. Leah had stood there dirty, muddy and shaken by her father's rage, but still safe in the presence of her loving mother and feisty grandmother. Savta had stood up to her father that day, not frightened by his rage. She had fought for Leah.

That was so many years ago. Homesickness for the life she had once known washed over her.

At the bottom of the trunk, she saw the corner of her pale blue bridal veil with its elaborate embroidery, its secret treasure hidden in its hem. Her medallion. The necklace of her mother and her grandmother. She felt herself slipping into her memories.

Clucking, she straightened up and shook her head hard, which made her slightly dizzy. "Pffth! No time for that this morning," she said loudly in a firm voice. "No time for that today."

Today Reuben would be coming, she thought. Certainly he comes today.

But before he came, Leah was going to the well, and when she got to the well, she was going to speak with those two women. For the first time, she was going to talk to Tirzah and her small laughing friend.

Without even realizing it, Leah woke up with a plan.

CHAPTER 19

Leah peeked out her window, intently watching the many women and children returning from the well to their homes. For the first time in many months, perhaps ever in all the time she had been in Capernaum, she would be glad to see Reuben. Leah had a plan!

"He should come this afternoon," she muttered to herself, distracted by worry over his delay for unknown reasons. "Today or tomorrow, Reuben will return to this house where he left me three long years ago."

The first few months when Reuben stood silent in her doorway with an armful of supplies, Leah had fallen to her knees, crying, desperate for food, pulling on the hem of his tunic, begging him to take her home. His replies were harsh and they hardened Leah's heart as well. She soon learned to speak polite words of ostensible gratitude when he came. She needed Reuben to survive, to save her from beggary.

But today was different. Today, hope was in her heart. There might be a chance for Leah yet. She had a plan, and she needed Reuben.

It was so important to talk to Tirzah and her small laughing friend before Reuben came and then left again for another long month. Yesterday the women had talked of a teacher, a healer here in

Galilee. Somehow, Leah had to find out more.

Only a few straggling women now walked by with full water jars balanced on their heads. Soon the two friends would pass by on their way to the well. They did not walk by until the other women had already gone home, preferring the heat of the day and each other's conversation to the morning coolness and noisy, idle chatter of the many women.

Leah knew their routine as if it were her own. She needed to act now, for if she waited too long, the women would come from behind and overtake her. Leah needed to be at the well when they arrived.

She had dressed with the greatest care, as clean as she could be without a bath. She had never met Tirzah and her small laughing friend face-to-face. Leah prayed that they would not be able to see or to smell her disease. The sky blue sash was wrapped twice around her skinny waist, the veil covering her hair all the colors of the sky over Mount Hebron. If only they would talk to her.

Leah started the short walk to the well. It was hot already. But her breakfast of bread and wine and hope in her heart strengthened her. Her excitement gave her a nervous energy she had not experienced for years. The well lay just ahead.

She met several women as she walked, none of whom she had ever seen before. She looked away, careful not to meet their eyes.

Thank goodness her neighbor was not among these straggling groups of women. Leah knew what her neighbor must think of her. A woman alone, with no means of support and a man who visited her once a month, was easily seen for a kept woman, a mistress. She felt shamed by the thought.

However, she could hardly defend herself by setting the record straight, insisting that she was not a prostitute but simply an unclean woman, expelled from the synagogue, reviled by all, disowned by her father, and abandoned by a husband who hated her and wanted her dead.

Thank goodness her neighbor had not walked by.

ೞ

Leah sat at the well, waiting. She had already filled her jar half-full and pulled it up, taking a deep drink of the cold water. She smiled. It tasted wonderful. Now, when the women approached, she would act as though she had just pulled the jar from the well.

And here they came! Her friends were reliable if nothing else. They were still some distance away, but Leah would know them anywhere. Leah was so excited, she thought she would faint.

"Wait, what if I do faint?" she spoke aloud, startled by that terrible thought. "It's happened before." She had often found herself sprawled on her dirt floor with no memory of falling. She had even fainted once before at this well, waking up with one eye gazing at a cloudless sky above her, and the other staring at the gritty dust of the street. At least she had never fallen from her roof!

She was paying for her nervous energy and exertions with a severe case of dizziness.

Leah tried to slow her breathing. Not knowing what else to do, she prayed. "Lord, if I faint I will lay here in the dirt alone until who knows when. Jehovah, keep me strong. Do not let me fall down like a dead woman!" She felt guilty about commanding the Lord God Almighty. But even King David had shouted at God when circumstances demanded it. "Awake, O Lord! Rouse yourself! Save me!" he had said.

"No fainting, Lord!" Leah mentally shouted, both at God and herself.

Her mother never spoke to the Lord like that. However, her mother had never fallen over in the dirt at the feet of strangers at the well. This required drastic action.

Leah concentrated on the careful words she had chosen to say to Tirzah and her small laughing friend. To act as though this were a chance encounter seemed contrived, but she didn't know what else to do.

As the two women reached the well, they smiled at Leah sitting there. The shorter girl was talking as usual, something about her oldest brother's wife's baby's rash.

"Now or never, Leah," Leah gathered all of her courage and remaining strength and stood up.

"Excuse me," Leah said. Her voice was as wobbly as her knees. She was suddenly unnerved by the realization that these were the first words she had uttered to anyone but Reuben in three years.

Both women turned toward Leah. Their look was not unfriendly, only curious. They weren't judging her, or recoiling in horror, or laughing at her. Leah took a deep breath.

"I'm sorry to interrupt, I hope you won't think I am being rude." Her voice would not stop shaking!

"I see you walk by every day to the well." Better to leave out that she sat hiding under her window grasping at their every word, hoping it would bring the smallest sense of normalcy to her own wretched life.

"I... I heard you the other day speaking of a young man who was lame. His mother's name is Rebecca. I thought I heard you say he was healed." Her words will stiff and halting. "I am sorry, I did not mean to listen to your conversation, I just heard you when you walked by." Her words limped along like the lame man. "I wonder if you, if you could tell me about the man who healed him, the, um, healer from... the man from Nazareth..."

A brief silence hung in the hot air, an eternity to Leah.

Then, the small laughing girl broke into a huge smile. In just the same way Leah had seen her do many times, she danced a few steps on her toes. "See, Tirzah, see? Remember what I told you that Jesus said? Remember? I just said this to you this morning! Jesus said, 'Give to every man who asks of you.' Or woman, in this case." She put special emphasis on the word woman. "Oh, Tirzah, who am I not to share this good news?"

Tirzah looked skeptically at her friend, her eyebrows arched into the middle of her forehead. She turned to Leah with a polite smile. "Do you know Rebecca?"

"No, no, I... I know of someone else who is ill. I wondered about all the people who go, um, to hear him and how... how that healing happened. And... about the leper. That's just... what I wondered." Disappointment at her stumbling words welled up in Leah. Why had she ever thought, ever dared, to talk to these women? She was light-headed with disgust at herself, her whole body shaking with nervousness.

The small woman turned to Leah. The grin was still on her face, but her response was one Leah never had imagined.

"What is your name?" Her gaze was direct.

A huge lump grew in Leah's throat. Her name? Someone wanted to know her name?

Leah shook her head as she tried to find her voice. "Please, can you tell me about this man from Nazareth, who heals lepers and lame men?"

The laughing friend answered her with an emphatic nod. "Yes, I can! I have gone to hear him teach many times. He is in Capernaum now. You can see him too!"

And despite Leah's imperious command to God, at the joyous words "You can see him too..." Leah fainted, sprawling in the dirt at the feet of the women at the well.

So much for answered prayer.

A blinding light pierced Leah's closed eyes. So brilliant, so bright!

Was she dead, she wondered dreamily, not for the first time and only for the briefest second.

"No, Leah, you are not dead, you are lying out in the sun," strong Leah mumbled testily. She thought about that for a moment, frowning. Then a second, more horrible thought came to her.

"Where am I?" She opened her eyes, squinting into the sun. She was cast into shadow as two faces leaned over her. She had fainted. She felt the dirt between her fingers. Had her two friends heard her incoherent muttering? Leah's embarrassment was immediate and complete.

The small woman spoke first. "Oh, no, are you all right?" Her face wrinkled up with concern. She and Tirzah knelt down in the dirt beside Leah. "What happened?"

Leah felt groggy. Even so, she scrambled to think of what she might tell these women. She needed to find out their secret about this healer. She was so close. "Lord, you let me fall over in the dirt," she prayed silently. "Do not fail me now." Her prayer was decidedly belligerent.

"I... I don't know what happened, really. I guess.... Well, I did not eat breakfast this morning and," sudden inspiration came to Leah. "I don't come to the well in the heat of the day, I usually come much earlier." God forgive me for these lies!

"Of course," said the small laughing friend. She and Tirzah each took an arm and pulled Leah to a sitting position. "Goodness, you were just standing there and plop! Down you went into the dirt like a stone into the well. Here, have something to drink." She jumped up and came back with a dipper of water from Leah's own jar. Leah

186

sipped the cool water, her eyes downcast. Relief rose up in her; they did not yet suspect her terrible illness. They did not know they had touched an untouchable. She felt better at once. They had not guessed.

"Do you live far?" asked Tirzah. "Do you have a husband or children who could help you home?"

"No, I will be fine, if I can only rest for a moment. No one," Leah paused to think, "No one is at my house right now but me. My husband returns later." That's somewhat true, she thought apologetically to God.

"Then we shall help you," the small laughing girl said emphatically, rising to her feet and dusting herself off.

Oh no, thought Leah. Now what? She just wanted to talk with the women. She didn't want them to help her.

The girl held out her hand to Leah, and, not knowing what else to do, Leah let herself be pulled to her feet. She still felt very weak. At least she hadn't hit her head on a rock and started bleeding all over the place, like the day of the ignorant doctor so many years ago.

"Why don't you sit down over here?" said Tirzah, pointing to the seat at the well. The two women busied themselves filling up their water jars. The small girl also lowered Leah's half-full jar and filled it to the brim. "How will I carry that?" thought Leah in sudden desperation.

"Don't worry," said the girl said, as though she heard Leah's thoughts. "I have to do all Tirzah's work too, since she is with child!"

Tirzah reddened and poked her friend with an elbow. "Jerusha!"

Jerusha.... Jerusha was her name! The small laughing woman was called Jerusha.

"Oh, Tirzah, one has but to look at you to know! You are so lovely. And soon your life will include another strong boy or beautiful girl, Yahweh be with you. You can't deny what everyone can see! Besides," she said in a confidential aside to Leah, "Tirzah fainted several times when she was carrying her first child. She never ate breakfast either! Remember how you used to throw up everything you ate all day long?" She laughed. "It's a common thing for us poor women."

Leah knew Tirzah was not angry at Jerusha, her small laughing friend, for sharing these secrets with an odd woman at the well. These two women loved each other. She felt intrusive at their shared smile.

"All right, here we go, which way?"

Leah was tempted to lie about the whereabouts of her small, shabby house. But what good would that do? And somehow she needed to ask them again about the crippled son of the unknown Rebecca and this man from Nazareth, the one that the laughing Jerusha called Jesus.

Leah's plan was not working at all.

Jerusha and Tirzah placed their water jars on their heads and each took a handle of Leah's jar. Leah walked to the right of Tirzah, praying she would be able to keep up. The women walked in silence until predictably Jerusha spoke, asking again what Leah had not answered before.

"What is your name?"

Unwanted hot tears came to Leah's eyes. When was the last time someone had asked her name? When was the last time someone had said her name out loud other than Reuben, who despised and hated her? What was her name? She didn't want these women to know anything about her.

"My name is Leah," she said softly. The two women exchanged glances but said nothing of the quaver they heard in her voice. Leah was thankful for this small grace.

"Leah, I am Jerusha and this is Tirzah," the small laughing woman said cheerfully, as though this stranger beside her was not in tears. "We're glad to meet you."

Leah's heart leapt at this simple statement.

"You asked about Jesus. He is preaching now all through Galilee and every few days he returns to Capernaum. This is his home, now. When he is here, he preaches on the shores of the Sea, over in the northeast side of the city. Do you know where the main street ends, down by the fishermen's houses?"

Leah shook her head no.

"You don't?" Jerusha looked surprised. "Well, it is not far from here. You turn right at the first street from here. See? It is just ahead of us, there." She pointed to a cross street a few houses away, a street Leah had never ventured to in three years.

Jerusha turned back to Leah. "Just keep on walking on that road. It is the main street through town. You will go past our synagogue first, then through the market. When the road ends, you will see an empty field by the sea. That is where Jesus teaches. Many can hear him there, and many, many will come." Her voice was confident. "For he says he is the Son of God, the Messiah, and I believe him."

Jerusha looked hard at her friend Tirzah. "Come with me, Tirzah, come listen to the Messiah."

Tirzah smiled. "We shall see," was all she said.

With a start, Leah realized they were approaching her house. The walk was so much easier when she did not have to carry her half-full water jar.

"This is where I live," she said shyly to the women, stopping a few steps away so they might not see her meager life inside.

The women set down Leah's water jar and took their own jars from their heads. Jerusha lifted Leah's jar and carried it right into her small house. She came out and walked back to Leah. "The way to the sea is there," she said, pointing down the street. "Turn right at the first street and just keep walking until you run into it. You will see the sea long before you reach its shores. It is there that Jesus preaches when he is in Capernaum."

"Thank you." Leah's voice was a whisper. She nodded and started the last few steps to her house. Jerusha's voice stopped her.

"Leah, this is what Jesus said. 'Come to me, you that are weary, and I will give you rest.' Leah, whatever hurts you, to hear Jesus is to find peace. I have heard his words. Leah," Jerusha paused. When she continued her voice was gentle.

"Leah, I saw how Jesus healed the lame man. I can see you are sick, very sick. Come and hear Jesus. Jesus can help you if only you believe. In my heart, I know this is true. He can help you. And if you need it, I can help you too."

"Why would you help me?" Startled, Leah was ashamed by the question she blurted out. What would this kind woman think of such an ungrateful spirit!

Much to Leah's great surprise, Jerusha walked up, took Leah in her arms and hugged her.

No one had hugged Leah in three long, lonely years, not since she stood outside Savta's little house weeping with her mother. Hot tears ran down her face again.

Jerusha pushed Leah back an arm's length to look at her, her grasp tight on Leah's arm, her eyes shining with joy.

189

"My mother taught me the words of old King Solomon, who said: 'Do not withhold good from those who deserve it, when it is in your power to act.'"

Leah's mouth twitched in the smallest of smiles. Those were the words of Savta, too.

"Leah, if I were sick and weak and fell over in the dirt, wouldn't you stop to help me? I would hope so! I think you would, for I can see you have a gentle and kind heart."

Jerusha put her arm around Leah's shoulder. "So, Leah, now listen to what Jesus says about doing good: 'Give and it will be given to you! A good measure, pressed down, shaken together and running over into your lap!'"

She reached out to Tirzah, pulled her close, and put her other arm around her. "And he has much for you too, Tirzah," Jerusha's voice was gentle. "Enough to run over into your lap..."

She nodded at Leah. "...and into your lap..."

And even with her arms on the shoulders of the two women, Jerusha danced, just the smallest step. "And into my lap, too!"

She looked at the two women on either side of her, first at serious Tirzah on her left and then at sickly Leah on her right, her face covered by her wide smile.

"Of course, some of us have bigger laps than others!"

She released tall Tirzah and skinny Leah from her strong embrace, picked up her water jar and started down the street, laughing as she left.

☙

As soon as Jerusha and Tirzah left her door, Leah got busy. God had answered her prayer, and now there was much to do. Her usual pain went unnoticed, for Leah had found a new remedy, one long forgotten. Hope!

She put water in the small iron pot on the fire. Since she had awakened to an empty water jar, Leah had not yet had a bath. And now, she had extra water, a full jar! It was important she be as clean as possible when Reuben arrived. She felt certain he would come today. What good news she had to share, news that someone might heal her.

When the water was warm, she hid behind the curtain to wash, change her bandages and comb her hair again. She hesitated. To wash her clothing was so difficult, so hard. Then, feeling reckless and hopeful, Leah put on her last fresh robe. She again twisted her beautiful belt around her waist and covered her head with her blue veil, as bright as the Mount Hermon sky in the spring. She tidied up the bowls she had used, dumped the soiled water on the tamarisk, swept the floor and then set the table with two cups and two plates. She got out the bread, the last of the honey, the remaining wine and sat down to wait.

All this activity exhausted Leah's body, but her mind alive with thoughts jumbled together, one after another. If only Reuben would take her to meet this Jesus. Together, they could go to see the teacher. For how else could Leah meet him, if not with Reuben? A Jewish woman could not approach any man who was not her husband, especially not a wise teacher like this Jesus. But Reuben could help her get through the crowds and ask the man from Nazareth to heal his wife.

Leah was so excited she could not sit still. If only Reuben would arrive soon. If she were healed, the life she knew as a daughter, wife, and Jew would be restored to her.

Soon, Reuben would arrive. Leah felt more alive than she had in years.

಩

Several hours later, Leah awoke. She had been sleeping where she sat, her chin resting on her chest, just like her aged grandmother snoozing in the sunshine of her home. Disgusted, Leah shook herself. What if Reuben found her like this? She stood, as stiff as an aged spinster or Savta.

Where was Reuben? He always came just before the Sabbath in the first week of the month. Had she miscounted the weeks? Perhaps. She was so confused lately. It was almost dark.

If Reuben was coming today, she mused, he would have already come and gone. Perhaps he saw me sleeping, thought me dead and left.

She scoffed out loud. "That's certainly possible. Death would make me even more unclean than I am now, and Reuben is as scared of being unclean as a child is to pick up his first grasshopper."

Leah tried not to be sarcastic as she thought of Reuben. She was dependent on him for the little she had. Without him, she would die.

And now, she needed him. For how else could she go to find the man from Nazareth except with Reuben? If Reuben even had the courage for that.

With a sigh, Leah realized it was becoming difficult to think of Reuben with even a shred of the respect a husband deserved from a good wife.

"Because Reuben is weak." She could not deny the truth of that statement, spoken aloud in the silence of her house.

It was not the first time she had thought this. Her mother had seen it from the beginning, recognizing his weakness, worrying about his hot temper. She feared his insecurities would leech away the confident exuberance and joy of her only daughter.

After they were married, Leah saw but would not admit what her mother already knew. Reuben was a weak man. Leah's husband was so self-conscious and uncomfortable around her. He had no backbone in the business with her father. He never questioned Leah on any household decisions, stoic in his agreement, relieved to stand aside and let her confident spirit lead.

Leah had not cared. Leah had not worried about what kind of man her husband was. She had only loved being married, being a wife, being a woman.

She had never loved Reuben.

And then, when the hardship of her illness came upon them, Reuben's true character came through. The moment she was struck down with her infirmity, Reuben began to withdraw. He only wanted a beautiful, healthy wife who could serve him, love him and bear him children. Even though he had not divorced her, Leah could not bring herself to count Reuben as a good, God-fearing man. Not for the first time, she wondered what had happened to her substantial dowry.

Reuben had supposedly taken her dowry to his family for safekeeping. Leah remembered just how angry her mother had been about that. Her mother had never trusted Reuben. "She was smarter than me," thought Leah, recalling how her mother had begged her father not to sign Leah's marriage contract with Reuben. The memory of her mother sprawled on the floor at the force of her father's hand still made her angry.

But her father had signed the contract, Leah and Reuben had married, and now Reuben had her dowry, all of it. It was probably long gone, sold away piece by piece.

All sold but the beautiful medallion. The necklace was still hidden in the secret hem of her bridal veil where her mother had hidden it three years ago, her passionate whispers begging Leah to never, ever tell Reuben she possessed it.

The veil was secreted away in the old chest that had come with the meager furnishings of this little house. Leah had never even undone the hem to look at it, so mindful was she of her mother's fierce warning. Leah had but to lift the veil to feel the reassuring weight of the medallion.

To feel the weight of the medallion was to feel her mother's love, her blessing for her only daughter.

"Sell it!" Talitha had whispered to her daughter.

Never, was Leah's stubborn reply.

She would not think about what would happen to the medallion if she died here alone in Capernaum. She would not.

She turned her thoughts back to Reuben. If her husband divorced her, the dowry was supposed to be Leah's. That was the law. If she died, however, the dowry was his.

When he left her alone three years ago, Reuben had most certainly thought he would not have to wait long to return to a dead wife, especially after the grueling five-day journey to Capernaum. She knew this now. Hadn't that last doctor said without cutting her up she would die, and die very soon? Surely this is what Reuben had planned. His wife would die, and he would be free.

But Reuben had not counted on Leah's stubborn spirit. She couldn't blame him. Even Leah got tired of her stubborn spirit from time to time.

Reuben stopped loving her when she became ill. When she was no longer beautiful and vibrant and healthy, he disowned her and then publicly shamed her. He had spent money on doctors to cure her, but was that for Leah's benefit or to show others his generosity? Most likely, it was out of his fear of his formidable mother-in-law.

Reuben put her away in a hovel so small and meager, it was nothing more than an old stable pretending to be a home. He sold her weavings to buy the paltry supplies he left her, but Leah was certain that he kept most of the money for himself. Leah lived like a beggar, like the poorest, childless widow.

Reuben was too weak to seek a divorce from the wife he hated, and too afraid to care for his wife with the illness he feared.

Reuben had separated Leah from her mother, with no word about her in three years.

Reuben claimed to be a man of God who hated sin and all things unclean.

"That was an excuse," Leah said out loud. "An excuse to himself, so he could be rid of me."

Was she being fair?

"Well, rather than let everyone know that he, a good Jewish man, was abandoning or divorcing his wife, he instead lied to everyone and hid me away."

Abandoning his sick, dying wife would be a secret between him and the God he claimed to worship.

"Perhaps God will be more merciful to Reuben than he ever was to me."

Was the God Reuben claimed to worship the same God Leah called Jehovah? That seemed impossible.

"Pah." Her voice was loud and clear in the silence. "The God I worship is loving, not cruel like Reuben and my father. O God, you blessed me with a mother who loved me. You comfort me with my memories and with mother's psalms. Although I live in pain, I do not live in sin. You have not yet brought me to death. You are a gracious God who loves his daughter, Leah."

She would not suffer another moment over the unhappiness Reuben brought her each month. Not one more moment. Enough was enough.

Leah sat down, ate her bread, drank her wine, and then, for good measure - since he had not shown up anyway - ate Reuben's portion, too. He was not coming today. But when he came, if he believed in God as he claimed he did, then Reuben would take her to see the Galilean they called Jesus.

CHAPTER 20

Where was Reuben?

The Sabbath had come and gone, as had two days more. Reuben had not darkened the door of her small house. Tirzah and Jerusha walked by daily, stopping once to check on Leah and ask if she wanted to walk to the well with them. She remembered her shock when, as she heard their voices approaching, those voices came right to her doorstep.

She had scrambled to her feet from her sitting position under the window to answer their knock. No, she had already been to the well. Thank you, maybe another day. Yes, it was hard for her to walk in the heat.

Leah was thankful that Jerusha did not walk right in and discover her empty jar.

She felt shame for her lies. However, to actually befriend people who were kind and decent, and who would certainly avoid her if they knew of her unclean state, was a risk Leah could not take. She felt far safer huddled on the floor, listening to the women as they walked by.

Yet the fact that they stopped to see her was a wonder, a treasure she held in her heart as securely as the precious medallion hidden in the hem of her bridal veil. Not an hour went by that she did not relive the words Jerusha spoke to her the day they met at the well.

"Give and it will be given to you!" Jerusha had exclaimed, her round face wreathed in a wide smile, her head thrown back in laughter.

Except for falling over in the dirt, Leah could recall no responses of her own. She pondered with wonder that someone had knocked on her door just to see how she was.

And Jerusha had hugged her! Oh, she would be so repulsed if she ever found out about Leah's unclean state, that she had touched someone who had made her ceremonially unclean. Leah prayed Jerusha and Tirzah would never find out her secret. She treasured their friendship, as meager as it was, as though it was a rare and precious jewel. If they found out about the real, shameful Leah, they would never be her friends.

Leah waited for Reuben to arrive with increasing worry, for her meager supplies of food, wine, and wood were almost gone. She recounted the days on her fingers. Yes, he should have arrived at least by yesterday, if not even two, three, even four days before. She did not know what to think.

However, she had none of the usual, frightened panic at the thought that Reuben might not come at all. Leah understood why. Although she was worried about what to do, she was not afraid of what might happen. For the first time in many years, Leah had hope.

But still, she could not help but wonder. Where was Reuben?

⁂

"Leah!"

The next morning, Leah was startled by Reuben's loud voice behind her as she sat on her small stool weaving at her loom. Days late, he had finally arrived in Capernaum from wherever it was he now stayed.

Her first reaction was not relief, but irritation. He could knock, Leah thought. This is my house and not his.

She stood up with difficulty, stiff from sitting, but she worked up a smile to mask her pain and her opinion from her husband. "Reuben."

He nodded at her and proceeded to set out down the supplies he had brought from a worn cotton bag: flour from barley, the cheapest available, and two flasks of oil for the lantern and for cooking. It made no difference to Reuben in the oil she ate or the oil she burned. There was a small sack of more barley for her to grind into flour herself. Dried fruit, dried fish, and several small wrapped parcels: she spied onions, figs, grapes and a small comb of honey. He did not bring her any more soap, even though she had asked for it on several of his visits. Her last small cake of soap was as thin as parchment.

Reuben stopped to look at her with narrowed eyes. Leah gazed back but did not move.

"Will you not serve me any of the food and wine I brought you today?" He sounded somewhat surprised. Normally Leah scurried about at his arrival, nervous at his towering presence and scowling demeanor.

Let's follow my husband's lead for a change, Leah thought to herself. She shook her head no, unblinking before his malicious stare.

His eyes were as black and unfeeling as coal under his bushy eyebrows, his words pompous. "Leah, I have come some distance today to bring you supplies, including the bread and wine you eat. You survive thanks only to me. The least you could do is to serve me food and drink when I arrive, as befits a wife to her husband."

"You are several days late in coming, husband." She hoped he did not hear the sarcasm she felt at the word. "Last time you were here, you ate as much I might use in three days. Since I have so little food, I must be very careful with everything you give me, just as you told me to do when you first left me here alone." She could not hide the smallest trace of accusation as she added, "For this time, I truly thought I might run out of supplies. I have waited for your return much longer than usual."

Reuben reddened. "I have been engaged elsewhere in the city since I arrived."

"Engaged elsewhere in the city? Here in Capernaum?"

Reuben's flush grew deeper at the slip. He shrugged and did not answer her. Oh, how she wanted to shout at him! Leah felt something strong building in her, a white-hot, livid rage boiling up, an anger she had not felt for many years.

She was angry that he tended to other business in Capernaum before he looked to see if his sick wife was dead or alive. She was angry at the meager supplies he brought. She was angry that he expected her to be grateful when he brought her so little. She was angry that he lied to her about the money he received for selling the cloth she wove. She was angry that he treated her as an insignificant, mundane chore. She was angry that he did not come as promised, leaving her to wonder if he would even return at all. She was angry at the lonely solitude he had forced upon her, and that he had taken her away from the only person who loved her.

Leah was angry.

"Reuben, what news of my mother?" The words burst out of her, loud and strong in the small house. Startled, Reuben looked at her. The question surprised Leah, too.

"I have no news of your mother. I no longer live in Caesarea Philippi."

"I'm sorry, I do not know where you live. Well, then, can you send for news? I wish to know how my mother fares."

Reuben looked at her, confused. He did not know how to respond to this side of Leah.

"Perhaps you could accompany me to Caesarea Philippi to see my mother. I wish to see her, Reuben."

It had been years since Leah had told Reuben she wished for anything. What I am asking is not unreasonable, she thought fiercely. I ask Reuben to do what any man of compassion would do.

He turned away from her before he answered. "No." It was the answer she expected.

All right, Reuben, Leah thought to herself. I will ask for something much easier for you, to see someone right here in Capernaum, a city you seem to know quite well. Let's see what kind of man you really are, since you've apparently been here for several days without even bothering to check on me.

She spoke again, her voice even and polite, hiding the anger she felt. "Reuben, there is a man here in Capernaum. His name is Jesus of Nazareth. Two women told me about him. Reuben, he is supposed to be a great teacher and healer, maybe you have even heard of him. The women say he is the Messiah. Reuben, he has healed many people."

Despite herself, Leah grew excited. "He heals people, Reuben! They say he is the one Jews have long prayed for. He healed a mother's crippled son and a leper. Reuben, I believe… I believe he could perhaps heal me."

Leah's sharp anger with Reuben was replaced with a profound hunger for this one thing. Oh, that she might be healed of this dreadful affliction, that her life might be changed! He stood with his back to Leah. She stood behind him, waiting. It took all her effort not to fall to her knees and clutch his robe in desperation.

"This Jesus, this Messiah... he is here in Capernaum. Reuben, please... I want you to take me to see this man called Jesus."

At this, Reuben whirled around to gape at her, his sudden temper evident on his mottled face. "I, a godly Jewish man all my life, take you - an unclean whore, scorned by all good Jewish people and condemned by God - to meet a Messiah! As if such a man exists anyway!"

A whore?" Leah thought. She could not imagine where that accusation had come from. A whore?

"What sort of Messiah would ever lay eyes on you? What teacher, what rabbi would ever speak to you, a woman, an unclean woman at that! Would any man ever touch your filthy, unclean body, woman? No, not to heal you, or curse you, or even dispose of you to your grave! No one would ever touch a woman like you. Never!"

Leah was caught off guard by the vicious fury in Reuben's voice. He was shouting, his face red, the threat of violence standing between them. Leah never forgot her mother's battered face at the hand of her father. She crumpled in the face of Reuben's sudden, ferocious rage, sinking to her knees in fear.

She had to make him understand.

"But Reuben, I want to be healed so I can be your wife. Don't you remember when we were first married?"

"I remember. I remember being an ignorant fool, doing only what my father and your father told me to do! Had I known what a sinful, lying, deceitful woman you are, I would have fled at the sight of you! You and your mother, thieves and liars, keeping me from what is rightfully mine! You have treated me with the greatest of disrespect, and it can never be forgiven!

"Rueben, please, I am sorry. I never meant to be disrespectful, to shame you." Leah did not really understand his anger, but she was desperate to make him see. "Please, Reuben, please help me."

"Help you?" Reuben paced in the small room. "Look at what I have done for you, Leah! Shelter and food. I did not abandon you with nothing. I fulfilled my duties as the law commanded. I have taken care of a woman dead to me for twelve long years. A woman who has never, ever been the wife I asked God to send to me!"

The smallest voice escaped Leah. She had to make him see. "Reuben, perhaps I might be healed, and be your wife again. Please, let us go see this Jesus."

Reuben looked at her and then strode to her household chest, pulling out every item and throwing them to the ground. He pulled out something wrapped in brown linen, what used to be a prized possession, her small metal mirror. A gift to Leah from Reuben on their wedding night, when he whispered to Leah of her beauty, his love for her, and their future together. Leah had not picked up the mirror in the three long years she lived here. To look in the mirror was to mourn what she had lost.

"Heal you, Leah? Heal you? How could any man - Messiah, doctor, witch - heal someone who has already died?" He grabbed Leah by the hair and pulled her up to a half-standing position, her body screaming at the sudden motion, her scalp burning in pain. Yanking her hair, he forced her to look in the mirror thrust before her.

The physical pain Reuben was causing was forgotten. The ashen reflection of a terrified old woman stared at her. Gray streaked her hair. Huge protruding eyes were set in a face so thin it might have been a skull. Cheekbones jutted above lips as thin as a reed, pinched as though always in pain. Red sores festered at the corners of the reflection's mouth. Above her ragged, baggy tunic, every cord in her neck stood out. Her collar bones looked like twigs that would snap between one's fingers. She stretched out her hand to touch her reflection and saw the wrists of a skeleton, so small the bracelets Talitha once wove for a little girl would slide off.

Leah did not recognize this woman.

The face of a dead woman stared at her from the mirror.

He gave her hair a final yank and pushed her away from him, throwing the mirror against the wall with a noisy clatter. "By all rights, you should be dead. Yet you are not. What else could keep you alive but your sin? But, Leah, you are dead to me."

He sneered at her. "I came four days ago to bring you supplies. But what did I see? I saw you, a woman who is all but a corpse, walking with two women. What kind of women would walk with you, a woman of filth and sin and shame? Whores? Gentiles?

Samaritans?"

Leah closed her eyes at the thought of kind Tirzah and smiling Jerusha.

"I could not believe that you who are unclean would even look at other women, much less speak to them. I left at once and went to the Capernaum synagogue, praying that God would take your soul from this earth, that God would take you from the vile state in which you live. And yet, my dead wife still lives."

He paused for a long moment and then continued in a tone suddenly reasonable. "After all, I am not a sinful man, Leah. I am not. I do not deserve to live in this disgrace."

Reuben turned to Leah, his voice triumphant. "Today, I am no longer your husband. I asked the synagogue ruler here in Capernaum for a divorce. A divorce, Leah. I went to him, told him where you live, about your filthy uncleanness, your sin, about the twelve years of marriage I have spent filled with pain and misery... and he commended me, Leah! He praised me for all I have done for you for twelve long years! I am an honorable husband! He praised me for my faithfulness and sacrifice. The synagogue ruler willingly gave me the divorce I asked for. I am a good Jewish man, like him. He knows all about you and your sin, Leah."

Leah felt the trickle of shame course down her back. Was this the synagogue of her friends?

"I am a good husband, Leah, and I have fulfilled my duty to an unclean, sinful wife who lives a half-dead life. I am not the demon here, Leah, it is you. You are evil, possessed. Only Satan could keep someone like you alive."

He looked at her for a moment. "Leah, I will return to my life among the living and you... you will die as you should have done long ago. No longer will you torture me."

Reuben stopped in the door. "You killed your father with shame. You will not shame me anymore. You are worthless and insignificant. No one, no one will save you or heal you. No true Jewish rabbi - much less a Messiah - would touch a woman like you. Unclean, unwanted, amê."

As he turned to go, he uttered his final words to his wife.

"You can die or you can live forever. I care not. All I know is I will never return."

CHAPTER 21

Leah awoke in a stupor, weak and beaten, too exhausted to even lift her head.

"Why should I?" she thought dully. After Reuben's final words, she had fallen on to her bed in shock and had not moved since. Her things lay scattered on the floor where Reuben had dumped them. The few supplies he brought sat untended by the door.

Over and over, her mind relived the horrific scene of that morning. Reuben was not returning. Reuben had divorced her. Reuben had condemned her to begging, to starvation and to certain death. Without the small supplies he left her each month, she would die.

How could she, already half-dead, find her way to a market to sell her cloth or to purchase her food?

Without Reuben, she would have no wool for weaving, no wood to burn, no oil for the lantern, and no food to eat. No matter how frugal she was, the little he left her would soon be gone.

How could she, the much-loved daughter of her mother, crawl to a corner and beg for pennies from those passing, their eyes averted from her tragedy?

Without Reuben, there was no hope to ever find the healer from Nazareth.

Only a few days ago, she had walked to the well to meet Tirzah and her small laughing friend, to ask about Rebecca's son, to find out about Jesus. They had given her strength, a sudden rush of freedom and a renewed spirit. Something took root that day she should never have allowed to grow. Hope.

Now, her strength and spirit had died right along with that fragile shoot of hope. Reuben was right; she should have died years ago. Why was she not dead? Why did God torture her and those she loved?

Leah turned her face to the wall in shame, thinking of Reuben's announcement in the Capernaum synagogue of a dying woman's sin and her uncleanness. He had publicly divorced his evil, sinful wife, a separation approved and blessed by the local synagogue ruler. Was there more than one synagogue in Capernaum? What if her two friends learned of her shameful existence? What if their husbands came home and spoke of the man from afar who divorced his sick, bleeding wife? What if they learned that woman was her?

She couldn't bear their horror that was certain to follow such repugnant news. When they walked past her house, they would stay as far to the other side of the dusty road as possible. Perhaps they would go to the rabbis to be made clean for touching Leah's water jar, for entering her shabby house, for touching Leah.

Jerusha had hugged her. A great sob tore at Leah's throat.

She had refused to admit until now that the last few months her illness had gotten much worse. She was shockingly weak, yet the bleeding continued unabated.

When you slaughtered an animal for sacrifice, the priests cut its neck and let it struggle and bleed until it moved no more. How much longer could Leah pour out her blood and survive? After she saw her horrific reflection in the mirror that morning, she understood why Reuben always expected to find her dead. What a disappointment to him that she refused to die. How laughable that she would suggest someone heal her when she lay at death's door.

Each day she grew weaker. The daily trips to the well were nearly all she could endure, the occasional trips to the public baths now non-existent. She wove less and less. She found herself sleeping so often that day and night ran together. The pain and bleeding were constant. She had become little more than a frightful, walking skeleton. She had fainted at the well in front of Jerusha and Tirzah.

203

The light in her small house wore the orange cast of a setting sun. She must have slept all day.

Why had she not thrown herself on Reuben's feet, beseeching him to at least bring her only flour and wood once a month, even if he divorced her? To throw his copper coins to her instead of a beggar on the street? Why had she not clung to his robe, crying out until he relented and showed her whatever meager mercy he might still have in his harsh, hardened heart?

Leah was so tired. "Mother, I am sorry, I am so sorry. I have always loved you. All I prayed for in this world was to see you once again."

At the thought of her mother, Leah cried herself back to sleep.

☃

What time of day was it? She had no idea. The sun was long gone. Her lantern was unlit, and it was pitch dark. Was it only this morning that Reuben had abandoned her?

As always, Leah was overcome by a shocking thirst. With every bit of effort she could rouse, she crawled across the dirt floor to her water jar. It was almost empty, but Leah greedily drank the last remnant, trying to shake every drop from the jar.

Oh, if the need for water was not always pressing upon her! The little she drank did nothing to quench her terrible parching thirst.

Leah was thirsty. She was tired. She was dirty, and she knew her bandages long ago needed changing. She didn't care.

In all the years of her illness, Leah had never felt so painfully sick, so appallingly weak. Sitting there on the floor, she felt a hot, heavy flow of blood run down her leg. Perhaps her fate was to never be cured of this disease, this sin that afflicted her, to die here alone in a foreign city. Perhaps it was to be as Reuben wished, as the Ethiopian doctor had predicted so many years ago. Perhaps she was finally dying.

Leah started to cry. She knew what she had to do, but she didn't think she had the strength to do it.

Leah needed to sell the medallion. She needed to go home.

The thought of selling the medallion was her final devastation. "My bones are filled with decay," she whispered.

For these three long years, she had never once mentioned the medallion to Reuben. Sometimes she would pick up the bridal veil, hidden in her chest. She could feel the reassuring weight of the necklace through the hem. She would touch the medallion through the embroidered cloth and hold it close to her breast, a comforting proof that someone had once loved her.

She was a young bride again, Reuben was her groom. He could not look away from her. He was enchanted by her beauty, by her gown, by her jewelry and the medallion. He was enchanted by his wife.

Her friends and family sang to her, the beautiful Songs of Solomon. "How is your beloved better than others, the most beautiful of women?" They sang those words about her.

Her mother had placed the medallion around her neck. "May God bless this woman, my Leah, my precious treasure and daughter." The necklace of her mother, of beloved Savta.

Her mother had prayed for her, her hands pressing down on Leah's and the medallion. "Everlasting Father, I entrust this child of my heart into your Almighty hand and everlasting love. Selah."

"Selah." Leah whispered the word in the darkness. It sounded alien and strange to her.

The time had come. Her mother had sent the medallion with her for that singular reason. Sell the medallion and save herself, her mother had said. It was Leah's final heartbreak, but there was no other way. She should have done it long ago.

Why, why had she not sold it three years ago? Why had she not kept that promise to her mother?

Leah set down the water jar she was still holding and got up slowly. Her aching body hurt, even more so from Reuben's roughness. She walked across the room to the chest that held her clothing, defeated. It stood open, her clothing still lying on the ground from Reuben's brutal rampage so many hours ago.

She had no choice. She would get the medallion out, lay down with it, feel its comforting presence, and at the first sad opportunity, sell it.

Maybe Tirzah and Jerusha could help her. Jerusha said she would help her.

Jerusha and Tirzah. Leah cried at the thought of the women she did not know, the women she loved so much.

She knelt down and pawed through the mess Reuben had left,

searching for the blue bridal veil. It was at the bottom, right where she always left it. Even in the darkness, she recognized it at once. She pulled it out and held it to her chest.

The edge was frayed and torn, loose strings tangled in her fingers. Something was wrong.

The secret hem that held the medallion, the one sewn with her mother's secretive, painstaking stitches, was ripped open. The medallion was not there.

Leah stared in disbelief. The hem had been torn apart roughly, as though someone was in a hurry. She felt both hems with frantic hands, but without looking knew the veil no longer hid the medallion. "Perhaps the hem caught on something," Leah thought. She pulled everything out of her chest, shaking each garment, waiting to see if the medallion would fall out, panic fueling her body.

Nothing.

Leah scrambled about on the floor, feeling each garment thrown about on the ground, crawling desperately to each corner of her small house, searching for the heavy necklace that was her birthright and her salvation, her pain forgotten.

Nothing. Nothing, nothing, nothing.

"No!" Her scream shredded the air and her heart, and she fell over on the floor weeping.

The medallion was gone.

Reuben had asked her about Tirzah and Jerusha. He had watched Leah walking from the well with the two women, calling them unclean prostitutes like her. He had probably stood in this hovel he called a house another day, watching her slow, feeble footsteps to the well alone.

While he waited, Reuben had searched her meager possessions, either out of boredom, or suspicion, or just because he could.

No robbers bothered her small dusty street of insignificant homes. No thief would ever think to come to a house as dilapidated as hers.

Reuben had taken the medallion. She had no doubt.

Leah understood why Reuben finally divorced her. His rage at finding the hidden medallion fueled his meager courage. The promise of the medallion's great worth, of its wealth to him if he abandoned his wife, was all he needed to make the decision that had tormented him for years.

Her husband had stolen the medallion, divorced her and left her here to die.

The final, unbreakable tie to her mother was gone. "Use the medallion," her mother had whispered in a fevered hiss. "Use it to keep yourself alive and bring yourself home to me!"

But Leah, in stubbornness or weakness, refused to do what her mother had begged. And now the medallion and its memories, its blessings and even its promise of salvation when there was nowhere else to turn... all were gone.

There was nothing left for Leah. She was finished.

What Reuben had so deeply desired, so urgently wanted for these past twelve years, Leah at last wanted, too: that God would take her from this misery into the darkness of death.

She lay in the dirt and prayed. "'Arouse yourself, O Lord, come quickly.'"

The psalmist's words dropped in the darkness like pebbles into a black well. "'Quickly come, Lord.'"

She hesitated and then spoke the words she feared. "Jehovah, take me to my death."

She waited and prayed her own prayer. "Please, Jehovah, please hear me." She could no longer live in such pain and heartache.

There was no answer.

Not even God would come near her.

She heard her mother's voice, the words haunting her like a ghost in the shadowy night:

"'My God, my God, why have you forsaken me?
O my God, I cry out by day, but you do not answer...'"

Leah pressed her face to the dirt. She closed her eyes and tried to picture her mother, but her face was faint, fading away like smoke on the wind.

Instead her father stood before her, fists clenched, his face contorted, screaming the vicious words of the psalm at his worthless, unloved daughter:

"'I am poured out like water and
All my bones are out of joint...'"

Her father was replaced by the evil glare and angry voice of Reuben:

"'All who see me mock me;
They hurl insults, shaking their heads.
My heart has turned to wax; it has melted away within me.'"

His face melted away too, replaced by the frightening, emaciated ghost that was Leah, whispering the final words of the psalm.

"'Lay me in the dust of death.'"

The dying Leah faded into the gloomy darkness, too, whispering the final words over and over, the dust of death, the dust of death, dust of death, dustofdeath dustofdeath deathdeathdeath...

A heavy blackness moved through the room, covering Leah. She felt its weight pressing down upon her, suffocating her.

She closed her eyes and once again, with all her heart, prayed. "Oh Yahweh! If you exist, if you are real, hear my prayer."

For there was only one answer left for Leah, only one final request of her God.

Death. In the blackest hours of night, the smell of blood and dirt in her nostrils, weak with disease and despair, Leah prayed for death.

CHAPTER 22

Tinges of purple and orange stole in with the night's last touch of gray, a gentle light creeping through Leah's small window. It was early. The sun was not yet hanging in the sky but its morning warmth touched Leah's face.

Her mind was foggy with sleep. Still shaking the cobwebs from her mind, Leah looked around. The water jar lay on its side. Her possessions were strewn about the house, remnants from Reuben's rampage from yesterday. What time was it? What day was it? Why was she laying on the floor in the dirt?

Goodness! Leah had slept for an entire day and night! She was still wearing the clothes she had put on yesterday morning before Reuben's unannounced visit. Leah could not remember the last time she had slept for more than a few hours without waking up to a terrible dream or a pounding headache or her relentless thirst. She not even rolled over since she collapsed on the floor last night, sobbing over the dreadful loss of the medallion.

She stretched out, feeling every ache in her body from her eternal illness, her slumber on the floor and Reuben's violence as he had dragged her about, shoving her face into the mirror. She thought of all that had happened the last few days, perhaps more than had ever happened in her entire life.

The healing of the unknown Rebecca's son, the kindness of Jerusha and Tirzah, her new-found hope in this man from Nazareth...

The unspeakable treachery of Reuben, the theft of her beautiful bridal necklace, her desperate groping crawl across the dirt floor, searching for her medallion.

Her fervent, resolute prayer for death...

God had not answered her prayer.

"'For you have delivered me from death, that I may walk before God in the light of life.' Our God is a God of life, my dearest daughter!" Leah could hear her mother's hopeful voice so clearly, it felt as if she was sitting in the dirt beside Leah, stroking her hair.

God was not a God of death. He was a God of life. Leah was ashamed both of her beseeching request to at last die, and of her relief that God had chosen to ignore it.

"Thank you, O Mighty Jehovah," she whispered, a little bit self-conscious. God had not answered her prayer. Thank you, Jehovah.

A new thought crossed her mind. She was divorced. If... when Reuben remarried, wouldn't she then be an adulteress? Maybe not. A shamed woman, anyway. She couldn't really remember how that all worked. She was not sure if she cared, anyway.

She would probably never see Reuben again.

"Reuben." She jumped at the sound of her loud voice with its decided tone of disgust.

Reuben had never been as strong as she was. Leah knew this. She finally understood why Reuben had dumped her so unceremoniously here in Capernaum three years ago. He was afraid of Leah's strong and willful spirit. She would be much harder to get rid of in Caesarea Philippi, especially with her mother living right around the corner. Reuben was not as strong as Leah, even when she was at her weakest.

And now, he proved himself to be what her mother suspected all along: the worst of men, a weak husband, one who would steal from his dying wife even as he was planning to divorce her, the lowest of the low.

Leah did not know exactly how she would survive without Reuben, but it would be a blessing, a relief to never lay eyes on him again. Despite herself, she smiled.

"Reuben, schmeuben."

Her voice was loud, as though to make sure God heard. "Lord, strike all my enemies on the jaw and break the teeth of the wicked!" Leah heard the smallest giggle.

It was her!

She laughed out loud at the picture of Reuben with a mouth full of broken, jagged teeth. Let him gum boiled barley for the rest of his days. She laughed some more, laughed until tears of relief ran down her face.

"Oh, Mother, you are right. There is a psalm for everything!"

Reuben hated Leah for her sickness and her spirit and her refusal to give up, to die like a good, sick wife should. He hated her with good reason.

For after a sound, dreamless sleep for most of the night, after sleeping longer than she had slept in years, there was no doubt about it. Leah felt better this morning.

Not good, for she had all her usual aches and pains plus a few more courtesy of Rueben dragging her about by her hair. But still, she felt better. Different. She felt…

Happy. Leah felt happy.

How was that even possible?

Leah had no idea. But for whatever reason, Leah's heart was light this morning.

Reuben had left her. Well, she would just have to find a way to sell her cloth without him. Then she could buy whatever she needed herself.

"I will profit far more without his help," Leah answered her own question before practical Leah could even ask it. "If I can sell my cloth, I can buy supplies. I went to the market nearly every day with Mother and listened to my father for many years brag about how to drive a bargain in the market. Surely I learned something."

Reuben had stolen the medallion. Well, it was given to her with a blessing. He could not steal that.

"Just as my mother's blessing cannot be stolen from me, may the curse of his treachery, his betrayal, indeed his sin follow him for the rest of his life."

Reuben had never been happy, and he would not be happy in the future.

"Good. Let him suffer."

Leah would die, and probably soon, but everyone dies. Even

treacherous Reuben would die someday.

"To go the way of the earth," as her mother had said. So be it. Savta had not been afraid to die. Her mother had not been afraid of anything, not death, not Leah's father, not Reuben, not even her daughter's unclean bleeding. Leah was not going to be afraid any more either. She simply was not.

And anyway, she wasn't going to die today. No, today, for the first time in years, Leah was happy.

She was not going to lie here in her bed either, waiting for starvation to set in. Or sit here and die of her eternal thirst as though she were stranded in a vast desert somewhere, instead of only a short walk to the neighborhood well.

She would much rather die tromping around with a half-full jar of water sloshing around on her head than die in her bed, whining about her thirst.

God had not answered her fervent prayer, for she was alive! She had asked God to take her, and yet she was not dead.

She was alive and thirsty!

"How long will you lie there, you sluggard?"

Leah laughed out loud at the sound of her own voice.

"Oh, Savta, now we know what a sluggard looks like. A sluggard looks like me!"

The time to wash herself, to change her clothes and bandages, even the time to eat breakfast was later. Right now, with the sun barely in the sky, it was time to set off for the well.

Leah needed water.

CB

Leah's trip to the well was every bit as slow and excruciating as it always was, but the long rest God had granted her somehow had strengthened both her body and mind. Good thing, for her mind tumbled around with thought after thought.

What if Jerusha and Tirzah have heard about me at the synagogue? She whispered the thought to herself.

"You will just have to hope they did not." Strong Leah took control.

Where are the cloth traders in this big city? How will I find them?

"You will find the market, it can't be far. Once you find the market, you will find the shops that sell cloth. Just ask someone, Leah, even a stranger. A stranger will only see a woman carrying wool."

But how can I carry the wool back to my house, or carry what I weave to the market?

"You haven't even sold anything yet, Leah. We will worry about that when it happens."

What if the leper this Jesus healed wasn't really very sick after all?

"It doesn't matter if you are a little sick or a lot sick, Leah, if you are a leper you are unclean. Jesus healed a leper. Remember the lame man, the son of the unknown Rebecca? Jesus healed him too."

So why couldn't this man heal a faithful, Jewish woman who has suffered from bleeding for so many years?

"That's right," she said aloud to the empty street. "Why can't this Jesus heal me?"

The morning coolness felt fresh on Leah's face. The unrelenting heat of the sun was hours away. She never came early, not wanting to face shepherds who might be watering their flocks, or the early-rising women or any others who came to the well at sunrise. She had been afraid of what people might do when they saw her.

Sheep and goats were already at the water trough for the livestock. But no shepherd men were there, only boys wandering around with their bleating charges, laughing with each other as they jostled for a spot. Leah sat on the stone bench on the other side of the trough, cheered by the sight of the young boys, noisy sheep and spotted goats. Why had she worried?

It was quite pleasant sitting near the sheep trough, the slurping animals paying her no mind, a lonely baa loud in the sunshine. She bent over and looked hard at her worn reflection in the rippling water.

"All right, so this is who you are now," she whispered. "You cannot change it, no one cares. The Leah you once knew is dead, but in her place stands a new and different Leah. Reuben is dead to you and you are dead to Reuben. Your life goes on."

She thought about all the things Jerusha had told her about this Jesus, the man from Nazareth. He preached right here in Capernaum and healed people. Jerusha said that the man claimed to be the Son of

God, the Messiah. Jerusha believed this. Could Leah believe?

"Leah." She heard the voice behind her. She stared into the eyes of Jerusha, Tirzah at her side.

Looking at them, Leah saw two strong and beautiful women; faithful Jewish women, married, respected and loved, women who might have heard all about the stranger at their synagogue who was granted a divorce according to Jewish law from his unclean, sinful wife. Amê. They had touched her, an unclean woman. Leah had defiled Tirzah and Jerusha, too.

The women grew blurry as Leah's eyes filled with tears, overcome with remorse. Leah had defiled the only women who had shown her kindness for so long. Surely they knew now what she really was; surely they would not want to even speak to her...

"Why, Leah, the sun just came up! Do you come this early every day?" asked Tirzah. She did not sound angry at all.

What could she say? Leah sat there in desperate silence, suddenly aware she still wore her clothing from yesterday, wrinkled from where she had slept in them, dirty from crawling around on the floor. She smelled the tinny, coppery stench of her blood; she should have changed her bandages instead of recklessly rushing to the well.

What if they had heard about the bleeding woman? What if they knew that shameful woman was her?

And why in the world were her friends here so early? She had not yet formulated her next conversation with Tirzah and Jerusha. It was too much for Leah to process.

"Oh, Tirzah, Leah is doing exactly what we are doing." Jerusha spoke before Leah could gather her thoughts. "Leah has heard the news! She has come to the well so she can finish her work and then go to hear Jesus the Messiah!"

At these words, Leah's heart leapt. She looked up at the women. "He is here?" Her voice was a shaky squeak.

"Yes!" Jerusha smiled her answer, spinning once around for emphasis. "He is here! He is teaching today and..." she looked happy as she gazed at her friend, her confidant, and the woman who was like her sister. "Today Tirzah will come and hear the Messiah with me!" She looked at Leah. "Jesus was at our synagogue yesterday. Today he is teaching on the shores of Galilee."

The synagogue! Jesus was at the synagogue! The synagogue, where the law was upheld and worshipped. What if Jesus, Tirzah and

214

Jerusha were at the synagogue where Reuben had publicly announced her years of uncleanness and then divorced her?

Amê!

The terrible, ponderous, dreadful word came to her unbidden. She closed her eyes in shame. If this Jesus was the Messiah, surely the synagogue ruler would have told him about the sinful abomination and the poor faithful Jew named Reuben who endured such evil for twelve years. This Jesus probably knew about her already. Jerusha and Tirzah probably knew, too. If they didn't, they soon would. They too would condemn her and shun her just as the world had for so many years.

Her only friends would hate her.

The fragile hope born in Leah shriveled away. At the thought of the synagogue, its harsh rulers and rigid laws, and the certain contempt and ridicule of her friends, Leah felt the full force of her shame. She was unclean before God and every other human. The very touch of her was a sin. Amê.

What was she thinking? How could she, Leah, go to this stranger for healing? All the condemnation she had endured before the uncompromising law of her God and at the brutal hands of her father and husband washed over her. Amê, amê...

She felt hands grasp her own in a tight grip. Jerusha knelt before her. "Leah," she said softly, "Will you come with us?"

Something inside her snapped.

How could she ever have thought these women might be her friends? The moment she went to this Jesus for healing, they would learn of her darkest secret. They would hate her, mock her, and join the line of people who thought she was better off dead. Why had Leah thought these women might befriend someone like her? The faces of Reuben and her father sneered before her. Jesus could only heal her of her terrible sin and shame in secret, without anyone ever knowing.

And now, that would never happen.

"Don't touch me!" she shouted, wrenching her hands free. "Don't touch me! You don't know what I am! Don't touch me!"

Stop, Leah thought desperately, stop! Please, God, make me stop. Seal my lips, Lord! But the floodgate had opened. She was unclean and Jerusha had touched her.

"You don't know what I am! Do not... Don't touch me!"

Leah laid her head on the edge of the trough and wept, her heart broken.

After a moment, she felt a light touch on her shoulder. She wanted to shake the hand off, but she was too beaten to even shrug. "Don't touch me!" she had shouted at this woman who had only shown her kindness. "Don't touch me!"

Leah felt dirty and humiliated. She was too tired to speak, to move, to even look at these women. She did not lift her head, her great gasping sobs shaming her even more. The hand left her shoulder.

Leah heard the footsteps to the well and the quiet murmur of the two voices. She felt the stares of the impudent, insolent shepherd boys. "Yes, you leave me, too." she sobbed. "Leave me, leave me!"

She did not raise her head, her shame was too heavy to bear. The ruler of the Capernaum synagogue knew about her. Jesus went to that synagogue and so did Jerusha and Tirzah. They too would know of her secret.

This Jesus would never heal someone like her.

Leah had shouted at the two women she had grown to love, the only ones who had shown her any kindness in three long years.

Her defeat was complete.

"Stand up, Leah, and come with us." Leah lay there, as unmoving as a stone. She felt gentle hands on her arm, pulling her to her feet. "We have your water jar," Jerusha said. "Come with us."

Just as before, the two women carried their own jars on their heads and shared the weight of Leah's jar between them. Jerusha and Tirzah did not speak. Leah walked a few steps behind them. The chirp of the morning birds welcoming the bright sun was the only sound in the dusty street.

Where is the woman who woke up this morning with so much hope and happiness, she whispered to herself.

"She was a fool," answered the practical Leah.

Why is she so easily beaten, cast into despair?

"Because she cannot bear to lose one more thing. These faithful and kind Jewish women are the only ones to speak to you in three long years. Soon they will soon hate you, condemn you and shun you like everyone one else. It's better not to hope."

But maybe they don't know about me. How can they know?

"Just like before, Reuben has publicly shamed you, this time in the synagogue of Tirzah and Jerusha. The synagogue of Jesus, Jerusha's Messiah, an honored and holy Jewish man."

Perhaps my disease will not matter to them.

"You are fooling no one but yourself," she answered herself with a snort.

What happened to the Leah who was better off without Reuben, the Leah who wanted to live?

"As he wished, she is better off dead. Beaten, defeated, dead."

When they came to Leah's barren courtyard, the two women set down their jars. As before, Jerusha picked up Leah's and carried it inside. Leah did not enter. She did not want to be in her house when Jerusha was in there. Her few possessions were still scattered about from Reuben's rampage and her own desperate search for the medallion.

Jerusha walked up to Leah still standing outside.

"Leah." Her voice was tender. "Jesus is here. He is preaching today, that's why we went to the well so early. Leah, come with us or go without us, but you must go. He will be teaching in the place I told you, on the shores of Galilee."

Leah could not meet her eyes. She pulled her head veil tighter, shook her head and without a word went into her small house.

"Blessed are the poor in spirit, Leah." She turned at the soft words. Jerusha stood in the doorway. "Blessed are the poor in spirit, the broken, for theirs is the Kingdom of Heaven. That is what the man of Nazareth says, Leah. That no matter how broken, how fragile, how poor or destroyed your spirit is, you will be blessed by God."

"Tirzah and I," Jerusha hesitated and then stepped inside. "We can see you are sick and alone and… broken. But Jesus blesses the broken, Leah, he blesses them. 'Blessed are the poor in spirit!' Not just the rulers or the teachers or Jewish men, but all kinds of people, Leah, even the broken. He is truly the son of God. And Leah, if you believe… Jesus can heal you."

Through stiff lips, Leah whispered, "How can you know this? You don't even know me."

"I don't, Leah. But I can see what I can see, and I know what Jesus says: 'Judge not, for in the same way you judge others, you will be judged.' What I see is someone sick who is all alone and who needs healing. Yet, in your eyes, life exists and fights to be free. I see it in your eyes, Leah. I know it in my heart."

She took Leah's hand in her own. "Come see Jesus, Leah. He is what he claims to be, the son of God. He blesses those who are broken. I know, if only you will believe, he will bless you. Come to Jesus, Leah."

After a moment, Jerusha's soft footsteps faded away.

Leah sat alone, transfixed. Bless the broken? Well, few could be more broken than she.

But if she went, and her secret was found out, what would happen to her? If she touched others in the crowd, they too would be unclean. She was afraid of both the public humiliation and the crowd's retaliation and punishment. "Amê, Amê!" shouted by a crowd of believers trying to see Jesus of Nazareth.

If she went with her friends, they would be treated in the same reviled manner as Leah. And how could she tell this man of her affliction? How could she give voice to her horrible shame?

And what if he really was the Son of God? If he was the Son of God…. Wasn't it the laws of God that required her to be separated from the world and all she loved?

She could not make sense of it.

If only she could meet the Man of Nazareth alone, confess her sin, ask for forgiveness, beg for mercy and healing, and then leave without being seen by staring, condemning eyes.

Unbidden, Leah heard her mother's voice. "I call on you, O God, for you will answer me."

Her voice took up the words as though she and her mother were singing them together. "Hear me and show me the wonder of your great love."

Her mother's voice was gentle. "His love is great, Leah. God will answer you."

She saw Jerusha's smiling face. "If only you believe, he will bless you, Leah."

God answers prayer, thought Leah. He says so in his words to his people.

Is this the answer to my prayers?

Who had sent these two women past Leah's door every day, sharing a conversation that brought Leah her only comfort and hope? Who sent them, if not God?

Who caused them to talk of miraculous healings by a Messiah

just at the moment they passed Leah's hiding window, talking about the renewed life of a cripple and a leper, if not God?

Who would plant the gentle seed of kindness in the two women's hearts, lead them to help the odd, lonely stranger that was Leah, if not God?

Everyday Leah knelt in prayer. So, if she believed in God enough to pray to him, why wouldn't she believe that God would answer?

Who else but God gave her the will to get up each day when she could have so easily given up? Leah had an inner strength, a fierce desire to survive. Where did that fight come from if not from God? No matter how beaten down, how weary, how close to death she was, who else but God always revived her?

Why wouldn't God's hand be in this? Why wouldn't God lead Leah to this alien city to meet the healer from Nazareth? God had answered the prayers of Deborah and Sarah and Esther and Leah of old. Why wouldn't God answer hers?

Leah knelt right there on the dirt floor. She prayed as her mother prayed, intense and passionate, the words of King David her own with their fervent hope and faith, words cried out to Jehovah that David and her mother loved.

"'When I am afraid, I will trust in you.
In God, whose word I praise, will I trust.
I will not be afraid.'"

The words of the psalmist strengthened her. "Jehovah, I will trust you," she took a deep breath, "and I will not be afraid anymore."

She sat remembering the verse's last words, the ones she had not yet spoken, words that resolutely nudged her, persistent, insisting they be part of her prayer.

"What can mortal man do to me?" Though she spoke out loud, her voice sounded as puny as a newborn baby's whimper.

She cleared her throat, lifted her head, and this time her voice was confident. "What can mortal man do to me?"

Resolutely, Leah stood to get ready. Jerusha told her to go and hear Jesus, and that was just what she was going to do.

The sun was already bright above the horizon, promising the

heat that would soon follow. Leah had a big day ahead of her and she still had much to do. What could man do to her indeed?

Mortal man beware! Leah was in a hurry.

CHAPTER 23

Leah recklessly ate a double portion of the bread and wine for her breakfast, followed with plenty of water. She always felt better when she ate more; she was just always so worried about running out of food. She used most of the water to bathe. Jerusha and Tirzah had left the water not even an hour ago, and it was already almost gone! Another rash act. But the rank odor of two days' blood was a grim reminder of the disease she carried. Leah wanted to be as clean as possible.

She dressed with care, forgoing the bright sash and veil of her youth for a common brown wool instead, one that would blend into the crowd she feared. She tucked a bit of bread into a pocket, wishing she had a water skin to bring. Perhaps there would be a well nearby. She tucked her small dipper in her pocket just in case. This would be the longest walk she had taken since she first walked to Capernaum three years ago. She was going to walk to the Sea of Galilee to see Jesus! If only she could walk that far...

"She sets about her work vigorously; her arms are strong for her tasks." The memory of Savta's laughter rustled in the room.

Strong arms! At last, a proverb that would encourage rather than pass judgment on her.

Leah stood in her doorway and took a deep breath. She turned to the right and walked to the spot where she had first overheard Jerusha and Tirzah talking about Jesus, a cripple man and a leper. She stopped, hearing the faint echo of Jerusha's joyful voice, "The amê! He heals the unclean, Tirzah!"

She stared down the unfamiliar street. Could she do this? She heard the soft echo of her mother's voice, Savta crowing in laughter: "She has strong arms for her task!"

Squaring her shoulders, Leah took the first steps of her journey into a foreign and unknown land, the fearsome first steps right outside her own front door.

ᘓ

Leah carefully recounted the directions Jerusha had given her to the place where Jesus would teach. She was a little worried, for after only a few steps from her house, the street was alien to her. Would she be able to find the Sea of Galilee?

As soon as she turned the corner of her quiet, dusty street, however, she entered a world filled with people. She lived right by the main thoroughfare in the village! Leah had not even known.

Only a few moments from the place she had lived for three long years were the busy sights of Capernaum. Roman soldiers marched on one side of the street. Fearful, she kept her head bowed low until they passed. A rich woman with the palest white skin wearing a gold and white gown floated by, four dark men in a foreign dress holding her white litter aloft from the crowd.

There was the synagogue, so close to where Leah lived. It must be the synagogue of Jerusha and Tirzah. She recognized the massive gray columns as though she had seen and not just heard about them, the newness of its construction still visible in the sheen of its marble columns. She pulled her veil tighter, the sight of this alien synagogue still enough to make her tremble.

She walked a short distance more before she found the market. A large square surrounded by shops of cloth, sandals, and perfumes, it was huge. Tents stood in rows in the middle of the courtyard, where noisy merchants sold flour and onions and leather and wool ready for the spinning.

The market was much larger than the one in little Caesarea Philippi. Before he hid her away, Reuben probably came to

Capernaum to sell his father's flax, her father's linen and her mother's beautiful weaving here. Her heart skipped a beat. The magnificent work of her mother's hands might be right here in one of these shops, but she knew she dared not stop to look.

The streets were wide and spacious, paved with a black stone. Down a side street, she saw the bright flags and tents of a caravan, the brown humped camels tethered nearby. Capernaum must be a stop on one of the many trade routes to Egypt or the Great Sea to the west.

Leah had to work hard not to lose herself in the sights and sounds. All this was less than twenty minutes from her house, even at her slow pace.

"Why did I never venture out of my house?" she wondered.

Because Reuben shamed you into staying out of sight, hidden and alone.

She scoffed at the thought of Reuben's professed kindness to her, bringing her food and wine, wood and wool from what she thought was a great distance. The market was so close, even puny Leah could make the trip. He could have left her money and she could have bought her own supplies!

"Even the kindest acts of the wicked are cruel." She spoke out loud, and an old woman sitting in a nearby doorway smiled at her. Another useful proverb, so much better than reminding herself what a sluggard she was!

She was thankful that Reuben was no longer part of her life. Her mother had taught her all she needed to know to survive.

After what seemed like a mile of walking, the houses grew fewer on either side of the street. She had fretted about having to ask a stranger for directions, but there was no need for her worries. The closer she got to her destination, the more the crowd grew.

She fell into the steady stream of people, who in the narrow street moved at such a slow pace that Leah could easily keep up. Everyone was headed the same direction, and what a mixed group of people it was!

There was a Roman centurion in all his military finery, gray hair gleaming in the sunshine. His erect stride was decisive and commanding, parting the crowd around him without a word.

A slump-shouldered, grim-faced man walked by, he and his followers pushing people out of the way. The kippah on his head was a rich gold color, embroidered with threads of a deeper hue, the same color as his long robes and tassels gracing the four corners of his fringed prayer shawl… One of the Sadducees in all his Temple finery, like those she had seen as a girl on pilgrimage to the Holy City with her parents. The dour man's entourage was followed by several of the Temple guard.

She had seen the Temple guard as a young girl visiting Jerusalem, sullen men carrying their shields and swords like badges of honor. "Why do we need guards in the Temple?" she had asked her father. "Isn't God all powerful over his enemies?" His face had been annoyed as he shushed her, slits of eyes peering at her as though she had spoken blasphemy.

Most of the crowd, however, held people just like her, except maybe healthier! Jewish men, with their prayer shawls around their shoulders, Jewish women with their children and friends, Gentiles in their foreign dress. There were rich men in finery and poor men in patched robes, but all were heading the same direction.

She heard snatches of conversations: "Cast a demon from a man."

"Shriveled hand just like new!"

"Lame Eri now walks, can you believe it?"

"Healed a deaf mute; sent him home to his family."

"Cast a fever from a woman."

Cast a fever from a woman! So Jesus healed women too! Her heart twisted when she spied a woman tenderly holding the arm of a frail older woman.

Oh, if she were healed, the first thing she would do would be to run to Caesarea Philippi to find her mother! She would run every single step of the way! Oh, Yahweh, please let me see my mother's face once more.

Leah caught her breath. As the crowd thinned out into a field, she caught sight of a shimmer of light. The Sea of Galilee! It sparkled before her in the sunlight, its deep blue surface glittering like thousands of stars in the sky.

On the far side, she could see a faint mountain. Why surely that was Hermon, the grand mountain of her youth, the mountain that looked down right now on Caesarea Philippi! The horrible trip with Reuben to Capernaum made her forget that the two cities were really not that far apart, only a three-day walk for someone who was not half-dead.

The crowd no longer carried her along. Leah moved at a much slower pace, grateful her goal was so near. She pushed towards the shore, careful not to brush against anyone.

A man sat in a boat anchored in the green sea, as the white gulls shrieked and wheeled in the cloudless blue sky above. He sat alone, his head bowed in prayer. The boat rocked gently as the waves slapped against its side, splash after splash a faint rhythm under the hum of the crowd.

Surely that must be Jesus!

Leah wanted to get closer. She pressed forward until finally she could move no more. She was only twenty paces from the man, and from this vantage point she would be able to see and hear everything. She claimed a small piece of ground and sat down with a thud, grateful to rest her aching legs and back. Some old men sat behind her talking as a woman coaxed four small children to sit down right in front of her.

Leah ignored her tired body. She wondered how anyone might approach this man when he was sitting in a boat. Leah had never been in a boat before. The Galilee looked wide and beautiful and forbidding.

"When will he teach?" the voice behind Leah said.

"Eh? Soon," another answered. "If Jesus comes ashore, there are too many who come only for the healing and not to hear his word."

Leah watched the man in the boat with some curiosity. She wanted to be healed, but she also wanted hear his word. She was anxious to hear what this man – the one Jerusha so emphatically claimed was the Messiah – would say.

She looked around again, but was relieved to not see Jerusha. Leah preferred to keep her shame a secret from her friend. If she could only be healed, Tirzah and Jerusha would never need to know.

Leah noticed a small group of men on the shore near the boat where Jesus sat. If anyone approached, the men would stand and listen, but not let them any closer. They were Jewish men, clad in the rough clothes of those that worked hard for a living. But Leah sensed from the jerks of their heads toward the man in the boat, from the confidence they had as they spoke to others and smiled at him, that these were the intimate acquaintances of the man from Nazareth.

Why didn't this Jesus surround himself by leaders from the synagogue and Temple priests?

She thought of old men that were the synagogue council of her youth, of the slump-shouldered crabby man she had just seen in the street, of the Temple guard stomping down the street. The men near the boat seemed like infinitely better company than any of the important ones. The men near the boat looked, well, happy.

Jesus stood. His followers sat down. At once, the mass of people was silent.

"Blessed are the poor in spirit, for theirs is the kingdom of heaven."

Leah's eyes filled with tears. The exact words Jerusha had said to her that morning! Blessed are the poor in spirit...

She, Leah, broken and worn, was blessed! Her God had not abandoned her. She could hardly contain herself that the first words she would hear Jesus speak would echo those of her friend.

"Blessed are those who mourn, for they will be comforted."

Those that mourn, Leah thought. O Lord God, is my mother mourning me somewhere, wondering if I am dead or alive? Oh, Jehovah, I ask that my mother would find comfort.

"Blessed are the meek, for they will inherit the earth. Blessed are those who hunger and thirst for righteousness, for they will be filled."

Oh to be filled! Didn't she, Leah, seek her God everyday in prayer and the words of the great kings David and Solomon?

"Blessed are the merciful, for they will be shown mercy."

Leah said a small prayer of thanksgiving for her new friends, so merciful and kind to her, a stranger.

"Blessed are the pure in heart, for they will see God. Blessed are the peacemakers, for they will be called sons of God. Blessed are those who are persecuted because of righteousness, for theirs is the kingdom of heaven."

The Kingdom of Heaven for the broken and the persecuted!

Blessed are the persecuted," thought Leah. Didn't my own people, my own husband and father, cast me out as unclean and unfit? Wasn't I left alone in the world, persecuted by silence and condemnation and the loss of all I loved?

"Blessed are you when people insult you, persecute you and falsely say all kinds of evil against you because of me. Rejoice and be glad, because great is your reward in heaven."

Leah felt a quiet joy awaken inside her. Her anger, her bitterness, her sadness, yes, even her pain… all were being edged aside by a quiet assurance that her Father in Heaven loved her even as the world despised her. She had been falsely accused! She had been insulted and reviled! Yet, her reward in heaven would be great. God loved broken, forgotten Leah. Someone loved her, after all.

Leah looked at the teacher, who was still speaking. If only she could remember every word!

"You have heard that it was said, 'Love your neighbor and hate your enemy.' But I tell you: Love your enemies and pray for those who persecute you, that you may be children of your father in Heaven."

The words cut straight to Leah's heart. "Love Reuben, who tore me from my mother and abandoned me in an unknown city? Love my father who disowned me and shunned me? Love my enemies and pray for those that have hurt me?"

The voice of Jesus continued. "If you love those who love you, what reward will you get? Are not even the tax collectors doing that?"

Leah thought of Jerusha's words. "If I were sick and weak and lying in the dirt at your feet, wouldn't you pick me up too, Leah? Jesus said to give and it will be given to you! A good measure, running over into my lap." She remembered Jerusha's laughter: "Some of us have bigger laps than others!"

For so many years, Leah thought only of how the world and her body and the law of God had judged and mistreated her. Not about others and how she treated them.

She thought again of Jerusha. Would she help a stranger lying in the dirt as Jerusha had helped her? Would she gladly get water for a thirsty woman sitting at the well, or tell a complete stranger about a man who healed the sick and the lame and the unclean?

"No." Leah spoke the word out loud. She closed her eyes at that unwelcome truth. She had been so worried about hiding her own shame from others, she would not stop to help a stranger. She had only prayed that God would help her in her misfortune. "I only prayed for me and the person I loved, my mother," she thought. "No one else, ever."

Jesus was still speaking. How could she remember every word

he said, when every word he spoke gave rise to new truths in Leah's heart?

"Therefore, I tell you, do not worry about your life, about what you will eat or drink; or about your body, what you will wear. Is not life more important than food, and the body more important than clothes? Look at the birds of the air; they do not sow or reap or store away in barns, and yet your heavenly Father feeds them. Are you not much more valuable than they? Who of you by worrying can add a single hour to his life?"

Was she more valuable than the gray sparrow flitting above her head right now, more precious than the shrieking gulls wheeling above the blue sea?

"I am," she whispered. "I am." All her worries about the work at her loom, the walk to the well, food and supplies, her loneliness, illness, living or dying...

As if in response Jesus said: "So do not worry, saying, 'What shall we eat?' or 'What shall we drink?' or 'What shall we wear?' For the pagans run after all these things. Your heavenly Father knows that you need them. But seek first his kingdom and his righteousness, and all these things will be given to you as well."

He paused. "Therefore do not worry about tomorrow, for tomorrow will worry about itself."

"Don't worry about tomorrow." Leah actually said the words out loud. She felt as though a huge weight had been lifted from her shoulders. "Don't worry about tomorrow!" She said it out loud again, this time with joy.

The woman with the four small children sitting in front of Leah turned around and smiled at her. "Don't worry about tomorrow!" she repeated after Leah, nodding in agreement before turning back to the man from Nazareth.

What worries about tomorrow does this woman bear, Leah thought, that she too seeks Jesus? Leah suddenly bowed her head, closed her eyes and prayed, right there on the shore of the Sea of Galilee.

"Lord, take care of this woman and her small children; feed them, clothe them, provide them with shelter and keep them in your care. Bring them ...joy. And Lord God," Leah paused, struggling to give this new thought words, "Thank you for how you have provided for me. Amen."

Surprised at herself, Leah smiled. She usually prayed the way her mother did, through the words of King David. She could not remember the last time she had prayed for anything but to ask that she be healed, she be fed, she be reunited with her mother, she be this, she be that. She could not remember being thankful for anything for a long, long time.

This prayer felt good, it felt right. It felt happy.

Leah looked up. Jesus was looking right at her, as though he had seen her praying. Her eyes widened as she looked all around her. Surely he was not looking at her. He was only looking this direction, not at her, not at insignificant, unclean Leah. There were hundreds of people all around. Jesus could not have seen her prayer, much less heard it.

"Ask and it will be given to you; seek and you will find; knock and the door will be opened to you. For everyone who asks receives; he who seeks finds; and to him who knocks, the door will be opened."

Leah froze, paralyzed by the words.

The voice of Jesus continued, but she could only think of the teacher's last words. She had just finished praying that someone else's needs be met, that God would protect the small family in front of her. In response to her prayer, Jesus told to her to ask, to seek, to knock. That she would receive, that she would find, that the door would be opened. She was motionless at the response to her prayer, the beauty of the promise before her.

As the day went on, Leah sat on the ground listening to Jesus of Nazareth, hiding each word in her heart, praying that every word would never be forgotten. If she were never healed, her life would still be changed for having heard the Messiah. The words he spoke would comfort her forever, words of love and mercy and grace. With every word he spoke, the joy in her heart grew.

As the sun set behind her, Jesus sat down in the boat. The men on the shore scrambled around, throwing in cloaks and parcels of brown leather, rolling out the sails and securing the nets. They were obviously experienced fisherman. As they completed their work, they jumped in the boat and left, sailing east across the Sea of Galilee. Several boats followed in their wake.

Leah stood with the rest of the crowd. She heard people all around her, their hands outstretched, begging, shouting for Jesus to return. Two men pushed past her, their arms lifting a man whose legs were limp and useless. Another man pressed forward, his deformed arm clasped to his chest. Women knelt on the shore, arms lifted up, pleading. "Come back, Messiah!"

Leah saw the press of the crowd, people begging Jesus for healing. But she stayed where she was. All Leah could think about were the words she heard that day. Her illness was forgotten.

"They will return to Capernaum," Leah heard the man speaking behind her. She turned around, anxious to hear more. She ducked her head, eyes on the ground, and pulled her veil tighter.

"His disciples, the men who got in the boat with him, they are from Capernaum," he continued.

Leah followed behind the two old men, hoping she could keep up to hear their conversation. However, the two old men walked slower than Leah on her worst days. It seemed both were a bit deaf, too, for she could every word from several steps away.

"His disciples are from Capernaum?" his companion asked.

"Yep. The boat they were in belongs to Simon the fisherman. His house is right down this road."

"Right down the road?"

"Yep. He owns that boat and employs several men to help him. You know him, eh?"

"Can't say I do."

"Sure you do, name's Simon, he married the only child of the old fisherman Obal."

"How is old Obal?"

"Dead many years, you remember. He died right after Simon married his daughter. Simon's lived in Obal's house ever since. Lives with his mother-in-law, eh?" The man nudged his companion.

"There's the house, see?" he pointed down the road.

"Which house?"

"That house. Old Simon married well, eh? After Obal died, Simon sold his boat, sold his father-in-law's boat, bought a bigger boat, and got a big house in the bargain. Nothing wrong with marrying well, eh?" The man elbowed his companion again.

"Helpful old Obal died right away," his companion snorted. "These disciples, are they all from Capernaum?"

"I don't know them all, just the fisherman Simon and his younger brother Andrew. And the two sons of Zebedee. Those boys left the nets and their father to follow Jesus. Zebedee has a couple of boats, one for him and two more, one for each boy. He was none too pleased, eh?"

His companion grunted.

"They say old Zebedee had a fit until he met the man from Nazareth. His wife made him go to meet Jesus, because he is her relative, some say. Don't know that for sure, but now the whole family follows. Except poor Zebedee who stays behind to fish."

"I'd probably rather fish, eh?"

"One of Zebedee's sons told him, 'We'll always have the sea, we'll always have the fish, but we won't always have the Messiah!' Can you imagine telling your father that?"

"A wise son brings joy to his father, but a foolish son grief to his mother, eh?" his friend elbowed the first man back to make sure he appreciated his humor, courtesy of King Solomon. Leah found herself smiling, too.

"Joy, grief, I can't tell the difference. My wife says I bring joy home every day when I leave and grief home when I return every night!" Both men laughed. Leah smiled at the thought of this old man and his wife, surely married in their youth, companions in life for many years.

He motioned to a house on his left. "When Jesus is here, he stays right there, at the house of Simon." The old men stopped in front of the house. Leah, a few steps behind, stopped too. "Simon has that big house because it was his wife's mother's, eh? The only people there are Simon, his wife, and their only child, a girl. Oh, and his mother-in-law. Simon probably follows Jesus so he can be healed of his own illness."

"What illness is that?"

"The illness of living with three generations of women!"

Leah let the old men walk on, their laughter fading away as they hobbled on. She stood in front of the house of Simon the fisherman, the crowds walking around her. Jesus stayed here. Perhaps people came to this very house to be healed.

When Jesus returned, would he come to this house? Perhaps she could just hide nearby and see him, talk to him as he entered the home of Simon and his wife. She stood in the street, gazing at the house, even as the thinning crowds pushed and jostled around her. She stared at the house, afraid to breathe. Jesus stayed here.

How could she meet this man, this teacher that was loved and revered by so many? She swayed slightly, an abrupt reminder that if she did not start her long journey back to her house now, she might have to spend the night sleeping in the street right in front of the house where Jesus stayed. She smiled at the thought and turned towards her house, her body weary from the long day but her heart light.

Jesus stayed in this house.

CHAPTER 24

Leah's thoughts of all she had seen and heard that day were soon overshadowed by a gnawing fear she might not be able to make it back to her house. She stopped every few minutes to rest, finding a house or building to lean against. The cramping spasms in her back and belly took her breath away, and she could tell her bandages were saturated with blood.

The orange glow of the sky told her the sun would soon set. The hot air of the afternoon was replaced by a cool breeze. Leah pulled her veil tighter to her, the chill of the approaching night blowing through her threadbare gown.

The sights and sounds she had gawked at earlier were now all replaced by one thought. "Please Lord, help me. Thank you for this wonderful day, but please... help me make it to my house."

She had been walking for a long time, past the houses, the market, the synagogue, each step a little slower than the last. The streets had turned back to dirt from the rough black stones. "At least it will hurt less if I topple over," Leah thought. "If Jerusha walks by and finds me sprawled in the dirt again, I wonder if she will haul me to my house a second time?" She tried to smile at her own joke.

The sweat ran from under Leah's veil down her face and neck

even as she shivered with cold. She was so thirsty. She had hoped to pass a well somewhere on the busy main street of Capernaum, but was not surprised that she had not. Wells were always on the side streets, out of the main traffic, far away to accommodate both women and livestock.

Almost two hours had passed since Leah had left the seaside. Getting back was taking much longer and was far more difficult than she had ever imagined.

Finally, Leah saw the corner she knew to be her own.

"Only a few more steps, Leah," she whispered to herself. "You can do it. Please, Jehovah, help me do it."

Her street, where that morning she had started her great adventure, was so close. She turned the corner and could see her small courtyard, just a few houses away.

But she could not help herself. She would have to rest or risk fainting. Crestfallen, she looked down the deserted street and then sat, leaning her back against the wall of the home on the corner.

It felt so good to sit down. "Don't fall asleep like a beggar in the dirt, Leah," she scolded herself.

I couldn't fall sleep, she snapped at herself. Her legs were throbbing harder than her heart.

If she only had a drink. Just a sip of cool water, to strengthen her. Leah looked around as though a water jar might materialize on the stoop of the house she leaned against.

"'Stolen water is sweet, she says, and bread eaten in secret is pleasant.'"

Leah smiled at the scolding words of Savta and leaned her head against the mud wall. As she rested, her thoughts turned back to the day. To hear Jesus speak was to hear the promised Messiah, Leah thought. She had heard his words of promise, words he seemed to direct straight to her. She had prayed, for herself, but for others too. It had been a long time since she had prayed for anyone but Leah.

Jerusha said Jesus healed a leper and a lame man. She must be right, or so many people would not come to him with their sick. All day she had overheard the crowd talking about the people Jesus had healed.

But the words he spoke! Surely a man like that was exactly who Jerusha said he was, the Messiah. Surely it was true.

"What's wrong with you?"

234

Startled, Leah opened her eyes to see a small brown face peering at her. He moved closer until their noses were almost touching, so close that his brown eyes were nearly crossed.

"Nothing," Leah's voice was a weak, raspy whisper. She could feel the heat radiating from the curious little face. She pulled her face into a semblance of a smile.

At once, his sturdy brown legs sprang to life like an arrow shot from the bow.

Leah remembered Reuben thrusting the mirror into her hands and seeing her ghastly reflection. She smiled again, she couldn't help it. She was very sick indeed if the sight of her smile scared away small boys.

She could hear his jumble of words through the open window above her head. Quick footsteps followed. Leah wanted to stand but had no strength to do so.

"Oh, my goodness, my dear, are you all right?" The woman's voice was not angry or judging. She sounded concerned - and kind.

Leah cleared her throat and tried to find her voice. "I live just a few houses away," Leah whispered, her voice gaining strength as she talked. "I am…. I'm not well today. I am sorry, I just stopped here a moment to rest before I walked the rest of the way."

The woman bent down and looked at her almost as closely as the little boy had. A smile spread across her face.

"Why, hello! I remember you. You sat right behind me today listening to the Man of Galilee! I sat right in front of you. Remember? 'Don't worry about tomorrow?' That's what Jesus said. And that's what you said to me!"

"Don't worry about tomorrow," Leah echoed. Of course. The woman with the four small children who had sat right in front of her that afternoon loomed over her.

"Oh, my goodness, and to think you live nearby. Why have we never met? Oh never mind! Right now, let's worry about getting you home. Eliza! Run fetch a dipper of water." The small girl hovering behind her mother's skirts broke into a trot, with an impish smile back at Leah. She was missing all of her front teeth, top and bottom, and had the biggest brown eyes Leah had ever seen.

The little girl shot through the door where two curly haired toddlers clung for balance, one sucking his thumb.

"Where is your house again? Just down the street, you said?

Why have I never seen you at the well? We'll get you some water and then we can help you walk the last little bit to your home."

Leah rested her head against the wall while the woman continued talking. She seemed to expect no answers to her questions. The non-stop words comforted Leah.

"Oh, wasn't the teacher wonderful today? Have you ever heard him speak before? I have. I just love it when he talks about 'those who are blessed!' Blessed are the broken, and the grieving, the hungry and thirsty. In this house, someone is always hungry and thirsty! And, oh! When he told us we are more important than the birds of the air, and right then those beautiful white gulls flew by in the blue sky, oh! And how he told us we cannot add one single hour to our lives by worrying! Oh!"

The small girl crept close to her mother and stretched her hands to Leah, a dipper of water in one and a small piece of bread in her hand. Leah grabbed the water and drank thirstily. Water, oh blessed water! She leaned her head on the wall in relief.

"Ah, Eliza, did you bring our friend a bit of food from our table? You are the sweetest girl a mother could ever wish for."

Leah took the bread from the small girl with the wide brown eyes. It was wheat bread, still steaming from the oven. Leah could not remember the last time she had eaten wonderful wheat bread while it was still hot. It smelled delicious. Leah popped the entire piece into her mouth. It *was* delicious! She swallowed it almost whole and felt the strength of joy surge up through her body.

The woman picked up the girl and hugged her with a tight squeeze and big smile. "You are the best daughter, ever!" Leah's heart expanded to see how much this mother loved little giggling Eliza.

"Thank you." Leah said in what she hoped was a stronger voice. "I think I can walk the rest of the way, it is not far. The water and the bread helped me. Thank you, thank you so much." Leah knew the woman could hear the complete weariness in her babbling, but she was so relieved by the kindness of this woman, the sweetness of these children, and most of all, by the nearness of her house.

The woman extended her hand and helped Leah to her feet. She did not let go of Leah's hand, but instead, pulled it to her in an iron grip. Leah could not have pulled her hand away if she tried. The woman's words were intense.

"One day, I went to hear the teacher from Nazareth. There weren't so many people there that day, and my children just ran up to him. He took each one of my children and blessed them! One of the disciples tried to shoo them away, but Jesus told him to let them be. 'Let the little children come to me!' he said. He held my four on his lap, one at a time, and blessed them and prayed with them. My children! And, Jesus laughed with them! My four little ones were crawling all over the Teacher, but he just held them and laughed... like he loved them. Like they were his own..."

The woman's voice trailed off. "Jesus isn't like any Jewish teacher I have ever seen."

Leah nodded.

The woman broke their silence. "There has never been a man like Jesus," she said passionately, still gripping Leah's hand. "Never a man like Jesus."

She looked at Leah, her gaze direct and unblinking. "Who do you think he is?"

Leah shook her head. "I am not sure I know," she said. "Never have I heard anyone teach like he taught today. A lesson of love and kindness and forgiveness. Those are words I have not heard for many years." Leah tried to soften the bitter edge in her voice. "My friend, she says this man is the Messiah."

"The Messiah," the woman said, releasing Leah's hand. "The Messiah, come to set the Jews free. My husband has heard that, too. Can it be?" She looked at Leah with shining eyes. "A Messiah to rule like King David, to restore the land to the Jews, to roust out the hated Romans and their gods and taxes and murderous ways! Oh! The Messiah."

She continued talking as though Leah had asked a question. "It's true, you know. What they say about Jesus. They say he has healed many people. Lepers, cripples, the blind, Jews and Romans, rich and poor, men, children... even women like you and like me. That's what they say about this Jesus." She froze in a sudden silence, as though entranced.

"Eleazar!" she hollered, making Leah jump. The small boy who found Leah first popped his head over the window sill. "Eleazar, come here." Obediently he trotted out the door.

She turned to Leah. "Eleazar will walk you home." The woman held up her hand to silence Leah's protest and bent down to her oldest son. "If anything happens, you help this lady sit and run, run, run back to find me, do you hear?"

The boy nodded, happy at this important mission given to him by his mother.

"Now go, and hurry! The lady is tired and wants to go home. And Eleazar, no talking! Come straight back home to me."

As Leah turned to walk away with Eleazar at her side, the woman threw up her hand in parting. "Remember! Don't worry about tomorrow. Jesus told you, you told me and now I tell you again… Tomorrow can worry about itself!"

With a laugh, the woman said to her son, "Come straight back, Eleazar!" She grinned at Leah and turned into her small well-lit home, the rest of her children clinging to her robe.

☙

At last Leah stood in her small house. She was so tired, she could not wait to lie down. She slipped behind the curtain to change her bandages. Oh, she had so little water left! Tirzah and Jerusha had carried a full jar of water to her house that morning. She recalled her reckless use of water, washing away two days of blood and dirt before she left to hear the teacher, drinking her fill before she made the long walk to Galilee.

"Shame on you, Leah, you know better than that!" But her scolding was good-natured, not cross.

She poured a tiny bit of water on a cloth, using as little as possible to clean herself and change her bandages. Pawing through the bags Reuben had left her, she pulled out some bread, dried fish and wine. She sat at her table, said her prayers and then ate every crumb as though she were starving. She lay on her bed, weary, yet overwhelmed with gratitude for her day and the help of the woman and little Eleazar.

She felt happy.

A favorite Psalm of her mother's came to mind:

"When I was in great need, he saved me.
Be at rest once more, O my soul,
    for the Lord has been good to you.
For you, O Lord, have delivered my soul from death,
    my eyes from tears, my feet from stumbling."

The Lord had certainly been good to Leah today.

"Selah." Leah whispered in the dark for good measure.

She lay silent in the dark, thinking, remembering Jesus, his head bowed in prayer as he sat alone in the gently rocking boat.

She was tired, but she had to do this.

Leah used all her remaining strength to crawl out of her bed and kneel. She bent her head and prayed for her mother, for Jerusha and Tirzah, for her neighbor and her children. It was hard, but she prayed for Reuben, that his heart would be softened... and... that he would be forgiven. She prayed to find forgiveness in her heart, to let her bitterness toward Reuben fade and her years of rage toward her father ease. She prayed she might find the peace that only forgiveness could bring.

"Help me to love my enemies, Lord," Leah whispered.

Leah asked God to continue to provide for her and - only if it was his will and his plan - to heal her. She prayed a prayer of thanksgiving, that she had been able to hear the Messiah that day, for those words that would comfort her forever. No matter what happened.

Leah crawled back into her bed and lay down. "You know, I'm not worried about tomorrow." The words were loud and confident, a silent shield to watch over her.

Smiling in agreement with the sound of her voice, Leah closed her eyes and slept.

CHAPTER 25

The crack was so loud, it sounded as though it were in the room. Leah's eyes flew open. She stared into the darkness, startled.

A flash of lightning hung in the air, so bright Leah could see every corner of her small house. "I need to sweep," was her first thought.

Pitched back into the blackest night, the answering thunder almost shook her from her bed. She heard the rain drumming on her roof. "What a storm," she thought. "Listen to that wild wind."

A disturbing thought flew into her mind. Jesus and his disciples! They had left in a boat that evening. Had they made it to safety? Surely they were not in their small boat on the sea in this raging storm.

She remembered the two old men talking about Jesus' disciples. "Fisherman," they had said.

They were fishermen, men who owned boats and knew the sea. "Wouldn't they know of an approaching storm," Leah thought, "and know what to do if they were in one?" Surely they were safe. The men called disciples, those seasoned fisherman that followed Jesus, would take good care of their precious cargo.

Leah sat up straight up in bed at another thought, as urgent to her as the first, gasping at the stab of pain it caused. It was pouring rain right outside her door, a rare occurrence. She struggled to her feet as quickly as she could. Hurry, Leah!

She pulled out her two bowls for washing, the iron pot, her other smaller bowls and both of her water jars. She set them all just outside her door where the water ran down from the roof in full force. "Oh, I might be able to fill up an entire water jar," Leah thought. What a blessing! Truly this rain was sent by God.

"And you didn't even pray for it, Leah," she added out loud.

Leah stood at the door, watching the violent wind and flashes of lightning, listening to the crashes of thunder. The rain fell so hard she could not even see across her small courtyard. She stared at the storm. "Don't worry about tomorrow, that's what he said," she thought. "And now I have water. Father God, O Holy One, keep those who may be in harm's way safe in this storm. Thank you for the rain and the water you have sent to me. Amen."

She smiled and spoke a final word out loud, happy. "See-LAH!" The thunder rumbled long and low in agreement.

Leah took one last look at the storm and returned to her bed. As she lay down, so did the wind. The hammering sound of the rain was reduced to a steady patter. The worst of the storm was over. "Lord, thank you for the thunder, the lightning, the wind, and most of all, the rain."

She closed her eyes and, to the sound of answered prayer drumming on her roof, returned to a sleep without dreams.

◌ঽ

The next morning, Leah found she had water several fingerbreadths deep in each bowl. She carried one of her water jars back into the house. One by one, she emptied the water from all the various vessels into the jar. It was half full, as much as she could carry in one day's trip. The two large bowls for washing bowls she did not empty, but carried behind her curtain, careful not to slosh a drop. She would have water to drink and to bathe today. What a blessing the storm had been!

Leah heated a little water to add to the water in the bowls. She washed herself, changed her bandages, dressed and ate her breakfast. She sat at her loom, where she would listen for her friends to walked by. She wanted to thank Jerusha and Tirzah, and see if they too had gone to see Jesus yesterday. She wanted to talk with Jerusha about Jesus!

As she sat there, she was surprised to hear a quick knock at the door. Little Eleazar stood in her open doorway, and behind him was his mother.

"Hello! I never even asked your name yesterday. I am so sorry! I am Elizabeth, and of course you know little Eleazar. Did you hear the rain last night? What a storm! I couldn't believe it! Oh, goodness, I see you are weaving! My, what beautiful work, my weaving is always so lumpy and uneven; it's hardly fit for weekday clothes for the children! Who taught you to do such fine work? And on such a small loom, too! So lovely!"

She took a breath but continued talking. "I just wanted to ask you, when we find out that Jesus is returning to teach, should I send Eleazar down to tell you? Jesus comes here all the time, you know. My husband always hears when Jesus is coming.

"They say he stays with one of the fishermen here in Capernaum, a fisherman who is now his disciple. Did you see him yesterday? That older man by the boat, that was his boat. His name used to be Simon, but Jesus changed it to Peter. Did you know that? 'Cephas.' That means the rock. My husband told me, he heard it at the synagogue. He goes to our synagogue. Simon, I mean Peter, not my husband. Well. He goes there, too, of course. I know Simon's, I mean Peter's wife, but not very well, she is older than me.

"If you like, as soon as we hear Jesus is coming, Eleazar can run down and let you know. Anyway, I am on my way to the well and thought I would check on you. I saw yesterday how the walk home..." For the first time, Elizabeth paused, just for a moment, before adding in a delicate tone, "how that walk seemed to tire you."

Leah stared at her. She wasn't sure which of the woman's questions to answer first. Leah stood up from the stool, the motion slow and painful. Her first steps were always hunched over, her knees bent and head low. It took a few steps for Leah to straighten up and face the woman standing there watching her. As she reached the door where the woman stood, she saw pity on the woman's face.

But instead of feeling ashamed, Leah's heart lifted.

The woman did not pity her because of Leah's illness or uncleanness or sin. She pitied her because Leah suffered. Leah could not help but smile.

"Hello, Elizabeth. My name is Leah."

ଓ

All Leah could think of that day was what preparations to make so she would be ready to go to Jesus when he returned. She listened all morning for the laughing conversations of Jerusha and Tirzah to float through her open window. She wanted to ask them if they too had heard Jesus.

Leah sat at her loom under her window all morning, but her friends did not walk by.

"They must not be coming," she mused. At last Leah picked up her water jar to go alone. What had happened to her faithful friends? Still, she might as well create a stockpile of water since she felt so good today.

As Leah was returning from the well, she was surprised to meet Tirzah walking alone. Leah nodded at her but was too nervous to speak first. Without Jerusha, Tirzah seemed less friendly, almost forbidding in demeanor.

"Hello, Leah." But when she spoke, Tirzah did not sound forbidding at all. She sounded... well, shy, too. And a little sad. "How are you today?"

"I am good, Tirzah, thank you." Leah wanted to ask how the pregnant Tirzah felt, where Jerusha was, and if Tirzah had been at the Sea of Galilee yesterday, but she could not find the words to say anything.

"Did you go to hear Jesus speak yesterday, Leah?"

Leah nodded her head yes. "It was wonderful," she replied, her voice almost inaudible at the wonder of the day.

"Did you see Jerusha there?"

Leah shook her head no.

"She came by this morning and said she could not walk to the well, she had to go at once to speak to some women about Jesus." There was a short pause. "I thought she would be back by now, but I guess I do not know when she will return. So I just came without her."

"Tirzah?" Leah tried to speak a little louder. "Tirzah, did you go to hear Jesus yesterday?"

Leah again saw something like sadness on Tirzah's face.

However, when she answered her measured tone was kind. "I have a husband and a home to tend to, as does Jerusha. I also have a small child and a baby on the way. I cannot waste… I cannot spend time listening to a teacher all day long. It's hard enough just to get to the synagogue. Jerusha, my beloved friend, does not always know what is important and what is not."

She hesitated and then added, "I am glad to see you today, Leah."

Tirzah turned and continued her path to the well alone.

❦

By the end of the day, Leah had everything ready. She created a small sack from a piece of woven fabric, tying it up with a string. In the sack she placed a large piece of bread, two figs and one of her cups. She was ready to travel! She used some of the rain water to wash out one of her tunics and then used the same water to wash out all her bandages. She made it up to the roof and laid all the items out to dry. She warmed herself for a few minutes in the sun, enjoying the fresh air washed clean by last night's rain.

She thought of Jerusha. Where had she gone? Who were the women she had gone to see about Jesus? Perhaps Jerusha knew of other puny, sick women like Leah, and wanted to let them know there was hope for them, too. Leah smiled at the thought.

She turned again to her biggest problem, one she had not yet solved. Jewish men did not speak to Jewish women. Never in public did a Jewish woman walk up to a Jewish man to speak to him, not even to her own husband. How could she approach Jesus? She had heard of him healing a lame man, a leprous man, the blind and the deaf and the mute. And a woman! He had even healed a woman with a fever.

How had that happened? Did the woman know Jesus? Did Jesus know the woman's husband? Did the husband beg his wife be healed, as Reuben had first asked for Leah years ago?

Yet this Jesus must be a kind man, for Jewish children never bothered Jewish men either! Jewish rabbis never hugged children. They might lay their hands on them in some sort of elaborate Temple ritual that usually frightened the children and cost a lot in sacrifices, but never would they hug them. Elizabeth said Jesus talked to her children. He took them in his lap, blessed them and... laughed with them! She thought of wide-eyed Eliza with all her missing baby teeth, handing Leah the bread that was the little girl's supper.

Leah knew this next thought was crazy. But even as her head said this was impossible, the feeling in her heart was so strong she could not dismiss it. After Leah prayed on the shores of Galilee, Jesus had looked right at her. There had been hundreds of people there, how could that be? But she had prayed and his next words were, "Ask and it will be given to you."

And the moment she said "Amen," she looked up to find him looking at her, to speak directly to her. He had heard her prayer. He knew the secret hope in her heart.

Impossible! But she felt this to be true in every bone of her skinny body. Jesus had heard her. And he had not turned her away.

Ask. Seek. Knock.

But what did that mean? Was he telling her to be brave and ask for healing?

How could she tell Jesus what was wrong with her? To publicly state her unclean condition would create an outrage in the crowd. Jewish law was explicit in its punishments. Leah shivered; she had heard of men stoning women for breaking certain laws. For a man to be ceremonially unclean because a stranger, an unclean woman, touched him - even an accidental brush - might be one of those reasons. She only had to remember standing in front of the synagogue council seven years ago to have her face burn with shame. Twelve years of uncleanness before God. Twelve years!

Leah did not know how she could ever meet Jesus. As hard as she tried, she could not find the answer to this problem. She did not know what she was going to do.

She only knew one thing for certain: Leah was going to find Jesus, and she was going to do something.

CHAPTER 26

The next morning, Leah woke up much later than usual, roused by a bright early sun instead of a gray hazy light through her only window. She had slept well, a rare night without bad dreams or waking pain. She lay in her bed for a few minutes, thankful for the blessing of rest, smiling at her laziness. She needed to get up, not loll around like a woman of wealth with servants.

She spoke out loud to no one in particular: "Do not love sleep or you will grow poor. Get up, you sluggard!"

The voice was not mean; it sounded happy and full of joy, joking about sluggards just as her beloved Savta had done so many years ago. "Look to the ant, you sluggard," Savta had shouted that morning when Leah startled her from her sleep. Leah smiled at the memory of her beloved grandmother, how the two of them had laughed until they cried.

"I'm alive for another day," she said, stretching her aching body. She took a deep breath, remembering the precious words of Jesus, the words he spoke in answer to her prayer: "Ask and it will be given to you; seek and you will find; knock and the door will be opened to you."

Her heart stopped at the immediate loud banging at her door. Goodness, she was still in her bed! Leah got up as quickly as she could and looked out her window. Standing at her closed door was little Eleazar. What loud knocking for such a little boy!

He spied her face at the window, and his small thin face broke into a wide grin. "Mama says she is sorry she sent me here so early. She says to tell you the boat that took Jesus is coming back across the Sea of Galilee. Jesus is coming back today, too! Mama says we are going to hear him again today and to tell you to go, too. Go to the sea, that's where Jesus will be. That's what Mama told me to tell you." He said this without pause and all in one breath.

It was just like listening to his mother, Leah thought.

"Thank you so much, Eleazar!" Leah's gratitude was heartfelt. Jesus was returning, and so soon, too.

The little boy smiled up at her, and then looked around as though to share a secret. "I met Jesus once. Mama says he blessed me! I sat on his lap, and I made him laugh!"

Leah looked at the innocent face with its sparkling brown eyes. Even children loved the teacher from Nazareth.

As though remembering his mother's certain instructions, Eleazar's eyes grew wide and serious. He shook his head once, a solemn firm nod, and then took off to sprint down the street. Leah gazed in wonder as he sped away, blessed by both the little messenger and his important news.

She turned to get ready at once. Leah felt as though she was moving as fast as little Eleazar, although unlike the boy, every step caused her pain. She changed her bandages, washed her face and hands, braided her hair and dressed in the common brown wool of the crowd. She bolted down her small breakfast, forcing herself to eat. She needed her strength! She wondered if Jerusha and Tirzah would be at the Sea, too.

Her veil draped on her head, Leah tucked the small bag of her supplies into her belt and began the long walk to the Sea of Galilee. Jesus was coming.

ൟ

"Walking to the Sea of Galilee is much easier than getting back from it," Leah thought, remembering her terrible trip two days before. "All I did was sit and listen, but still I was worn out. Listening and thinking must be work I am not used to."

The market was quiet as she walked by, booths shuttered with only a few merchants milling about, setting out their wares.

She plodded forward, single-minded in her determination. This time, no crowd jostled her in their rush to get to Jesus. The street belonged to Leah.

She soon arrived at the same place where she had first heard the man from Galilee. The same sea sparkled before her, an aquamarine jewel lined with sandy brown shores and shining black rocks. How beautiful the day seemed, the air so fresh after the rain. A few groups of people stood about, some alone, some in groups of two or three, talking, eating, laughing, waiting for the Teacher.

Just like Eleazar had said, there were the boats tied up on the shore. But where was Jesus? Neither he nor his disciples were anywhere in sight. Where were the people?

"Think, Leah!" She looked around, as though someone could guide her. Should she wait here? Eleazar said this is where Jesus would be. Maybe she should just sit down and wait with these people, too.

Perhaps Jesus would go to the synagogue to teach instead. Isn't that where most rabbis taught? Leah quailed at the thought. The synagogue! Maybe Leah could wait outside the synagogue, hiding somewhere where no one might see her.

Then it struck Leah. No wonder so few people were here, the streets eerily empty, the market booths still closed.

It was still early in the day, not even the third hour yet! Jesus was probably still at the home of his friend Simon Peter, preparing for the crowds that would swarm around him that day. Leah should have waited at least an hour or more before she started her trek to the sea. Even the market was not open yet!

It had been so long since Leah had been part of the world, she had forgotten the starts, stops and times in between that measured people's days.

Leah shook her head in disgust. Perhaps she should just sit down and wait here. But what if Jesus did not even come to the sea today? Not knowing what else to do, she turned to walk to this Simon's house. She wondered how many people knew Jesus stayed at the house of the fisherman.

It took her a few minutes to hobble the short distance to the house of Simon now called Cephas. She tried not stare. There were a few men standing outside. Leah felt as though they all looked at her with a wary distrust. She shrank into her veil, a finger of fear in her belly.

Strong Leah prevailed. "Don't be silly!" she scolded herself. "You are just a woman walking by on the street." She ignored the obvious, that no other women were loitering outside the fisherman's house.

She walked past the house, came back, and, trying to make herself as insignificant as possible, stood on the edge of the property. At some point Jesus would leave or come to this house, she knew it. She would just stand there and wait until he did.

If she had to, she would stand there all day.

CHAPTER 27

Leah's back ached, but to sit in the dusty street outside this house would mark her as a beggar. She had earlier resolved to wait here all day if she needed to, but her strength was dwindling fast. She had scarcely been there for an hour!

What should she do? She was afraid to eat her bread in case she really needed it later. If only she had the money to purchase a skin to hold water! She was so thirsty. Sometimes when she got very tired, she fainted. It was one thing to faint alone in her own house, or at the well with only women, sheep and goats for company. To faint here, today, would be certain catastrophe.

By now, a lot of people had gathered outside the house of Simon Peter. A steady stream of people walked by, claiming their spots by the Sea of Galilee. Everyone was waiting for Jesus.

People were everywhere. Leah shrank into her veil and hunched her thin shoulders, trying to make her gaunt frame as insignificant as possible, careful not to make eye contact with anyone.

So busy was Leah with her worries, she did not notice the approaching commotion until it was upon her. A man was running, pushing people out of his way. He wore an outer robe of the wealthy, a finely woven linen with rich hues vaguely familiar to her. Talitha's colors.

Beside him, a Roman soldier half ran and half-strode, his long, muscular build matching the first man's step for step. He was a commander of the Roman army, a centurion! Had he come to arrest Jesus? What was happening?

"It is Jarius, the synagogue ruler!" A man beside her spoke to no one in particular, wonder in his voice. "Why would he come here?"

The synagogue ruler! Leah shrank back, hoping no one would notice her. Was this the ruler who commended Reuben for staying faithful to his sick wife for twelve long years? Was this the man who gave Reuben a divorce from his unclean, sinful wife, and praised him for his faithfulness? The ruler from Jerusha and Tirzah's synagogue?

What was left of Leah's waning resolve grew as weak as her legs. She had to escape before the synagogue men found her. She wanted to see Jesus, but not with the synagogue ruler and his council of judgmental and angry men nearby.

However, the ruler had eyes for nothing but the house of the fisherman. She had never seen a synagogue ruler run. As he passed by, his linen robe billowed behind him. It was wrinkled and stained, odd for a man of his position. Leah could hear him panting, out of breath, sweating as though demons were on his heels. He did not stop until he reached the courtyard gate.

Before he could enter or even call out, Jesus stood at the door.

"My friend." Leah's heart stilled at the sound of Jesus' voice. As though to mirror Leah's heart, all the people stopped to stand silent, waiting for his next words.

The ruler stood at the front of the crowd, mute.

"Jarius." Jesus walked out to the ruler. He was followed by the men who had been with him two days ago. Several women came out too, standing on the portico of the home, watching.

The man looked at Jesus for a moment and then fell in the dust at Jesus's feet. Even the synagogue ruler bowed before Jesus! The Roman centurion stood beside Jarius, his head bowed low in deferential reverence. The soldier wiped his eyes as though he was crying. A hardened Roman warrior, shedding tears! Leah forgot her pain and fear, mesmerized by the scene unfolding before her.

"Jesus," the ruler's voice shook. "Jesus, my little daughter is dying. Please come and put your hands on her so that she will be healed and live. She is my only child, Jesus. She is only twelve years old. Jesus, please come. She is dying!"

"Twelve years old," Leah thought. "Twelve years old, a little girl."

She was struck by an odd thought. "Twelve years ago I had hoped for a son or a daughter of my own. Instead, I was given this horrible bleeding disease. Twelve years. My shame began when this man's little daughter was born."

Twelve years was only a series of fleeting moments and precious memories to the father of this beloved little girl. It was an eternity of torment and suffering for Leah.

Jesus pulled Jarius to his feet. He turned and said something to the men behind him and then walked to the street in step with Jarius. Several of the disciples walked ahead of and beside Jesus, as though they were shielding him. They were followed by the Roman centurion and even more men who had been standing in the street.

A few people waiting near the sea shouted to others and began running. Jesus had been spotted. He had spoken only a few words, and yet at once – from nowhere – came a crowd.

Jesus, the ruler Jarius, the disciples, the Roman centurion and the sudden crowd were walking towards Leah, who still stood at the edge of Simon Peter's property. The disciples in their practiced formation formed a protective hedge around the teacher, creating a path through the crowd for Jesus.

Something bubbled up in Leah. It was not anger. It was not fear. Leah burned with a fierce and strong desire. What was it?

Courage!

Ask! Seek! Knock!

This was her only chance. There were so many people pushing and jostling to walk beside Jesus, all in a hurry to get to the ruler's house. No one needed to know! Leah burned with this sudden revelation. She knew the man from Nazareth could heal her with a touch. No one would ever know of her shame.

He could heal anyone. Not just a crippled man, not just a leper or a woman with a fever, not just the ruler's little daughter! He could heal her. If she believed it would happen, God would answer her prayers. Jesus could heal Leah.

Ask. Seek. Knock.

Leah's small, thin body worked to her advantage as she slipped ahead of the disciples. No one noticed the gaunt woman with the hollow eyes who lingered at the edge of the street. All eyes were on

Jesus and Jarius. Leah watched the first disciples go by.

"Now!" Leah couldn't help it, she said the word out loud. As Jesus passed, she reached out to touch the edge of his prayer shawl.

Her prayer was a whisper. "Heal me, Messiah, heal me."

The tassel grazed her fingers for the briefest instant, its touch as soft as a mother's caress, an exquisite, fleeting moment.

Leah gasped and looked at her hand, expecting to see a charred ruin, great bubbling blisters of flesh. She felt as though she had thrust her hand into a raging fire. She closed her eyes, the roar of the fire in her head, its heat racing up through every limb, to the top of her head, down to every fingertip and toe. A great pain stabbed like a knife, twisting in her belly, her back, her womanhood. In this briefest moment of agony, Leah thought she would fall to the ground, writhing in terrible pain. She opened her eyes but only saw blackness...

And then, just as swiftly... nothing.

Nothing was not quite the right word. Her constant pain was gone. It was an odd sensation, unfamiliar. How did she feel? Leah felt different. She felt... well, strong! And powerful, as though she could run to the sea and swim across and back. She felt alert and agile and quick. Every part of her body could feel the pulse of her beating heart.

She felt alive.

And Leah did not know how she knew this, but she did. The bleeding that was always with her? It was gone. Just like that. The bleeding of twelve years was gone. Just the touch of the robe of Jesus had banished her illness from her body.

Leah was healed.

"Who touched me?" The voice rang out over the crowd.

The crowd stopped as though it were one body.

Leah stood like a statue, a pillar of salt like the wife of Lot, unable to turn around and lift her eyes to face that voice.

"Who touched me?"

Leah's beating heart stopped. How did he know?

One of the disciples nearest Jesus snorted. "Master, these people are crowding and pressing against you. Everyone is touching you! Come, we must hurry."

"Someone touched me. I know that power has gone out from me."

The crowd stood silent, save for the gasping breath of Jarius, who stood pulling on the arm of Jesus, desperate to make him follow. Jesus laid his hand on the ruler's shoulder.

What should she do? She could not hide. Everyone knew Jesus was searching for the person who had touched him, who had sought his power without asking. What had he said? "Ask and you shall receive." *Ask*.

"Oh, Leah," she whispered. Leah's guilt and remorse was immediate. She had not asked, but she had received. She had taken without asking! This must be her sin, to believe and to receive, but to be so bold, so disrespectful, so... shameless that she did not even ask this great man if he would perform a miracle of such amazing kindness for an unworthy woman he had never met.

All the shame she had ever felt came raining down upon Leah's head. She had shamed herself before Jesus.

Jerusha's voice sounded in her head. "Blessed are the poor in spirit, Leah, for theirs is the kingdom of Heaven. Jesus blesses the broken, Leah, and gives them a good measure, running over into your lap! Jesus blesses the broken, Leah."

All these years accused of a sin I did not commit, she thought to herself. Confess this sin, confess and ask Jesus for forgiveness and for mercy. Ask.

Leah took a deep breath. The crowd gasped as she turned around and stepped forward.

They fell silent as she walked up to Jesus. Her knees were so weak from fear, it was a relief to fall in the dirt at his feet. The only sound was Jarius's ragged, heavy breathing. The crowd stood silent, watching. Leah remembered her friend's gentle words, encouraging her: "He blesses those who are broken, Leah."

What had the man called Jesus? She looked at the dusty hem of Jesus' robe, for she could not bear to look at his face. Master, Leah thought. The disciple of Jesus called him Master.

She took a deep, shaky breath. "Master." She took another breath. "I touched you... Master."

Jesus did not speak. The crowd was silent.

"I touched you, to be healed. For twelve years I have suffered a disease, a horrible disease. None could cure me. For twelve years I have had a..." Leah could hardly speak the words, "...an issue of blood, a disease... a bleeding that has left me unclean, unworthy and alone." It sounded so terrible to speak the words aloud.

Still Jesus did not speak. Leah struggled with what to say. "I have no one who could ask you to heal me. No... man to ask you. My husband left me here to die three years ago. Just this week he went to the synagogue here to divorce me according to the Law of Moses, because... because of my bleeding and uncleanness." Leah's voice shook. "I was expelled from the synagogue, disowned by my father, separated from my mother, divorced by my husband, and abandoned in a strange city to die. I am alone, and yes, I am unclean in the eyes of our God. I am... amê."

She felt the horrible shame of that word. "Yes, Master, amê. I touched your robe without asking so that my shame could remain a secret." A sob escaped her, that before all these strange eyes, before all these people, these men, her shame would be so public. "I knew that just a touch of your robe would heal me. Then no one would know of my shame."

Leah lifted her head to look up at Jesus but was startled to see the wide, shocked eyes of the synagogue ruler Jarius staring at her in disbelief. "Even in his sorrow," Leah thought, "this man is outraged that an unclean woman kneels at the feet of this great teacher."

She forced herself to look at Jesus, fearful, but saw only sadness in his face. And compassion, a deep, quiet compassion. He was silent, waiting for her to continue. She took a deep breath.

"Master, I have been unclean, unworthy for so many years. They told me you are the Messiah and that you bless the broken. When I went to hear you at the Sea of Galilee, you said, 'Ask and you shall receive.' But Master, I did not ask, and you healed me anyway."

Leah began to cry, remorse and sorrow, shame and joy all surging within her to one fierce emotion, compelling her to say what she knew she must. The words choked her but she struggled to speak them loud enough for Jesus and the crowd to hear.

"Forgive me. With all my heart, I am sorry. Please, Master, Messiah, Son of God... forgive me for my sin."

Leah pressed her tear-streaked cheek to the dust and closed her eyes. The crowd was utterly still. Everyone had heard of her shame; those that she had touched were now unclean; she had touched the Master for mercy without asking for his grace.

Leah felt Jesus crouch down in front of her. He laid his hands on her shoulders. He was touching her, she who was still ceremonially unclean and sinful! She shook with fear that she would make the Master unclean in the eyes of God.

His hands felt very heavy, like the entire world pressed down on her. The weight covered her, comforted her, protected her from all that was evil. She could hear Jesus whispering. She could not understand what he was saying, but she knew. With his hands pressing down on her shoulders, Jesus was praying. Jesus was praying for her. They stayed like that for an eternity of moments.

Jesus touched her face, forcing her to look at him. His eyes were pools of mercy, kindness and love – all the good things in the world Leah had missed for three long years in Capernaum. He picked up her hands from the dirt and helped her to her feet. With his hand on her shoulder, he spoke loud enough for the crowd to hear. His steady gaze never left Leah's face.

"Daughter, your faith has healed you. Go in peace and suffer no more."

She was healed.

Jesus forgave her.

He called her daughter.

Leah thought she would faint, but this time from happiness. She heard her mother's voice: "O Lord, you have delivered my soul from death, my eyes from tears, my feet from stumbling, that I may walk before the Lord in the Land of the Living!"

Jesus had delivered her from death and from tears. Leah was healed and forgiven.

Jesus had forgiven her!

But before she could say anything to the Master, a man pushed his way through to where Leah stood with Jesus and Jarius. He was followed by a heavy-set man, sweaty and panting, gasping for air.

"Jarius!" The man took Jarius by the arm and shook it, panting for breath. "Jarius, your daughter is dead."

This man also wore the rich embroidered garments of the wealthy Temple select. Jarius stared stupidly at the man without moving.

The man took Jarius by the shoulders and shook him again, as though to rouse him from sleep. "Jarius! Your daughter is dead." Jarius shook his head, uncomprehending.

"Don't bother the teacher any more," the man's voice broke. "Your daughter is dead."

The crowd held its breath.

The long moment of silent was broken by a scream of anguish, echoing eerily in the silent street filled with people. Leah knew the ruler would have fallen to the ground if the other man did not still hold him in a tight grip.

Jarius wrenched away from the man. He tore his robe open and then fell to his knees, hands clasped to his forehead, rocking back and forth, silent in his agony. The only sound was his ragged breath.

Kneeling in the dirt before Leah and Jesus, Jarius began weeping, great rasping sobs loud in the eerie silence, his face wet with tears. His daughter was dead.

The twelve-year-old girl died while Jesus healed Leah of her terrible disease. Leah's joy disappeared like a wisp of smoke in the wind.

"Jarius," Leah heard the low urgency in Jesus' voice. He pulled Jarius to his feet. "Listen! Don't be afraid; just believe, and she will be healed." The compelling intensity of his voice pierced Jarius' shattered state. He nodded.

Jesus took Jarius by the arm. The two men began walking. Voices broke out all around, and the people surged to follow Jesus and Jarius in one fluid motion. Leah was buffeted by first one man and then another, the skeletal woman and her ceremonial uncleanness already forgotten.

Leah was pushed in all directions as she tried to free herself from the mass of people. She elbowed her way to the edge of the street, where her shaking knees forced her to sit down on the step of some stranger's home. She sat unnoticed and ignored in the wake of Jesus walking away.

Leah was healed. The ruler's daughter had died. Jesus left with Jarius. Leah was alone, forgiven and free to go.

The Master had called her daughter. He had healed her and forgiven her. Now, he was leaving to comfort this man, this man mourning the death of his only child, his little daughter. Just as Leah's mother might have mourned her only daughter.

Jesus had called Leah "Daughter."

Leah sat alone in her confusion as others from the sea ran by to catch up with the crowd. What she had asked God to do for so many years had happened, but she could not find joy in her healing. She could not go in peace. She could not forget that the moment an unworthy, unclean woman was healed… a little girl died.

Leah was alive. The daughter of the synagogue ruler was dead.

As her thoughts tumbled about, Leah realized something else. Jarius was the ruler who had given Reuben the divorce. She had seen it in his eyes when she told Jesus how she had bled for twelve years, and that her husband had just divorced her.

Jarius knew she was the sick woman with an unclean bleeding. She was the woman divorced by the stranger in the synagogue. Jarius had not been horrified that an unclean woman knelt at the feet of Jesus. He was as dumbfounded by their shared fearsome circumstances as Leah was. The unclean, unknown bleeding woman divorced by her husband had been healed while his own precious, innocent daughter was dying.

Not dying. She was dead. The ruler's daughter died when Leah had been healed.

One body was made new after twelve years of a dreadful disease. The other body lay lifeless, its future stolen by the finality of death.

Leah put her hands on her head, pressing her temples with all her new strength, trying to still the pounding inside her. It was too much to comprehend, too much to bear.

She cried out loud, not caring if anyone heard her. "O Jehovah! Almighty Father, Holy God! Abba, Abba!" Leah wept. "For a little girl to die at the moment I was healed! O God, O God!"

Leah sobbed for the tragic fate of this unknown girl, for the husband that had abandoned her, the father that disowned her, the mother who had needlessly suffered for three long years, for the Master that healed Leah and called her daughter.

Didn't this contradict everything that Jesus taught about love and mercy and peace? This pain was too great, too tragic. A new life for Leah. Death for a little girl. Twelve years of tragic pain, twelve years of loving joy. Tragedy and joy. Leah's heart was ripped in two.

In the face of such a terrible loss, she did not know how to be grateful for her miracle. She did not know what to say to God.

"Daughter," Jesus called her. "Go in peace," he said. He could have gone to heal this little girl, but he stopped to talk to Leah, to pray over her, to free her from her shame before the crowd. She was not worthy, surely Jesus knew this!

Why had God let this happen?

As she sat there, tears running down her face, Leah pondered the words Jesus said to Jarius. "Don't be afraid, just believe and she will be healed!"

What did Jesus mean? The man said Jarius' daughter was dead.

But Jesus said she would be healed. "Just believe," Jesus said to the ruler. "Don't be afraid."

Don't be afraid...

"I believe. I am not afraid," Leah whispered. She remembered her joyous psalm of only two days ago. "'When I am afraid, I will trust in you, God. I will not be afraid.'" She wiped her tears on her sleeve. "I believe in your promise, Master. I am not afraid."

At once, Leah knew what she needed to do. She stood up, supple and quick. For the first time, Leah felt the strength of her newly-healed body. She stretched her once beaten frame, flexed her arms and arched her back. She looked down the street and felt strong legs break into a run to catch up to the crowd following Jesus.

For Leah knew if she did not go to the place where the little twelve-year-old girl lay dead, she would never, ever be able to go in peace.

CHAPTER 28

Leah stood in front of a beautiful mansion painted pale yellow with ornate columns of gold lining its façade. The home of a wealthy man... the home of the synagogue ruler.

The crowds outside the ruler's home were overwhelming. She could not get close enough to see inside the massive courtyard gates, but she had pushed her way through to stand in the shadow of the house's impressive balcony.

Leah had easily caught up with the crowd following Jesus and the synagogue ruler Jarius. As she ran, she heard snatches of conversation. People recognized her.

"She touched Jesus! She is healed!"

"She bled for twelve years!"

"With only a touch of his robe, she was healed!"

"Jesus called her daughter!"

"He told her to go in peace!"

Over and over... "Jesus healed her." Sometimes the words were spoken with excited surprise, other times with awe. She did not care.

Only moments ago, those same comments would have caused Leah to run, to hide, to shut herself away. But she did not care what people said. Jesus healed her! He called her daughter! She grinned at everyone she saw. "Like a mad woman," she muttered.

Indeed, she was so overjoyed at the strength and spring of her legs, she had to stop herself from pushing people out of her way. She felt as strong as the young girl who once ran to the foot of Mount Hebron, or who pulled the beater of the loom back and forth, sturdy arms working in tandem with her mother and grandmother. She felt wonderful... except for the synagogue ruler's daughter.

Leah would flame up with a joy as bright as dry leaves on a hot fire until the thought of the dead girl would come to her. Then the fire extinguished as quickly as a brown leaf might burn into an ember, carried away by the comments of the crowd like gray ash on the wind.

"Poor little girl, she was so beautiful."

"Dreadfully sick for two days and two nights."

"So many doctors. They could not heal her."

"Only twelve..."

Leah was healed! She was sick for twelve, terrible years and now she was healed.

"Raging fever, so terribly sick, so fast."

"Even terrible seizures. Her illness consumed her."

"She died this morning."

The little girl was dead.

"Jarius' wife never left her, not for a moment, for three days."

"He wasn't with her when she died."

"The girl died while Jarius was with Jesus."

Everyone in the crowd seemed to know about the synagogue ruler and his sick daughter. When Leah arrived, there was not only a crowd already at the ruler's house, but also the somber music of the flute players and wails of the professional mourners piercing the noise. She wanted to cover her ears and shut out the dissonance of the flutes and the mournful wailing, the noisy hum of people murmuring, talking and even laughing.

It was earsplitting, thought Leah. Not at all mournful and sad. Was she the only one outside this sad house grieving for the dead girl?

The little girl was the only child of an important man. The paid mourners must have been ready to begin the moment she died. Before Jarius even knew his daughter was dead, the old women had probably started their loud, keening dirges, their trilling elegies on

261

reedy flutes.

Oh, how sad for Jarius to return to his home where others already stood mourning the death of his only child. How bitter to face a crowd of vultures watching to witness the grief of their synagogue ruler.

Leah wondered where the ruler was. Surely he was inside with his daughter and with Jesus. "Don't be afraid.' That's what Jesus told him." What had Jesus meant by that?

She listened to the crowd talking all around her, murmuring over and over their wonder at the man called Jesus.

"He healed the centurion's servant without even seeing him."

That must have been the Roman centurion who ran beside Jarius, the hardened soldier who wept at the death of the little girl.

"He preached in the synagogue of Jarius. Remember when he healed the old man's hand there on Sabbath?"

Jesus laughed with little children and showed mercy to the aged.

"He made that lame man walk. Eri, the son of Rebecca, he walks!"

Jerusha's story of the lame man, the son of Rebecca, that led Leah to seek Jesus.

No one spoke to Leah, but she felt their eyes upon her. Even as they spoke to each other about the miracles of the Teacher, they cast furtive glances of awe and fear toward the thin stranger that stood among them waiting for the Lord.

Leah did not care, for Jesus had healed her and called her daughter. Let the world wonder! She would never forget the feeling of his hands upon her shoulders, warm and protecting. The world would never frighten her again. Jesus had prayed for her, forgiven her and told her to go in peace. But first, she had to find out what was happening inside the walls of the synagogue ruler's house. If she had to, she would wait here all day.

Unlike a short hour ago, this time she had the strength to do it.

ɔ

The abrupt silence of the mourners' wailing and flutes hushed the noisy crowd, too. The sudden absence of the harsh, grating noise was as loud as the discordant racket. A quiet anticipation fell over the expectant crowd. The mourners, the people who had been inside the courtyards of Jarius, streamed out into the street, one aged woman after another.

A fat man in the courtyard shooed out the last flute player and latched the gate. It was the same man who had stood sweating and panting in the street when the richly-robed man told Jarius his daughter had died.

A voice from the crowd broke the silence. "What's happening?"

Emboldened, another voice cried out, "Where is Jesus?"

"Be quiet!" the fat man shouted. He disappeared into the mansion.

Be quiet? What was happening inside that house? It was unheard of for the mourners to stop until the dead were buried. The mourners made their way through the press of people, wide eyes set in faces of awe under black veils. They whispered to one person and then another. Hushed murmurs ran through the crowd.

"Jesus put the mourners out."

"Jesus told them the girl is not dead, but asleep."

"But the girl is dead, she has been dead for several hours!"

The conversation passed person to person, one by one, each exchange a furtive whisper.

"They had already called for the mourners! The girl is dead."

"They say Jesus went in with Jarius to see the girl and her mother."

"Jesus made the mourners leave, Jesus put them out."

Those standing apart from the whispers pressed close to hear.

"The three disciples went in, too."

"The girl is dead, I say! I heard she was dead."

"Jesus said the girl was only sleeping!"

Leah felt an odd flutter in her chest.

The crowd was no longer noisy and pressing. There was an unbroken, persistent hum, like bees at a hive, a hushed tizzy of people nervously waiting. The crowd stood for a long time that way, whispering, wondering, waiting. What was happening inside that house?

The courtyard gate swung open, unlatched by the Roman centurion. He did not look like a battle-hardened soldier at all; he looked as though he had been crying. But he smiled at the crowd and then knelt on one knee, his outstretched arm holding the gate open, his head bowed low in respect.

Jesus and the three disciples walked out. The crowd was motionless. Leah had never heard such an enormous silence.

The four men did not speak. As though on cue, the silent crowd parted, making way for the Master and his disciples. No one spoke to Jesus; he strode down the street with great purpose, nodding and even smiling at those along the way. Yet no one dared approach him. His disciples looked straight ahead, eyes wide in faces of awe, staring at the back of the man they followed, silent and unmindful of the whispers of the crowd.

Leah watched the men walking away. What had happened inside that house?

She turned at the sound of commotion behind her. Several men stood at the gate. The man in the rich robes who had told Jarius his daughter was dead was babbling something to another man. A beautiful woman with curly hair stood at his side, wiping her eyes on her veil, a weak smile on her face. The Roman centurion stood there, a broad smile on his bronzed, craggy face.

A murmur passed from person to person, growing in volume as it rolled through the crowd like a wave rolling up on the shore. Leah could not understand the repeated phrase, the buzz of voices building.

"What are they saying?" she blurted out to the man next to her. He shook his head. They found themselves pressed together in a crush of people behind them.

"What are they saying?" The buzz grew louder as people asked the question again and again.

The moment each cluster of people heard the response from another, the crush released its binding grip. People fell back and shook their heads in disbelief. The wave was receding, only to return with even greater strength, a noisy crash in the sea of people.

Leah's knees grew weak. She could not believe the words she heard.

"The girl lives!"

"The daughter of Jarius lives!"

"The ruler's daughter lives!"

"She lives," Leah whispered to herself.

The wave rumbled on through the crowd, rising and falling. "The girl lives, the girl lives!"

Leah's eyes filled with tears as she remembered Jesus' words to

Jarius. "Your daughter is not dead. Don't be afraid, only believe."

She stood motionless for a moment. Then, as quickly as she had run to the house of the synagogue ruler, she turned and sped back toward the house of Simon Peter.

This time, Leah had no hesitation whatsoever about pushing people out of her way.

൫

The four men were approaching the gate of Simon's house when Leah caught up with them. She slowed her pace, panting. She had run the entire way.

She could run!

Jesus and two of the men entered the home's courtyard, pausing to speak to a few men. The youngest man stopped and was talking to a man only a few paces away from Leah in the street.

Leah wanted to call out to them, to stop them, but the only man she knew for certain was Jesus. To shout the name of Jesus! She could not bring herself to speak the name of someone so... so...

What should she do? She didn't know what to do. What to do!

Leah closed her eyes and heard her own strong, stern voice. "Jesus called you daughter! Be brave, Leah!"

She opened her eyes and walked up to the young man, the disciple of the Messiah.

"Sir." The young man was younger than her, maybe the age of Jerusha. Please, let him speak to her. He recognized her at once. His nod was kind.

"Sir, may I please ask you, please..." Leah realized she did not know what to ask the young disciple of Jesus.

"What is it, my friend?"

At the sound of his voice, Leah's again eyes filled with tears. She thought she would start crying. He called her friend! Leah took a deep breath. Her words came in a rush.

"Please... What happened to the ruler's daughter? Please tell me. I am the woman Jesus healed, and the little girl died while Jesus stopped to talk to me. Talked to me, an unworthy, unclean woman! The Master healed me, and the little girl died. So, please, I beg of you, tell me if what the people say is true. Does the girl live?"

The young man gazed at her for a moment as though debating

265

what to say. Finally he nodded. "Yes. She lives, the daughter of Jarius lives." He looked at her, and at once his eyes were fierce and blazing. "The daughter of Jarius the synagogue ruler was dead, but at the command of Jesus Christ my Lord and Master, she lives!"

They stood there, staring at each other. What was there to say?

He looked at Leah and shook his head in disbelief and awe. "She lives, the daughter of the ruler of my own synagogue lives. Jesus spoke to her and brought her back from the dead. Yes, friend, the girl, the daughter of Jarius the synagogue ruler… she lives."

"She lives." Her voice was a whisper.

Leah stood in silence, looking at young man. Go in peace, that's what Jesus had told her. Leah knew she would have peace for the rest of her days.

Slowly, a smile covered her face, wide, glorious… happy.

There was no stopping the words that bubbled up in the long-silent Leah. "She lives and I am healed! Oh, please, I am not worthy to speak to him! But please, tell the Master that I, Leah, a good and faithful Jewish woman, thank him. That I will follow him, worship him, believe in him for the rest of my days. Truly he is the Messiah. I believe, with all my heart, I believe!

"Please tell him, for I must leave to find my mother, to tell her the good news of my forgiveness and my healing and of… Jesus." She said the name reverently, but she could not keep the smile from her face.

"I go in peace, just as Jesus told me to! I am free of my suffering, just as Jesus said! Jesus said my faith healed me! I believed in him, and he healed me!" Leah tried to stop her babble. I sound like Elizabeth, she thought, hysterical with joy. She took a breath and tried to slow her words.

"Jesus called me daughter, and I will follow him forever. I leave to find my mother, but please thank him for me! Please tell the Master…" Leah knew she was jabbering again. But suddenly, she could hardly get the words out.

"Tell the Master I am thankful, I am so thankful…" She felt the tears in her eyes. Words were inadequate. What could she say?

Of course!

"Please tell my Master I left singing the words of King David: 'Forever more my heart will sing and not be silent!' I will never be silent about Jesus Christ the Messiah!"

She could not help herself. She grabbed the young man's sleeve and shook his arm for emphasis. "I will not be silent! I will give thanks forever!"

Leah's joy was so great, she laughed out loud. "Forever and forever more!"

The young disciple smiled too, a look of understanding on his face.

Leah laughed again. Her heart light, her legs strong, her body healed, she ran all the way back to her small dilapidated Capernaum house.

CHAPTER 29

Leah could see the mountain looming larger, its brown rocky crags graying to the faintest brush of white snow at its peak. Mount Hermon. How she had missed Savta's Old Gray-Haired Lady. The mountain seemed so close. Surely the city of her childhood would soon appear.

"Patience, Leah, patience." The woman beside her patted Leah's shoulder, smiling at the jittery anticipation of the thin, restless woman walking beside her.

Leah took a deep breath and tried to smile back. What she really wanted was to run off and leave the slow pace of the woman, her husband and two children.

But Leah would never leave this woman without a proper farewell, this kind soul who had been so good to Leah.

Leah had liked her the moment she laid eyes on her two days ago. She was a friend of Tirzah's making her way to Damascus with her small family.

"Yeah, Leah, patience! Patience!" The five-year-old girl jumped up and wrapped her arms around Leah's neck in a tight embrace, clambering up a bit higher for a better view as she rode piggy-back at the expense of her new friend. But Leah and the girl laughed, both ignoring her mother's admonitions that the wee girl behave.

"Patience," Leah thought to herself.

Was it only four days ago that Leah stood alone and frightened in a crowd of people, sick and bleeding, straining for a glimpse of the Master, knowing what she needed to do but afraid to do it?

Much had happened in four days. Patience.

"'A fool is hotheaded and reckless,' my daughter." The words were a soft whisper in Leah's head. But if her mother knew Leah was only a few hours away, surely she would certainly give those tiresome proverbs a rest and run to meet her daughter on this dusty road!

"Patience," Leah said out loud. Her new friend smiled and shook her head at the small girl clinging to Leah's back.

What little patience Leah had was at once been tested by her new friends. Despite their unbridled joy at the miracle of Leah, Tirzah and Jerusha had been horrified when Leah announced she was leaving for Caesarea Philippi the very next morning. After three long years, she would not wait another moment to see her mother.

"You cannot go alone, Leah!"

"There are bandits on the road."

"But I have nothing to steal!"

"There are bad men who sit and wait for the traveler who is alone!"

"There are men who would take more from you than money, Leah."

"But I would stay on the main road during the day, and hide myself away at night. I would be safe."

"Criminals on the road would hide from you instead of the other way around, Leah! You would be helpless against such men."

"It's true, Leah. You cannot travel alone."

"But I cannot wait! I must go to my mother. I must leave now. She has had no word of me for three years!"

"Let us help you! We will figure something out."

"Leah, Jesus did not give you your life back only for you to throw it away. We will get you there, and quickly, trust me. Patience, Leah."

"And your mother would not want you to be hurt traveling to her. After all, your mother has waited for you for such a long time, Leah. She will wait a few more days."

"Wait, Leah, wait one day. We will help you. I will start asking right now. Trust us."

As much as Leah wanted to argue with Jerusha and Tirzah, she knew they were right. To travel alone to Caesarea Philippi would be both foolish and dangerous. She knew they only cared about her safety... and about her.

Leah marveled at the thought that someone cared about her.

❧

The first day of her new life – as she had taken to calling that day – Leah left the young disciple to run all the way from the house of Simon Peter to the doorway of her small, ramshackle house. She stood panting, a stitch in her side, surveying the wreckage of Reuben's frenzied rage and her own desperate, fumbling midnight search for the medallion.

The remnants of her old dilapidated life stared back at her.

Leah walked in with slow steps, looking at the four walls that had imprisoned her for three years. The water jars stood in the corner, empty, one rolled over on its side. The food and other meager supplies from Reuben were still sitting where he had unceremoniously dumped them. Both trunks stood open. Her few possessions lay in the dirt, tunics in a heap, her basket of bloody rags lying on its side, the mirror tossed in the corner.

She bent to pick the mirror up. Leah stared at the watery reflection in the wavy metal surface. This was not the face of a gaunt, sick stranger. Familiar brown eyes stared back at her, eyes set in a face with wrinkles and thin lips, framed by fading brown hair with streaks of gray... a familiar face, strong and fearless. She set the mirror thoughtfully in the trunk.

She sat down on the stool by her loom, under the same window where she had huddled for three long years, clinging to life, clutching at hope.

Leah wanted to go home, to go home to her mother.

But it was mid-afternoon, the sun already casting long shadows in the street. Too late to start that journey today. She would have to leave tomorrow.

But she knew she could not leave until mid-day, when her two friends made their trek to the well, chattering, laughing, and loving each other as sisters do. Tirzah, so quiet and kind. Jerusha, so full of life, so giving. They had saved Leah, for they had led her to the

Messiah. She had to share the good news with them before she left.

"One more day, Mother," she whispered. "Then I will come home."

She looked again at the small house. Her prison for three years, where she had been held captive by her illness, her body, her shame and her fear. This house, this shack, this old beat-up, run-down has-been of a stable, this prison...

This was her home! She had a place to live, a place that was hers alone.

"I have a home!" She felt as though a dam burst within her, a pent-up happiness that could no longer be contained.

Leah's hands and feet flew as she made two trips to the well, filling both jars to the top with the cold, clear water. And with every step she sang a joyous psalm of Almighty King David, repeating the refrain over and over again: "'Give thanks to the Lord, for he is good! His love endures forever!'"

The joy bubbled out of her.

Back at her home, she stopped to drink the cold water until she had her fill, chewing a piece of dried fish between her thirsty gulps. She would never be thirsty again, never!

She got to work setting her home to right, storing supplies, folding clothes, straightening and sorting. She used copious amounts of water to wash down every surface in the small dwelling, years of dust and neglect replaced by a fresh start. She swept the dirt floor with such vigor, the dust made her cough. One brisk, meticulous stroke followed another, until the dirt was as compact as a woven woolen rug. She even fixed the weary shutter, hanging on its single hinge all these years.

She carried a heavy bundle from her home, asking the first woman she met where she might find a stream. It was so close to her home! Leah washed everything she owned except for the tunic on her back, relishing the strength of her arms beating her worn gowns against the rocks, and the firm grip of her hands wringing the cold water from each garment.

Leah carried the wet bundle home and sprinted up the steps to her roof, laying everything out to dry in the sun. The weight of the rocks to hold down the garments were like pebbles in her hands. She spotted a familiar face across the dusty street.

"Hello! Halloo!" Leah laughed. "Isn't the sun wonderful today?"

Startled, the neighbor woman looked around before she spotted Leah grinning down at her. She lifted her hand in a hesitant wave, but then smiled at the joy that was Leah. "Hello yourself! Yes, it is a beautiful day!"

Leah raced down the steps two at a time, executing a Jerusha-esque spin in the center of the room before picking up the heavy iron oven. She skipped out the door to the little courtyard with the oven in her arms. She admired the profuse blooms of her tamarisk. "I must continue to water it every day," she said to no one in particular. Leah looked about and then decided the oven would work best in the corner opposite from the tamarisk. No more hot fires smoking up her home!

She prodded a small fire in the oven to a hot blaze, stepped inside her home and returned with the small stool and a covered basket.

Leah watched with satisfaction as each stained and bloody bandage burned, stiff dry cloths reduced to a fine gray ash that blew away in the wind. She kept the fire hot until not one single shred or vestige of her illness remained.

She ground some barley into the finest flour, mixed in water and oil and set the loaf in the oven to bake. She would bake another later that night. She wanted plenty of bread to take with her on the journey to Caesarea Philippi.

Leah smiled at the sight of her home, pristine and neat. Her chores were complete.

Time to do some work on herself!

Leah did not walk, she ran to the public bath, where she sat in the hot water for over an hour. Such a wonderful sensation, to be clean and fresh and new! She offered the attendant all of her supply of figs, a token of her belated thanks for the years she had come without any gratuity for the old woman. But at the happiness on Leah's shining face, the old woman who tended the baths shook her head no, smiling in return at the thin woman. Leah pressed three figs into her hand anyway.

Leah ran home, her hair damp under her veil, stopping every now and then just to twirl around on the spot with joy. She was in the middle of one such twirl when she heard a familiar voice.

"Leah!"

"Elizabeth!"

"Leah, what has happened to you? You look, you look… different! Better! Wonderful!"

Leah told her the entire story right there on the street. This time, Elizabeth was the one who could not get a word in edgewise.

"You are the woman! I heard about you, I heard!"

"I am the woman."

"Jesus healed you."

"Yes, Jesus healed me." Leah picked up Elizabeth's hand. "Elizabeth, thank you for giving me water and food when I needed it most, for helping me home… for telling me when Jesus would arrive. Without you, I might never have known that Jesus had returned. I am lucky to have collapsed under your window! You are a wonderful woman with such a beautiful family. Thank you."

Elizabeth's eyes filled with tears.

"And it is true, Elizabeth. I know it in my heart. The teacher that healed me, it is as you thought. He is the Master, the Son of Man, the Messiah."

"The Messiah!" Elizabeth's voice was a whisper. She wiped her eyes and smiled. "The Messiah."

"Mama!" Eleazar, Eliza and their two small brothers ran up in a small pack, the two smaller boys jumping up and down and tugging on both women's tunics. Elizabeth and Leah burst into laughter.

Leah put her arm around Elizabeth. "Thank you for caring about me," she whispered in her new friend's ear.

Elizabeth nodded, and with her small entourage tugging on her robes, turned to her home that was only a few doors away from Leah.

℞

On the morning of the second day of her new life, Leah stood outside her home, waiting for the two women to walk by as they had for the last three years. She could not wait to see them.

Leah felt even better today, strong, vibrant, rested. The night before she was certain she would not be able to sleep one wink. Instead, the moment she finished her prayers and crawled into bed, her eyes did not open until bright sunlight shown through her window.

Leah woke to fresh bread for breakfast and abundant water

from her jar. She dressed in the bright veil of her youth with the richly woven belt wrapped around her waist, her hair braided, the ever-present smile on her face.

If the other women passing by were surprised by the friendly wave and hello from the reclusive woman who had hidden away in the small house on their street for years, they did not show it. Leah was cheered by their smiles.

"This is such a nice street full of wonderful women," she thought to herself.

She waited for what seemed an eternity for the last two women.

"Please, Lord, let them walk by," she thought. "How else can I find them if not walking to the well?"

At last, she spotted them. Jumping to her feet, she ran to meet them in the street.

They stopped, amazed at the sight of her.

Leah stopped too, looking at the women in silence.

She had listened to their conversations for three years, private things meant for their own ears only, not to be shared with an uninvited, unknown recluse. She had been unclean; she had touched them and made them unclean. She had lied to them and brushed them off when they tried to help her. She had counted them as her friends when really they were strangers.

And yet they had saved her, for they had introduced her to Jesus.

She owed them everything.

Leah knelt before them, looking up at their shocked expressions.

"Jerusha, Tirzah," Leah took a deep breath. What could she say?

Then, the words flooded out. "I am healed! You told me about the Messiah! You told me to go to Jesus, to believe! And it is as you said, I am healed! Without you and your kindness to me…" Leah could not finish the amazement she felt, that these two women had been so kind to her. "You were so good to me, a stranger. You told me about the Messiah, and he healed me! Thank you Jerusha! Thank you, Tirzah! Thank you!

"And forgive me, please, I beg your forgiveness, for I touched you when I was unclean. I had a disease, an issue of blood for twelve years. When you touched me, I made you unclean, too. But the Master, he healed me. He called me daughter, and told me to go in peace. I am cured. And it was you who told me of the Master."

Leah looked up at Jerusha, tears in her eyes. "I ask you to forgive me as the Master forgave me. For Jerusha, you are right. The man from Galilee... the Teacher... Jesus of Nazareth is the Messiah."

Much to the amazement of the crying woman kneeling in the dirt, her two friends burst into tears, Jerusha loud and noisy, Tirzah silently wiping her eyes.

Jerusha turned to Tirzah. "I knew the woman Jesus healed was Leah, I knew it," she said between her sobs. "I knew it had to be Leah."

Tirzah nodded. "Everyone is talking about yesterday's miracles, about you and the ruler's daughter. It is as they say. Truly he is the son of God."

"Oh, Tirzah!"

Tirzah smiled at Jerusha's joyous outburst. "Yes, it is as you said, too, Jerusha my sister."

"I knew the woman they talked about had to be Leah! I knew it. Praise Jehovah!"

They spent the entire afternoon together, first walking to the well. They stopped long enough only leave Leah's water jar at her home, insisting she come with them to Tirzah's home, refusing to let her leave to Caesarea Philippi alone.

"The dangers are too great! Something terrible might happen to you!"

"Patience, Leah. We will help you."

Leah felt at ease the moment she stepped into Tirzah's bright and tidy home. Tirzah's grandmother sat in the corner, spinning thread, nodding with enjoyment at the animated conversation of the three women. Tirzah's small daughter played with delight in the midst of so much activity, running from knee to knee, climbing from lap to lap.

With each chapter Leah told, Jerusha and Tirzah added to the story. They knew the ruler's daughter, Abigail was her name. Tirzah and Jerusha knew Jarius and his wife and daughter well. He was the ruler of their own synagogue. They knew Simon Peter, and the two other disciples. From Leah's description, the young man she talked to was probably John, a fisherman and the son of Zebedee, one of the first and youngest disciples, a cousin of Jesus.

They cried over Leah's painful story. They shed tears over Reuben's evil treachery and tortured hatred of his wife. They nodded with sad eyes over Leah's long illness, how Leah's mother had sacrificed so much to care for her for nine long years, and how desperately Leah missed her mother. All three women wept together remembering how Tirzah's own mother had died two years ago, how Jerusha had conceived but lost a baby.

Leah was embarrassed, but told them how she knew many of the things they told her. She told them of her isolation and fear, how their brief conversations were her only comfort, a shred of hope unwittingly shared with a sick, wretched woman huddled under her small window.

Silent tears flowed at her story, for such a horrible life of pain, isolation and loneliness.

"Still, Leah, you never gave up hope. You never gave up on God. You are an amazing woman. Who could have stood what you have endured these long years?"

Leah flushed at Jerusha's praise. "It is not true, because after Reuben divorced me and left me... alone, and I was so sick, that I prayed for... death." Leah looked down, ashamed her faith had fled her that night. She whispered her admission again. "I prayed for death."

"Leah." Jerusha's voice was soft. "Even King David grew discouraged," She took Leah's hand. "Even the greatest people of faith sometime lose hope. But you never gave up on God, Leah."

Leah nodded. It was true; her mother had said the same many times. Even the source of Talitha's never-ending praise, the mighty King David, sometimes grew discouraged. Even people of great faith could be worn down by the world, until God reached down to revive them once again.

Jerusha and Tirzah clapped over her wedding, were shocked over the theft of the medallion, scoffed at the doctors who tried to cure her, gasped at the father who disowned her, scorned the husband who abandoned her, and smiled for the mother so fierce in her protection of her daughter. The three women talked and cried and laughed together all afternoon, plotting Leah's return to Caesarea Philippi and her mother.

Leah was healed. She was happy. Her new life had begun. Her heart desired only one more thing. Her mother.

"Patience, Leah. We will help you."

Patience had never been Leah's best quality, but she nodded. Leah had friends who cared about her. If they told her to be patient, she would.

Or at least, she would try.

⍥

Early on the morning of the third day of her new life, Leah was still asleep in her bed.

"Leah! Leah! Wake up, Leah!"

Leah leapt from her bed in the small home that no longer felt alone and lonely to her. Jerusha and Tirzah were peering through her window, grinning, pounding on the wall, hollering. "Leah, hurry!"

Jerusha was babbling. It was a two-day walk to Caesarea Philippi. They would wait to leave if Leah could come right now.

What?

Tirzah's words were quiet and measured. Could Leah be ready to leave on such short notice? Her husband had found a friend who was leaving today, this morning. Could she leave now?

Could she! Leah and the two women left her small home behind only moments later. Indeed, she had been ready to leave from the first moment of her new life.

An hour later, Leah met some wonderful strangers, a young couple and their two children. The woman Tirzah's childhood friend, the man a cousin of her husband. Despite Leah's protests, Tirzah gave the man money for Leah's room at the small inn where they would break their journey.

"No, no, please Tirzah, it is not necessary!" Leah shook her head for emphasis. She did not want Tirzah's charity.

"But where else would you sleep? Sharing a room with these two rambunctious heathens? You'd be better off in the stable!" The two children were tumbling around and wrestling with Tirzah's daughter, all three shrieking with laughter. Tirzah nodded at the man. "Please make certain she has a spot of her own."

Leah shook her head again, this time in disbelief at this unexpected, loving generosity. "No, Tirzah."

Tirzah smiled her quiet smile and shook her finger at the man. "Make sure!"

He threw up his hands and laughed. "I will, Tirzah."

Tirzah then took Leah's hand, pressing a few coins on her. "You must have a bit of money, just in case. Just in case, Leah! You will pay me when you return. You do not need to, but I know you will."

"I can't! Tirzah, please. No."

"Yes."

Leah had already learned you could not argue with the stoic, strong-willed Tirzah. "Thank you," Leah whispered.

"We're just looking for a way to make sure you come back to us. If you owe Tirzah money, we know you'll come back." Jerusha's voice was teasing. Her new friends wanted her to come back.

Leah had not thought about when or even if she would be back. She had no other thought than to get to her mother.

"Oh, Tirzah, Jerusha…" Leah searched for words to say goodbye. She had no words for their kindness. They were true friends, even more wonderful than she had imagined.

They silenced her at once. She tried to tell them, yet they would not hear it.

"It is an honor to know the woman that the Messiah healed," Jerusha said in a reverent voice. "What if you had not heard us talking about Jesus? Oh, it truly is a miracle! God brought you here through the despicable Reuben, to be cured by the Master! To be a witness, a testimony to Jews everywhere! Oh, Leah!"

"God's hand was in this from the beginning, Leah," Tirzah added. "I believe now what Jerusha has known all along: this man Jesus is the Messiah."

The three women had gathered in prayer, asking Jehovah that if it was his will he might grant safe travel for Leah and speed her to her mother. Jerusha said that was how the Master prayed in the synagogue, that all things be to "His will."

"Amen," the women whispered.

"Come back to us soon, Leah." Jerusha had embraced her in a tight hug and kissed her on the cheek. "We will miss you so!"

"We cannot wait to hear all about your mother," Tirzah told her. "Tell her hello from us. Be safe, Leah."

"Be safe, Leah!"

Leah smiled at the two women who had changed her life.

CS

That was yesterday morning. Now, the Old Gray-Haired Lady loomed before Leah just as she remembered it, a massive gray monument whose white snowcap stood in stark contrast to the bright blue sky. The snow looked so pure and clean. "Perhaps I will feel that snow between my toes someday, after all, Savta," Leah thought.

Leah had walked this wide road many times with her family. She knew they could not be more than two miles away. Two miles! Two miles to her mother. She turned to the woman beside her.

"We are close, now. Just ahead there is a fork in the road. From there it is only a short walk to Caesarea Philippi."

It was a fork in the road that Leah knew quite well, after all. Hadn't she sat there on two occasions, startled by shouting and cymbals and silly doctors hoping to frighten the bleeding out of her?

Fear is never the answer, Leah thought.

She remembered the years she hid from her father, from the Law of Moses, from the world. She remembered the three years of isolation, staring hungrily out her window at a world she had grown afraid of, too frightened to creep out her own front door.

"Fear is not the answer. The only answer is faith. And forgiveness. And hope." Leah whispered to herself and then smiled. "And courage!" For she knew it had taken all of her faith to find her courage, a courage she never knew she had to ask for a forgiveness that changed her life

Wouldn't those doctors be surprised to find out what really cured her! The touch of a robe created a new life in Leah. Such knowledge would put them out of business!

She laughed at the thought and turned to her new friend.

"Once we get to that fork, please, I must go on ahead. I will be walking where I walked as a girl; I know it is safe. You will soon see the people of Caesarea Philippi on the road, children playing, women going to the river. It is safe. There I must leave you and say farewell until we meet again. Because once we get to the fork, I... I won't be able to wait another moment. I cannot thank you enough for bringing me to my home..."

The woman smiled at her and then at her husband. They knew her story and the reason for her urgency. "I promised Jerusha and

Tirzah I would take good care of you! But yes, when we get to that fork…"

"When we get to the fork in the road!" Leah danced a few steps on the spot in a good imitation of Jerusha.

She could see the town of old Panias, a faint sketch on the horizon, the pencil outline of the small brown buildings growing bolder with each passing footstep. She had walked this path many times. She could smell the approaching freshness of the Jordan River. The fork in the road was only a few footsteps away. She turned to the woman.

"You have been so good to me. But I cannot wait another moment," she whispered to the woman. "I must run the rest of the way."

The woman smiled. "God speed, Leah. I pray we will meet again someday."

With a shy nod at the husband, Leah broke into a run.

"Goodbye! Goodbye, Leah!" Leah smiled at the voices of the two children running beside her. They stopped at their mother's voice calling them back, still calling their farewells.

Soon she would hear the voice of her own mother. Please, Jehovah, if it is your will, let that be so.

"'God has listened and heard my voice in prayer. Selah.'" Her mother's voice and the words of King David's prayer bounced around in Leah's head as she sprinted down the road, quavering and disjointed.

Would God hear her prayer again?

"Fear is not the answer, Leah." Strong, confident Leah was in control. "Faith is the answer. Don't be afraid. No matter what happens, you will always have the voice of your mother in your heart."

Leah looked over her shoulder and waved at the children, but she did not stop running. She was running, running to the sound of her mother's voice.

CHAPTER 30

Leah stood gasping for air, clutching a stitch in her side. "I haven't run that far since I was ten years old," she thought, panting. She had not stopped running until she turned the corner of the street that led to her mother's home.

She stood still now, gazing at the house. It was not shuttered or abandoned or empty. It looked just as she remembered. She walked slowly to the open courtyard gate.

Leah remembered the time she had stood at the door of her childhood home, huddled on the ground, crying in the dust, her father's fist above her, her mother's battered face knotted in pain.

"Don't be afraid," she thought. "Faith, not fear. He is not here, he is dead. Dead now for many years. It is only your mother there now. She waits for you inside. She waits for you."

She walked through the gate into the courtyard.

A pretty girl sat on the same stone bench of Leah's youth. A younger girl sat beside her.

"Sisters," Leah thought, followed by a second, more urgent thought: "Who are they?"

"Hello," said the older, smiling at Leah.

"Hello." Leah was uncertain as to what to say next.

"Are you looking for my mother?"

Leah shook her head, confused. "No, I am looking for my mother. She lives here." She wrinkled her brow.

"She lives here, I mean, she lived here before. I have not been here for three years, and I thought my mother would be here. This was my home," Leah forced herself to say the words, "years ago."

"You used to live here? We have lived here for three years. I was only six when we moved in. Me, my two sisters and my parents live here." The older girl was lovely, confident in her beauty and place in life.

Like I was once, thought Leah.

Were these children somehow related to one of her brothers? Their daughters? But she would know about a nine-year-old granddaughter. "Do you live here with your grandmother, too? Is your grandmother's name Talitha?" Even as she asked, she knew the question made no sense.

"No!" laughed the younger girl. "My grandmother is Sarah, and I am Sarah, too!"

"Sarah?"

Yes! I am four! How many are you?"

"Hush, now," scolded the older girl. She smiled at Leah. "Our father is Simeon and my mother and grandmother are both named Sara, too.

"Like me!" At the look on the older girl's face, the younger clapped a hand over her own mouth to keep any more outbursts from escaping.

The older girl frowned but her tone was kind. "I do not know of a Talitha, but my mother will know, I am certain. She will return from the market soon."

Leah backed away, a slow weakness spreading through her. "I am sorry, my mother lived here. Do you, do you know what happened to the woman who used to live here?"

The older sister shook her head. "No, but please, wait and talk with my mother?" She smiled at Leah. "Would you like some water? It is hot out today."

As if in answer, sweat ran down Leah's forehead from under her veil. Leah started to tremble, from her hard run and the heat and the harsh realization that she did not know where her mother was.

Her mother did not live here. Where was Leah's mother?

Leah backed to the gate and gripped it, trying to steady her wobbling knees. She felt as though she could not breathe.

"No. Perhaps. I mean, no, thank you, I don't need any water. Well, I don't know. I may return later to talk to her. To your mother. Thank you."

She felt behind her for the gateway and backed out, never taking her eyes off the two girls seated in the courtyard of her mother. The little one waved, giggling.

They had moved in to Leah's home almost three years ago, right after she left with Reuben. Where could her mother have gone?

Leah would not, she would not even think about the second thought screaming to be voiced. So much could have happened in three years.

Where was Leah's mother?

Leah took a deep breath and plodded away with slow, measured steps, forcing one foot after the other. After all, she could not just stand in the middle of the street with a bewildered look on her face.

Leah had imagined her return to Caesarea Philippi so many times. In her mind, she would run to her childhood home, stand in the courtyard and, without even knocking, watch as her mother flung open the door. They would rush into each other's arms, reunited at last, weeping with tears of joy.

Leah had not imagined any other scenario. As such, she was lost.

And afraid. She could not help it.

"I will not be afraid, I will not be afraid," she muttered, willing herself to believe. "Fear is not the answer. Faith is."

She wondered where her trudging steps would take her, for she had no idea of where she should go.

"I wonder if Reuben still lives here in Savta's house?" The thought had never before occurred to Leah. If there was anyone she did not want to see, it was Reuben. Although she had prayed for him by the Sea of Galilee less than a week ago, she was indignant at the sudden thought that Reuben might still live in the home of her beloved grandmother, the home they had shared during their marriage.

But surely he did not live right here in Caesarea Philippi! Her mother would have hounded him to his death, demanding to see Leah, forcing him to take her to her daughter. No, Reuben could not live here.

Unless Leah's mother was not here anymore to hound him.

If her mother were not here, Reuben might have indeed returned to the home of their bitter marriage, the little house of Savta. If Leah was dead – as Reuben wanted everyone to think – and her mother was... gone...

Then the house would by law belong to Reuben.

She shook her head at the blasphemous thought of the husband that had abused her so calling the house of Savta his own.

Perhaps as Reuben slept in their old bed, the spirit of Savta came back to whisper nightmares in his ear every night. Leah smiled at the thought, refusing to give any credence to the other:

Where was her mother?

Leah walked slowly. She needed the answer to the question she was afraid to ask. Despite her sluggish steps, she found herself standing before the house of her beloved Savta. It was the house she had shared with Reuben, where she had laid sick for nine long years, tended to by her mother, hated by her husband.

Flowers bloomed out front. The shutters were thrown open, and a small goat was tethered to a rope in the little courtyard. The small house did not look deserted, but neat and well-tended. Someone was living here, just as someone lived in the house of Leah's childhood.

Leah licked her lips nervously; as strong as she felt, she did not think she was quite ready to face the hatred of Reuben, to hear any news of her mother from his lips.

Who lived in Savta's house?

The mid-day street was deserted. Leah stood with her shoulders hunched together, motionless, unable to breathe, alone in the dust of the baking late-day sun. The clicks and hums of a noisy locust in the nearby cedar tree echoed in the still, silent street.

It took a moment for Leah to realize there was another sound, faint and familiar. Clack. Clack.

She moved closer, holding her breath.

Clack. Clack.

Leah's slow steps took her to the front of the house. Through the open door, Leah could see a cloth of brilliant colors spread out before the arrow-straight back of the dark-haired woman sitting at her loom. Her song continued in tandem with the rhythm of her loom. Push and pull. In and out. Clack. Clack.

Leah heard the echo of her own childish voice in her head. "Re-joice. Re-joice."

"'Put your hope in God.'" Push and pull. The woman was singing.

"'For I will yet praise him, my Savior and my God.'" Clack. Clack.

"I put my hope in God," Leah thought.

Leah saw the beautiful veil of vivid colors resting on the woman's shoulders, her shining black hair shot through with gray. The work of steady hands, bright tones of red and gold and orange, unfurled before the woman, a rich cloth all the colors of a Mount Hermon sunset.

"'My Savior and my God.'" The voice was strong and confident. Push and pull. In and out. Clack. Clack.

"Se-lah. Se-lah." Leah's voice was so quiet, it was nothing more than a whisper in the warm sunshine.

But the loom stopped. The woman did not turn around. In a voice so soft Leah could barely hear, the woman spoke.

"O Jehovah, I praise you, for surely you have returned my daughter to me."

Leah was rooted to the spot, eyes overflowing with tears. "Mother."

Talitha stood and turned around to face Leah. A long silence stretched between them. "I cannot believe my eyes. My daughter stands before me... Is it a dream? For I see you are well. Is it a dream, or are you real?"

Leah nodded. "I am real, and I am well. I have been healed by a man called Jesus of Nazareth. He is the promised Messiah, the son of God, the Christ. He healed me, Mother, only a few short days ago. In more ways than one, he healed me."

Her mother nodded but did not move. There was no sound except for the hum of the buzzing locusts.

The loud bleat of the goat made both women jump. Talitha and Leah both burst into laughter and ran to each other, weeping tears of joy, reunited at last.

ଓଃ

It was long since dark, and still they talked. There was much to tell.

"I was so afraid when I did not find you at home, Mother."

"As soon as you left, I sold the house. I did not want to live there. Your brothers agreed when I told them they could share in the proceeds. They did not want to live there either, in that house of bad memories."

"They do not support you!"

"Oh, when I am old and frail, they will take care of me as we did for Savta. Remember how she lived to the end of her days in this very house?" They both smiled at the memory of Savta. "And you lived here, too, and now me. All three of us have called this house our home.

"Your brothers and I agreed on this. I like it better this way, rather than living with them. I sell my cloth to them and they sell it for a greater price. I like my independence, and they are still nearby to look after me. Your brothers..." Talitha's words were gentle.

"Leah, many times your brothers traveled to Great Caesarea on the Sea to search for you, for that is where Reuben said you were going. They could not find out anything; no one had heard of Reuben or you. It is such a great, large city." She sighed at the sad memory.

"So they started asking in every city, the synagogues, the merchants, even strangers. But when we had no word for so long, your brothers agreed that if Reuben ever were to return without you after such a long absence, it would be with blood on his hands. Your brothers vowed to never let this little house of Savta return to Reuben, or to even let Reuben return to our little town. No one has heard from him since he left with you, not even his family."

Leah was touched. Perhaps her brothers were not like the father she feared. Perhaps they had lived in anxious worry of his rage and hatred just as she had. "I cannot wait to see them, and their wives and my nieces and nephews, too."

"They are changed men, Leah. After your father died, their lives changed. Leah, they lived in fear of their father all their lives. He beat them when they were young, berated them when they were older. They lived in fear of his anger and his fists. I could not help them!"

Leah placed a gentle hand on her mother's shoulder at the sight of her raw pain.

Her mother wiped away her tears. "'It will make men of them,' he used to say. At least you were spared from that dark side of your father, except for that day after the synagogue."

Leah shuddered, remembering the physical pain of that day. She could not imagine that her two brothers had endured such fear and rage all of their lives.

"When your father died, your brothers vowed that they would never be like their father. And praise Jehovah, they are such kind men! But I saw some of your father's rage in them when they were searching for you to no avail. They are good sons, good men, Leah."

Leah realized she knew nothing of her brothers, and yet they had spent countless days searching for her. "I cannot wait to see them, Mother."

Talitha nodded and wiped her eyes. "They will be so happy you are alive. I am sorry, it was hard not to think the worst, especially since Reuben has never returned."

"Reuben will not return here, especially if he ever learns I live."

"No, I do not think he will ever come back. Even his own family has disowned him."

"I am so sorry Reuben stole the medallion, Mother. You were right about him. I am so sorry."

"We had no choice, he is the man your father picked for you. And to think how he abandoned you! Oh, Leah, what if you had died alone! What a monster! If only I had known where you were."

Her mother was weeping. "You were so sick when you left. I was so afraid you had died, Leah. I was so worried. I am sorry I let Reuben take you away! I have begged Jehovah for forgiveness everyday since you left with him. I cannot forgive myself that I let you go!"

"Mother…"

"It is a miracle to see you again. I am so sorry, my daughter!"

"It is a miracle, Mother. Reuben left me without money or means, and I was… I was afraid to leave my home. I was sick so much of the time. And afraid, afraid I would be found out. I had no one to help me, and could not send word to you. And even though I promised you I would, I could not bring myself to sell the medallion! I am so sorry, Mother."

"Oh Leah, I am so sorry you were alone and so sick for three terrible years. I am sorry!"

They had laughed through their tears at their repeated apologies to the other.

"If I ever see Reuben…"

Leah heard the anger in her mother's voice. She laid a gentle hand on her mother's arm. "Mother, this is hard to understand, but Jesus is a Master who preaches forgiveness and love. I do not know what God has in store for Reuben, but…"

Talitha's eyes were intent on Leah's.

"But I do know I have forgiven Reuben. This is what Jesus said: 'Love your enemies and pray for those who persecute you.'"

"How can you forgive him? Look what he did to you!"

"Mother, if Reuben had not left me in Capernaum, if I had not been alone all those years… I would not have found the Messiah. For truly that is what he is, the Messiah."

"But to forgive Reuben for what he did to you?" Leah heard the doubt in her mother's voice.

"'Go in peace.' That is what Jesus told me. Any anger, any hatred I have towards Reuben… I must let that go. Anger, hatred and even fear… they no longer have a place in my life if I want to have peace in my heart.

"I am grateful. I am happy! I am here with you, I am healed. God is good and so is my life.

"And someday you will meet the two women who helped me, Jerusha and Tirzah. For Jerusha heard Jesus and shared the story of a crippled man made whole with Tirzah. Because I was eavesdropping on their conversation, I heard them talking about Jesus, too! They are wonderful friends, and I owe them so much. Jerusha led me to Jesus."

"How did you meet them?"

Leah clapped her hands as she told the story. "And then, after I fainted in the dirt, they helped me home. They were so kind to me. I was so sick!"

"My poor daughter."

"I will never forget the words of Jesus that Jerusha spoke to me: 'Blessed are the poor in spirit, for theirs is the Kingdom of Heaven.' Then, when I sat beside the Sea of Galilee, I heard Jesus say the same words and more! I heard the words that gave me the courage to seek him: 'Ask and it will be given to you; seek and you will find; knock and the door will be opened to you. For everyone who asks receives; he who seeks finds; and to him who knocks, the door will be opened.' Ask! Seek! Knock! I knew whether I was ever healed or not, I had heard the Messiah."

Her mother shook her head. "The Messiah? The Son of God? I cannot believe it after all these years!"

"It is true, Mother, he truly is the Son of God."

"Can it be?"

"Oh, yes! It is true. Mother, I only touched his robe, and I was healed."

"Healed by only a touch of his robe?"

Leah told her told her mother how she stood in the street waiting for Jesus to walk by in the crowd, that only a touch of his robe healed her, how he knew that she had been healed. She tried to remember every word the Master had shared with her, how he prayed for her and told her to go in peace.

"Because I believed, Jesus healed me."

Leah told her how she sat by the fisherman's house and cried when she learned about the death of the ruler's daughter. A twelve-year-old girl, dying when Leah's twelve years of illness was finally cured by only a touch of a robe. The words Jesus spoke to the ruler: "Your daughter is not dead. Don't be afraid, only believe." The long wait in front of the ruler's mansion, the mourners, the centurion and the crowds.

Leah told her of the miracle, confirmed by the young disciple with eyes ablaze at the wonder of his Master. The two women were silent for a long time, pondering the miracle of the ruler's daughter who died and then lived. For what could one say? A new life for Leah, a new life for an unknown little girl. A new life for Leah's mother. New life through the man from Galilee, Lord, Master and Jesus.

"He is the Son of God, Mother."

"Truly, he is the Son of God." Talitha whispered the words.

Talitha put her arm around Leah and spoke words so familiar to Leah, the words of the king and the psalmist, the words Leah's mother always used in prayer, familiar and reassuring.

"'Be at rest once more, O my soul,
For the Lord has been good to you.'"

Leah nodded and picked up the passage.

"'For you, O Lord, have delivered my soul from death,
My eyes from tears, my feet from stumbling.'"

She added softly, "He delivered my soul from death, Mother. From death. Selah."

Her mother gazed at her daughter for a long moment, then shook her head with a look of disapproval on her face. "Leah, you know that is not right."

Leah looked at her mother, a question on her face.

"I believe King David would have said... "Selah! SEELAH! SEEEE LAH LAH LAH!"

Leah's reserved, gentle mother was shouting!

They laughed and cried long into the night.

CHAPTER 31

Leah arched her skinny back, wiggled her toes and stretched out her thin arms in satisfaction. How wonderful she felt! She looked around her old bedroom, unchanged after all these years. The wide smile that never seemed to leave her was already spread across her face.

Across the room, her mother's peaceful profile came into Leah's foggy morning view. She still slept, her breathing steady and even.

"Good," Leah thought.

The first night, they could not stop talking and finally pulled a second straw mat into the room, crying and laughing until sleep finally overtook them.

Yesterday was just as memorable. Talitha summoned them all in the mid-afternoon. Her brothers and their quiet wives sat gape-mouthed in quiet shock at the sight of Leah. Then, much to Leah's amazement, all four cried, even her two quiet sisters-in-law.

Their last memory of Leah was of a seldom-seen skeletal woman suffering from illness and the wrath of her father and husband. Leah was the woman they had never expected to see alive again.

Standing before them now was a joyous woman, healed of an illness none could cure. Leah's oldest brother, strapping with broad shoulders, gray hair and a strong jaw, wept longer than anyone –

which soon was cause for much gentle teasing from the others.

Who knew her brothers had such tender hearts, Leah marveled to herself.

The tears finally came to a halt at the clamoring chaos that seven children aged four to fifteen brought to the small house, all clamoring to see their grandmother and their new Aunt Leah.

She had never seen any of her nieces or nephews until now. Not even Talitha had been brave enough to face the wrath of her husband by exposing her grandchildren to the fierce recriminations of the Law during the years Leah lay alone, branded as an unclean outcast. The year after her father died, Reuben kept everyone but her mother away. She remembered her sisters-in-law would sometimes stop in to see her, but only when Reuben was away. Leah had been too sick to do more than acknowledge their presence with a nod, anyway.

"I hate them both. My father and Reuben. I curse them forever. I will always hate them." Leah had been startled by the loathing in her oldest brother's voice. She shook her head and gathered her family close.

Leah began the story of Jesus, a Messiah and healer, the son of God who preached forgiveness and peace. She told of two strangers, two women who heard his word and shared it with Leah. She told of the crippled man and his mother, the leper, the woman with a fever. She saw the looks of surprise and then of awe at the story of her healing. They were silent at the miracle of the ruler's daughter, until all their questions broke out at once.

"He touched a leper and made a blind man see?"

"He teaches by the Sea?"

"He healed you with a touch?"

"He raised a little girl from death?"

"He is the Messiah?"

Leah answered all these questions and more. "They say he is the Son of God... and I believe it. To hear him speak is to hear the truth of God. I believe that Jesus is all the people say he is and more. He is the Messiah."

"Messiah." The whispered word of awe ran from one person to the next, until shouts of joy and laughter took over. "The Messiah!"

It was a day of feasting, stories, laughter and tears. Leah realized now how terrible her brothers' lives were at the hand of their father. Physically beaten and mentally berated, she wondered at their kind hearts and generous capacity for love to their families, her mother and their long-lost sister.

The afternoon stretched into evening and then into the darkness of night. Finally the youngest children were slung over shoulders of parents or older siblings, sound in their sleep and oblivious to the noisy farewells and promises to meet on the morrow.

Leah's heart swelled with gratitude. So much had been given to her in less than a week! Her health, beloved friends, her mother, a wonderful family... Her life was good, and she was grateful.

Leah looked again in wonder at the profile of her sleeping mother. She had wondered if she would ever see her mother again. Now, all her prayers had been answered. God was so good.

She rolled over and got up, grabbing her robe and veil, careful not to disturb her mother. After long nights like the last two, let her sleep as long as she wanted.

She opened the door to see the sunshine creeping across Savta's small courtyard. The brown goat tethered to his rope bleated a morning inquiry.

"Bah, yourself," she said.

She went inside and knelt at the stool before her mother's loom to pray, feeling the peace promised by the Messiah steal over her. She took a deep breath and bowed her head, feeling the serenity of the presence of Jehovah. Her voice was reverent.

"'I will exalt you, my God and King;
    I will praise your name for ever and ever.'"

The words of King David, taught faithfully to her by her mother, never failed to bring her into the presence of the Lord.

"'Every day I will praise you, forever and ever.'"

Forever and ever. Leah remembered standing outside the home of Simon Peter the fisherman, recalling the words she practically shrieked with joy at the Lord's young disciple. "Tell my Lord and Master I will not be silent!" She had been so happy that that the ruler's daughter lived, that she had been healed, and that her bruised heart had found peace. "I will give thanks forever more," she had shouted. His ears probably still ached.

She grinned in spite of herself, but then remembered how solemn and worshipful she wanted her prayers to be – like her mother's. Leah took a deep breath, bowed her head and resumed the poetry of David.

"'Great is the Lord and most worthy of praise.
  His greatness no one can fathom.'"

A thin squeaky voice interrupted Leah.

"One generation will commend your works to another;
  They will tell of your mighty acts."

Leah's head jerked straight up.

The reedy voice cackled. "What's that? Yes, Lord. Leah will tell of your mighty acts."

Leah shot straight up, her eyes open wide. She looked left, then right, then over her shoulder. What was *that*?

It took a moment before Leah shook her head in amusement. Goodness. The long-gone voice of her beloved grandmother had sounded so real. Jesus might have healed her body, but it appeared her mind was somewhat worse for wear. She was hearing things. Leah raised her eyebrows and answered her grandmother's quavering, but imaginary, voice.

"Now, Savta, we both know you prefer King Solomon's scolding to the King David's praise." Leah tilted her head. No one answered her, of course. Not Savta, or the Master, or mighty Jehovah, not even her mother, still sleeping in the next room. Savta never quoted the psalms, anyway. Leah's mind and memory were failing her.

She heard her own childish voice asking her mother in amazement, "Savta knows all the psalms?"

"She knows them all and she taught them to me," answered her mother.

For goodness sake! Now she was hearing both Savta and her mother, when one stood beside the Lord in all his glory and the other slept in her bed on the other side of a thin wall with a curtain for a door.

"You need to concentrate a little harder when you pray," Leah chastised herself. Silently, so all those imaginary voices would not start babbling at her.

She bent her head, squeezed her eyes shut and returned to the holy words of King David, the words mother recited so often.

"'They will speak of the glorious splendor of your majesty.
They will tell of the power of your awesome works.
I will proclaim your great deeds, celebrate your abundant
    goodness and joyfully sing of your righteousness.'"

Leah sighed, feeling the tranquility of the prayerful words.

"Yes, Lord, Leah *will* proclaim your great deeds. She *will* tell of your great power! She is my granddaughter, after all."

Savta!

It was hard to be humble before God with Savta shouting at Him at the exact same moment, Leah thought somewhat crossly. She wrinkled her forehead with fierce determination.

"All your saints will extol you, Lord. That includes my grandmother Savta."

The cackle clearly did not hear the words of her granddaughter.

"Yes, Lord. My Leah will tell of the glory of your kingdom and speak of your might. All will know of your mighty acts! My granddaughter will tell them!"

The singsong voice was so real, Leah scrambled up from her prostrate kneeling.

"Pffth! Yes, sometimes my little dove is stubborn. But I will not rest until she does what you have called her to do. Yes, my Lord. Leah must speak, for you have touched her with your mighty hand. She will tell of your glory to all. I know she will."

"Savta?"

Leah jumped. The sound of her own tentative voice was so loud in the morning stillness, she had startled herself. She looked around again.

No one was there, of course. Beloved Savta was dead. Her mother still slept. Leah was alone.

Leah turned around slowly, making a full circle of the room. She felt her shoulders start to shake. The laughter rumbled up from somewhere deep inside, gasping chuckles that turned into tears of hilarity.

Oh, Savta.

Her mother would think she was crazy. Come to think of it, her mother would be right.

Leah wiped her eyes, squared her shoulders and spoke to the empty room.

"All right, Savta. I get it. I will speak of the might of the Lord, and what he has done for me. I. Get. It." She started to giggle again. "And pffth, yourself. I am not stubborn. Just a little slow."

She listened, but this time, Savta did not answer.

ଔ

Leah watched her mother's strong hands push the stone in its mill, over and over, until the grain lay crushed in a fine brown powder. She had already fired up the oven. They would have delicious wheat bread for lunch today. Leah's mouth watered at the thought.

She had not yet decided what to say to her mother. But there was no doubt about what she had to do. There was no other way. She had no choice. She was disgusted that Savta had to tell her. She should have thought of it herself.

"It would have come to me eventually, Savta," she muttered somewhat crossly.

Talitha dusted off her hands, dipped them in the water bowl and then dried them off. They sat down together, Leah at the ancient loom of Savta, her mother at the loom of her marriage. Her mother hummed as she pulled the threads taut, her brows drawn in concentration with her work. Leah looked at the profile she loved, her mother's hands busy at her artistry, her back straight and ready for her work. How could she possibly do what she knew she must?

She took a deep breath. "Mother."

"Yes?"

Leah told her. Her mother did not even act surprised.

"I expected as much. How could you not?"

Leah smiled at her mother in relief. "Wonderful. I am so glad you understand."

"Of course I understand. But I will never be parted from you again, my daughter. So I am ready."

"You are ready. Wait. You are...What?"

296

"I am ready."

"Ready for what?"

"Why, to go with you."

"Mother! I cannot ask you leave your home. The walk is long, my house in Capernaum is quite small and... I don't know what will happen and... I think you should..." Leah voice trailed off as she felt her excitement growing. "You are ready! Goodness! Are you sure?"

"Pffth!" Talitha sounded just like the imaginary voice of Savta that very morning. Leah felt a bubble of joy within her.

"Of course I am sure, Leah. I am ready. There is no other choice for me, my daughter. I will stay with you in Capernaum. I want to go where you go. It will be wonderful."

"Are you sure, Mother? Because that would be ...well, wonderful!" Leah could not think of a better word.

"I am sure. I am going. I could not stay here. I can think of nothing else but you. You will not go without me."

Leah nodded. She did not want to be separated from her mother either, but she would never ask her mother to come along, to leave all she had known for her entire life to live in Capernaum. Leah could not ask her mother to abandon everything to follow the Master.

"What I have known my whole life is you, Leah. I want to be with you, now, if you will let me." Her mother always seemed to know what she was thinking.

Her mother was coming with her to Capernaum.

"Thank you, God," Leah whispered. "Thank you, Jehovah." She looked at the woman she had loved since the first moment she knew what love was. "Mother, thank you. I am so glad we will be together. I love you so much."

Leah's next words were urgent. "Mother, there is something more... you must hear the Messiah, the man from Galilee."

"Well, Leah, why else would we go?" Leah heard the excitement in Talitha's voice, saw the eagerness on her face. "I want to hear him. I want to see him. As a matter of fact, I plan to walk right up to him and thank him!"

Leah knew her mother was not afraid to talk to anyone. She remembered her mother throwing Reuben and the last doctor out the door. Her mother was never afraid.

But her mother had a pensive look on her face. "But Leah, how does one thank someone for the gift I have been given? What can I possibly say?"

Leah shook her head. She did not know how to thank Jesus either.

Leah's mother started smiling. Leah grinned back. She had smiled so much the last three days, her cheeks hurt.

"Yes, Leah, you must return to Capernaum and I must go too. We have two entire days of walking to figure out what to say the Messiah! God will tell me what to say. After all, 'The mouth of the righteous brings forth wisdom.' We will pray for wisdom."

"Pray for wisdom!" Leah crowed.

"Or maybe we will just bow before him in silence. After all, 'even a fool is thought wise if he keeps silent.'"

Leah giggled. Savta's proverbs! "Don't you mean, 'A fool is discerning if he holds his tongue.' I heard that one often enough!"

Talitha grinned. "I think Savta shouted this one at you every single day. 'A chattering fool comes to ruin!'"

"How about, 'The mouth of a fool invites ruin.'"

"'A fool's mouth invites a beating.'"

Leah wrinkled her forehead, thinking hard. "'But the way of a fool seems right to him.' To her. Um, to me!"

Her mother tilted her head. "'And so a fool exposes her folly.'"

"Well..." That was it. Leah was out of Proverbs. "I quit! I give up! I can't think of any more!"

Talitha smiled, satisfied. "Of course you cannot. You can never out-proverb me. But just so you won't feel bad..." her voice took on a high and squeaky tone, just like the one that had interrupted Leah's prayers that morning: "Pffth! Do not despise your mother when she is old!'"

Talitha grinned at her daughter. "At least that's what my mother used to say to me!"

ᙢ

A small caravan of Jewish travelers was leaving the next morning, passing through Capernaum as they made their way to Jerusalem.

Talitha and Leah made their farewells to their astonished family that evening, with long hugs of good-bye and fervent promises to return soon. The surprise was short-lived. Capernaum was a short journey and everyone, from Leah's oldest brother to youngest niece, wanted to hear the Man of Galilee teach. Leah knew her family would most likely join them in Capernaum before they made their way back home to Caesarea Philippi. Leah could not wait for her family to meet Elizabeth, Tirzah and Jerusha.

"Sister, my wife and I will be there within a fortnight," her oldest brother whispered in her ear.

Leah smiled at the sound of the word "Sister."

Her sisters-in-law promised to look after Savta's small house. The small goat would move to the younger brother's home to be tended and petted by the many grandchildren.

"That's the last milk from her for a while!" laughed Talitha.

It was a night of food and wine, hope and prayers, love and laughter, joyous, heartfelt laughter.

Talitha and Leah were still laughing the next morning as they started the dusty walk to Capernaum to find the Messiah, arm in strong arm, the Old Gray-Haired Lady brilliant in the sunlight behind them, the joy of Savta in their hearts.

Made in the USA
Lexington, KY
22 November 2014